"A changewind is the random wrath of God . . ."

Zenchur explained, "It is a storm. It is every storm that you have ever seen and more. It destroys worse than the worst kind of storm imaginable, yet it does what no other storm does. It also *creates*.

"Only the freaks and the monsters have looked upon the changewinds and survived in the wastes, belonging only to each other, to tell the tale. Believe me, you do not want to see a changewind—ever!"

Charley shrugged and shook her head. "What the hell is a changewind?" she repeated.

"A random force that does the one thing everyone fears everywhere," the mercenary responded. "It changes the rules."

Ladai suddenly made a sharp comment in her strange tongue and he nodded. "It has come," he said softly. "A bad one . . ."

CHANGEWINDS I:

WHEN THE CHANGEWINDS BLOW

JACK L. CHALKER

ACE BOOKS, NEW YORK

This book is an Ace
original edition, and
has never been previously
published.

WHEN THE CHANGEWINDS BLOW

An Ace Book/published by arrangement with
the author

PRINTING HISTORY
Ace edition/September 1987

ISBN: 0-441-88081-9

Ace Books are published by The Berkley Publishing Group,
200 Madison Avenue, New York, New York 10016.
The name "Ace" and the "A"
logo are trademarks belonging to
Charter Communications, Inc.
PRINTED IN THE UNITED STATES OF AMERICA

10 9 8 7 6 5 4 3 2

For Eva

· 1 ·

The Girl Who Was Afraid of Thunderstorms

THERE IS SOMETHING almost other-worldly about a huge shopping mall; enter it and you leave heat or cold, night and day behind, and enter a futuristic Disney-like vision of a future world which is all antiseptic, insulated, and artificial yet somehow it caters to all your basic modern needs. It is the synthesis of the ancient bazaar, the communal marketplace, the soda fountain, the drive-in, and the town square and more. Its vast interiors with their wasted space, careful fountains, phony waterfalls, plastic park benches and canned music which may be *The 1001 Strings Play the Best of the Rolling Stones* but somehow sounds like the same elevator music the parents and grandparents of those denizens of malls heard in their day. To many of the youth who are too young to be allowed in the adult bars and clubs and too old to be in by eight o'clock it is a massive singles bar as well.

Wednesday night wasn't the best night out, even in the mall, and it was tough on a school night to figure out an excuse to get there that parents might accept, but teens have had many centuries of evolution to get to a point where they instinctively know how to manage such urgencies when they have to, and Sharlene "Charley" Sharkin certainly felt like she had to.

It wasn't anything to do with the mall itself, but rather what it filled in her life. She was seventeen and due to graduate in five months, an occasion she was looking forward to with great anticipation. She was bright, athletic, and had good grades for the most part, but she hated school and all it stood for. Her parents had all sorts of plans for her, all of which included college and perhaps beyond, but the thought of four or more

1

years of additional school was just *gruesome,* that was all. She could see herself putting up with some secretarial school—she was already a lightning typist and did some word processing on the school computer for office brownie points—or maybe even a medical technician's course, or paralegal, or something like that, but nothing more. College wasn't like regular school in one way: if you didn't get it and later regretted it there was nothing that said you had to be eighteen and not twenty or even older to get in.

She had a nice, round face with just a bit of an overbite set off by mid-length Clairol brown perm-curled hair, no beauty but cute and she knew it. She was slightly chubby and thought she was fat and hated it but not enough to really work at dieting or giving up all the nice foods that made life worthwhile. She'd been a skinny, athletic kid but it had just started to come on and stay there, particularly in the past year or two, but at five foot three and a hundred and thirty-six pounds she didn't *feel* out of whack. She'd really let herself go since—well, since Tommy.

She had just turned sixteen, and was real popular with the boys, and the night of the junior prom Tommy Meyers had brought out this bottle of high-proof whiskey he'd gotten someplace and before she knew it Tommy had popped her cherry for good in his brother's borrowed conversion van, and while nothing had come of it she'd gone through *months* of nervous fear wondering if she was pregnant, or had caught something, or who knew what, and it'd scared her far more than all that blood. The experience made her something of a leader among her friends, of course, but it'd also given her a reputation among the boys as an easy girl and she'd had more than her share of troubles from *that.*

She'd let herself go after that, giving up most of the athletics and pigging out on whatever she wanted, particularly chocolate. If it hadn't been for Sam moving into the city she might have gotten really depressed, but even though Sam was a real straight arrow she didn't care and there was no closer friendship.

And now Sam was gone.

Samantha Buell was certainly her best friend in the whole world and the only person she felt she could confide in. Sam had needed a friend when she'd moved here with her mother a little over a year ago and they'd hit it off, the original thing they had in common being that they both went by nicknames that sounded more boy than girl—although Sam just called it "unisex." They liked the same rock bands, the same TV shows, they swapped romance novels—although Sam was more of a reader than she was—and they both *loved* roaming the mall and trying on all sorts of outrageous fashions. They spent a lot of free time together and talking on the phone and all that. They were the same height, and while Sam had a better figure she had a little bit of extra weight herself. Still, they looked enough alike to be mistaken more than once for sisters, and they were both also the only children of well-off professionals, spoiled without really realizing it.

Not that there weren't real differences, the least of which was Sam's slight but noticeable New England accent contrasted with Charley's southwestern twang. Sam's folks were divorced, and she lived here now with her mother who was a lawyer who worked for some federal agency or another. Environment, she thought, but she'd never really gone into it. Sam's dad was a contractor in Boston and they still got along pretty good—Sam would fly out to stay with him part of the summer and some of the long holidays and he called a lot—but maybe three thousand miles was a lot of distance for so-called "joint custody."

But Sam's voice was, well, unique. She had one of the deepest, most asexual voices Charley had ever heard in a girl, although not unpleasant or irritating. It was just, well, *asexual,* the kind of tonal voice that was stuck between the half octaves and could easily belong to a boy her age although it didn't sound wrong in her, either. Sam said that her grandmother—her dad's mother—had the same kind of voice. She could actually shift that voice even lower a bit and you'd swear she was all male, too, or higher a bit and sound feminine and sassy. Sam had hoped that this odd ability might get her into acting one day.

She'd always been something of a tomboy type, fooling around in Dad's workshop as a kid. She particularly liked carpentry and was really good at it, but her Dad had always tried to steer her away with some ingrained sexist ideas about what was properly boys' work and girls' work while her mother, who wanted her to be like the first female President or a great doctor or something was appalled by Sam's taste for manual skills. Charley, on the other hand, wouldn't be caught *dead* if not dressed in the latest style. Until she'd met Charley

the only real concession she'd made to unmistakable femininity was long, almost waist-length straight black hair.

Still, under Charley's skilled eye and guidance, Sam had
lately taken to trying all sorts of new and feminine fashion,
taken a real interest suddenly in perfume and cosmetics and
stuff like that, which somewhat pleased her mother and also
started getting her all sorts of attention from the boys. So far
she hadn't done much, though; Sam had some real hangups of
her own. Back in Boston she'd gone to this private all-girls'
school, and two of her classmates had done it before they were
past sixteen that Sam knew about. It was sheer stupid bad luck,
but one of them had gotten pregnant the first time out and the
other one had come down with VD. The odds against both of
'em, or even either of 'em, having anything like that happen
was small, and maybe that was only the two Sam found out
about, but it had scared the hell out of her. She was still a
virgin and not real inclined to changing that in the immediate
future. That was why a best girlfriend was an essential. They
protected and supported each other. Together, somehow, they
were safe.

And now Sam was gone.

At first she hadn't thought anything of it, when Sam hadn't
shown up for school on Monday. Charley had been away
visiting relatives all weekend, and had been too damned tired
to feel sociable on Monday. On Tuesday she'd called over to
the house and gotten Sam's mother's answering machine and
left a message. No big deal. Maybe somebody got sick back
east or something. Later, she heard it had been in the news over
the weekend and in the Sunday paper, but they'd thrown out
everything but the comics.

But today, in school, she'd been called out of first period
English to Mr. Dunteman's office—he was the administrative
vice principal—and waiting there had been this strange man
who introduced himself as Detective O'Donnell of the Juvenile
Division and said he wanted to know if Charley had heard from
Sam in the last few days.

"Huh? No. Why? Has something happened?"

"We—don't really know. When was the last time you saw or
spoke to her?"

"Uh—Friday. Here. I went away that night for the weekend
and didn't get back til Sunday night."

"Uh-huh. And did she seem—different? I mean, did she

seem out of the ordinary in any way? Nervous? Irritable? Depressed? Anything like that?"

She thought a moment. The fact was, there *had* been something wrong. She'd sensed it rather than been told it, but it was noticeable enough that she'd asked Sam if there were any problems.

"She seemed—you know, tense. Yeah, maybe nervous. I figured at first it was just her period or something but it wasn't like that, really. She looked, well, kinda *scared*. But she said everything was okay when I asked her about it. She just sorta' shrugged it off and said she was havin' some problems and that she'd tell me when I got back. I *did* kinda get the idea that she wanted to say more but when she found out I was goin' away, well, she just tried to laugh it off. Why? What's happened to her?"

O'Donnell had sighed. He was big and craggy and built like cement block, with curly red hair and real pale blue eyes. If you'd been ordered to build an Irishman he was about what you'd come up with.

"She left school normally—we know that much," he told her. "She caught the first bus home, got a few things—her mother wasn't back from work yet—and then left. We don't know anything beyond that. She simply—vanished." He paused as he watched her look of horror grow. "These things *do* happen, Miss. All the time. It's my job to piece everything together and see if we can find her before something very bad happens to her."

"You think she—*ran away?* Not Sam! The only one she could run to would be her Dad and he'd send her right back here. I *know!*"

"We don't honestly know. She certainly hadn't made any long-range plans to bolt; there's no sign of it. Everything points to a sudden decision to just take off. She went home, packed a small suitcase, went down to the Front Street Bank's automated teller with the backup of her mother's card and withdrew the maximum three hundred dollars allowed by the machine."

"Yeah, her mom gave her the card just in case she needed money when her mom wasn't around but I don't think she ever used it for more'n twenty bucks. Three hundred . . ."

"That's really not that much when you consider it," the detective had pointed out. "Enough to buy a ticket to most places but only if you had money or people at the other end.

We checked the airlines and bus stations—no sign, although that doesn't always mean much. She didn't have a driver's license?"

Charley shook her head. "Nope. Flunked the test three times. She was just too scared behind the wheel."

"And no boyfriends? Particularly new ones? No major infatuations? You're positive?"

"Positive! She's not gay or nothin' like that—she liked boys and all, but if she had anything going she'd'a told me. No way there was anybody she'd do *this* for, not unless it happened between Friday morning and Friday afternoon."

"Stranger things have happened, but I admit it's unlikely unless it involved someone in school and we can account for everyone but her. Very well—if she contacts you let me know *immediately.* I'll give you a card, here, with my name and number. It looks very likely that something scared her very badly. Something she couldn't or wouldn't confide for any of a thousand reasons to either her best friend or her mother. She panicked. She ran. No note, nothing. But her resources are quite limited. If she uses any of her mother's charge cards we'll find her and I think she's bright enough to know that. Her cash will be running low if it isn't gone already. She'll only have a few choices, and they're crime, or falling prey to the seamier side of society, or she'll have to contact somebody she trusts. You're a likely candidate for that. If she does, try and get her what she needs and find out where she's staying and then call me. And, if you can, find out what in the world could scare her so much that this was the only way out."

She had promised it all, but the truth was that if Sam called she didn't know *what* she would do, and she suspected O'Donnell knew that, too. What the hell could have *scared* her like that? Caused her to run rather than go to her mom or best friend? Had Sam been less honest than she seemed? Had she, like, gotten knocked up? No, that wouldn't do it. Hell, she might get grounded for six months but her mom would still have worked it all out and Sam would know that. Her mom was pretty busy but she was all right deep down—much more modern than Charley's parents, anyway.

Sam always said she wanted to be an actress; she'd been in the drama club and was set for a pretty good part in the class play coming up in April, but she had few other real interests. Setting off for Hollywood on impulse just wasn't her style.

It was hard for Charley to imagine Sam out there on her own in any event. Hell, she was scared to go out alone most times. Like, she was even scared of thunderstorms. Well, maybe she'd find out now.

Charley had gone through the day confused and depressed and then went straight home. She'd gotten the mail and found a small envelope addressed to her and postmarked locally with very familiar handwriting and she'd torn it open. Inside, on a piece of notepaper in Sam's handwriting, had been a nervously scrawled message.

> *Dear Charley—Sorry to get you into this but I got noplace else to go. Can you meet me at the mall at seven o'clock? Just go browse at Sears. Look normal, then at seven go back to credit like you was going to the ladies room. Don't tell nobody or let them see this note. Don't let nobody follow you. I'm OK so long as you don't bring nobody. Love and kisses, Sam.*

Charley was afraid at first that she wouldn't make it in time. Her Dad had a bunch of stuff to talk about and wasn't in any mood to let her out, but she'd convinced him it wouldn't be long and that she really needed to pick up something for school tomorrow. She barely had time to change into an outfit more appropriate for the mall—the satiny blue pantsuit and the mid-calf boots with the fold-down leather fringes. And it'd been like six-thirty when she'd gotten the okay, and while it was only a ten-minute drive to the mall she had to park and go to Sears and spend some time browsing, too, so it'd look natural when she went to the jane. There was also the level of paranoia the note induced.

"Don't let nobody follow you. . . ."

Like, who would be following *her?* Well, okay, the cops, maybe—if they figured one runaway teen was worth a stakeout. Or, maybe, whoever scared Sam so bad. They might figure it like O'Donnell and keep an eye on her best friend, right?

Damn it, she's got me seein' cars and mysterious people in trenchcoats!

The worst part of it was, she had to wear her glasses and she hated that. Made her look like some dumb librarian. But she was fairly nearsighted and needed them to drive, and she'd had her contacts in all day at school. Not like Sam—Sam only needed glasses to read close up, and she'd look like an idiot, face at arm's length from a book, rather than wear them in school.

The mall was pretty crowded for a winter Wednesday, maybe because it was unusually warm tonight for this time of year, and Charley saw one or two kids she knew, but the time didn't allow for her to be anything but single-minded. If somebody was following they'd just have to follow, that's all. What the hell could happen in a place crowded like *this*, anyway?

She made her way to Sears, then went and looked at some of the clothes there. She knew she didn't have Sam's acting talent and she probably was giving the most unconvincing show of her life, but she had to try. She glanced at her watch—five after seven! Past time to go to the bathroom.

Had she delayed long enough? Had she delayed too long? She went on back to the business office and then around the corner toward the restrooms. You sure knew where *they* were in a big mall. Most times the biggest department stores had the only bathrooms in the place.

The restrooms were near the end of a corridor that wound up at an "Employees Only" door to the warehouse part, and there was a branch corridor just before them leading to some offices. She went into the bathroom expecting Sam to be there, but it was empty. She wasn't sure if she should just stay there or not, but she sure as hell wasn't gonna stay there all night. She really did have to go—this Jane Bond shit didn't really make it at all—and so she decided to just do everything normal. Maybe Sam wasn't there tonight. Maybe something happened, or Sam figured the note would come earlier, or maybe this was just a way for Sam to check and see that she wasn't being followed.

She gave it fifteen minutes, during which one pregnant lady came in and nobody else, and then decided to get out of there. She opened the door and heard, behind her, in a loud whisper, "Charley! In here—quick!"

She turned and saw a small, chunky figure in boys' blue denim jeans and matching jacket holding the employee door open. She hesitated a moment, then went to the door and out just before the pregnant lady exited.

Charley stared at the other. "Christ, Sam—is that really *you?*"

"Yeah! Come on! I want to get us out of here and someplace where we can talk. Hurry up!"

As close as she'd been to Sam she wouldn't have recognized her from any distance. Gone was the long, straight black hair, replaced with a slightly curly sandy brown cut, extremely short, like a boy's, and combed straight back with a side part. She was also wearing a man's style rose-tinted pair of glasses and dressed in the stiff denim that completely concealed her figure and some cheap sneakers and high black socks. It was a fairly simple disguise but by its subtlety very effective. No fake beard or shit like that that would never be convincing. The fact that Sam was one of those people whose face by itself could be either male or female depending on the hair and body and the like helped, too. It was also a natural disguise—her voice was already unusually low, and it didn't take much effort to get it low and raspy enough to sound like maybe a thirteen- or fourteen-year-old boy.

They wound up outside, then walked across the parking lot to the theater entrance. Sam bought two tickets to the newest Disney cartoon, knowing that for the late show there'd be very few people there and none they would know. Not with a "G" rating.

Sam was right. There were like a dozen people in there for the Wednesday late show. They took seats on a side aisle near the back, away from the rest. Sam put her arm around Charley. "Just act like we don't care about the movie, which we don't," she said. "Nobody ever notices much about a boy and a girl makin' out in the back of a theater."

"Okay, I'll play along," Charley whispered back, "but what the hell is this all *about*? Why'd you run? Where you *been*? Everybody's worried sick. . . ."

"Long story," Sam responded. "I'll tell you as much as I can. Some of it'll sound crazy and maybe I am, but it's damned *real*."

It hadn't been all that sudden, only the final act. For months, almost since moving out west, she had been having strange experiences. First it was the dreams—lots of them, long and elaborate, sometimes several nights in a row with no break, and always involving the same things although never quite the same.

Charley knew about the dreams. The most frequent one involved the demon and Sam, who was always driving a red sports car around a twisting mountain road along a coast, although Sam couldn't drive and they were hundreds of miles from any coast.

It always began with a dark figure, sitting alone in a comfortable-looking room that none the less resembled more a medieval castle than anything modern. There was a low fire in the fireplace and a few goblets about, but everything was indistinct, as if in a dream. She saw his form, but not really his face, masked in shadow, but it was a strange form of a fairly large man in flowing robes and wearing what might have been a helmet with two large, crooked horns emerging from each side. She saw him, though, not as a vision, or a completed scene, but as if she were there as well, sitting opposite him in a chair of her own, looking at his dark form with her own eyes. Somehow, she was aware that the goblet near her on a small table had until recently contained some kind of drug, and that the dark figure's mysterious, hazy, dark presence was partly due to that.

Suddenly there was a rumble and crackling, more like an electrical short circuit than anything else, but it seemed to overwhelm them, to carry them, not physically but mentally, through a dizzying, blinding, multicolored ride like an out of control carousel, although the dark form in the chair was still there, silhouetted against the swirling maelstrom.

And then there had been darkness, with scenes illuminated now by flashes of lightning and accompanying clashes of thunder, and a view from a great height down to a frothing ocean below beating itself against black rocks, and a low range of mountains forming a jagged and serpentine coastline, and, in the distance, two small lights approaching along that coast. They were not the storm, but they were of and with the storm, and they moved swiftly inland to a point where storm and lights must meet.

And now she saw herself driving that red sports car, but not from the point of view of the driver. Rather, she saw herself from the height during the flashes of lightning, and now they were nearly on top of it, and the dark, horned figure whispered fearsomely in a tone that somehow still cut through the noise of storm and surf, "Now! I was correct. The equations are perfectly in balance. She is the one we seek and she sleeps in the stupors of overindulgence. Minimum resistance, maximum flow, calculated odds of success in the ninety-plus percentile. . . . Now!"

And from the cloud a great bolt of lightning shot out, and while it struck just ahead and on the ocean side of the road the car suddenly slammed on its brakes and spun, aided by the sudden rain, and . . .

All then was blackness.

That had been the first of them, repeated many times with little or no variation, but it had not been the last. At first she put them down as mere fantasies, as nightmares, maybe, or possibly even a sign of a good imagination, but then the dreams progressed and she began to see a pattern both in when the dreams came and in their progression.

Always in the night. Always when thunderstorms approached and then raged around her.

But during this season of the year she felt she'd almost licked it. No thunderstorms, no really bad dreams. Not until last Thursday night, when this freak warm front had moved in and clashed with the very chilly winter air and set off a rare winter one.

Charley frowned. "I don't remember a thunderstorm last Thursday."

"It was real early in the morning. Like two or three. You'd sleep through an atomic bomb anyway. You can check it in the papers, though. We had it—and I had another real mean one."

"You mean you're running from a *dream?*"

"Not—exactly."

She had awakened to the sound and fury of the freak storm, and lay there, eyes wide open, feeling wide awake and afraid to go back to sleep, but even though the storm raged and she was fully conscious, through the thunder, through the roar of rain and hail on the roof and the rattling of windows by heavy winds, the voices intruded and the room seemed to fade. It was also quite dark, but she was seeing through another's eyes, a visitor without influence or control; an interloper who should not have been there, wherever "there" was.

It was the hall of a medieval-like castle, damp and somewhat dark, illuminated by torches and by a fire in the great fireplace. She sat in a large, lushly upholstered chair at the head of a long table, an elegant if greasy and overcooked meal in front of her. She knew it was a woman's body, and probably royalty; long, feminine arms reached out for food and wine, with long, delicate fingers unblemished by any sign of work or wear, with crimson, perfectly trimmed and shaped nails so long they could not have withstood doing anything serious.

There were others at the table. A large man with a full beard and shoulder-length hair, stocky and rough but dressed in fine clothing including a cape. Several others, mostly rough-looking men, some accompanied by young women dressed in satin and gold, were also there—and a few others.

One was a tiny, gnarled man who must have been no more than three feet high, dressed in gray and brown with a rich black beard that seemed to go down almost to his feet, sitting there on a very high stool to be at equal height to the others. Another wore a crimson cloak and hood but seemed to have a frog-like snout extending from it and two round, yellow eyes that never blinked but, cat-like, reflected the torchlight. Yet another had a long, distorted, puffy kind of face, huge round blue eyes, and a rhinoceros-like horn rising up from the center of his forehead, and a woman whose hairless head seemed covered by a bony gray plate and whose arms ended not in hands but in claw-like mandibles. There may have been more, but the onlooker did not focus on them but rather on eating.

Finally the hairy man closest to her asked, "Highness, has the problem of the simulacra been disposed of?"

From behind her a voice, that voice, responded, "My Lord Klewa, we all know that nothing is certain except that the unthinkable must be thought, but there was little danger. So far we have found only a very few in all our months of searching that even slightly posed a danger and we are dealing with each in turn. The odds of that ever being a factor were always slim—the enemy would have to find a simulacrum and somehow transport before we could find and destroy them, and we had the only model for such loci searching anyway. You have no idea how many levels up we have gone and continue to go. Just when we believe it is no longer possible my storms find another, but so far away. . . . Even so, I shall deal with each.

"If you wish certainties, then kill yourself," the strange one continued, "for that will produce a certainty in this world, at least. If you desire minimum risk, we have gone far further in that regard then anyone could imagine. But risk there will always be, and should be, for gain without risk would make a prize meaningless. So vast is our enterprise that we risk

disrupting the fragile fabric of our reality and might cause the changewinds to increase and turn on us as well, but consider the goals and the alternatives. Be at ease.''

And then she *spoke, with a voice not unlike her own voice, strangely deep, although the tongue was strange and musical and not at all like English or any other language she had known, and the tone was softer, gentler, maybe sexier than she'd ever used.*

"My Lord, why these questions now? You know my talents, and you know the skills of Protector Klittichorn. None of you entered into this alliance blindly, and our ideals and goals are of the highest order. The small brains who blindly struck down your own son to preserve their evil statist values would also have at me. We unite and triumph or die, or we do nothing and thus only die ever so slowly but no less certainly. But if we die, let it not be from faint hearts when all goes well. Speak your mind freely here, for we are equals at this table.''

"Equals, aye, except for him,'' muttered the gnome-like man in a surprisingly deep, gruff voice. "We would follow you and your ideals to the death, My Lady, but not to deliver ourselves into the hands of another oppressor.''

"The Protector is a brilliant man who has the same dreams as we,'' she responded. "I have complete confidence in him, and, of course, there is no real chance of true victory without his tremendous skills. I regret that he has not the pleasing personality of court and politics, but I do not doubt his motives. He has always served me faithfully and well, and if you have any doubts then you must discard them. All of us must trust one another and give our bond; it is the only true thing of value between us.''

Suddenly the scene began to fade, jumping in and out, becoming disjointed and impossible to follow, like hearing three seconds out of every ten in a conversation. Another voice seemed to be cutting out the connection, with intermittent words here and there in a totally different tone and appearing to come from much farther away.

. . . *bee* . . . *kow* . . . *low* . . . *bap* . . .

There was a sudden dizziness, first one way, then the other, as if someone were tuning a radio and she was the dial. It stopped almost as quickly as it began, and again there was a sense of contact with someone or something far away, but with a difference. This time she was lying there in the dark, fully aware of herself and her surroundings, her skin tingling oddly, and there was a sense that now the situation was reversed and that someone, or something, was looking at her or through her to the room beyond.

"There is darkness. She is awake and her eyes are open but there is darkness." There was a sudden slight tickling sensation as if cobwebs had been run up and down her body. *"Hmmm . . . Nothing really wrong. I was afraid for a moment she was blind or something."*

"It's nighttime, you idiot, and she's in bed in a trance," came another voice.

"Who are you?" she called aloud to the voice in her head. "What do you want with me?"

The voice either did not or could not hear, and ignored her. It was inside her head, yet distanced. A man's voice, but not any of the men at the court dinner she had witnessed. Someone new, someone different, almost clinical-sounding, like some of her doctors. More interesting, if a bit more frightening, the words were certainly American English.

"I have her construct now. It is identical in every detail. Astonishing. There must not be one point of similarity in background or origin yet there is an identical genetic code." A sigh. *"Too late. The storm is passing and the lock of hair is not sufficient for more. But—does he know of her? He must—the storms are passing through and she's next. Still alive, Cromil! The first one we've found before he's killed her!"*

"The one in the red car was barely dead," the other noted optimistically. *"At least we're catching up."*

The man ignored the comment. *"Too late to do more now, damn it! Time for preparations. We must not let him kill her if we can. In our hands, she would be a great weapon. One test, no more. It already fades. . . ."*

Suddenly, eerily, she was entirely back in the room, the storm already going away, her senses abnormally keen and sharp.

And then someone began to run his fingers through her hair!

It was terrifying, horrible. She wanted to scream, but dared not. The sensation faded in a moment but it was some time before she could move, dared to sit up, to turn—and find no one there.

Charley didn't know what to believe but she could understand her friend's terror. "Jeez! That's why you looked like hell and were so shook up at school Friday."

Sam nodded. "Yeah—but what could I do? You were goin' away for the weekend, and my mom would have all kinds of pop psychology bullshit. I mean, I didn't have any proof or nothin'. Hell, maybe I *was* nuts. I didn't know. But when we got out of school, well, something else happened. Just comin' out the door, kids all around, I thought I saw this big guy out of the corner of my eye, all black and stuff, maybe ten feet away. I turned, but there was nobody there. I got spooked. I got on the bus and sat up front, almost behind Miss Everett. I was lookin' out, and I know it's nuts, but I saw him again. Out of the corner of my eye, like before—standin' on the street. In a crowd. But when I looked around, he was gone."

"Just nerves."

"Yeah, that's what I told myself, but then I looked up for some reason straight into the rear view mirror. You know what I mean—shows the aisle and seats? And he was there, sittin' in the back, and he didn't disappear. I turned, and there was nothin' where he should'a been but empty seats. I turned back to the mirror and there he was."

"What—what did he look like?" Like, was this a loony tune or was this strait jacket city?

"He—he didn't have any real features. He was all black, kinda like a cardboard cutout of black paper, but he moved. He breathed. He was *alive!* And, I mean, I had to get off that bus. I walked the last three blocks, and when the bus passed I kinda saw him on it still. I got into the house, I didn't know what to do, but I knew it'd be dark in an hour and Mom wouldn't be home for three. Besides, they'd got me in my own room in my own bed. All she'd do would be to get me off to the funny farm where I'd be cooped up, and I figured he'd find me easy there. I looked out the front windows and I saw him, across the street, by the mailbox, just standin' there. I didn't know what he was doin', but I figured he was either just keepin' an eye on me for somebody else or he was waitin' til dark and I just wasn't gonna give him no chance. I panicked. I stuffed one of Mom's overnight bags with whatever I could find quick, grabbed the cash card, and got out the cellar window and out through the backyard. I snuck six blocks to Central Avenue, hit the automatic teller—I forgot you couldn't get much from one— and then caught the bus to the mall. I knew I'd given him the slip—no sign of him, not in the mirror of the bus, not anywhere. All I wanted was to shake him—and I did.''

She blew a hundred and ten bucks on the boy's denims and shoes and another forty in the Hair Palace, a unisex hair salon. "I told them it was for a school play," she said. "That I had to look like a boy 'cause the role was a girl pretending to be a boy. The glasses were fifteen bucks. Plain lenses. I washed the stuff at the little coin-op at the motel over on Figuroa. I finally dumped most everything I brought with me in the dumpster. Then I started hidin' out here in the mall. There's all sorts of places if you really want to, and don't mind gettin' locked in. They got a couple of security guards but they're easy to dodge and they only go to midnight, eight on Sundays, then they just lock up tight and go. The water fountains work and the employee rest rooms in the mall security area ain't never locked. Durin' the day I been hustlin'. You know—carrying groceries to cars down at the Food Mart, helpin' little old ladies with shit, that kind of thing. I been doin' maybe twenty, thirty bucks a day in tips.''

"And, like nobody's *recognized* you?''

She grinned. "Nope. I even been real close to some of the gang from school, mostly by accident—no use in pushin' things—and they never gave me a glance. You'd be surprised how many kids are around durin' school days, too. Nobody ever says nothin' unless they're at the arcade or like that. And everybody's been treatin' me like a boy. I even use the men's room. I always wondered what a urinal looks like. No wonder they can be in and out so fast. Only thing wrong is the mice.'' She shivered. "You'd think a classy place like this wouldn't have things like them hiding around. At least they should get a cat or something. And I'm *dying* for a shower!''

Charley stared at Sam in the darkness as an evil cartoon cat was chortling over plans to do in a very strange-looking duck in France or someplace on the screen. "You nuts? You gone stark raving mad? Sam, you can't keep going on like this! Your mom's probably worried sick by now, the cops are all over looking for you, and sooner or later somebody's gonna notice.''

The fugitive sighed. "I know. I know. But I can't go home yet—I'll never feel real comfortable there again, and what if this character doesn't care who he hurts? I know it sounds nuts, like spook city, but it's for *real*. When I get out of this and have some breathing time I'll call Mom and tell her I'm okay. It won't stop her worryin' but at least she'll know I'm not kidnapped or dead or somethin'." She paused, sensing that it wasn't getting through. "Charley—I'm scared. I've never been more scared in my whole life. I'm—doing this—'cause I don't know what else to do."

"Sam—you just gotta come home. You just *gotta*. You're not cut out for this. Sooner or later somebody's gonna find you out anyway, or somebody else will spot you for what you are and you'll wind up in some strange city all doped up and turnin' tricks or somethin' like that. Jesus, there must be a hundred rapes a year just in *this* town! This ain't TV and you're no karate queen!"

"I made out so far. It's different when they think you're a boy. I found out how different just around here. But—you think I *like* this? I never thought ahead. I had to run and hide. Whoever it is, though—they haven't found me here. Not yet, anyway."

"Look—your mom and the cops can help."

"How? From a black figure who's only visible when he wants to be seen? From fucking thunderstorms that can put *something* in my own bedroom with me? You're sayin' go back and stand in front of the guys with guns who want to kill ya 'cause if you run through the door and get away from 'em you just *might* run into a guy with a gun someplace who wants to kill ya."

"They're just *dreams*, Sam! Just *dreams*. They're just all in your head. And a black figure who's seen only in mirrors and once in a while when you're alone—that's creepy but it's right out of a horror movie. Those things just don't *exist* in the real world. I may not be a real brain but I know better than to believe in elves and fairies and Santa Claus and the Boogeyman."

Sam sighed. "I kinda thought you'd say that. I *know* that's what Mom and Dad and the cops would say—what almost *anybody'd* say. Okay, forget the dreams, forget the Boogeyman, forget everything I told you. Just promise me that you won't give me away here. Not until I can get clear and get settled someplace. A day. Two days tops. Will you promise me that?" She stared at her friend in the darkness of the movie house. "Charley—if I have to go home now, or to the funny farm, I'll kill myself. You can't *know* what it was like. Don't force me to do that. *Please!"*

Charley didn't really know what to do. Sam needed help—a lot of it. That was for sure. Help she couldn't give. She needed a really good psychiatrist and a lot of time. On the other hand, Sam was still Sam and she was still her friend, and there was such a note of desperation there that Charley felt Sam might well kill herself at this point. She needed advice on what to do and there was no way she could get it. Anybody she told about this would be hell-bent to recapture Sam, and if anything happened to Sam as a result of what she did she'd never forgive herself.

"Okay, okay, keep cool," Charley responded, trying to think. "Look, there's not much I can do tonight, and I got school tomorrow and Friday. I was supposed to go to a movie with Harry Friday night, but I can break that without my folks knowing. Look, I'll pick you up here. We'll do this boyfriend-girlfriend bit so it'll look right. I'll pick you up in front of the Food Mart say . . . seven-thirty. We'll go someplace and try and really figure it out. If anything happens before then, call me and I'll see what I can do. I *swear* I won't tell nobody nothin'. All right?"

Sam seemed somewhat relieved. "All right. Friday night, then. You better get home now—I'll get by."

Charley kissed Sam and squeezed her hand and then, hesitantly, got up and walked out of the theater. The mall was already mostly closed down, and she had no trouble finding her car. She got in, started it, and pulled out toward the exit light, trying to think, to figure things out, and not paying any attention to the rock blaring from the car radio.

"And here's the latest from Action Weather. Cool tonight, lows about thirty-five in the city and lower than that in the suburbs, with light snow possible above the six thousand foot mark. In spite of this, unseasonable freak thunderstorms continue in the area due to an unsettled mix of very cold air aloft and relatively warmer air near the surface. High tomorrow around fifty. This is Doctor Ruben Miller with Action Weather. . . ."

A car's lights turned on behind her and slowly pulled out toward the exit traffic light. *Just nerves,* she told herself. *Most people would be leaving now who hadn't already left.*

She turned onto the street and couldn't help but see the lights of the other car turn the same way. She began feeling very paranoid, very silly. Sam was, well, *sick,* that's all. It'd take a shrink to figure it out, but Sam never really liked it out here in the southwestern boonies or being this far from her dad, she was too straight arrow to even date in the usual ways, and she was hemmed in by her lack of wheels to get out and enjoy things. She'd gone so far into that fantasy life she couldn't quite get out anymore, Charley decided.

Still, she couldn't shake some of the paranoia that rubbed off Sam like dirt. Was that the same car still following? What if she made a turn?

Feeling stupid, she turned onto a side street well before hers just to get a little peace of mind. She went about a block and then saw headlights turn in from the main street. She made a left, then another right before the other car could possibly see her, then pulled over and parked just ahead of a big black car that would partially shield her from view.

A car passed on the cross street; a dark blue Ford. It was impossible to see who was driving, but that was certainly the car. She pulled back out, then threaded her way through the development and back toward her house again. She chided herself for being so spooked and came up to the stop sign on her street, then forward to the middle of the block where her house was. She almost panicked when she passed a blue Ford—*the* blue Ford—parked at the corner across the street from her house. It looked like there was somebody in it, but she couldn't really make him out.

Unnerved now, she parked in the driveway and got out, wanting to be inside as quickly as possible. It was probably a cop—all the cops on TV seemed to drive big, dark cars like that. O'Donnell or his boss had decided to bet a couple of men that Sam was still in town and would be likely to contact her best friend, that was all. It was scary, but it sure as hell wasn't no mysterious dark figure you could see only in mirrors or any magic princesses.

A mall is a strange place at night, full of half-lit halls and ghostly stores and vast, deserted airspace. There were bars or roll-down security fronts on the stores, of course, and after Security left at midnight all of the entrances and exits also were wired, although, of course, a few key doors had safety bars just in case someone got trapped inside. Some malls had twenty-four-hour security inside, but, fortunately, this wasn't exactly a major crime area and the place was pretty secure against burglars and vandals. All the stores closed at nine; only the theaters were open later, usually until eleven or so, and they had a separate outside exit allowing them to have their final show without disturbing the mall routine.

By ten the merchants were gone and the cleaning crews were out in force. It was pretty impressive to see them work a whole mall in such a short time, but everything was on such an impressive system that they almost never strayed past midnight. The theaters had their own crew that came in at seven in the morning; their first features were the matinees and it was more efficient to clean them during the unused morning time than pay overtime to a night crew.

The first security personnel arrived about seven, give or take a couple of minutes. They checked the locks and made the rounds once to make certain that all was well. Around seven-thirty some mall personnel showed up, checking all the settings and turning on the lights, fountains, and the rest, and soon after the early merchants would begin to show, starting with the food stall people and then the rest. By nine it was all ready to go once again. Only on Sundays, when the mall was only open noon to six, did anything vary. Then, starting at six, a veritable army of cleaning and maintenance personnel mo ed in and it was often after midnight when they left.

Behind the facade, however, were miles of service corridors, storerooms, and other areas that were the nuts and bolts of running such a place. There were even some classroom-sized rooms and a small complex of offices. By now Sam had explored them all and discovered the areas where virtually no one went on a regular basis, and there, well hidden from even the most chance encounter, she'd made something of a nest using some removable seat cushions from stored chairs and other things picked up along the way that nobody would miss. Saturday night she'd made a valuable find, in fact, although she hadn't yet had to use it, where the day cleaning crew who picked up while all was open changed. It was a nice red security badge with a male name on it—George Trask, whoever he was—and a number but no photo. She always wore it when getting in or out of here, though, just in case.

She had run in terror and run to the only place she could think of, but when it became clear that she had not been seen or followed and she had, at least temporarily, some safety, the focus had changed. The more nights she got away with it, the more confident she became, now often staying awake late and sleeping late, sneaking out into the mall itself well after it was alive and going. By Monday it had become something of an adventure, although she knew full well it couldn't last. She also had to know what was going on, what was being said about her, how large the hue and cry, and that was the reason for the note to Charley. She wasn't sure what Charley could do, if anything, but it was better than being alone.

She also felt frustrated. She didn't want her mom to worry, or her dad, either. He was probably flying out now if he wasn't already here yelling and screaming at her mom and the cops and everybody else. Better they should worry than find her dead, though.

She would have liked to have reassured them, but what the hell could she say? She'd tried the truth with Charley and Charley had reacted like it was psycho city, so explaining this to her parents was just impossible. She needed to get away for a while, far from here, and sort it all out. Maybe north or east into the real cold where they didn't have thunderstorms this time of year. Someplace where she could get some kind of menial job that would keep her going. Damn it, she knew carpentry and construction. There had to be something out there someplace. Not much chance for a girl, but she played a mighty convincing boy if she did say so herself. She had the walk and the moves and the vocabulary down pat. Hell, she had it down so pat she'd gone right past some people she'd been in school with for a year and they never noticed, and she'd even gotten friendly with a couple of fifteen-year-old girls who hung out here.

She'd kind of fantasized being a boy off and on and she had to admit it had its points. Boys didn't have to spend an hour and a half just getting ready to go out in public; they didn't have to suffer lewd comments from passing pickup trucks or worry much about being alone on the bus or why a guy was being nice. In a sense, they were just more invisible in everyday life.

She acted the part well enough but she wasn't a boy, and on Thursday evening that was driven home to her hard. Everything was closed, she was getting her damned period, and there wasn't a reachable tampon in sight. Some blood had seeped through, soaking her panties and getting on the jeans. She had spare panties but she knew she had to work on that jeans stain before it set. The one small washroom that was open had some soap but the basin wasn't big enough for that. *Okay, Sam, you figured out the rest up to now—what the hell do you do about this?*

And so she found herself, at two in the morning, stark naked in the middle of the main concourse of the mall, sitting on the edge of the fountain and soaking her pants and underwear. The fountain was turned off for the night, but there was a pool of water there maybe two feet deep. It was also surprisingly warm—well, tepid, anyway—and quite clear. At the bottom she saw what seemed to be hundreds of coins thrown in by people over the week—they generally fished out the stuff on Sundays. Mostly pennies, but there was occasional silver in there and she found herself slipping into the fountain and combing the bottom. She came up in the end with only three dollars and fifty-five cents in non-pennies but it was okay.

She finally decided to hell with it and gave herself something of a rinse and she felt a lot better for it. Her flow was still intermittent; by tomorrow she'd buy something that would keep it from betraying her.

When she got out, rinsed out the clothes and laid them out to dry as much as possible, she found herself feeling a lot cheerier but not at all sleepy, even though she should have been dead tired. She looked out at the silent mall and felt a kind of kinky thrill. In a few hours this place would be jammed with people, but here she was, stark naked in the middle of it all. She decided to have a stroll around the mall. She'd once had a dream about touring a mall stark naked, although, of course, all the stores were open in the dream. Even so, it was sort of like living a brief fantasy and it was kind of funny.

Most of the stores kept lights on at low levels, but a few were completely dark, and their display windows reflected her form. She stopped at one and stared at herself. She sure didn't look like a boy now, and for the moment she didn't want to. She'd never been thrilled with her face—her ears were too big and her nose was wrong and her teeth were too big and prominent and she had a kind of chubbette face, or so she thought, but there was nothing wrong with her body. It amazed her that breasts like hers could be so effectively concealed by that stiff denim jacket, although she'd paid a price for it in rubbing and chafing. Nice body curve, too, and pretty good hips if she did say so herself. Her ass looked fatter than it should be, but that was about it. She struck a few sexy poses and kind of liked it. She was getting turned on by all this and she didn't fight it. She tried to imagine herself as a boy now, though, and couldn't. No, she could play one all right, but she didn't want to give up what she was seeing now.

She passed close to one of the security cameras monitoring the staff exit and suppressed a giggle. Couldn't *she* give 'em something to really look at! Not that she would. If anybody saw her like this now, she'd just *die*. Suddenly the thrill was gone. What if somebody *did* show up now? What if some merchant or security man or mall supervisor had to come in real early for something? They hadn't yet, but suddenly the possibility loomed like a certainty in her mind.

She went back down to the fountain where her clothes were. In the dry mall air the undies were almost dry although they looked like veterans of a chainsaw massacre; the jeans, however, seemed as wet as ever. They generally took an hour on high in the dryer at home. Hell, it might be a long time before they were dry enough to wear, damn it. Still, scrubbing the fresh stain with some hand soap and water had done wonders. It was still there but wasn't much and certainly didn't look like blood anymore.

Outside, as if very far away, she heard a faint rumble. *Oh, God! Not a thunderstorm! Not now!* To be heard much at all inside *here* it must be right on top of her! *They* were still looking for her, that was for sure. They'd lost her once but they wouldn't give up if they thought she was still around the town. She knew that. If the cops were still looking, then *they* were sure as hell not gonna give up.

She felt sudden panic. What would she do if *they* found her in here right now? Visions of mad slasher movies started running through her head. The jeans were still so wet they'd be more a hindrance than a help. Being chased, naked, through a deserted mall by *him* . . .

What was that? Some kind of noise over by the book store . . .

She grabbed up everything and made for the staff exit, being careful to avoid the camera and other more actual traps and back to her hiding place. She could hear the storm a bit more here, closer to the outer walls, but she could do nothing but huddle, shivering in the dark, eyes glued to the door of the storeroom.

Oh, God! Please, God! Steer them away from me! I'll do anything, anything, but please don't let them find me tonight! Just send the storm away from here, away from me!

And, although wide awake and terrified, she seemed to hear the Horned One's voice, as if in a whisper far away.

"Damn it, I almost had her, but something is deflecting the storms, interfering with the focus. I can't seem to get a fix. This requires too much energy; I am drained. But we will find her, never fear. If not this night, another night. This one must be dealt with. She has tapped the Power. Potentially she is the most dangerous one we have yet encountered. . . .

And all the while the object of this ghostly conversation sat crouched against the wall in the corner of the storeroom, naked, helpless, and terrified in the dark.

· 2 ·

The Maelstrom

MORNING DAWNED BRIGHT if a little crisp over the valley. Inside the insulated mall the canned music was turned on and a chorus of massed violins was playing a soft, melodic version of *Beast of Burden*. In the storeroom, Sam had gone to sleep after several hours in spite of herself but her real gain was perhaps two hours of rest and she felt like she'd been run over by a truck.

Even so, she felt some elation. Once again, somehow, she'd beaten them, if only for a night. One thing was sure, though— she had to get out of here now. *They* knew, or at least suspected, that she was here. They'd be back, again and again, until they found her. She wanted to meet no dark figure in this mall at two the next morning.

Still, it was now Friday. If Charley hadn't decided to stay out of it and if she really wanted to help she'd be there tonight, maybe with a car.

The jeans were still damp and badly wrinkled, but they would do. The socks might as well be abandoned. After days in them they were beyond the help of merely soaking. She never liked the feel of them anyway.

First things first. She'd have to get out of here and find enough light to count her money and see just what she did and didn't have. She didn't feel much like eating right now, but she needed tea or a Coke or something with a jolt in it to get her going and keep her moving today. It was gonna be one damned long day.

She managed to dress and slip out and into the mall proper. She had to pass a few people in back as she always did, but so

25

long as you looked like you belonged nobody ever said much, particularly if you were going out. She headed first for the now open public restrooms. Nothing like a well-lighted stall for privacy, although the men's rooms weren't as nice as the ladies' rooms and had far fewer stalls.

She sat down and pulled out the crumpled mass of coins and bills and flattened and counted them. A hundred twenty-seven sixty-five. Not much. She still had her mother's bank card but the odds were they changed that just in case she was kidnapped or something. Still, it might be worth a try tonight. Friday night—if the number hadn't been changed it'd be Monday before anybody'd find out it was used again and by that time she really would be gone while they searched here. Not bad. Nothing to lose, anyway.

A pocket-sized pack of maxi-pads solved the immediate problem and just in time, too. That and some Panadol for the cramps, although it only helped a little. She was one of those unlucky ones who got it bad, at least for a day or so. Charley was luckier in that regard; she hardly ever had it bad. Sam always wondered if it was because she was oversexed or something or if it was easier once your cherry was popped or if the combination would turn her into a nymphomaniac or something. Hustling much was out today; her lack of sleep, period, and nerves combined to make her unfit for much of anything. She picked up a couple of donuts and a Coke and managed to get them down. It helped only in that it was an improvement over no donuts and no Coke.

It was tough to stay awake and kill a whole day without doing much. She browsed a lot, but the fact was that time really crawled and she was feeling just miserable. Worse was seeing all the things she'd like to buy, things she really needed—like more clothes and a jacket at least—but didn't dare pick up. By the time Charley was due she was in pretty bad shape. Still, she spotted the little red Subaru wagon cruise by the entrance slowly, then stop by the curb, and she practically ran to it and jumped in. Charley pulled away almost immediately.

"Jeez! You look like warmed over shit," her friend commented. Charley was dressed like she was going on a real heavy date—lipstick, makeup, perfume, fake fur jacket, nice satiny blouse and short skirt, even pantihose and heels. She even had her contacts in—at least, Sam *hoped* she did.

"This has been one of the worst days of my whole life," Sam responded honestly. "No sleep, cramps, you name it. Glad to see you dressed up for me, though."

Charley laughed. "I had a couple of days to work this out and some of the gang at school were willing to help out, too."

Sam had closed her eyes but one opened. "You didn't tell nobody else about me, did you?"

"No, relax. There's a group going up to Taos to ski this weekend and I just begged my folks to be included, since the weather's been so weird and we have a four-wheel-drive wagon. I think they're happy to get me out of town and someplace safe for the weekend. It's not the first time—you know that—and Monday's a school holiday. The cops seem to have given up on you but my folks are still real paranoid about me since you vanished. It was almost World War Three just to go to the bathroom alone after they found out about you yesterday."

"Yeah? And what's the group gonna say when you don't show up?"

Charley laughed. "Oh, if necessary they'll cover for me. They think I'm sneaking out this weekend to spend it with a new and secret boyfriend. Remember my reputation at school. I'm a woman of *experience*, remember. I'll give my folks a call later on tonight and again tomorrow night and lie and that gives me until Monday night before I have to be back."

Sam leaned back in the seat, too exhausted to even be concerned anymore. "I just need someplace to sleep and get myself together if you know what I mean," she sighed. "A hot bath and a bed."

"I've got some money for the weekend and I got my own Visa, remember. When the bill comes in next month I'll just kinda tear off the bottom of the form and lose it and stick it in the pile to be paid. We'll get you a motel tonight but tomorrow I think we'll go up to my folks' cabin by the lake. Dad bought it years ago but we hardly ever use it. I think there've been more relatives stay there than us. Nobody'll be up there now and maybe not for miles. I figure it's as good a place as any to start. We got all Saturday to work something out."

Charley was still a little paranoid from Wednesday night and decided to see if anybody was following. Not that she could do much if they were, but it would give something of an edge. She took a number of turns and spent a good fifteen minutes at it

until she felt sure she wasn't being tailed. Then she headed out
to the freeway and headed north, out and away from the city.
Only then did she look over and see that Sam was out cold,
dead to the world. She looked so damned—*helpless* out like
that.

For Charley, it was just helping out a friend and a little touch
of adventure that broke the boredom of day to day routine. She
found a small motel off the highway and registered as "Mr. and
Mrs. Sam Sharkin." She had to use her last name since it was
on the credit card. She didn't know why she put that down
instead of passing Sam off as a more credible little brother or
something, but it kind of added to the adventure, to the sense
of doing something naughty.

Sam was still out cold and it took some doing just to get her
awake enough to get her inside. The room was small but
comfortable, with a full bath and a queen-sized bed. Charley
went back out to get her suitcase and lock the car, and found
that Sam had gotten awake enough to strip and was running a
hot bath. She certainly needed it, so Charley took the
opportunity to call her parents and lie enthusiastically. They
seemed satisfied, relieved that she was out of town and with a
group and told her to have a good time. She felt much better
afterward, and turned on the TV. She was a woman now, damn
it, and a bit too old to be towing her parents' line all the time.
What they didn't know wouldn't hurt them.

Sam was in the tub so long Charley got worried that maybe
she'd gone to sleep in there, but then her friend struggled in,
dried herself with a towel, and flopped down on the bed. "You
bring any tampons?" she asked.

"Yeah, sure." Charley got one from her suitcase. "Don't
leave home without it. How are you feeling?"

"Dead. Like a pool of warm shit and my head's poundin'
something fierce. Dead—but *clean*." She said the word like a
religious fanatic talking about heaven. "You?"

"I'm okay. A little tired but not like you. What happened to
you? You looked so good on Wednesday." She got up and
turned off the TV—nothing much on anyway—and the lights
and crawled back into bed. She'd brought pajamas with her but
somehow they just didn't seem right.

Sam sighed. "Just my nuttiness screwin' me up again."

"Tell me—if you want." It might be easier if she could get it
out of her system.

Slowly, Sam described the previous night in the mall, sparing nothing.

"You *actually* walked nude around the *mall?*" The image had an erotic kinkiness to it that appealed to her, although she was sure she couldn't have done it.

"Yeah. It was kinda fun, but then the thunder came and I panicked and then the voices in my head started again and that was the end of that. The worst part was being all alone." She shivered.

Almost instinctively Charley put her arms around Sam and drew her close. "Well, Charley's here now. You're not alone tonight."

Sam clung to her tightly, and Charley, a bit embarrassed, realized that her friend was softly crying.

It was a small, very dark cloud in the night sky, nearly impossible to see, yet if it could have been seen from the ground it would resemble a swirling, seething mass that pulsed almost as if it were alive. It flowed like an amoeba across the dark sky, faintly pulsing with electrical energy that made it appear almost to have a broad, comic, if still demonic face, the internal flashes of lightning illuminating two small areas almost as if they were eyes.

It settled first over the mall and remained there for quite some time, drifting a bit this way and that as if trying to catch a scent. Then, finally, catching a hint of something, it began to move out, away from the mall, stopping again over a residential neighborhood where it swirled in sudden confusion for almost an hour. Then it seemed to find its direction again and slowly moved northward. It was tenacious but ponderously slow. It headed northward now, following a road below, but it was no longer going with the prevailing winds and the energy drain was enormous. Even as it moved, it shrank, losing little bits and pieces of itself to the atmosphere. With single-minded determination it ignored this, but the effect was to slow it even more. The fight against the other elements was too great, its dissipation too fast. Even as the scent grew stronger the cloud grew weaker and weaker, until, perhaps just short of its goal, it weakened sufficiently that it could no longer maintain its structural integrity.

For a brief moment, the swirling mass gone, only two

*bright, terrible spots of light remained suspended in the air,
and then suddenly they were shattered by the prevailing winds.*

Saturday dawned bright if a bit crisp and cool, and the
brightness was reflected in Sam's attitude as well. She had slept
for eleven straight hours and she felt hung over, but she also
felt a tremendous lessening of the tension she'd been under for
a week. Charley checked out and then they went over to
MacDonalds and had what was essentially a brunch. Charley
was never very hungry and nibbled on a cheeseburger and
fries, but Sam was ravenous, putting away two quarter-pound
burgers, a fish sandwich, fries, and a shake. It was as if she
hadn't eaten in a week. Still, by the time they were off again it
was almost like the old Sam was back and it was the two of
them out for a lark.

In Amarillo they found a mall and made good use of
Charley's credit card. Sam declared the old denim outfit unfit
for further human consumption and hit a western-wear store for
a new if similar outfit in a young boy's size, cowboy boots,
leather belt with antique copper buckle, and even a Stetson.
Considering the season, the addition of an imitation sheepskin
jacket was welcome. She also got a small overnight case of
fake leather, with a shoulder strap, which looked pretty
masculine but could double as a purse, and some boys'
underwear. She also hit a barber and got a haircut so short it
was called "the military cut" in the style book—very short and
flat on top and almost shaved on the sides. She still looked
fourteen but, dressed that way and with that cut, just about
every outward trace of femininity was erased. In fact, with her
cool, tough, male act, Charley thought Sam was kind of cool
and cute and sexy, not butch but convincing.

It was a bit over two hours more on back roads before they
reached the cabin. It had been so long since Charley herself
had been there that she had to check all sorts of landmarks and
even then missed the dirt road turnoff twice. The cabin itself
was a single-room log affair about a mile and a half off the
main road and sheltered from view by both the land and the
trees. Fortunately, it was locked with combination locks the
numbers for which were in Dad's address book, so they were
able to enter and look around.

"It's not much," Charley admitted. "It was supposed to be
hot shit when we bought it but they never developed the so-

called getaway wilderness resort they were selling in the brochures. Some folks camp around here in summer but I think we're the only ones that ever built anything within miles of here. Dad sued the hell out of them and got the cabin in a settlement. This was used as the sales office years ago and it's the only one with a well and septic system. You still gotta pump it up by hand over there, though, and add water to the toilet to flush it. They powered the place in the old days with a generator and they took that with 'em. No electricity."

There were, however, kerosene lamps, a wood stove built out of a fireplace, a sink with an old-fashioned handle pump where the faucets should be, a bare toilet that once had a curtain around it, some cabinets, pots, pans, and an old and squeaky but serviceable double bed. "Used to be my folks' but it either got too squeaky or too small for 'em so they moved it here," Charley explained.

Sam looked around. "Real country primitive, that's for sure. Matches the outfit, though. How long's it been since anybody was here?"

"Oh, a couple of cousins used it like for a week last year, I think—there's wood in the woodpile out there that we can use that I guess is from them. I don't think my folks have been here since the one and only time I was, which was like *years* ago. The river out back's supposed to have good fish in it, leastwise in the summer and fall. I don't know why Dad hangs on to it 'cept I guess you can't get much for it. Ain't exactly the great vacation spot of the universe or even Texas. I guess maybe he like figures he fought for it and it cost him, so he's keepin' it on principle or something."

They took turns trying to make the pump work. It took several minutes to get any water up, all the time screeching like the wail of the dead, and when it did come it was very rusty, but after pumping what seemed to be gallons it cleared enough so neither felt nervous about drinking or using it.

Charley had prepared for many of the cabin's obvious lacks. They'd stopped at a grocery store and picked up a pretty good assortment of stuff, although very little in the way of meat and nothing frozen since there was no refrigerator. Still, with the kind of stuff you could buy freeze-dried or boil-in-bag these days you could get by pretty good without it for a while.

They spent the day cleaning up and more or less playing house for real, and it struck Charley after a while that even out here and with the act down they had just sort of naturally assumed sexual roles, with Sam doing the logs and heavy stuff and she doing the cooking and making the bed with the linen she'd brought along. It was almost like they were acting like— well, her mom and dad—and it hadn't been deliberate. It was kind of fun, really; if Sam had really been a boy it might be different, but this was like a pleasant fantasy game and far preferable to making the hard choices ahead.

Sam came in from the car with a small brown bag which she'd obviously already opened, then pulled out a fifth of vodka. It was open, but still three-fourths full. "And what's this? Lighter fluid?"

"It's from home. There's so many bottles in the club room they'll never miss it. At the time I kinda figured you might need it, but to tell you the truth I forgot about it. I could'a got some grass from Louisa but I knew you couldn't stand the smell of the stuff."

Sam sighed. "I never really touched much of any of that. Too scared, I guess. What's it taste like?"

"Not much of anything, really. You just mix it with juice or pop. It just makes me real silly and it makes you feel good for a while. Too much can make you sick in the morning, though."

Sam looked back outside. "Well, we got a nice fire in here, it's hot as hell inside, dark and cold outside; we got no TV, no radio 'less we want to sit in the car, and not much else. Maybe I can stand bein' silly once."

And they *did* get silly, partly because they had no real way to measure the stuff and partly because the early attempts caused no real effect quickly and by the time they had enough to really feel it it was pretty cumulative. They sang and they danced to the songs they sang and they laughed at really stupid things and Charley got up on the table and did a silly strip tease and just like the last time she'd gotten drunk she got real turned on. She had no inhibitions at all and it was all impulse, all feel, now, not thinking. Sam, too, seemed real vacant and giggly and pretty unsteady.

They were both pretty giddy and helped each other to blow out the lamps and make it to bed. Charley snuggled up close to Sam and started gently rubbing the other. She sensed Sam stiffen. "What's wrong?"

"I—I dunno. I have these funny feelings inside and I'm all mixed up. It's all—*wrong*."

"You want me to stop?"

"That's just it—I *don't* want you to stop. I—I had *other* dreams, not just the bad ones. Ones I never told about. You dream about boys. I know you do. Mine had you and me in bed, like this, only in my dreams I was a boy and you was you and that made it all right. . . ."

In any other circumstances Charley would have reacted differently, but she was high as a kite and horny as hell. "Okay, just for tonight, then, let's do a fantasy. You're the boy and I'm the girl and we're here all alone. Jus' relax and pretend and ol' Charley'll show you just what to do."

It wasn't clear how long it went in the darkness before they both passed out from the booze, but it was day when Charley awoke with a splitting headache to the sounds of Sam throwing up into the toilet. Charley didn't feel that sick, but her head was throbbing and the room was slightly spinning and she could do nothing but lie there and try not to move.

She didn't remember much about the night but she remembered—enough, and it started her thinking and worrying. She was slightly troubled about herself, wondering if this was anything much inside her head or not. She sure as hell fantasized about boys, but she'd gotten turned on by looking at a girl or two and it hadn't bothered her much. Hell, when she'd been fourteen she'd had a real, if short, adolescent crush on Mrs. Santiago, her English teacher at the time. Months later Mrs. Santiago had been replaced with Mr. Horvath. Sam, though—she was such a damned straight arrow it must be killing her inside, or would when she stopped being sick and really sobered up. She and Sam were physically only a month apart in age, but emotionally Sam was closer to fourteen than seventeen going on eighteen, and she'd had that split home and since being separated so long and so far from her dad Sam had turned him into almost Superman in her mind so no boy could ever compare or measure up.

Boy, Dr. Joan Herwitz—she was the phone-in psychologist on the radio—had lots of cases like this. Sam got a crush on Charley but it went against everything her straight arrow upbringing and church groups believed. So she couldn't handle it, and finally invented this weird fantasy world and dark mysterious ghosts and talking thunderstorms. Man! These were *heavy* thoughts! Sam was running, all right, but not from the darker dreams and fantasies but rather *to* them. The solution startled Charley but it also cheered her. It explained *everything!* The trouble was, would *Sam* buy it now and deal with it? It was Sunday. There was only one day left.

Still, they had to survive a rough morning first. Charley had one of those awful problems—she *desperately* needed to take some industrial-strength Tylenol she had with her but to do so involved pumping some water and the screeching of the pump was unendurable. It was also very cold in the cabin; Sam was covered with goosebumps but first things came first and upchucking had a way of forcing itself to the head of the line. Even so, once her stomach was empty she felt much better if dizzy and lightheaded. Still, she had enough sense to know that building a fire was essential and she managed to throw some wood in the stove, light some paper with a cheap lighter, and toss it in. It would take a few minutes but at least things would be livable.

She found an unopened bottle of orange juice that was slightly cold because of the cabin's temperature and got the pills from Charley's purse and brought them to her. It was only then that they both discovered that Sam, the bed, and even Charley were something of a bloody mess and Sam felt bruised and scratched up inside. It confused her. "Jeez—my period's pretty well over and I never had flow like *that.*"

Charley had to laugh even though it hurt to do so. "Long fingernails," she muttered. "Sam, I popped your cherry last night. Don't worry—it'll never happen again. Hurt a little inside?"

"Uh-huh."

"That'll go away, too, and shouldn't ever come back." She sighed. "I guess if we can heat a little water we can wash ourselves off but I didn't bring but one set of bedding. I figured it was only a couple of days. Best we can do I guess is wash 'em in the sink when my head slows down. They'll still look awful but at least they can be used."

By the early afternoon both were feeling much better, although the after-effects lingered on in upset stomachs and generally feeling drained. Sam, perhaps because she'd cleared her stomach, seemed to get over it faster than Charley, much to Charley's chagrin, although the mental effects of the binge were dwelling inside the fugitive.

"So what do I do now? Go to San Francisco or Greenwich

Village or somethin'?" Sam muttered unhappily. "'Cept I don't wanna go to any of them places."

"Oh, come on, Sam. Like, you never even *tried* it with a boy. Hell, I been pretty straight lately myself but I'm no saint. I got all sorts of urges and attractions and most of 'em I don't let out unless I'm high or drunk or whatever, but some I do. Don't you see? That's what's happened to you. You been so scared of letting go, lettin' your hair down when you had it and, well, *sinning* a little. You're scared you won't be the Virgin Mary and you're not. Nobody is. You're almost scared of makin' friends or gettin' into a little hell raisin' and that's got it all bottled up inside. I don't know if you really swing that way exclusive or not and I don't think you do, neither. You don't have the experience yet to know."

Sam sighed. "I always felt I should'a been a boy, that somebody screwed up someplace. I never felt comfortable around boys 'cept my dad, of course. Even my *voice* wasn't no girl's voice. But when I was naked in front of that store window I kinda liked what I saw there, too. Fact was, for the first time in my life I liked me as I was, if that don't sound crazy."

Charley shook her head. "I understand."

"But it didn't change nothin'. I still felt the same towards you, and when you not only didn't turn me in but picked me up and went to all this trouble it was like, well, you felt somethin' for me, too. And since we been together I felt, well, *safe*."

Charley hesitantly chewed on her lower lip, thinking hard, then said, "And you don't see the connection? It's been buildin' up inside you and it scared you, that's all. When I went away for the whole weekend leavin' you alone around the house you had your shadow man. When you looked at yourself in the mall and turned yourself on you got panicky and had another dream. I bet almost all of 'em happened after something stuck in your mind about your own feelings or me. And since we been together there's been nothin'. Don't you see, Sam? Them dreams, them voices, they're not real. They come for you when you get hung up and feelin' guilty and all. They're in your *head*, that's all. They're scarier even than what you're really 'fraid of so you don't think about that no more."

Sam thought it over. "They're so *real*. And the thunderstorms—they're real, too. Thunderstorms at high altitude here in the middle of winter."

"Yeah, I guess the storms are real, but they're real with you or without you. It's not like they never happened before—I heard the weather guy on the radio. Come on, Sam! Lotsa folks are scared by things that don't make no sense. Me, I'm terrified of spiders and I ain't too fond of tall buildings, neither, even when I'm inside 'em. You step on spiders and leave 'em outside to catch flies and I bet back in Boston you went in lots of tall buildings and never thought 'bout it. You got thunderstorms which I always thought were kinda neat and exciting so long as you was lookin' at 'em from inside someplace. You just put your storms and your fears together and it *still* wasn't enough. Your shadow man didn't come durin' no thunderstorm, did he?"

For the first time there was a glimmer of doubt in Sam's mind. "You really think so? That this was all for *nothin'*? But everything was so *real*."

"I guess it can be. But it's out in the open now, at least between the two of us, and I don't *care*. You told me and showed me and I didn't run screamin' away or nothin'. Look, you go home, you see a shrink. Your mom's into all that liberal cause shit; you'll wind up gettin' one that'll say just what I'm sayin', I'll bet you. We won't tell anybody else about it." She was thinking furiously now. She'd hooked the fish and didn't want to let it slip away. "Maybe we'll go off to college together. How's that sound? We'll room together and raise a little hell ourselves."

"But you hate the idea of college!"

"Well, like maybe I can stand it with a good friend, huh? It'll freak out our parents but they'll love it. Come on—what do you say?"

Sam thought hard about it. "I really want to believe it, Charley. But what if I go back and it all starts again anyway? *They'll* get me sure, then, and you better believe I'll be grounded for months."

"And if you don't? Where you gonna run, Sam? Sure, you look and can act like a fifteen- or sixteen-year-old boy, but ten years from now you're *still* gonna look fifteen or sixteen. Nobody'll hire a kid that young with no ID, no background, no experience, no family. Nobody you could ever trust workin' for, anyways. You can't even get a job for the minimum at *MacDonalds*, for Christ's sake, without a Social Security card, home address, parental permission, you name it. Only thing you could do would be to turn yourself back into a girl with everything hangin' out and sell yourself."

"I—I couldn't do that."

"You get hungry enough or fall into the wrong hands and you damn well will, or you'll die—and what's the difference if your shadow man kills you or you freeze to death hitchin' or starve to death in Denver? Hell, you can't even *drive*. There's bastards out there pickin' up *boys* for the last ride, you know, and if they find out you're a *girl* they'll find your body in a ditch someplace years from now if ever."

"But what if my dreams are *real?*"

"They're *not,* damn it, but real or not they'll follow you and you know it. You don't face it, it'll get you. I can just see you hitchin' on some warm day in the middle of nowhere when a thunderstorm comes up. *There* you face it alone. Back we face it together."

"Charley, I—I really want to believe you but I *have* to know. Before I can go back, I just have to."

Charley looked out the window. It was a clear sky, only a few high wispy clouds, but the winter sun was coming close to the horizon. "Then let's face them now, huh? All night if necessary, or until we freeze our tits off. Together."

Sam looked suddenly nervous as Charley pulled on designer jeans, a lavender cashmere sweater, her calf-length boots with high, thick heels, then got her fur coat. "Put on your boots, coat, and hat and we'll see just how nasty this all is. If they're so hot to find you, then they should accept a call."

"*What?*"

"If you love me, or *think* you love me, then you'll do it. For me."

"But—what if they come?"

Charley sighed. "Well, if you can conjure up a storm it'll show there's some ESP or that kind of stuff and if you can do it here you sure as hell can convince other folks. Besides, didn't you tell me that you thought you sent it away from the mall? If anything really shows up, push it back."

She didn't really believe any of this, but clearly Sam did. It was better to play the game out.

"Come on," said Charley. "Prove to me that you can screw up this pretty day."

They walked down the dirt road until they cleared the trees, Charley leading. She wanted as unobstructed a view of the sky

as possible, convinced that there was no way to imagine storms
or demons in a sky like this. There was a chill in the air but it
wasn't unbearable, partly because there was almost a dead
calm; the sky pale blue with only those high, thin, wispy
clouds and nothing else visible as far as they could see.

"Here. This is far enough," Charley said firmly. She
stopped and looked around. "Well, I don't see no shadow man
and I don't see no storm clouds. If you can conjure up anything
in the here and now then you got a hell of a power."

Sam looked uncomfortable, feeling vulnerable, but she was
unable to back out at this point. "So what do you want me to
do?"

"Call 'em. Just look up in the sky or towards the horizon
and just sort of like *think* them to come. Just tell 'em, 'Here's
Sam Buell! If you want me come and get me!' Do it over and
over for a few minutes and see if anything develops. Either it
works or it don't. If it don't you're home free."

Sam looked up at the very pale sky with perhaps no more
than an hour's light left in it. She had real problems with this
because she was not at all convinced that it was all in her head,
but, damn it, Charley was right. She had to *know*, and this time
somebody else was watching, too.

She stared at the clouds, took a deep breath, then closed her
eyes and thought, hard, *Who are you? What do you want with
me? I'm sick of running from you! If you want me come here,
now, and have it out, or get away forever and let me alone!*

She tensed, then after a few moments opened her eyes. It all
looked the same. Nothing had changed. She felt, suddenly,
very emotional, even angry, and tears welled up inside her.
"You bastards!" she screamed at the sky. *"You storms and
shadow men! Come and get me! Now! Or the hell with you!"*

Very slowly, the wind began to pick up. The temperature
was certainly dropping, at least in wind chill, and what had felt
pleasant at the start now began to feel pretty cold. Still, nothing
else had changed and the wind was more natural than the calm
had been.

"Come on," Charley muttered. "My fingers are turnin'
blue. Let's get back up to the cabin and thaw out."

Sam nodded, and they started back up the road toward the
cabin. "I dunno if I feel happy or sad," Sam muttered. "On
the one hand, this proves nothin'. *They* always picked the time
and nine out of ten times it was after dark. Only the shadow

man was daytime, and he only scared the shit outta me,
followin', waitin'—until dark, maybe. Still and all, it's lookin'
more and more like I'm really a nut case and that don't 'zactly
make me wanna shout 'Hallaluja.'"

"Yeah, well, it proves *something,* anyways. Look, we'll do
one more night even if we have to sleep on them sheets. If
nothin' happens, then you come home with me tomorrow.
Man! That wind is really pickin' up." She looked over her
shoulder and up at the sky. *"Ohmygod!"*

Sam froze just before the door of the cabin and turned to
look and saw immediately what Charley was seeing.

The sky was alive!

The thin, wispy clouds were now suddenly in motion, rapid
motion, and they were moving in a circular pattern around a
broad arc of sky, moving outward to form a circular collection
barrier around an invisible blue center, thickening every
second, growing dense and ugly with every increase in speed.
It was as if they were at the point where the eye of a hurricane
formed, the motion violent and building all around them.

The circle of thick clouds now began to grow inward,
toward the center, in a spiral pattern. Charley stared at it in
sheer terror, for the first time experiencing what Sam surely
must have felt. "Sam! Send it away!" she screamed as the
noise grew and the ominous, distant rumbling of thunder
sounded. *"Send it away!"*

"Back off!" Sam screamed at the sky. "Get away! I called
you, I send you back! *Get away from me!"*

For a second the entire sky seemed to freeze and there was a
momentary stillness that was almost as frightening as the
spectacle, but then enormous claps of thunder answered the
frightened girl and it started up again. "It's too strong! Damn
you, Charley! Why didn't you *believe* me?"

Charley was too stunned and frightened for any rational
response. Sam took her hard by the hand and pulled her.
"Come on! Get inside the cabin! It'll give us *some* protection!"

They got inside as the storm continued to build. Charley was
shaking and Sam wasn't much better, but she was more
accepting of what was happening and trying to think fast.

"The car!" Charley muttered. "I'll get the keys! We can try
and outrun it—"

"No! That's how they killed that—other—girl!"

"We can't stay *here!* It'll suck up this whole cabin and make pieces out of it and us!"

Even now the cabin was shaking and things were rattling and falling all over the place, and Sam realized that Charley was right. They had no damned chance at all in here. "*Under* the car!" she shouted. "Ain't that where you hide if you get into a big storm? No storm cellar!"

Charley finally got some wits about her and grabbed her purse. "Not *under!* Inside! It's grounded!" There were sheets of rain coming down now, and wind so great it felt like the cabin was going to shake apart, yet they both hesitated. Suddenly there was a horrible, gut-wrenching, tearing sound near the bed and a small section of roof just broke off like ripped by some giant hand.

It took both of them to get the door even open, and then they ran for the car. The storm itself had only a superficial resemblance to a natural storm now; it contained not only the grays of its violence but seemed to seethe with electrical power, pulsing like a living beast, each pulse a different color—crimson, violet, emerald green, yellow—there was no end to it.

Outside it was a sea of mud in a tropical storm; even the air temperature had warmed incredibly and it felt now like a muggy summer day. Sam made it to the car and had her hand on the door when she heard Charley scream and turned and saw her friend fall forward into the mud. Sam rushed back to her fallen friend and pulled her up. They both just made it to the car when a strong finger of lightning came down and struck the very area where Charley had fallen, sending up a short burst of smoke and mud.

They got inside the car and automatically locked the doors. Charley was a mass of mud and Sam was drenched. Charley had lost her purse in the fall and she disregarded the mud and pushed open the glove compartment knob. "There's a spare key in there! We gotta get out of here!"

"No! Don't touch nothin' metal, not even the keys! Lightning strikes the car and you'll fry even if me and the car don't! You think it won't follow us no matter where we go anyways? If it can't get the wind to blow us over . . ."

"Damn it, we got to do *something!*" Lightning was striking all around them with the regularity of a piston engine and the car was being rocked by the wind as if it were under assault by some powerful yet invisible monster.

"We hang on if we can! I had the dreams, remember! They can't keep this up real long! If they could they'd'a had me long ago! They ain't God—just the next thing to it!"

They both suddenly shrieked as a bolt hit the car and they could feel the electricity crackling in the air and even see it dancing around the hood of the car. A few loose metal objects—keys, an old film can, a loose part of a seat—flew up to the roof and stuck there as if magnetized.

The radio crackled and buzzed, although there was no automobile power being fed to it. Suddenly a clear voice in American English said, somewhat tinnily out of the speaker, "If you want to live, then calm down, shut up, and listen to me!"

"It's *him!*"

"Who? The one with the horns?"

"No! The other one! The one that thinks I'm a lab animal!"

"I'm moving the damned magnets on this thing by external force but I can't maintain it for long with all this damned storm interference, so listen up!" snapped the man on the radio through numerous and loud snaps, crackles, and pops.

"You called him. He'll never have you as exposed as this again," the voice noted. "He can't keep this up for long but he can hurl trees at you and smash in that car and overturn it and get you exposed before he runs out of steam. I want to save your life. You must believe that, and it's him or me. The other girl—I don't know who you are but he can't tell you apart in this mess so you're in this, too. Now, listen up! Hold hands, close your eyes! Lean back! Clear your minds as much as you can and will yourself to come to me! You'll feel the pull. Don't resist it—and don't let go of each other if you both want to wind up alive and in the same place!"

The car shook so violently that the entire left side rose a few inches and came crashing back down. There was a sudden, violent pounding all around and they saw the front and back windshields begin to crack under hail the size of oranges. Even the roof seemed ready to cave in, and the hailstones were like iron balls against the hood.

Charley looked at Sam in fear and anguish. Sam grabbed her hand tightly and shouted above the roar, "Let's do it! I don't know about him but it's better than any chance we got here!"

42   Jack L. Chalker

It was impossible to ignore the terrors being visited on the car or suppress the fear, but, somehow, through it all, they both seemed to see something in their minds, a tiny point of bright light that grew larger and larger by the second. There was the sound of shattered glass and Sam felt pain in her leg, but at that moment the light, which seemed to be enormous and approaching them, somehow, reached and engulfed them.

The sound abruptly ceased with a silence so deafening that it was in many ways as scary as the storm had been. Sam couldn't stand it; she opened her eyes, and almost immediately shut them again.

They were floating in air, in the center of the storm, with the swirling, charged, multicolored clouds of violent energy all around them as far as the eye could see, not only on all sides and above them but also below. There had been nothing, no place at all.

Sam opened her eyes again, and after a few moments of vertigo got used to it. She looked over at Charley and saw her friend's eyes tightly shut, lips quivering. *"Char- leeeee . . . !"* she called, the sound thin and echoing into infinity.

Charley was in the grips of total, unreasoned terror, the only rational thought in her head, going 'round and 'round in a never-ending loop, was *God damn all fucking radio psychologists!*

"Charleee . . . Open your eyes! It's—beautiful!"

"I—I can't!" But after a moment she did so, since she was suddenly hearing nothing but Sam's voice and did not feel any other sensations, not even wind. When she saw the maelstrom it almost took her breath away. She tightened her already solid grip on Sam's hand. *"Are we—are we dead?"*

"You're too damned filthy to be dead and I'm too wet!" Charley responded, the eerie echoes of their voices almost mixing in the distance. *"I think we're moving, though. Down!"*

It was true. The storm was no storm anymore, if it had ever been, but rather it seemed to be a long tube, or perhaps a giant funnel would be a better term for it. It had such a uniformity of broad bands of lighter cloud, or whatever it was, separated by thin bands of darker stuff that it was hard to really tell movement. Charley looked down once and decided she didn't want to anymore, but she could look straight ahead, at the bands, and when she had looked long enough she began to see, or thought she saw, a scene, a picture, that flipped every second or so to become slightly different, like viewing a movie one frame at a time.

Woods . . . clearing . . . paved road beyond . . . even telephone poles, all against a stormy-looking sky. It was looking out from the car's position—it was the cabin land! But there was no car and no cabin and the image was ghostly, two dimensional, not at all real.

Dark band. Same scene, but suddenly the telephone poles were gone. *Dark band.* A few differences in trees, subtle differences as each band came floating by. Slowly, ever so slowly, the road was dirt now, then a track, a mere trail. Trees changed subtly, not only in number and position but in shape and kind. And now it was a true winter scene, with snow suspended in air while the ground was getting progressively covered.

"Stare straight ahead and watch!" Charley called, pointing but not taking her eyes off the scene.

There was something now in and among the trees. It emerged after a while—time had no meaning in this long descent but it seemed to be going on forever—as some sort of deer, maybe an elk, clear in the stormy twilight and making tracks, one snapshot at a time, in the snow. They watched it walk, but as it did, with each still frame, it, too, subtly changed. The antlers became horns and then bony plates, the dark brown skin changed to tough and leathery, the short tail grew long and thick, the legs thickened and became three-toed and clawed rather than hooved. All this took time—hundreds, maybe thousands of snapshots—and each time the creature looked complete and whole, not in the midst of any transformation.

Now it was no elk nor anything like an elk, but rather a creature like a dragon, larger and meaner looking than anything they had ever seen, and it was no longer walking in snow at all but across a swampy region, the trees now more Amazonian jungle than west Texas woodland and hills. Now it, too, was gone from view and the land continued to change. Unfortunately it also continued to darken, and soon there was nothing left of the scene but a few fleeting impressions of things that stood out in the storm clouds and the night.

The storm itself had now grown dark and ominous once

more, the walls closing in on them where at the start the thing had seemed a mile across. But the storm was still alive; red, pupilless eyes like burning coals started suddenly out at them from below, then leaped out into the maelstrom itself, floating as they were floating but maneuvering toward them.

They were ugly, horrible beasts, three in number; monstrous creatures, resembling dogs, that seemed almost as big as they were, with gaping mouths dripping something yellow. They were still well below, but they were coming, charging toward them as they fell to meet the things. Both girls screamed and tried to flee in horror, but there was no way to break this fall. The creatures had to be even larger than they appeared; *huge* in fact, because they were growing as they approached yet there was still some distance between the three beasts and their obvious prey.

Both of them stopped screaming only when they saw the others emerge from the walls, closer to them, between them and the beasts. Shadow people, with no features, like two-dimensional black cardboard cutouts, but *alive,* and, from their looks, not unarmed. The beasts tried to dodge the newcomers, and Charley had the strangest feeling that those six terrible eyes were fixed not on Sam but on *her* and on her alone.

The three shadow humans worked quickly, one drawing a shadow sword, another placing an arrow in a shadow box, a third with a great, long, sharp spear. All three struck their dog monsters almost simultaneously and with great accuracy, but the beasts, while wounded and suddenly howling in agony a strange, supernatural howl that echoed forever down the spout, kept coming, kept staring not at Sam but at Charley. She could practically smell their breath, but the three shadow hunters were not done turning the tables on the fearsome hunters, falling upon the beasts, stabbing, spearing, gripping their foes and dragging them down and away. One beast let out a great scream and suddenly vanished, dissipating like smoke in the wind, while the other two were now being dragged down, away from the girls, at an accelerating rate until they were just tiny dots, then gone.

All returned to normalcy for a moment, but then below them at the point on the storm wall they were facing, another figure seemed to grow, a figure that was anything but cardboard and two-dimensional or even black. It was the figure of a large man, imposing, well built, wearing flowing robes of crimson and gold, his face sporting a full snow-white beard that was trimmed oddly as if an inverted V-shaped notch was cut from it, and on his head was a crown from which arose two long, sharp, slightly curved horns.

Sam gasped, knowing that this was the one she feared the most, her tormentor and would-be murderer. They were falling—or he was rising—at a rate that would bring them face to face in a matter of seconds.

Suddenly there was an odd sound like a giant spring suddenly uncoiled at great speed, and between them and the horned figure there appeared a thin, transparent pink barrier.

"*That will hold him only for a minute or so,*" said a familiar voice nearby. They turned and saw another figure, this of a small man with long, unkempt white hair, a bulbous nose and oddly chubby cheeks, like a doll's, dressed in similar fashion to the Horned One, only in robes of silver and emerald green. This, then, was the voice from the car radio. "*I'm going to have to face him down,*" he told them. "*I don't think he wants a full calling out right now, so I can stall him long enough to get you down to someplace neutral and out of the way. Trust Zenchur. He's a scoundrel but he stays bought and he'll be expecting you and know what to do, and he speaks English.*"

Both of them were beyond shock at this point and it brought a curious clarity of mind, almost like this was normal. "*But what's this all about?*" Sam called to him. "*And where are we going?*"

"*What's the difference? You're going there anyway,*" the man in green responded pragmatically. "*He's through the barrier already. Stand by. When I divert him you'll get a real sudden push.*"

The Horned One raised a hand and the barrier vanished, and he continued until he was level with them, perhaps ten feet away from the girls. The one in green, however, stood suspended in the maelstrom between them and their immediate nemesis.

"*Enough!*" said the Horned One impatiently in that sinister, terribly cold voice Sam had heard in the dreams. "*This is not your affair, Boolean. You are out of your league here. Stand aside. She is mine,*" he said emphatically, holding out a thin, almost skeletal hand and pointing, clearly, not to Sam but to Charley!

This is nuts, Sam thought, thoroughly confused. *This is* my *nightmare, not Charley's!* And, just as suddenly, she realized what was going on. There *was* a fair resemblance between the two of them, and the Horned One knew he was seeking a girl. Whatever power or sense he used to track his prey, the two of them, together, touching hands, confused it. Charley was also still pretty well covered with mud, but her hair and dress made it very clear she was female, but Sam looked like a boy and with the very short hair . . .

He thinks Charley is me!

The man in green, who clearly knew different, did nothing to correct the impression. Instead he said, *"I am making it my business. Do you want to have it out now over her? You think you're ready for me? You think you can finally beat me in something?"*

The comments clearly infuriated the Horned One, but he hesitated. *"You would fight me for her? Risk everything?"*

For an answer, the small man in green raised his hands and there was a pyrotechnic light show that was almost blinding in its brilliance. At the same moment, both Charley and Sam felt a tremendous push on them, forcing them suddenly and very quickly down and away from the duo. It was so sudden and forceful that it took their breaths away in spite of the green one's warnings, and it was no longer an eternal floating sensation but more the feeling of going down the biggest hill on the roller coaster.

The walls continued to close in until there was no more space between and they were inside the clouds themselves.

Lightly but very suddenly and unexpectedly they hit the ground and rolled, letting go of one another's hand in spite of themselves, tumbling to a stop.

Wherever they had been going, they had now arrived.

· 3 ·

The Mother of Universes

WHEREVER IT WAS, it was dark and hot and incredibly humid; a layer of gray mist so thick you couldn't see a thing in it lay over the land and extended perhaps two feet up from the ground it clung to. Sam groaned and managed to get first to her knees and then to her feet and look around. The night sky appeared totally clouded over; at least, there were no stars visible, nor any moon, although it wasn't pitch black. She could see the thick carpet of mist well enough, although it seemed that it was not from any light source on high but rather that the mist itself was faintly glowing.

"Charley?" she shouted worriedly. "Are you anywhere in this gook?"

For a moment she was worried that they had not landed together, that the last moment when they'd lost their grip on each other it had sent them to different places and left them both alone. Sam's hand hurt like hell from what seemed like *hours* gripping Charley's hand—and it might well have been that long.

She heard something moving not far from her. *"Oh! Jeez! That you, Sam?"*

Sam frowned. "That you, Charley?" The voice just didn't sound right, but then she saw a familiar form, still caked with mud, rise eerily from the mist.

"Yeah, I *think* so. Damn! My voice sounds funny. Are my ears stopped up or what? *You* sound okay."

Sam frowned, but went over to her friend and helped her to her feet. "Your voice sounds as deep as mine! I don't know. Maybe I—shit!"

47

"What's the matter?"

"That chubby-cheeked bastard! He saw that Old Horny mistook you for me. He looked, saw a boy and a girl, and since he was after a girl he made the obvious mistake. Old Greenie, then, figured he'd keep it up I bet. He wants old Stick Head to keep goin' after you, that's what! Both of 'em don't give a damn about *you*—it's me they both want for some reason. So Greenie, he cast a spell or something to make you sound like me. Keep it up as long as possible. You don't sound to me like I sound to me, but I bet to anybody else your voice and my voice now sound pretty much the same. You still got the accent but who's gonna know the difference *here*? If I keep my voice on low and keep dressin' and actin' like a boy then anybody sent out lookin' for me'll go for *you*."

Charley didn't like any of this. She was scared, confused, and totally off-balance, but what Sam said made sense considering the crazy low voice she was hearing in herself and the fact that those *things*—she shivered at the memory even though it already seemed like a dream—only had eyes for *her* and even that fancy wizard with the horns had pointed to her. It wasn't at all comforting; she was nothing to them, a sacrificial lamb, no more, no less. She had become the target and it wasn't even her nightmare.

"I'm dreaming this. Somehow this is all a dream and I'm back home or in the cabin or something sound asleep," she muttered in that strange-sounding voice. The whole thing *did* have a dreamlike, nightmarish quality about it, and to think otherwise was to believe in monster storms called at will and shadow people and wizards and magic spells, none of which she'd believed in for many, many years. She believed in Halston and Gucci and I. Magmun's and they seemed very far from here.

"Sam," she said very softly, "I'm scared. I'm filthy, wet, miserable, and scared to death."

"Yeah. Me, too," sighed the other. She looked around. "*Now* what are we supposed to do, I wonder? Wait here to be picked up or move someplace or what? And if we're supposed to go someplace, where in hell *is* it?"

"I don't know. If this is a dream, why can't we conjure up a bath tub? Talk about gettin' mixed up. I dunno if I'm in *Alice in Wonderland* or *The Wizard of Oz*. A storm sucks you down the rabbit hole. . . . Can't even get our damn fairy tales straight."

Sam knelt down and felt the ground. They had landed relatively gently for the apparent speed, but it felt like pretty hard rock down there, covered perhaps with moss most places. It was firm, but her hand was wet when she ran it around on the surface.

Off in the distance there was the sudden sound of thunder and an area of the sky was illuminated, briefly. Charley started, then turned quickly back to Sam. "Don't you *dare* call it!"

Sam looked out at it. For some odd reason it hadn't the unreasoned fear she had always felt when seeing or hearing such things; instead, it inspired wary caution, as if it were a person, directed by an intelligence, that she had to avoid. Somehow that made it easier to take—particularly since she'd evaded or fooled that intelligence more than once now. But that had been on essentially home turf. This place—wherever this place was—was something else again. Still, she was thinking fast and surprisingly clear considering her experience and how tired she was feeling.

"I don't think it's the same here as back home," she mused.

"No shit. Tell me something else that's brilliant."

"No, no! I don't mean *that*. You don't have to worry 'bout me callin' no storms, 'cause I bet that's one of the few easy ways Old Horny can find me here. If he could find me here the same way he could back home, then what's the use of sendin' us down here, changin' your voice, and all the rest? Here's got to be different. If I don't call him he's got no more chance of findin' me than if he was lookin' for anybody else. He don't know where Chubby Cheeks plopped us 'cause he was kinda busy. Now he's gotta find me the hard way. The same way somebody normal would try'n find somebody else back home."

"Yeah, that makes sense. But your Chubby Cheeks knows where he dropped us and even which is which. That's okay for you—he wants you alive for something—but it sure as hell paints a target on me. I'm stickin' to you like glue, girl, 'cause if I'm ever separated, your savior there could just let some of Horny's agents bump me off and then he thinks he's home free and you're off the hook."

Sam sighed. "I'm sorry I dragged you into this, Charley, I really am. But it was *your* idea to call that damned storm."

"Yeah, but how was I to know it'd actually show up? This isn't *real!* It *can't* be! It just *can't* be!" And then Charley dissolved into tears.

Sam didn't know what to do except try and comfort her friend. Common sense said to stay the night right here. Charley was right about one thing—old Chubby Cheeks knew just where he dropped them and they were supposed to be met by somebody. Move too far and they might not meet—and *then* where would they be? Lost in some damned weird world where they didn't know the rules, that's where. And Charley was worried she couldn't cope with Denver!

Still, staying here, in this crap, wasn't too comforting. She was dead tired—they both were—but what lived around here, hidden by this glowing fog? Damn it, what the hell were they supposed to *do?*

Ultimately, it was decided by practical matters. They were too tired, still too much in shock, and it was too damned dark to make a try for someplace better than they were in now, if in fact that place existed. Still, it was not hard to sit there, just your head and shoulders above the mist, and imagine monsters moving underneath. They clung to each other and comforted each other and, eventually, they went to sleep in spite of themselves, so exhausted that not even fear could hold it back.

Sam awoke suddenly with a start and sat up. It was still quite dark and still, and the mist was still there—in fact, it seemed to have risen some. She was soaked through again by the mist, and it was clammy and uncomfortable, but she put it from her mind. Charley still slept, protected beneath it, but Sam had always been a lighter sleeper and she had been on the run and under tension for more than a week. There was something—an odd noise—coming across the dark to her, approaching.

It was somebody whistling. It was a casual but firm and loud whistle, and whoever it was was whistling a bright, fast tune.

It was *Yankee Doodle!*

She tensed, alert, and used the mist as a cover so that only her eyes and the top of her head were visible. Protecting Charley and herself became the only purpose in her mind. She reached down and shook the sleeping girl, who mumbled and murmured but suddenly came awake and sat up. "It wasn't a dream," she said, more amazed than anything else.

"*Shhhh!*" Sam hissed the warning. "Listen and stay low."

The whistler continued to approach, and now, too, she could

hear the sound of hoofbeats as well on the rocky ground, as if a horse was progressing ever so slowly through this stuff. Now she saw them—two people eerily illuminated by the glowing mist, only their upper torsos showing because of it. One was a woman and she wasn't wearing any clothes! She was a light brown color, and there was something odd about her face and hair, and although it was hard to tell it looked like she had the biggest tits Sam had ever seen.

At first Sam thought that the other was a woman, too; the clean-shaven face was set off by what looked like a *mane* of hair cascading up and then around the head and down to and below the shoulders. This was the whistler, who suddenly stopped and looked around, appearing very unconcerned about anything lurking in the mists, and called out softly in a voice that was unmistakably a pretty fair male baritone.

"Come out, come out, wherever you are," called the man with all the hair. He had a thick, somewhat gutteral accent that sounded vaguely east European, but his English was clear. "I do not have eyes to see in this mess. I know you are around, watching us. Do not be afraid—I am Zenchur and this is Ladai. We were told you would be expecting us."

"Can we trust him?" Charley whispered nervously to Sam.

"No, but what other choice we got?" Sam stood and was instantly spotted by the newcomers. "Hey! You from the green guy with the chubby cheeks?"

The man started, then looked a little confused. "What is 'chubby cheeks' meaning? I am hired to get you to someplace safe and to help you. Or would you rather stay here?"

Charley got up, and the sight of her also seemed to surprise the man, while the woman just looked suspiciously at both of them. The man frowned. "*Two* of you! I was only told of one. This will double the price. Well, come on—we must be away from here by dawn. There will be others looking for you that you do not want to meet, I think."

They moved hesitantly forward, wary but knowing they were helpless in this situation to do more. Suddenly, both girls stopped and just stared at the female member of the duo. Now, up close, they could see that it wasn't a woman at all.

Her hair flared out in front, then seemed to be pinched back to the back of her head, becoming a thick mane of dark brown hair running completely down her upper back. Her ears, their exteriors covered in brown fur, were pointed and seemed to move independently of one another, rising up stiffly from the side of her head in animal fashion. Her eyes were extremely large and bulged slightly outward, and were like two huge black orbs floating in a brown rather than white sea. Her nose was somewhat flattened, but the nostrils seemed to move slightly in and out as she breathed. Her hands had three thick, very long fingers and an even thicker thumb, and seemed to be all fingernail from just beyond the knuckle joints; her breasts hung down huge and fat—although she seemed quite thin otherwise—to or below where her navel would have been, if she'd had a navel. And at the hips, and beyond, she merged into a long body whose top they could barely see but which seemed to reach out in back of her as long as her torso was tall, yet she stood shorter than the man who was of no more than average height and only five or six inches taller than the two girls.

"Is that—is *she* a centaur?" Charley breathed softly.

"Ah!" responded the man. "*That* is the word. Yes, centaur in English. They call themselves *ba'ahdon,* which sort of means human being. It all depends on how you look at it, yes?" He paused. "She speaks no English, but she is good people. They do not understand why we do not fall over when we walk."

The speaker was himself certainly what *they* would call a human being, but he, too, was decidedly unusual in appearance. For one thing, his huge head of curly reddish blond hair ballooned out as if permed and framed his face as it dropped below his shoulders. He had no sideburns nor any trace that he ever had to shave; his face was smooth as a woman's although it had clearly seen a lot of exposure as its lines and wrinkles around the eyes demonstrated. It was a large, squared-off face with steel gray eyes and frankly androgynous, a fact emphasized by his twin earrings which hung down from pierced earlobes, each ending in a copper oval in which there was a maltese cross. He had an olive brown complexion that was most certainly dark even without exposure to the sun but now was deeply tanned. He wore frontier buckskins with fringe ornamentation, the jacket ties not fully done and revealing a surprisingly hairy chest for one with no noticeable facial hair. It was almost as if somebody had stuck Farah Fawcett's head on the body of Davy Crockett, Sam thought crazily.

Zenchur turned to the centauress and said something in a

singsong tongue that sounded sort of Chinese or something, and she nodded. Then he turned back to them. "Come. Follow us. We have not too far to go but it is best that we go there. It is very unlikely that you can be traced to this spot, but one does not live long by not taking the unlikely into account."

They began walking, the centauress leading the way and the three of them following.

"If you please, sir," Charley said as they walked, "can you tell us just where we are?"

Zenchur chuckled. "You are in Akahlar. That is the name of the world in the dominant language and it is used generally. There are more than six thousand languages, you see, so there had to be some standards."

"Yes, but—where is Akahlar? Is it another world than ours or what?"

"Another world, yes—and no. You come from the Out-planes and it is hard to explain things to you since I do not understand them myself. You are almost where you left yet you are as far away from your home as if you were on a distant star. It is—how you say?—a layer cake. Many layers. Hundreds. Thousands. You fall from somewhere near the top of the cake or in the middle or like that through to the bottom. Is the asshole of creation. People, things, falling down here all the time and stick here because there is no farther place to fall. Well, there is, but this is last layer where people can live. Every once in a while, when big storms come, some more drop through, but not like the old days."

"But you—you're a native? You're from here?"

"From here, yes. Native—there are no natives of Akahlar. All our ancestors come here from someplace else long ago. Used to be giant storms all the time go far Outplane before they stop, but no more. Oh, we still get big storms, but there is too much out there now. They break up, get weak. We still get some—one here, another there—like you two, but not big groups, whole tribes, towns, like ancient times."

"You speak English quite well," Sam put in, feeling left out of this. "Is it spoken around this place?"

"Some places, yes. Not many. I learn it because Akhbreed sorcerers use it. Is good to know the tongues they use. They like it because it is so hard to learn, so confusing. I am good at languages and I buy this one not long ago. I know sixteen very well and another ten or so enough to get along. Ladai, she is also good. Knows ten or more, I forget. Fortunately, we both know one the same so can talk. She can do ones I can not handle. The throat will not make the sounds. You understand? That is why we work so well together.''

Sam thought she had enough problems with English. "Are we gonna hav'ta know all those languages to get by here?"

Zenchur laughed. "Oh, no, but the more you know the better it is. I get this job because I know English. Ladai and me, we need them in our work."

"Just what is it you do?" Charley asked him.

"Sort of—what is the term? Mercenary, I think. No, that is not quite it. They are paid soldiers. I fight, when I have to, but I do not like it if I can keep away from having to do it. People pay me to do these things they need to have done that they cannot or will not do themselves. When no one pays me I think up my own little jobs to get pay. Free some extra valuables from ones who will not miss them, that sort of thing. Better working for someone else, though. Same danger, same trouble, but if you get caught you are not alone."

Sam thought about it and saw just what he was. "And Ladai—she does the same? You are partners?"

Zenchur chuckled. "Partners. Yes, I think that might be the right term. You see, our sort of work—requires—that we live away from most, from civilization. When we go to cities, to lands, it is to either spend money or on the job. Then go, usually run, sometime chased, back to the wastes. You never know where you might have to go. I am Akhbreed. You are Akhbreed. Akhbreed not very welcome in lots of places. If you are not Akhbreed—Ladai, for example—you are not welcome in Akhbreed places. I can do little about Akhbreed law. It stinks. But I can go where few Akhbreed can follow. Akhbreed have the power. Akhbreed sorcerers have the greatest power of all. Like gods. Akhbreed does not see any of the other races as human. They take what they want, all the best, leave the garbage to the rest. Akhbreed have massacred whole races here for petty reasons, for greed. Enslaved others. That is why I do not mind stealing from them or causing them problems."

"But you said you were an Akhbreed," Charley pointed out. She was getting very tired and the short distance was turning into a very long hike in the dark.

"I am sometimes ashamed of it. If one race tortured and enslaved your people and drove them off your lands would you not hate that race? Yet I was trapped, with a storm coming, many years ago out in the wastes. I had no chance. Two *ba'ahdon* found me, wounded, half dead. They took me to their camp, brought me back to health. I lived with them long time. Got to know them. How could I go back and be Akhbreed again?"

"But couldn't you go back and tell 'em that these are good people? Work to bring everybody together?" Charley couldn't help thinking this sounded a lot like the Indians and the white man in her own southwest in the frontier days.

Zenchur looked at her strangely. "You must have interesting Outplane. If anyone were to go back and say that, they would be called traitors to their kind. If they kept it up, they would be publicly tortured, mutilated, then killed or given to the sorcerers to be made monsters. The kings and queens of Akhbreed do not permit disagreements."

Suddenly the mist ended, at least just ahead of them, and a grassy hill came out of it and went up and then out. There were some trees and bushes there and what seemed like a rock wall rising imposingly into the darkness. They walked along the bottom of the cliff side for a bit, then entered an area that really could not be seen from outside and which, even in daylight, would betray no hint that it was there. It led to a fissure in the rock that zigzagged back underneath and either led to or became a cave. Well inside the mountain it opened up into a large cavern lit by torches. There was a definite airflow here, and in the center of the cave there was a pool of clear water.

To one side, in a natural depression, was a rather basic camp, with two tents, on obvious fire pit, atop which sat a cold cauldron, all of which sat upon a thick layer of straw with many rugs in front of the tent to add insulation from the cold and damp cave floor. It looked pretty damned primitive but at least it was *someplace*.

Ladai's full form was visible from the moment they entered the torchlit area. The lower body was not really all that much like a horse's; the legs were far thicker than a horse's legs and ended in large hooved feet that, while proportionately small, reminded them more of an elephant's feet than a horse's. The lower body was relatively short—certainly not much longer than the upper, more human body—and sloped slightly down, terminating in massive hind legs that none the less were shorter than the forelegs by several inches. The mane continued along the back all the way and merged with the tail at the base of the spine where it became rather like a straight, thick head of human-looking hair reaching almost but not quite to the ground. She was not just the old idea of a human upper mated to a horse's lower; in fact, she was an entirely separate creature that seemed to be less hybrid than something new and different but a single whole. Nor was she massive like the centaurs of legend; on the whole, she was about the size of a Shetland pony.

Zenchur and Ladai exchanged more conversation, and she went and started up the fire in the fire pit using one of the torches. Soon it was burning quite well, the smoke rising in a steady diagonal to the roof of the cave and then vanishing somewhere. It had certainly been well thought out; Charley bet that no smoke ever was visible from outside.

Ladai went and brought a loaf of thick, black bread and an amphora and some hand-fashioned but sturdy-looking cups. She poured some of the contents of the amphora into each of the cups, handing one to each girl, then broke the bread.

Both *were* hungry, and the bread was fresh and with an odd but very sweet flavor to it. The liquid in the cups was thin and refreshing, more like white grape juice than wine although they both knew it probably *was* wine of some sort. It had an aftertaste almost like honey, and in their condition it was irresistible.

When they had finished, Charley went over to the side of the pool, knelt down, and stuck her hand in the water. It was quite warm but not hot.

"You wish to wash off the grime," Zenchur said. "By all means. Just stay close to the sides of the pool. It is mostly safe but there is a sharp drop perhaps six paces in. Plenty of room for bath. Ladai bathes in it, and if it is safe for her it is certainly safe enough for you."

She wanted to very much, and so did Sam, but here, in front of Zenchur . . . Neither of them wanted to bring it up, but it seemed to occur to Ladai even though she obviously had no problems with exposure and the centauress said something to Zenchur. He chuckled. "Ah—modesty. You will have to get cured of that out here, although it is an Akhbreed trait. You go ahead—I will go into the tent here. I have—how you say it?—I have to make a long-distance call."

And with that cryptic remark, and with something of a flourish, he turned and entered the nearest tent.

There wasn't much to use for soap—Ladai offered them a rough, shapeless white mass that didn't smell like much and didn't work all that well, either—but the water was warm and they both needed it badly. Ladai collected their clothing and took them off toward the cauldron. The clothes were in as bad shape as they were, so they didn't protest too much, although Charley figured it was good-bye to the fake fur jacket. They were a hell of a long way from a dry cleaner's, she figured, although it was warm enough around here that maybe she wouldn't need it. After all, it wasn't like mink or anything, anyway.

With the neutral, bland soap or whatever it was and no washcloths, they generally had to help one another scrub and get off the grime, particularly Charley's. She longed for her herbal shampoo and rinse but rubbing the soap stuff in and then ducking under and kneading the hair out took out the dried-in mud fairly well. Sam, at least, had less of a problem, with her very short hair, and what mud she'd encountered was mostly on her clothes.

They finally pulled themselves out, feeling clean and *much* better. Ladai, who seemed to be cooking or burning something very hot and bulky—the black smoke was billowing up from the fire pit and even tainting the air away from it—came away from her activities and brought them two thick towels the size of good hand towels which Charley suspected might have been cheap rugs, as well as a rather primitive brush and comb for Charley's thick, wet hair. They worked, anyway, at least for the basics, although Charley was going to have a time getting her hair completely dry and right.

"I guess we ought'a get our clothes and wash 'em as best we can, too," Sam suggested. "They might hav'ta last awhile."

Charley looked around and frowned. "Where *are* our clothes?" She stood up and went over to Ladai, who looked up at her from stirring the fire and smiled. "Our clothes," Charley said slowly, then remembered that the centauress couldn't understand them. She made as if to put on pants and a sweater and repeated, "Where—are—our—clothes?"

Ladai smiled sweetly and pointed to the fire pit. Charley looked down and could see the remains of a jacket and boots being charred to bits. "*Sam!*" she screamed. "*She's just burned all our clothes!*"

Sam was up and over there in a flash and saw the unmistakable remains. It was no use reaching in there to get them—the fire was incredibly hot, far too hot to get close to, and what was left in there was beyond help anyway.

Zenchur came out of his tent, frowning. "What is going on out here?"

Both girls instantly reacted with a shriek and covered as much of themselves as possible with their hands and arms. "She burned all our clothes!" Sam complained.

Zenchur sighed. "Yes. Sorry, but it was necessary. The appearance of any clothing or artifacts which you could not get here would be like standing up in the middle of town and saying, 'Here we are!' Even a fragment could be taken and any competent alchemist could indentify it as coming from the Outplane."

"But what do you expect us to do? Parade around stark naked?" Charlie asked, feeling terribly embarrassed.

"No, we will find other clothing for you. Do not worry so. It must be a very strange world you come from. One in which you can openly try to overthrow the king but where the sight of a naked body arouses anyone and incites instant attack. I hope you will not be incited to attack me if you see me naked on this trip." He seemed genuinely bemused by their reaction, yet irritated by its inconvenience.

"Look," he sighed, impatient now. "If I wanted either or both of you I could take you. I would not do so for—many reasons. Not that you are unattractive or undesirable, mind you, but this is business. I am your protector, not your attacker."

When neither of them moved a muscle but just stood there with their arms doing a bad job of covering what they wanted to cover, he got impatient. "I cannot afford such foolishness. I am tempted to let you stand there indefinitely until you get hungry or thirsty or have to go to the bathroom, but I cannot. I have no schedule to keep but something must be done and it must be done yet tonight. If you fight me or fail to trust me from this point you may yet die. I had not thought to need this so soon, but, very well." He reached into a leather pouch hanging from his belt and pulled out a small box. He opened it, and immediately there was a golden glow from it. They watched, not knowing what to do.

He removed the thing from the box, a glowing opaque, oval-shaped jewel perhaps the size of a half dollar, then held it out, waist high. He stared at them, not at the jewel, and if they had bothered to notice even Ladai was looking away.

Although there was no light source for the thing, a pencil-thin ray of the same golden color shot from it and made a small spot of light on the floor of the cave. He suddenly brought it up and let it shine for a moment on Sam's forehead. Charley frowned and looked for a likely place to run, but then he shifted the locus from Sam's forehead to hers.

She felt a sudden shock, then very strange and tingly, but it was another moment before she realized that she could not move a muscle. She was frozen, a statue, in this absurd and embarrassing position.

"The difference between common magic and sorcerer's magic is that common magic comes from an outside source, and belongs to the one who owns the source and knows how to use it. I have no magic powers, but this does. It has gotten me out of many scrapes and at times saved my skin. It was payment by a magician and alchemist for a particularly ugly and dirty piece of work I had to do for him, but it is the most priceless payment I have ever received. It debases it, almost, to use it for so silly a reason. Now—look upon it, both of you."

They did, compelled to in spite of themselves, and felt a numbness come over them. They could see only the gem, could not take their eyes off it.

"Come," he commanded, and they stood up and followed, eyes staring ahead, walking right into his tent.

The tent was larger on the inside than it looked; the floor was covered with rugs, there was a large chest to one side with an ornate gold dragon design on it, an enormous, mattresslike layering of rugs covered with silk, and, off to one side, a disk of polished wood with an intricate design carved in it, raised up on four ornate wooden legs. Five small incense sticks burned around it, each relating to a point on the disk's design.

"Stand before the disk, one on each side," he commanded, and they did so. "Now," he said, sounding somewhat relieved, "when I put this away you will have your wits back, but I want no more hysterics. Were I to focus this once more on your faces and tell you that down is up, black is white, and we are mice in a giant cheese you would believe it and try to eat the ceiling. If I said you both worshiped me like a god and wanted only to be ravished by me you would plead for my favors. I will demonstrate if I have to but at your peril. Such things have been known to permanently damage the mind." And, with that, he placed the jewel back in its case and slipped it back in his pouch.

Instantly they felt some release and both had a slight headache, but they were terrified. Right now, either one of them would do whatever he said rather than be subjected to that thing again, although Sam, in particular, felt disgusted. Not even in the midst of the storm had she ever felt as weak and small and helpless as she did here. And *this* was supposed to be the *good* guy!

"Hold hands, do not look at me, and stare at the center of the disk," Zenchur told them. "Just keep staring. He might not be immediately available."

Not all the fight was out of Sam. "Who's *he?*"

"My employer."

Sam took Charley's right hand in her left and squeezed it and they both stared at the center of the funny diagram carved into the wood. *He* was apparently on hold; things happened almost immediately.

There was a sudden shimmering just above the center of the disk but not touching it, and then it thickened and took on a definite shape outlined first in golden sparklies, but it soon became the form of a man, slightly transparent but in full, realistic three dimensions. The image was a living hologram of the green-robed wizard from the maelstrom, perhaps ten inches high.

"About time," the sorcerer snapped, the voice a bit thin and proportionate to the image, yet very clear. "I dare not risk keeping this open any longer than I have to. Ladies, we have several problems and we must deal with them quickly. I know you have a lot of questions but the answers to most will have to wait, perhaps until we can meet in person. All you need know is that you, with the short hair and the deep voice, are a target here just like you were. The fellow with the horns is very powerful both in magic and in temporal power. I'm also powerful—maybe his superior in magical power but I don't have much of a temporal base. In this case Satan has the army and the Pope has none. Nevermind. He was too gutless to try me back there, so he's lost track of you and unlike on the old world he can't just whip up a spell of location. If he tried that in Akahlar he'd risk whipping up a changewind even he couldn't handle.

"He knows I've got you, so he'll put all sorts of temporal and magical tails and shadows on me. I can probably get to you and protect you but then we'll be back where we started because he can follow. If he finds you, Short Hair, he'll kill you without hesitation or mercy. Believe that. Oddly, that's an advantage since he has strict orders to his minions that they are not to harm you but merely to capture and summon him. That's because only he can tell if it's really you. I could run some interference in the tunnel but that wouldn't have fooled him for long if I hadn't been there in person. As such, he's put out a very high reward for you, alive only and held until he can come to you. Every damned crook and politician in the business will be drooling over it, even his enemies. Trust only Zenchur. He is the only one who knows that the greatness of his reward will be matched only by the horror if he sells me out. What *is* your name, anyway? I can't keep calling you Short Hair."

"S—Sam. Samantha Buell," she managed. "And this is my friend Charley—Sharlene."

"You're not even related? Remarkable. Sam and Charley. Huh! Who'd have thought it?" He sighed. "All right, Charley, I don't know if you are here by accident or choice but you are here and you are stuck and as such you are going to be useful to me and to your friend. You might have noticed old Horn Head and his beasties both got confused, a common occurrence with them. That's why I had to alter your voice. I was afraid you'd say something and give the show away. The fact is, he doesn't know a damn thing more about you than I do and only what he saw. He knows what Sam looks like if Sam's looking like a young woman. I need Sam alive. Not only for now but for the far distant future. Alive and physically unchanged by magic or any other forces. He thinks Sam was a boy, possibly your brother. He'll be looking for an attractive young lady with a deep and distinctive voice. They all will. Sam must continue to be a boy to all outward appearance and that leaves you, Charley."

"You're gonna make her the Judas goat! They'll *kill* her!" Sam protested.

"Perhaps—but remember that everyone hunting for you

knows there is no reward and perhaps some punishment for killing you, and if Horn Head comes without me running interference he'll know it's not. That gives you a chance, which is more than you have on your own. I can't fill the countryside with Sam clones. For one thing, it takes a small part of Sam to do it right and there's only so much of her. Understand, though, I don't want him to catch you, Charley. If he does he'll catch on fast to who the real one must be. We will protect you all the way as if you were the real quarry. In the end, not only your friend's life and future but your own as well will depend on you carrying it off. I can help a little now. Interlock the fingers of the hands you are now holding. Go on—do it.''

They did so, although it was a bit awkward.

"There is feminine in the most brutish male, and there is masculine in the most gentle and beauteous female. Sam, I can't change you physically—I wish I could but I cannot and he knows it—but I can make some temporary mental adjustments and Charley stands right next to you now. Put your clasped hands into the center of my image. Go ahead—I'm not going to turn anybody into a toad."

Hesitantly, they both did as instructed. There was a sudden tingle and the image of the sorcerer seemed to mix with and grow out of the two hands clasped together. There was suddenly a sharp and painful shock through both hands that made them cry out but they could not pull their hands away from his image. Sam felt a wave of nausea and dizziness and would have fallen to the floor if not frozen there; Charley felt the same sensation but in addition a thin, burning sensation that started at the top of her head and went slowly and methodically down through every part of her.

"Okay," the sorcerer said with satisfaction. "You're probably both going to pass out when I break the contact, so I'll say the rest of my piece here. I've been able to get away with this because Horn Head doesn't know where I am yet or where you are at all, but since I have to be public shortly that will end. Within a few days he will have narrowed down and figured out the rough area where you had to land, so you will have to move. Zenchur will take you to a place where you can be safe and be taught something about this world and trained in what might be needed of you in the future. Horny can't touch you there but if he learns of your presence there he sure as hell can make it hard to get out again. When it blows over and the hue and cry is yesterday's news to all but your enemy and us, then we must meet. We must do what he fears most. I do not understate this. If we fail, it is entirely possible, even likely, that it will mean the destruction or total domination not only of this world but every world—your old world, too—by the blackest of evil. The odds of our survival, let alone success, are quite small, but the alternative is far worse than death. But if we succeed the prize, *your* prize, will also be great, and Charley will share.

"Zenchur—one last thing. I have now done the calculations and the clumsy and heavy-handed attempt on this pair by my adversary has triggered the largest and deepest changewind in a decade. I have calculated it will penetrate the Malabar District just beyond the Brothers. It might well proceed a great distance before going Outplane—it's that bad. Sit tight a full day and night more before moving and take its aftermath into account when you go. I go to alert those I can—or care to. Farewell, and may the winds be with you."

The image flickered out, the hold was released, and, as the sorcerer had predicted, both of them fell unconscious to the floor. With Ladai's help he got them apart and to the other tent, where they were laid side by side on silk-covered rugs and silk pillows. Looking down at the pair, Ladai could only shake her head in wonder. "It is incredible. And at such a distance! What power he must have!"

Zenchur nodded. "And that is why we must do as he says even though our hearts are not in it. I *knew* I should never have done that job for him, Jewel of Omak or no Jewel of Omak. It was payment for services rendered but the bastard now owns my soul. He *knew* about this! He *knew* even then! That is why he threw in the spell that allowed me to learn his accursed tongue."

Ladai nodded sadly. "Still, they seem quite nice, if very shy and very frightened girls. In a sense, they are more victimized than we. Their shyness in front of you was actually quite touching. They took me as an equal, yet were embarrassed and frightened by you. It would be well if they continued to fear the Akhbreed and showed no hatred or fear toward the other races. It shows what this world *might* become. See them now. They look so tiny—so helpless. What in the name of the Five

Netherworlds would cause two such powers to go to such lengths to have them?"

"Just the one," Zenchur told her. She had understood none of the English conversations and was very curious. "That one. The other is the decoy. I have no idea what this could be about, but I am not certain which I envy least—the one they want or the decoy." He sighed. "At least they won't need the Jewel of Omak with us anymore. Our employer has seen to that."

The pair left them to their dreams, and they were vastly different dreams, many in number and vivid in their realism.

For Sam, the dreams were adventure stories with, for her, an odd perspective. Time and again, through many variations, she was the hero; a small but handsome man in sword and cape, battling various monsters both human and inhuman, saving the innocent and the helpless and rescuing the fair damsel in distress who then threw herself at "him" in gratitude and love. They were a boy's dreams, romantic dreams, of brave knights and muscled warriors vanquished by power and skill and guts.

And through it all ran a thread that somehow her mind sorted out, and she understood and she believed. You are a man, born heir to a kingdom that only males can rule, but a great sorcerer stole your soul one day to advance the cause of a greedy rival to the throne and placed it far away, in another world, in the body of a girl. Now you are back in the land of your origins but still in that alien female body but your soul rebels. Henceforth you will let your soul guide you; you will look, act, talk, think like a man and all things womanly you must put aside or you will remain trapped in that body forever. None who do not now know your secret must ever know. You must put aside all womanly things and convince everyone, even yourself, that you are male. Only that way is redemption.

But for Charley, the message was quite radically different, as were the dreams.

For Charley, the dreams were exotic and erotic, almost a 1001 Nights scenario, in which she was the beautiful slave girl coveted by all, or an exotic and mysterious femme fatale desired by all men and using her charms to twist them to her will. They were romantic fantasies of the power of beauty, of being so alluring that men would risk their lives and their honor over her and for her while she risked very little. They were curiously mixed, with dreams of power intermingling with dreams of subjugation and domination, but they were all intensely erotic.

And, deep inside, she knew that this was what she wanted. To be glamorous, sexy, uninhibited, erotic, in all ways totally feminine, totally female.

Charley awoke first to find herself extremely turned on. She had awakened turned on quite a few times since puberty, but never this intense. She just lay there and felt herself up, mentally pretty well switched out. The same girl who was so shy and terrified the night before of even revealing her naked self would at that specific moment have been unable to resist the ugliest nerd who might have walked in.

Charley's active moaning awakened Sam, who for a brief moment had that flash of utter confusion when, opening your eyes and seeing strange surroundings instead of a familiar room, you did not immediately remember where you were.

Then, abruptly, it all came back and she sat up, and as she supported herself on her hands she felt a slight dull hurt on the left palm. She looked at it and saw a tiny, odd-looking cross-shaped cut just below her thumb. It wasn't very much, but it was slightly bruised and not yet quite scabbed over.

She looked down at her body and hated it. It was a prison, a shell that kept her trapped. Still, a rush of hope and possible power went through her. She was a *man,* damn it. She would behave that way and let no one know the secret shame. She heard Charley moaning and chuckled. The new Sam could give her what relief was possible, but somehow the thought was no longer attractive but seemed rather like kissing your sister. Well, time to get her up, anyway. But when Sam turned and looked at her companion all such thoughts drained from her along with some of her color. It wasn't Charley there beside her! It wasn't Charley it was—Sam!

"Wake up!" Sam snapped. "What's going on here, anyway?"

Charley opened her eyes and smiled. "What's the problem?"

"Charley—that *is* you, isn't it?"

"Yeah, sure. What . . . ?" Sensing that something was definitely very wrong, she jumped to her feet. "What's happened, Sam? What *now?*"

"Your face—your hair, your eyes, your build . . . We always kinda looked like sisters, but, Charley—you're *me!*"

Sam pointed to a scar on Charley's abdomen. "That's even my appendix scar, and my birthmarks. A few of the freckles. Holy shit!"

Charley grabbed her hair, which was uncharacteristically trailing down her back, and brought it forward. It was nice, thick hair but it was straight and black and down almost to her waist—like Sam's had been before she'd cut it and run.

Hearing them, Ladai entered carrying a fairly large but manageable hand mirror. She had anticipated the problem again, as usual. Charley almost grabbed for it and looked at herself in the mirror, then all the way down. She stared in the mirror, then at Sam, back and forth, unable to believe it. Other than hair, they were absolutely identical, twins in every way except that one. Body hair was similarly missing; Charley's underarms were smooth and her legs even smoother, while Sam's underarms were fairly bushy and she had never shaved her legs.

"Well," she sighed at last, "he *said* I was the decoy, didn't he?" She looked at her right palm and saw the small cross-shaped cut similiar to the one on Sam's left hand. Something—something had been exchanged. Blood or whatever from Sam had gone to Charley and triggered the marching orders. "At least I got your figure, and it's the easiest diet I ever been on. I wonder if it's permanent?"

"Well, at least we still talk different," Sam noted. "You got my voice but you still got your accent."

"And you have yours," she retorted. "But you are talking at your low end normally, in your most male voice. Are you doing that deliberately?"

"No. I hadn't noticed until you said something. But it's—convenient. Charley, once we get some proper clothes and get moving I'm staying a man. You're gonna have to think of me that way, too. From this point on I'm Sam and I'm your brother. Okay?"

"Uh—sure. If I got to look like you I guess one of us ought'a be safe."

"You know you're talkin' high and a little whispery. I never knew it sounded that way. It's still real low but it's kind'a sexy and definitely female. You suddenly got the moves, too. Just standin' there. Jeez—I never knew I could look that sexy in the old days. Well, that's the old days." She shivered. "It's kinda damp in here. I wonder if we're ever gonna get any clothes?"

Zenchur took the cue to enter as Ladai left. He had pants and boots on but no shirt, and did he *ever* have hairy arms and legs! Somehow his presence no longer elicited in them any embarrassment at all. It wasn't that something had changed that they recognized; they simply didn't even give it a thought.

"I see you have found what your sorcerer has done," the mercenary noted. "I will not ask you how you like it because it makes no difference. Charley, you can still be Charley—the enemy knows only the looks, not the name and family history. I received explicit instructions before you had your encounter. Ladai is fixing a light breakfast; while she does, come in to my tent and we will find you suitable clothes and adornments."

They followed him and again were in the larger tent, this time at the two trunks. "The one on the left has typical Akhbreed male garb. The one on the right is similar but female. Select what you like—there is a large mirror over there in the back. Dress comfortably—we cannot leave today."

Sam looked through her trunk and found it an odd assortment. She wasn't sure what she expected—Peter Pan outfits or whatever—but the pants were mostly loose but leather, the shirts very thick wool or cotton with large wooden fasteners, the boots mostly high-top range-type or chukka boot height. Clearly whoever assembled the grouping had in mind disguising the female figure; much of it was stiff and reinforced in the places that would conceal the breasts and blur the body shape while still looking natural. Most if it looked fairly worn, although it all smelled clean and new. An interesting touch, actually—anybody out looking for her would naturally look for brand new-looking outfits. All the stuff had a handmade look.

Several things were immediately obvious when sorting through the pile as well. There was no real mass production of clothes, no big machines to make them, and nobody here had invented zippers, underwear—at least for the men—or opposing shoes. There were no left and right boots, for example. The harder fabrics had some cotton or wool lining in the seat to cushion extremities on leather, but it was still gonna take some getting used to. She picked a cotton outfit and low chukka boots to start—no socks, either, but they had a soft fur lining. It was clear, though, that if she couldn't tolerate the stiff stuff or it wasn't appropriate she was going to have to create a makeshift minimizer to tie around her breasts, and as for pissing—well, she doubted they had stalls around here so it was gonna have to be real circumspect.

Charley's trunk contained a far different assortment. It was quite a bit tighter, for one thing, and maximized what Sam's assortment minimized. The pullovers were mostly cotton and cleverly stitched to give some breast support, and the lone pair of pants was of similar material and would never be in danger of falling off her hips no matter what she did.

There were a few gorgeous skirts, mostly slit to mid-thigh, made of silk or satin, with tie-on matching halters that supported but stretched just enough that you could see her nipples through them. There was an outfit that looked for all the world like a mink bikini. There were several bottoms with no obvious tops, suggesting that often here, if the weather permitted, women went topless. She knew she couldn't do it on her own, but if *everybody* was doing it, well . . .

They did seem to go in for capes here. There were quite a number of matching capes even for outfits that had no tops. There were no clearcut bras or an equivalent to pantihose or any other sort of underwear. Footware seemed to consist of sandals, sandals with thick heels, and a kind of high-top boot that laced up almost to the knee. As with the male shoes, there was no right or left.

There were also three smaller boxes in the trunk. One, to her surprise, contained cosmetics—recognizable cosmetics in the generic sense at that. The two lipsticks were in copper cylinders, true, but they weren't bad. There was also a kind of rouge, eye shadow, a nail file made out of some dull, heavy metal, even two small baked ceramic jars of what proved to be nail polish. The brushes were independent and not the sort you'd buy in stores, but they were there. She had a sudden urge to really do herself up, to see just how sexy she could make this Sam body and how much she could erase any traces of maleness from the face and distract the rest with the other parts of the body. But first she decided to see what the other, larger boxes contained. The other contained ceramic jars with a funny kind of writing on each, but they proved to be perfumes, a couple not to her liking but the others seemed great. There was also a pad, powder, and a couple of jars of nice smelling but mysterious paste-like stuff. There was also a brush, a comb, and a small polished surface that made a decent mirror.

The third and final box contained an odd assortment of

jewelry. There were bracelets and anklets and necklaces and earrings that hung down as teardrops like quartz almost to or maybe below her jaw line. None of it was fancy, no jewel-encrusted stuff—but it was mostly bronze or yellow-gold and not at all bad.

Sam was comfortably dressed and ready to eat while she was still deciding and trying on several of the outfits. She loved trying on outfits anyway, always had. Finally Sam asked, "You noticed anything odd about this stuff?"

"Huh? No. I think I'm gonna be *dying* for a bra and panties under some of this before too long, and I'd *kill* for some pantihose, but it's not that bad."

"It all fits. Perfectly. I—we—got crazy wide feet. Always drove me nuts findin' shoes that I could get into. These fit. Perfect. All my stuff minimizes me just like they had my measurements. All that stuff you been tryin' on fits you, too. Even the stuff with built-in cups are perfect."

"So? Old Greenie hoped he could get you here, right? You got to figure he prepared. Like, that burnin' of the clothes."

"Yeah, but there's one for each of us—and Zenchur said he only expected me. He was real surprised when you popped up—that wasn't faked."

Charley shrugged. "Maybe he thought of the boy disguise, too. He didn't know your name or nothin' 'bout you. So he fixed up this for a real *femme fatale* type and he fixed the other as a disguise just in case. No big mystery."

"Okay, I'll give ya that. He just sorta thought of everything. But, Charley—*how'd he know my size?* In everything, too. Far enough in advance to age this shit so it don't look new and get even the shoe width and breast sizes right. He didn't know my name—or says he didn't. If he didn't know my name or nothin' at all about me, how come he knew my shape and size and all better than *I* did? Hell, better even than my mother?"

Charley shrugged. "Beats the hell outta me, but I still ain't sure I believe I'm *here* yet. We got a lot of answers to get, that's for sure. Let me just use the pullover here and slip on this skirt and sandals—they clash but I'm not goin' noplace—and we'll get something to eat and try'n make sense of all this. Maybe Zenchur can give some of the answers. I think he knows a lot more than he's lettin' on."

Charley let her go and set about choosing an outfit. It was all sort of fun, like a Flintstones makeup kit, but when she sat in

front of the mirror it was not her face that stared back and it
jolted her. *This isn't any game*, she thought, feeling suddenly
chilled. *Somehow this is really happening!* Images suddenly
arose, of her Mom and Dad, her home, her other friends at
school. What would they think when she didn't show up again?
When they finally found the cabin demolished and the
bloodstains and the Subaru all smashed and crushed? And now,
here, in this God-forsaken hole, she sat and it wasn't herself
she saw in the mirror.

My God! she thought, suddenly a frightened and nervous girl
even younger than her years. *What have I done?* She wanted
her Mom and Dad very badly then, and her own face and lousy
figure back, too. God, how she just wanted to go home!

She started crying softly. She'd never been the crying sort,
but she'd never been in a situation like this before or felt so
completely helpless and alone. It didn't last very long, but she
needed it. Finally, she wiped away the tears and took stock of
herself. She was stuck, and she could either give up or just go
along for the ride and make the best of it. The body wasn't half
bad; if only Sam didn't have such a boyish-looking face.
Well—the long hair helped. Maybe she could use this and see
just what she could make out of it all.

She had no idea what kind of a world they were in, but if
there were men like Zenchur around there were certain
universal things you could assume as well. If she was gonna
see that world, then that world was gonna see her looking
right.

· 4 ·

A Hard Wind's Caress

THERE WAS NO day or night inside the cave, only a certain eternal quality that insulated you from the world. Sam felt a sense of safety here such as she hadn't known in a very long time. Even the storms did not seem able to penetrate this spot, where there was only the water and the rock and the flickering brightness of the torches. She wanted to know about this world, this place that had brought her to it against her will for reasons still unclear. She wanted to know, but she felt no impulse to leave.

"This world is not like your world," Zenchur told Sam as they sipped strong, black tea and nibbled on sweet rolls. "It is, in fact, like *all* the worlds."

"You said you never left this world," Sam responded. "So how can you know much about mine?"

"I know about many of them because so many like you fall from them here. Not like it used to be, but regularly enough to get some pictures. Yours is a stable world. The rules are known and are always the same. Nothing ever falls up, rain is always wet, snow is always cold—yes?"

She nodded. "Yeah, I'll grant you that. But you gotta have some rules here, too. I mean, we're stuck on the ground here, the fire's hot, and it all looks real normal."

"Here, yes, because we are on the lip of a hub. But when we move out it might not always be so. It is hard for me to explain and it will be harder for you to believe until you witness it. Tell me—if you had a map showing your world, its nations and peoples and mountains and seas, would that map not be true many years later?"

71

"Sure. I guess some of the nations and people might change or move around, and the names seem to change a lot in places, but the maps I started out in elementary school with are still pretty good."

"Well, that is not possible here. The maps, and more than the maps, change. You see, long ago there was nothing but a single tiny block containing everything that ever was and ever will be. It grew heavier and heavier and heavier until it was too heavy to remain together and too—unstable I think the word is. It exploded and created everything else. Can you grasp that?"

She nodded. "Yeah. I wasn't too good in school but I seem to remember that the one thing the church and science agreed on was this big bang that started it all. It created the universe, whether by God or something else."

"Good, good! But it did not create the universe. It was far too powerful for that. It created the *universes,* in layers, like the layers in a fancy cake. One on top of the other." He picked up a charred stick and drew a funnel shape on the cave floor. "See—this little bottom point is where it all started." He drew a series of lines bisecting the funnel from top to bottom. "Each of these—thousands, millions, who knows how many?—is a universe. Yours is up towards the top someplace. Mine is down here, not at the bottom but as far down as you can get and still live and breathe and have our kind of life. Up near the top the distance between them is great and you are rarely aware of any others except perhaps in dreams, but down here we have a smaller universe and things are packed more closely together. Here many universes lie almost on top of each other—layers with no cake, as it were. Akahlar is not one world, it is many."

She stared and shook her head. This was getting too much like school. "But if you got all them universes on top of each other like this, then what keeps it all from gettin' to be a jumbled mess?"

"No two can occupy the same wedge at the same time. That would be chaos. But the forces still coming from the core, from the place where it all began, keep things in motion here. Whole sections of Akahlar drop out and are replaced by others." He drew a circle, then an inner hub, then drew spokes out from the hub to the sides. "There are forty-eight of these. They are not true circles but close enough. Each two spokes creates a wedge and that wedge is *someplace.* The forces that strike us from below, at the tiny point, cause the circles not to turn but to change. One land drops out of a wedge, another drops in. If you are there you do not notice it. If you are *not* there you do not notice it. But where a city by a sea was the last time you were through there might now be a mountain lair for dragons. Twelve wedges to a wheel, as it were. Hundreds of combinations. Such changes keep us in constant turmoil. The weather changes, there are always storms and changes in most everything.''

"Jeez! How do you ever keep anything straight?"

He smiled. "Never underestimate intelligence, my young friend. The races who think and build and create are the ones who can adapt. Tell me—on your world, do not people live where it is freezing cold all year, and others where it is an eternal steaming jungle, and still others where it is a hot and near lifeless desert?"

"Uh—yeah, I guess so. Sure."

"That is why they survive. There are literally thousands of races, not all even close to our kind as are the ba'ahdon. All fell to this point in ancient times when the changewinds blew strong through the whole of creation, before everything stabilized and got built up and solidified. Each is a little slice of a real universe, and each universe has exacting rules—but they are not necessarily the same rules."

"Seems to me everybody'd get lost or all mixed up or somethin'. Couldn't tell nobody from nobody else."

"Well, most races cannot breed with most others. It is possible that even you and I are different enough that we could never produce offspring, although we appear close enough that it is possible that we could, too. It is rather—what is the word?—*insular*. Everyone sticks to their own kind and their own ways and defends their land against the others. There is some trade, of course, but how can you even have a lot of trade when you do not know if your trading partner will be there next week or next month? Many races believe themselves superior, higher than the others, and so would not consider the others human or worthy of respect. Some may even delight in *eating* other races. For thousands upon thousands of years there was just a lot of little worlds. That is, until the Akhbreed conquest."

She frowned. "How the hell could you conquer something like *that?*"

"You don't. What you conquer are *these*," he replied,

pointing his stick at the hub of the wheel. "The loci—the hub. These do not change. They are constant always no matter what wedge you come from. They coexist in all our universes. They were mostly uninhabitable messes, however, until the Akhbreed came with their powerful sorcery the likes of which none had ever seen before. Many of the other races possess magic, some have great power within their own wedges, but this was different. These people could do *all* the magic, and they could do it anywhere. They created order in the hubs and established kingdoms for the Akhbreed. Because all hubs coexist in all universes that are down here, they could step away into any wedge they chose. They are brutal, ruthless, powerful, and they believe themselves the anointed superiors to all other races who exist for their benefit. They alone can trade. They alone have stability. They alone can force their will by sending armies against the wedges that resist them. The forty-eight kings and queens of Akhbreed rule Akahlar because of it and keep the rest down, their power based in their god-like sorcerers. That one whom you saw last night—he is an Akhbreed sorcerer. You have just a small taste of his power."

Sam's head was spinning a bit at this. "I sure don't understand this and I ain't sure I believe what I do understand, but *him* I understand. And the one with the horns and the thunderstorms? He's another one?"

Zenchur stiffened. "Do not even speak of him so. Yes, he is of the same kind, but he is not in the service of the Akhbreed. He is what the Akhbreed call a rogue. He serves no Akhbreed kingdom. If they could locate him and gang up on him to destroy him—you do not kill Akhbreed sorcerers, you destroy them—they would. This one of whom we speak is very powerful but rebels at the Akhbreed dominance, as do I. He is their sworn enemy, and he plots to destroy the Akhbreed kingdoms and end their dominance. He offers liberation from Akhbreed tyranny to those who follow his cause, and as he is the first of that rank of sorcerer to offer his power to them he is a formidable foe, since the forty-eight Akhbreed kingdoms are bound together only by their common belief of racial superiority and their power. Otherwise, they hate each other, and the sorcerers of one are jealous and not at all cordial towards others of their kind from other kingdoms."

Sam shook her head. "Jeez! Lemme get this straight now. You got tons of races and they're all kinda bossed around and made to work for the ones who look like us 'cause the ones that look like us got the power. But our kind don't like each other, neither. They kick around all the others but they don't like the fact that all them other kings and sorcerers got the same kinda power they got. Is that about right?''

"Yes. Very good. But because they hate each other they are vulnerable—if a sorcerer of high enough power could combine with the magic of many other races as well as building a physical army that could outnumber and outfight the Akhbreed troopers, they might well fall one hub at a time. This one of whom we speak is the first of his class to offer such power to the other races. All hate the Akhbreed; some will be convinced to support him. He builds to strike at the heart of the tyranny. He has some command of a weapon that could even weaken or possibly destroy the Akhbreed hubs—if he could control it. Until he can he dares not risk it, for it is as dangerous to him and to his followers as to the Akhbreed. He is the master of the storms and can summon the changewind of old, the sort that can alter or destroy even the hubs. We get a few every now and then, randomly, in different parts of Akahlar, every year, but he can cause them. If he ever learns to control them he will smash all the tyrants of Akhbreed.''

Sam frowned. "This is nuts. The way you're talkin', the guy who's tryin' to kill me is somebody doin' a good thing, and the guy who's tryin' to save me is defendin' a real evil system. This is nuts! Kinda like discoverin' that the Russians are your friends and protectors and the Americans wanna string you up when you're an American who likes the American way." She paused a moment. "I can see where some might be scared, but seems to me that this guy would have the support of everybody who ain't us. But he don't, right?''

Zenchur nodded. "Right. It is partly because he is Akhbreed, and the other races have learned through bitter experience never to trust one, and it is also that it is known that such tremendous power, like the gods, is impossible to have without corrupting your very soul. Every Akhbreed sorcerer is in some way insane. You can see the problem. Do you trade in a tyrant for a god? Which is worse—to be dominated, or to be owned? Every Akhbreed kingdom overthrown will make his domain greater and greatly increase his already unbelievable power. It is the ultimate dilemma. Without one such as him there is no hope of ever breaking the bonds that enslave countless millions

of other races, but with one such as him one might long for the
good old days of Akhbreed rule. It is dividing many races and
many leaders. This last business will not win him many
converts, either. Just to get at you he expended enormous
power and that power has created a hole, a vacuum, in
Akahlar. Such vacuums do not remain unfilled for long. He has
of necessity created conditions that will bring a changewind to
us. We must wait until it passes and hope it does not come this
way."

Charley stepped out of the tent, hearing only the tail end of
the conversation. She was wearing some of the jewelry and a
colorful slit skirt and sandals but was topless. Sam couldn't
figure just what Charley had done, but she looked *damned*
good. "What's a changewind?" she asked curiously.

Zenchur looked at her and frowned. "A changewind is the
random wrath of God. It is a storm. It is every storm that you
have ever seen and more. It destroys worse than the worst kind
of storm imaginable, yet it does what no other storm does. It
also *creates*."

"Wow!" breathed Sam. "I was in a hurricane once and I
seen a coupl've tornadoes. I don't wanna be in any of 'em, but
I'd sure like to see one of these things—from a safe distance,
of course."

"Not even an Akhbreed sorcerer will look at one of these
storms," Zenchur responded. "One who looks upon the
changewinds too closely gets some of its curse. Only the freaks
and the monsters have looked upon the changewinds and
survived in the wastes, belonging only to each other, to tell the
tale. Believe me, you do not want to see a changewind—
ever!"

Charley shrugged and shook her head. "What the hell is a
changewind?" she repeated.

"A random force that does the one thing everyone fears
everywhere," the mercenary responded. "It changes the
rules."

Ladai suddenly made a sharp comment in her strange tongue
and he nodded. "It has come," he said softly. "Not close, but
close enough. To Malabar, the hub to the southeast, and its
attendant wedges. A bad one."

Charley looked at him strangely, then at Ladai. "How does
she know?"

"No traveler though this world is ever completely untouched by the changewind, and, once touched, you *know*."

Suddenly Sam felt a tremendous throbbing in her temples; her ears stopped up and the cave and those in it seemed to vanish. Charley, Zenchur, and Ladai saw her suddenly get straight to her feet, looking not at anything they could see but somewhere else, and then Sam cried out—and fainted.

Zenchur was fast enough to break her fall, but even as Sam was lowered to the cave floor she seemed to come to, in a sense, her eyes opening wide, still staring at something none of the others could see and hearing things that none of the others could hear. Inside her, she felt awake, alert, the scenes she was now seeing clear and vivid to her as if she stood there with them. She knew somehow that she was not really there, but as much as she wished that it was a dream she also knew with absolute certainty that it was no dream but reality she was witnessing. Somehow, in some way, she was getting her wish whether she wanted it or not.

The coming of the changewind.

Terror wafted in on a nice spring breeze, filling the air with intangible charged particles of fear. As always, the animals felt it first, stopping whatever they were doing and then raising their heads to the northeast, almost as one, looking for what could not be seen.

The horses froze in the fields and turned to look, as did the cows. The dogs did more, emitting after a while a low growl, and the barn cats turned their ears back and arched their spines as if facing some immediate and tangible threat. Even the chickens, ordinarily too dumb to get out of the summer hail, stopped their incessant cackling and darting about and turned to look; turned to look at the northeastern horizon.

It was a clear, warm day, the kind of day that comes but once in a while in early spring but which lifts the spirits and tells all that the majesty and life of summer is approaching. The sun shone brightly down on the small village and its farms and fields and illuminated the golden coating on the great castle that seemed carved out of the hills in back of the settlement, making the greatest and grandest of the buildings shine like some majestic fairyland jewel. The sky was a pale blue, broken here and there by fluffy cumulus clouds too white to hold the threat of moisture. It was the kind of day that wouldn't dare be rained on, yet it was suddenly bathed in silence.

The lands of the hub were places of pure magic yet also places where such magic should never intrude.

People, of course, were the last to notice, as usual. Still, eventually, they noticed the silence, and the animals, and soon they, too, began looking fearfully to the northeast.

Perhaps it's nothing, they told themselves, trying to gain some measure of confidence and fight back the fear that was growing inside them. *Perhaps it's not coming our way. There hasn't been one through here in generations. This is a charmed village, a safe place, in the solidity of the hub, protected from all harm by the sorcery of the Akhbreed and even from the changewinds by the great Mountains of Morning.* So they had told themselves and each other for generations.

The changewind blew down from its far north origin, though, ignorant and uncaring of such things. It had been riding well high in the weather patterns and had not touched ground or near ground, making it more a fearsome sight than something of lasting effect that might be seen and felt and known by those over which it passed. So far it had a pretty clear run along the air currents across the plains, but now it was caught in the twisting currents at the base of the Mountains of Morning and sucked in toward them. They were ancient, massive peaks, all purple in the distance and snow-clad, and they stood as a formidable barrier to all save the changewind. It was too dense to rise over the mountains, and too stubborn and powerful to allow them to get in its way.

Nothing really could be seen from the castle or the village as yet; it was still too far away. Yet it could be felt, and sensed, even by those inside the castle who had grown fat and complacent over the decades of stability, and on Akahlar stability was everything. Even they could not ignore the behavior of their animals, or some of the signs from their instruments.

The Royal Sorcerer made his way to the forward battlement, his blue robe flapping in the breeze, a tiny green monkey remaining expertly perched on his shoulder in spite of the sudden movement. The sorcerer had a large bronze telescope mounted there, pointing to the north and east, and he swung the thing but did not look in it himself. Rather, it was the small green monkey who looked in it, as the sorcerer moved the telescope, scanning the horizon, yet from the sorcerer's head movements one would swear that he was indeed peering in and looking hard, not for anything direct or obvious, but just for the signs he knew would be there.

In the valley between the twin peaks they called the Two Brothers he found his signs, although they would have meant little to the untrained eye. Just a bit of a glow, pale crimson, beyond the peaks, and the peaks themselves framed slightly with a blue borderline, as if superimposed upon another scene beyond. It was enough. It was more than enough.

"Captain of the Guard!" the little man yelled, and a soldier came running. "There is a changewind coming. A high probability, too, given the wind patterns aloft, that it will come straight down the valley. Alert His Majesty and Colonel Fristanna at once. Waste no time in preparing the shelters and sounding the alarm to the people."

This was bad; a lot worse than either he or the king had originally thought. This was going to be the storm of the century for this old place.

The Guardsman did nothing right away. Finally, licking his lips, he said, "Are you sure?" Ordinarily questioning or in any way failing to immediately carry out the order of an Akhbreed sorcerer would be unthinkable, but the sorcerer had just introduced the unthinkable and forced consideration of it.

The little man in blue fumed. "Why do you hesitate? Time is of the essence! If you don't do as I say now you will see the changewind close up, from down there, outside the castle and Keep!"

Galvanized, the Guardsman turned and ran off. Within two minutes the sound that all dreaded, highborn and low, rang out from the same battlements as Guardsmen turned the cranks on the howler boxes sounding a terrible siren call that reached for miles and penetrated the very soul.

The man in blue looked down to see the castle's company springing into action. One, an officer, already mounted and ready to move, looked up and saw him. "How long, wizard?" he shouted. "Do we have a time frame?"

"Hard to say," the little man shouted back. "Certainly an hour, most certainly not two. Keep an eye on the Brothers. If they change, then you have at best five to ten minutes. Understand? Watch the Brothers!"

The officer nodded, turned, and began shouting orders.

The sorcerer himself could do little. He of all the people was most vulnerable to the changewind; it might well be attracted to him like a magnet, and he knew his only real duty was to get inside and behind proper insulation until it passed. He sighed and looked out on the peaceful valley and the town below. A simple place, with rolling green fields newly fertilized and planted with summer maize, oats, corn, and other grains, the vegetable regions newly tilled. Off to the west were the groves of grapes, hardly ready as yet for the harvest but promising a very good year. He sincerely hoped that they, at least, would be spared.

The low stone buildings of the town with their thatched roofs newly repaired after a harder than usual winter looked somehow unreal, like a painting in the Great Hall.

There would be little time to gather much in the way of personal belongings; those who dallied might well be caught outside, for when the howlers howled again it would signal the closing of the refuges and the closing of hope for anyone and anything left outside.

Below the Golden Castle, at the base of the hill that supported it, great teams of men and oxen turned massive gears that had been moved only in drills for the past fourteen years. Below, great doors slowly swung outward, revealing a massive cavity that went not only into the hill but down below it. Not even hills were safe in a changewind; not even mountains.

With the aid and none too gentle encouragement of the cavalry, the village began to move toward that cavity. The women and children first, of course; they were the least expendable. Then the men, some pulling hastily filled carts, others not bothering, while the farmers themselves herded cows and horses and as many sheep as they could quickly round up from the nearby meadows.

Malachan was only fourteen, but that was old enough to make him a man in the village. He had been still in his mother's womb the last time and knew of such things only in legends and tales told by his elders, but now one was coming and he was of age, subject to his father's orders, and it was partially his responsibility to see that all living things that could be saved be protected. The rest could be replaced or rebuilt, if need be. He was aware of the tales and legends of the change-winds and knew it might not be needed, that in fact they might gain better than they lost, if they but protected what could not be risked.

Up on the battlement, the Captain of the Guard stared at the Two Brothers, which no longer seemed so distant or so permanent, and then he gasped and his heart leaped to his throat. For a brief moment he was paralyzed, this man who had fought a hundred battles and faced a hundred foes, by what he now saw.

The Brothers were melting, melting down like ice on a hot summer's day, turning purple and white to a burnt orange color and revealing suddenly a huge pass through the Mountains of Morning, and beyond that pass the sky turned an ominous, yet beautiful cyan, a massive violet that was moving and twisting and writhing like something alive, and which flashed with bright sparks as it did so. Beyond it, on its fringes, the regular clouds coalesced into a dark, nasty storm that rumbled lightning and thunder and accompanied the swirling mass.

He broke free and ran to the far end, shouting as he did so. "It's through! It's through! Sound the alarm and take cover!"

A wind came suddenly up from nowhere, rustling through the grasses and causing the trees to sway and speak the roaring tongue. And from the ground and the houses and the trees and the very air there seemed to come shapes; indistinct, wraithlike shapes large and small, gentle and fierce, and they rushed through the air as well, beating the wind to the great enclosure, going over the heads of the people and animals still going in.

The siren call of the howlers wailed. *Ten minutes! Last warning!* But ten minutes was not ten at all, but five, for they had to be closed and all well below in the insulated, packed shelters by the time that mass got here, if indeed it was coming. Men dropped carts and abandoned what they had been carrying and ran for the great opening, and even the animals seemed to quicken and run for that last place of escape.

Malachan prepared to run as well, when he heard a plaintive wailing cry off to his right. He stopped and then made for it, quickly spotting a very frightened small cat hunched up against the side of a house and mewing in terror. He picked it up and it clung to him, and he petted it for a moment, then turned, aware now that the howling had stopped. Clutching the kitten, he made as fast as he could for the doors which were even now beginning to close.

It was not much distance; it was designed that way, but the

usually clear and easy path to it was now littered with carts and dropped and spilled goods. Here a treasured picture, there an old clock, and over there bottles, some smashed. It was like running an obstacle course, and on top of that the kitten's claws were dug through his clothing to his skin.

Still, he was going to make it. Perhaps at the last moment, but he was going to make it. The doors were only three-quarters shut, and he was small. At the same moment he made to leap a smashed basket of what looked like bowls and dishes, the kitten decided it had had enough and launched itself away toward the closing great doors. The action was enough to disorient him briefly, and he tripped over the box and fell hard on the ground. It didn't take him long to recover, although he was scraped and skinned up a bit, but it had cost him precious seconds and all his momentum. He looked at the doors and saw they were almost closed, and took off again on a run, screaming, "Wait! Wait! Just a few seconds more!"

But the forces turning the great gears that controlled the gate ignored him, as was their duty, if, indeed, they had heard him at all.

He was but three steps from the doors when they closed tight with a mighty clang and echoing roar that seemed to rebound across the entire valley. Malachan hurled himself at the doors and beat upon them with all his might, shouting loudly, but it did no good at all.

He wasted little time once he realized this, running back and then over toward the road leading up to the Golden Castle. There would still be someone there, probably until the last minute. There were ways in and down from there, he knew. The Stormholders and Guardsmen would have their own privileges.

The wind was picking up, reaching almost gale force, however, and it drove him back. The air was full of dust and debris, and everything loose began to shake and shimmer and take on a life of its own. He knew now it was no use; the storm would be upon him before he could reach the top gates, and by that time no one would be left. He tried to think.

If you are caught by a changewind, and have any warning, go as low as you can, below ground if possible, and cover yourself with earth, they'd taught him. *Let no part of your body be exposed to the air and wind.*

He looked around. That was easy to say, but hardly useful

right now. The defense of the village was predicated on and dependent on the Refuge carefully built below and lined with the best of insulators. Even the golden coating on the castle was an insulating substance that might work if it were not directly hit, but it would do him little good. He knew that you had to stay away from such substances if you were on the outside, since any forces that were repelled would build up and concentrate there.

And so he found what shelter he could against the conventional winds behind a stone wall and peered out at the coming great storm. It was both beautiful and awesome. It was preceded by a rolling bank of black clouds that seemed to advance like some great carpet, a carpet fit for a king or a god. Lightning flared out from this leading edge, dancing along the ground and sounding mighty reverberant thunderclaps throughout the valley.

The changewind also had its attendants; more clouds, racing with a speed he had never seen before, giving off not only lightning but darker shapes, funnel-like clouds marching beside the changewind and sucking up whatever they trod upon.

In the center of it all was the changewind, most beautiful and awesome of all. Everyone was properly frightened to death of it, but none had ever spoken of its great beauty and majesty. Swirling clouds like violet oil in a sky full of clear water; that's what it looked like at first. The closer it got, though, the less color it seemed to have and it became paradoxically more and less complex. A sea of infinite stars, blinking and wavering, in a vaguely violet universe unlike any known to any people of his own world. It was a vastness that covered, engulfed, all that it rolled across. The air was thick and heavy, drawing the great wind down until nothing but it could be seen in the center of the valley. The changewind, finally, rode only a hundred feet or so above the ground and influenced all that was below it. Had it reached the ground it would have been grabbed by enormous friction, slowed, and absorbed, its effect major but localized, and it would have quickly died.

This one would not oblige.

Malachan knew nothing of its physics, which was just as well, for in truth the learned wizard who had first spied it had vastly more questions than answers, but he understood well that it was coming and that there was no way really for him to get out of its way.

Strangely, he found himself suddenly drained of fear, taken up only in the awesome beauty and wonder of that force he could neither comprehend nor do anything at all about. He knew he was going to die, and he only hoped that his reincarnation would be swift and his judgment fair, for he had been a good boy. For a brief moment he thought of his family, all safe inside and huddled there in the torchlit darkness, and knew that his loss, when discovered, would bring them grief. He hoped it would not be too much or too long. He would get his experiences in the next life; this was almost worth the price.

The changewind advanced into the valley and did what it always did. All below its pulsing form took on an eerie glow and became outlined in brilliant, electric blue. Grass, trees, everything—even the very air seemed altered and illuminated with a glow. The grape vines shimmered and writhed and changed, becoming strange, gnarled trees with dark, huge blossoms unlike anything he'd ever seen before. The maize field shimmered and melted and part of it became water, pushed by the storms. The rest became taller, wilder grasses in spots, and yellow sand in others.

The changewind began to pass over the thatched cottages and stables of the village. They glowed and flowed and changed as well, becoming blocky, multi-story structures made of some reddish-brown material, a form totally alien to him. He could already see beneath and beyond the changewind to a fierce rainstorm on the back side, while over on the edges there seemed to be clearing and even the start of breaks in the clouds.

And then it was over and upon him. Curiously, there was no sensation, no pain, nothing. Just a light tingling sensation, nothing more. He held out his arms and saw that he was bathed in the changewind glow. He grew, and his clothing burst and then seemed to melt away within him. His arms became thick and muscular, his fingers long and powerful, with steel-like claws as nails. His skin turned thick and brown as he watched, then was covered down to the wrists and even on the backs of his huge hands with very short thick brown hair like an animal's.

Below his waist the hair changed, becoming thick and woolly, and his legs throbbed and twisted and changed as well.

They were animal legs, although not exactly like any animal he had ever known, and they terminated in great, cloven hooves which would be fine for running but provided less than the best balance standing still. He went backward a bit, but found himself well supported on his long, thick brown tail.

Malachan was less terrified than horrified at what he had become. Death he could accept, and had been willing to, but he had not died. He had become some sort of monster.

The changewind was past now, and proceeding far up the valley, losing force as it did so. It was already rising, and losing some of its consistency. It would not travel on much farther. Malachan stood there, stunned, as the torrential rain came down upon him, masking and taking with them his very real tears.

The backwash of the storm was quickly through, though, and the clouds grew thinner and then began to break up. Sunlight dared peer down on a vastly different scene. It would be quite some time, perhaps months, before the climatological changes stabilized and it was possible to really see what the changewind had made of this wonderful place, but it certainly was no longer the paradise that a previous changewind helped create.

The Golden Castle still stood, its golden sheen now a metallic blue-black, but it would be quite some time, perhaps days, before the assembled populace could free itself from the Refuge the way they got in. The great doors had held, but in the process they had melted a bit and been fused into a solid metallic wall.

The place was not without some familiarity. The Two Brothers no longer stood out in the distance, but the vast wall of the Mountains of Morning otherwise remained pretty much as it was. There was now a vast lake leading from just in front of the village back almost as far as the eye could see, yet it was not wide; patches of real green could be seen in the distance.

This side, however, had not fared so well. The soil was sandy, and rocky as well, and the vegetation was wild grasses, some waist high, and nasty and twisted plants unlike any known here before. Over where the grape vines were, intermixed with the trees, were strange looking bushes bearing large and beautiful pink and crimson flowers that looked like giant roses.

Hesitantly, Malachan moved toward them, and as he got

within five or six feet of the first it barked at him. All of the flowers barked at him, and snarled, like a pack of angry dogs, and the beautiful bushes shook and flailed out blindly. He backed off quickly, very confused.

He looked down at himself and then at the vicious plants and shook his now massive head. He simply did not know what to do. He was still Malachan—at least, he *thought* that at least that part of him remained unchanged. Changewinds could alter anything, inside and out, even the very soul, but this one seemed to have limited itself to the physical.

He looked at the lake, and the menacing plants, and knew he could not go there. He looked back at the transformed village, so alien now, and beyond it. The last of the storm was leaving, but where the two lines of hills had once come together there was now unbroken plain littered with tall grasses and equally tall bright, huge flowers. *Everything* had changed, everything but the castle itself, and it would never be the same again any more than he would. He just wished he knew what to do.

He was still trying to determine this when the laborers and cutters up at the castle broke through and managed to peel away the remains of the armored doors at the top. Within minutes, a large troop of cavalry rode out, stopping just outside to survey the new scene and take it all in. The real survey, however, had to come later. Theirs was a different mission that had to come first.

The leader peered through field glasses, panning the scene, looking for what his duty required, and he finally found it. It wasn't hard, not against this new landscape and being the size and shape it was. He put down his glasses and pointed. "Down there, to the left and behind the village. See it?"

His sergeant squinted, then nodded. "Yes, sir. I had hoped we had gotten them all this time. Pray the gods this is the only one."

"We don't know if it was human or animal," the lieutenant shouted to his men, "or whether it will attack or flee. Weapons ready, then move down. Shoot first and study the thing later!"

Malachan saw and heard them, too, and for a moment didn't know whether to stand there or flee. When he saw that they had their weapons out, though, he turned and began to run at full speed through the tall grass.

He was fast, very fast, as if made for this sort of country, but the skilled men and superbly trained horses were faster and smarter and more experienced. He quickly realized that he could not outrun them and stopped, marveling that he was hardly breathing hard at all, and waited, his massive hands raised in a gesture of surrender. They were all around him in a minute, but none too close.

"Please!" he bellowed as they stared nervously and uncomfortably at him. "I am Malachan of the old village! The doors closed on me just a few steps before I could enter! Have mercy! I am hideous, but I am just a fourteen-year-old peasant boy!"

That startled some of the newer men, but not the officer and the sergeant who were more experienced. It was usually kids.

"I know, son," sighed the lieutenant in a sad, almost tragic-sounding voice. "I just hope you're old enough to understand. Understand that what we must—do—now *is* out of mercy."

"*No!*" wailed Malachan as the missiles struck and penetrated even his powerful body, again and again, with great pain, until he was so helpless that the officer had no problem administering the *coup de grace*.

Up on the charred battlements, the sorcerer Boolean examined his old area. The telescope was gone, of course—sort of. What stood in its place was a very odd sort of weapon mounted on a similar tripod, a weapon not known in this land before, but one the Akhbreed sorcerer understood full well.

"Well I'll be damned," the wizard said under his breath. "Have to melt *that* one down for scrap pretty damned fast. Can't have 'em getting too many ideas of *that* sort around here. Things are rotten enough already." He turned and looked out at the changed landscape, the new lake, the missing hills, the strange trees and grass, and shook his head.

"Well," he sighed, again talking to himself, "there goes the neighborhood."

Sam awoke, sweat dripping from her, the scene fading gradually and being replaced by fuzzy images that resolved into the concerned faces of Charley and Zenchur.

"They killed him!" she shouted, slightly in shock. "They hunted him down and killed him! Just a kid who got caught in some bad luck! The bastards! The dirty bastards!"

"What did you see?" Zenchur asked curtly. "Tell me all of it—now!"

Ladai spoke to him a bit sharply and then brought some dry wine for Sam to drink. Once she had a bit of it down, she felt more and more in control of herself, and with a little prompting she told them the entire story.

Zenchur nodded. "It sounds right, although I can't understand how or why you would have such a vision, particularly of Malabar where neither of the ones involved in your own affairs here have much interest or influence. The Akhbreed tolerate no one not of their own kind to live in any of the kingdoms, and none may remain overnight except right on the edge, as we are here."

"But—but it changed *everything!* The houses, the plants, the dirt, the water, even that poor boy. Even if he was a victim, why'd they hav'ta *kill* him? Why not just send him off someplace?"

Zenchur sighed. "It is complicated. The Akhbreed believe themselves the superior race to all others. Therefore, it is unthinkable to them that any of their kind would even wish to live as some sort of—well, monster. They killed him as a mercy—to keep him from suffering in an inferior form. He was also probably one of a kind in Akahlar—that happens a lot with the big ones. He would be a freak, an outcast, and none would take him or accept him."

That was not an answer either girl could accept, and they were beginning to like this place less and less with each passing discovery. Still, Sam wanted to understand. "Where did those changes come from? His form, the houses, the barking bushes . . . ?"

Zenchur shrugged. "Practically everything is possible, you know. If one little thing went differently, if your ancestors had arisen from different stock than they did, our whole race might have looked like that. The houses, the land, everything was probably consistent with beings of his kind. They may even exist somewhere on an Outplane—there are far too many to know. They call it probability theory. Sorcerer's mathematics. Ask one sometime about it if you get the chance—and somehow I suspect you will meet one or more sooner or later. More to the point now is why you had this spell, this vision, and how."

She shrugged helplessly. "In my dreams—back home. The dreams always brought visions—I guess of this place—and always when it stormed. I guess even this far away and buried this deep a storm like that triggered it off again."

Zenchur rubbed his chin thoughtfully, then muttered to

himself in the singsong tongue of the Akhbreed, "The Horned One, and a girl from the Outplane who is linked to storms. Of course! Why did I not think of this from the start? By the gods—what do I do now?" He paused a moment more, then sighed.

"All right," he said in English. "You saw the Chief Sorcerer of Malabar there. Did he seem to be aware of you? Did anyone give the slightest hint that they were aware of your presence? Any? Think! It is important!"

"It was like I was a ghost, not seen and not being able to say or do anything. I was just *there,* that's all. Besides, they were a little too busy to bother much with me."

"And you sensed no one else there? No other presence, or guiding force?"

She shook her head. "Nope. It just—*happened,* is all."

"Very well. That is some consolation, anyway. Just relax here. I must discuss this with Ladai." He walked over to the centauress who was relaxing by the pool. The distance between them and Sam was a good twenty feet or more but the cave made it fairly easy to hear everything in the mercenary's low conversation with his strange companion.

"I don't like this," Charley commented sourly. "I wish I could make out that language of theirs."

"*Shhhh . . . ,*" Sam responded. When Charley seemed not inclined to shut up, her friend mouthed, *I can understand it.*

And she could, just as she had understood the comments in the Akhbreed tongue that Zenchur had muttered to himself. She had not understood many of the conversations between Zenchur and Ladai before, since they had been in some other, less formal, tongue, but now the mercenary was using Akhbreed, the same language of Sam's dreams of the past, the language which, somehow, she instantly understood.

"We cannot go on with this," Zenchur told Ladai. "Our distrust for that horned bastard kept us neutral in this so far, but we no longer have that luxury. If we deliver her to Boolean it is more than possible that the entire rebellion will be crushed and Akhbreed dominance assured for another thousand years or more. *We*—you and I—will be the instruments of perpetuating this foulness! This I cannot accept!"

Ladai understood him, apparently used to him speaking in his native tongue when he was angry or upset, but she answered in their common speech and Sam could not make out any of it.

Zenchur nodded. "I agree. We cannot just kill them—Boolean would know and there would be no place to hide from his wrath, for one thing. And, no, I can't have either of us leaking the facts to others because that would destroy our reputations for never betraying a commission. We would be finished. Yet, somehow, they must die."

Again Ladai said something unintelligible.

"Yes," he responded, sounding somewhat pleased by whatever suggestion she'd given. "You're right. If they are placed in a position where they are certain to be exposed, and the odds are overwhelming, then what can we do? Besides, they are ignorant of all of this. If the name Klittichorn should be spoken rather regularly it might well attract just the wrong attention on its own." He kissed her. "My dear, I believe we will have another of our honorable failures."

Charley thought the unintelligible scene a bit charming if very kinky, but Sam's expression told her that it was far more than that. Still, she knew better than to press it right now; if the odd couple's conversation could carry, so could any other.

Zenchur came back over to them, ever the friendly protector. "I will have to leave here for a while in order to make arrangements for mounts and the like to get us into Tubikosa, the capital city of this hub. Because of the changewind we will need up-to-date information on just what damage it did and where. I am a competent navigator but we will have to engage a trustworthy pilot who is also up-to-date. That means the city, although I detest it and had hoped we would not have to travel there. The changewind makes it essential that we do so. Ladai will stand guard and you will be all right. Take some time to look through the trunks and choose a selection that could fit in no more than two of the saddlebags in my tent. Um—you can both ride horses, can't you?"

"Never been on one in my life," Sam responded, " 'cept the pony rides at the fair when I was little. But I'll make do."

"I'm a pretty good horsewoman," Charley told him. "We'll have to teach Sam what she needs to know."

Zenchur shrugged. "Very well. I will secure a particularly gentle horse for Sam, a first rider type. Now—farewell." And, with that, he walked to the cave entrance and was gone.

"I don't like that," Sam muttered, almost to herself. "Come on—let's go look through the trunks."

Charley frowned. "But it's okay. He's gone, and she don't speak English."

"Yeah, maybe, but I'm not about to make the same mistake he did. Come on."

They walked into the tent and Sam stood there for a minute or so, as Charley watched in frustration. Then Sam peered out of the tent flap and looked back. "It's okay," she whispered, "so long as we keep our voices down. She's still just lyin' there playin' with her reflection in the water." Quickly she told Charley of the conversation in low tones.

"Damn! What the hell do we do *now?* I mean, if you're new on a horse you're a sittin' duck and you know it. All he has to do is get one that's got a mean streak or is easily spooked and it can look real natural. Horse bolts or panics, you fall and break your neck, and he's off the hook, right? And I'm all alone and stuck here as witness to the terrible accident." Charley sighed. "But how come you understood him at all?"

"Lucky break. He don't speak it like I know it but it was close enough. Sort'a like hearin' an English farmer instead of American. It's the same language I heard in my dreams and I understood it then. I guess I still do. Maybe I can talk it, too, but I ain't gonna try until I hav'ta give away the fact I know it. Couldn't make out Ladai's speech for nothin', though."

Charley sighed. "Well, that's a break, sort of, for what it's worth. Too bad we can't talk to Ladai. I know they're partners and all, but she seems so sweet and understanding. . . ."

"Bullshit! She was givin' him the ideas on how to knock us off without gettin' caught at it. Look, I was out there talkin' to Zenchur long before you got there. The guy's *weird*. Got some sort'a guilt complex or somethin'. His family's rich—maybe nobles, I dunno. Lots of money and power, though, that they got partly from the sweat of labor by the nonhumans. He got to know and like some of 'em, found out they was regular folks and all, and got a real heavy conscience. When he could he just ran away rather than keep livin' under that system. Tried to live with some of the other races but they didn't trust him none, run him out. He was on the run when he nearly died and got rescued by the—whatchamacallit?—horse people?"

"Centaurs."

"Yeah, that's right. They took him in 'cause they can look

deep inside you and read your feelin's. Not your mind, but whether you're happy or sad, in love or whatever, that kind of shit. They just know, somehow, who their friends are. He lived with 'em a long time and just real flipped out. Went native. Ladai—she ain't his business partner. She's his wife."

"Wow! *Kinkee* . . ."

"You bet. He thinks he's one of *them*. They believe in that reincarnation stuff, and he thinks he's one of them horse types reborn by accident or whatever as a human. He believes it so strong I think she believes it, too. She's got a few screws loose herself 'cause she went for him in a big way, too, but their marriage wasn't all that popular with her folks or tribe or whatever it is. So they got kicked out, and they been workin' the dirty job and mercenary racket all over ever since. So now they got in over their head and they're gonna try and shake it so's they can get back to ignorin' the world and its problems. And I'm what they gotta shake."

Charley sat down on top of the trunk and tried to think. "So what can we do? We stay with them, we're dead. We sneak out and, like, we're alone and friendless in some crazy world where we don't know a damned thing and where I can't even speak nobody's language, we don't know the rules, and everybody wants our heads."

"Yeah, well, maybe so, but I got to figure we got a better chance on our own, small as it is, than we do stickin' with *this* pair. At least we're Akhbreed—the bosses—and we're in a land of Akhbreed where I can probably get by in the language and we won't get tossed out or strung up 'cause we ain't got four legs or six arms or whatever. Trouble is, our disguises ain't gonna help much if these two know about them. Damn it!"

Charley looked suddenly horror-struck. "Sam! I—I couldn't kill them! Even if I thought we could get away with it, and they're pros, I just *couldn't!*"

It was Sam's turn to sigh. "Yeah, I know. I mean, maybe if he was in the *act* of tryin' to kill me and I had a gun or somethin' maybe I could, but not cold."

"Not at all! I just don't think I could kill another human being, or even one with a horse's body."

"Then we're gonna hav'ta run from them all the time, too. That's just the way it's gotta be."

"Yeah, but—where to? We can't run forever without gettin'

in real trouble and you know it. This ain't Texas or Denver, you know."

"I know. The only thing we got is that we know the names of both the one who wants us live and the one who wants me dead." She suddenly stopped, an idea coming into her head. "Say! It's crazy but it don't cost nothin'!"

"Huh? What?"

"Well—Zenchur said that if he could get us and maybe him, too, sayin' the name of Old Horny that somehow that crud would hear his name and maybe find us."

"Yeah. I remember him tellin' us not to even *talk* about that guy."

"Uh-huh. Don't you see? Maybe it works for the other one, too. The green guy. Zenchur called him Boolean. Maybe if we say it enough times he'll hear us and figure somethin's wrong."

Charley shrugged. "Makes as much sense as anything else has so far."

"Well, let's give it a try. Just over and over while we go through the trunks and do the packin' and all."

"And if he don't hear us and do something?"

"Then we get the hell out of here tonight. Grab what food and water we can and just go. If he's got the horses we'll use 'em, I guess. If not, it's on foot."

Charley got up and opened her trunk, then looked into it. "I dunno even what I should *wear*, let alone pack."

"Well, I got a look at that Malabar and that's supposed to be the next Akhbreed kingdom to this one, so I know kind'a what they wear. You ain't gonna like it, though."

"Huh? What'd'ya mean?"

"Well, you ever see pictures of them strict Moslem countries on TV or in school? It ain't that bad, but it's bad enough. Lemme look through your trunk. I bet there's a couple of outfits right there someplace. Yeah—here's one down here. Thought so."

"Oh, *no!*"

"Just try it on and start chantin' 'Boolean' over and over. I'll show you how it goes on."

· 5 ·

The Road to Tubikosa

THE CHANTING OF the name didn't seem to have much effect except to bore both of them fairly quickly. The outfits Sam picked for Charley quickly took over the latter's attention. They were basically one-piece outfits, kind of like Indian saris, but they were made of some very thin, ultra-light material that conformed well to the body's shape and were tied off at the waist to bring it into shape there. The wrap started below the arms leaving the shoulders bare but went down almost to the ground and, without slitting or pleating, gave little play. You could walk in it fairly well and there was enough stretch in the material to allow comfortable sitting so long as you didn't cross your legs, but it would be hell if she had to run for it. Still, it was relatively easy to get on and the fasteners, while snug, were carefully and invisibly built in with the material somehow adjusting to whatever body shape it needed.

It felt like fine silk, but was so lightweight it was almost like having nothing on more formidable than a negligee, although when you tried to move in a way it wasn't designed to let you, it won. The stuff was *tough*, which was somewhat reassuring. The material was plain, but the three in the trunk were lavender, crimson, and emerald green and were quite attractive. There was also a long, wispy black transparent scarf, more gossamer than anything, that was worn on the head and tied off under the chin. "I think that's important," Sam told her. "At least, the women I saw in that—vision—all had their heads covered. 'Course, their dresses were plainer material— mostly cotton, I think—and the scarfs more the usual type, but I think this is what we got that'll be okay. Beats the other type

94

which were kind'a Mother Hubbard dresses all to hell, anyways."

"The sandals, I suppose?"

"Most all the women had bare feet where I saw, but I didn't see inside that castle or any of the higher class people 'cept the wizard and some soldiers so I can't really tell. Up to you but I'd pack the sandals til we needed 'em for protection. You slip and fall in that outfit and you'll hav'ta be helped back up."

"I'll go along with that. Who knows? Maybe bare feet are sexy here. At least we'll have a chance for Zenchur to see it and make comments before we have to split. What about you?"

"Well, since I'm the brother, one of these Robin Hood outfits in brown ought'a do okay. The top's loose and everything's kind'a bloused, so it should give me the look. Black's strictly for soldiers, from the looks of it. The high-ups might wear fancy stuff but the common folk mostly wore this kind of outfit in earth tones, with a wide belt and these short boots. Wonder what this sucker is?"

Charley looked at it, thought for a moment, then gave a slight laugh. "I think I remember that one from last year's drama class. You didn't take that, did you? We all dressed up in those old Elizabethan outfits to do scenes from Shakespeare. If I remember right, that's a codpiece."

"A what?"

"Think of it as a boy's bra. It holds and protects your prick. Hmmm . . . Pretty stiff at that. You don't have anything to protect there, but if you wear it it'll sure look like you do if those pants are as tight as they look. Tie it off above the hips, then—yeah, okay. Now pull on the pants."

"It feels like I got a rubber ball between my legs."

"Well, you'll get used to it. It's *perfect!* With a bulge like that and the rest disguisin' your other parts it kind'a advertises your sex like a good padded bra. Take a look in the mirror."

"Uh—yeah, okay. I see what you mean. I hope it stays in place when I walk or run, though. Be kind'a embarrassin' seein' there's nothin' there to hold it."

"You'll manage, and I'll keep an eye out. I wish I knew some of the language, though. I can't play deaf and dumb—the first time somebody shouts a warning or a pot drops I'll jump. I know English and Spanish 'cause half the neighborhood spoke it when I grew up, but that stuff you and Zenchur talk—that's like Chinese or something."

"Yeah, I know. I thought I only knew English til this came along. But you'll just hav'ta keep your mouth shut and let me do the talkin', I guess. I been tryin' to go through my head and teach you some words and phrases, but it just don't come out right. It's a whole different kind of talkin' that just don't work like 'good-bye' means 'adios'. Seems like they got a hundred ways of sayin' 'good-bye' dependin' on the situation or the words before and after. And lots of our words they don't have words for at all. It's like, well, you say somethin' that takes a sentence with us and then there's one big word that puts all the sounds together just right to make, like, well, a song, and it says it all. How in hell do I teach *that?* There ain't no way I could learn this sucker by myself."

"I know, I know, but it's like driving me *nuts*. Not so bad now, but when we get out in the world here I won't know like 'there's the ladies' room' from 'There's robbers and rapists back there.' I—"

Sam held up a hand. "I hear somethin' in the cave. Maybe Zenchur's back. I'll go out and stall; you get yourself the way you want and we'll see what he says."

Zenchur *was* back, looking all business. He may have been crazy but he wasn't dumb. When he saw Sam he nodded approvingly and said, "You really *did* see it all, didn't you? That is precisely the right outfit for Tubikosa and most of the surrounding hubs. Other kingdoms have far different rulers and so far different rules and dress, but that one is good everywhere, just marking you as being a southerner. All right—I have secured a horse and wagon as well as a spare from a farmer nearby who is quite blind to anything if money is produced. The wagon will allow us to move most of the supplies we have and will need so we can take both trunks, and it should allow for your lack of expertise with horses. The city is a good day's ride from here, so get a good night's sleep."

"If I can," Sam responded.

Zenchur went over to Ladai and began talking in that language they both used that she couldn't understand. Sam had to regret that the mercenary wasn't upset or agitated again. She would love to have known what was being said.

Finally Zenchur came back over and sat down, looking a bit tired. "Ladai cannot accompany us, of course. It is forbidden for any not of the Akhbreed to be inside the city or any town after sundown, and the kind of pig sties that they have for such people are below any standards of decency. She will close up here and join us on the road out from the kingdom."

Charley emerged and immediately caught Zenchur's eye dressed as she was. "Ah! More accuracy!" he exclaimed. "It is perfect for the city, although I'm not certain that something plainer but looser might not be appropriate for the trip. Still— we have the wagon. Ah! I see you have the scarf as well. That is good. It is considered something of a sacrilege in these more conservative kingdoms if a woman ever appears in public with her head uncovered—or a man with his head covered. The makeup, the jewelry, gives the correct impression, too, I think, although I suspect you hit upon it by accident."

"I could'a used some press-on nails but like I did my best with that Stone Age Emery board and file set," she responded. "I just feel so damned *helpless* not speakin' anything but English, though."

"A good point," he agreed. "That is where you are both vulnerable, I fear. More than likely him who seeks you will have supplied some English phrases to the rogues and scoundrels who are looking for you to claim the reward. Do not feel too hesitant about using English when you must, since they will not understand it or recognize it—they are merely being taught sounds—but some will undoubtedly come up to you and whisper an English phrase, possibly a question requiring a response. If you *do* respond you give yourself away, see? Both of you should remember that. Hopefully we can find some second-rate magician down on his luck with some language spells there that can give the two of you working knowledge of something useful, but until then you must depend on my translations and do *not* react to any English spoken to you by any not now present. Do not drop your guard! The price is most certainly good enough that they will kidnap you and ask questions later."

"Thanks a lot," Charley responded sourly.

"I should warn you, though, that the way you are gives you a good cover but at something of a price. Women in these conservative kingdoms do not wear jewelry or makeup and dress rather plainly in public, you see. To do otherwise marks you as an—what would be the word?—*entertainer*. That is, I am afraid, not a position of respect."

"Well, that's not so bad. I can't sing or dance much, but I can fake it."

"Uh—Charley," Sam said slowly, "I don't think that's exactly what he meant. I think he means like an entertainer of men—one at a time."

Charley looked blank for a minute, then said, "Oh. You mean—*you mean I'm dressed like a two-bit whore?*"

"No, that is not the word," Zenchur said, unfazed by her reaction. "I am trying—*courtesan* is too much of the noble sort—prostitute? I do not know what this two-bit means."

"Cheap," Sam told him. "As cheap and common as you can get."

"Yes, that is about it. Oh, I see your reaction, but here it is something of an honorable profession, you see, for those who are, pardon, too slow and unskilled to do much of anything else. It is, in fact, one of the few businesses here run by women, since when one is too old or loses one's looks she becomes a manager of younger ones or a housekeeper for them or something like that. You see, true basic unskilled labor is something that Akhbreed just do not do. Young girls who are ignorant or orphaned or who refuse arranged marriages or the like do not have the menial jobs to fill and all must contribute. Unless you are very old or disabled you must have a function, a job. Few are natives. Most come from distant hubs or from some of the Akhbreed settlements in the wedges. Many of the wedge settlements come from different Akhbreed stock than the ruling race, as is obvious to look at you. Many do not even know the Akhbreed tongue and if you are not raised with it you do not learn it more than a little to get by. It is a very difficult language. So it would not be unusual if you did not know Akhbreed. In some circles it is considered an advantage."

"Oh, great! A great cover, huh? But every damned man I meet is gonna figure he only has to wave some money around and I'll sleep with him. Oh, no! I draw the line at that!"

Zenchur grinned. "It is not a big problem. You see, it is improper to make a direct offer, as it were. As you are passing through, they will think you are along with us for serving business clients, as it were. The offers would be made to either your brother or to me."

"My *what?* Oh—I see. Yeah. It's hard to remember how much alike we look now."

"Yes, and since the brother cannot speak Akhbreed, either, then they would come to me. You look quite lovely. I am certain to get offers not only to lie with you but to purchase rights to you. I shall, of course, refuse.''

"You better! What's that about purchasing rights?"

"Akhbreed are all free by definition and cannot be bought or sold. However, you would be under a contract if it were for real and someone else could purchase that contract. An employment contract, essentially. Without it you would be illegal to sell your services and that is a crime with very hard punishments."

"Sounds like slavery after some lawyers got done changin' the words," Sam noted.

"No, no. You do not have to agree to such a contract and you do not have to agree to its reassignment. Of course, then you would have two weeks to find some other form of work or you would be arrested."

"Are there any male—*entertainers?*" Charley asked him sarcastically.

The sarcasm was lost on him. "Why yes, there are, certainly."

"That what you're gonna make me?" Sam asked, not liking this a bit. She could see a scenario where Charley was sold into a brothel, helpless without friends or language, while she was somehow compromised and taken away.

"No, no. One is enough. I will make you an apprentice for their purposes. An apprentice—trader. Basically a hired hand, a helper. With my type of business and my wanderings it will draw no attention." He paused a moment. "Come. We have some light left. Would you like to see what this place really looks like?"

Charley looked a bit anxiously at Sam and saw that Sam was suddenly tense as well, but then the object of all this said, "Sure. Why not? You sure we won't be spotted?"

"It will make no difference, as no one likely to see us is likely to have anything to do with us. Come—follow me."

"It'll have to be damned slow in this dress," Charley grumped, but went along.

Sam was genuinely curious after all this time cooped up in a cave but she was also wary. Zenchur had more than enough time to betray them and perhaps have people lying in wait for them outside. She decided to go along partly because it really didn't matter—better to know now than be kidnapped sneaking out later and let the bastard completely off the hook. If this

Boolean was half as powerful and half as devious as they'd pictured his kind to be then *something* would happen in their favor. If not, then there really wasn't much hope anyway.

It was hot and very humid just beyond the cave entrance; they were sweating in no time.

The eerie mist was still there; maybe it was *always* there, for some reason or other. It stretched out for miles from the rocky outcrop, featureless, with nothing seeming to grow up from it or in any way disturb it, but it was not endless. Off in the distance rose low hills of green and what looked like pleasant pasture land. For all Charley could tell, it might well be right out of Lincoln County in northern New Mexico, with perhaps the high mountains just beyond the horizon. It appeared overcast almost everywhere.

"The mist is a natural phenomenon," Zenchur told them, sounding not at all tense or threatening. Maybe he was having second thoughts about double-crossing a sorcerer. "It surrounds the hubs and in a sense insulates them from the wedges. That green region you see beyond is a wedge. It looks like Habanadur, although it's been awhile since I was there. The people are herders, primarily—impossible to describe unless you have seen one, I am afraid, but not particularly pleasant to our eyes. They herd large, hairy herbivores called *blauns,* and exist entirely by drinking the blauns' blood and milk."

Charley shivered, and saw that Sam wasn't reacting too well to that one, either.

"They are a rather fierce race when provoked, and quite tough," the mercenary went on, apparently not taking notice. "The Akhbreed kings treat them with some respect and they act as soldiers and enforcers for much of the region. They consider it pragmatic; they still hate the Akhbreed but fear the magic too much. Of course, most of the other races identify them as tools of the king and hate them as much or more than they hate the Akhbreed. You can see why unifying such people seems impossible."

They made it up a trail—Charley needing some helping hands—to the top of the bluff and looked inland. This land was quite rocky, with thick forests and probably rushing streams. It looked lush but wild, yet, looking in toward the mountains and forests, it seemed like the overcast thinned and there were hints of sun.

"Is it always this cloudy?" Sam asked him, remembering his comment about frequent storms and bad weather.

"No, not always, although it is cloudy more than clear most places outside of the hubs, except in desert regions and places like that. This is part of the after-effect of the changewind. You saw it. It will influence the weather for vast regions."

Sam nodded, then turned to look back out over the mist. "Hey—wait a minute!"

The other two turned and looked out as well. The green, rolling hills in the distance were gone; now there was an enormous wall of snow-capped peaks reaching into the clouds and beyond, reflecting back a hazy purple cast to them.

"What happened to the hills?" Charley asked. "There were no mountains there a minute ago!" She turned and looked back at the forest as if to reassure herself that she was still somehow at the same location, then back. The forest was still there, and so were the mountains.

Zenchur chuckled. "That is Maksut, or so the Akhbreed call it. Those people produce among the finest furs of Akahlar. I know it well."

"Yeah, but where the hell did the *hills* go?" Sam wanted to know.

"They're still there. Both of the lands you saw are not mere slices of things but entire worlds of which only a small portion overlaps here at any time. If you wait—perhaps a few minutes, perhaps hours, or even days, it will be a portion of another land that you see. That is the ever-changing nature of Akahlar. They appear, and disappear, around the hubs—sometimes here, sometimes elsewhere, sometimes not at all. My trade is navigator. I know the ways to tell where I am physically in Akahlar at any given time—with some work, of course. I can plot a course between two definite points on the globe, short or long, and get you there. I do not, however, know what will occupy that point at any given time, or the points in between. Maksut, or Habanadur, or a hundred others. Only the Akhbreed with their Pilots can choose their path and their destination exactly, and the Pilots do not tell how they do it. I can get to the exact same spot—but I may be worlds away. That is why one cannot travel long out there without Pilots. They are Akhbreed who work with the locals, each Pilot guild assigned to a particular wedge. When I fled my homeland I was without a Pilot and

without navigational skills and only sheer luck and the hand of
the gods kept me from death."

That's why he's taken us out here, Sam thought to herself.
*He suspects we might not fully trust him and he wants to show
us just how impossible it would be to even survive on our own.
And he's making a good case for it, damn his soul!*

"In the morning we shall go inland—that way," he told
them, pointing to the forest behind them. "The hub is large,
but it is not as primitive as it looks. There is a major road just
beyond that hill, and in a hub all roads tend to lead either to the
capital city or to the border. Come—we will be hot and wet
enough tomorrow. Let us enjoy the coolness of the cave while
we still can."

They went back down and inside, and Charley in particular
felt frustrated that she and Sam couldn't immediately get
together. That time would come much later.

It was quite late when that opportunity came with some
certainty, and all of them were supposed to be asleep. Charley
and Sam felt tired, too, but there was much to think over and,
perhaps, to do.

"Okay, is he crooked or square with us?" Charley asked.

"Crooked," Sam responded flatly. "That little show today
was to show us just how at his mercy we are. To tell you the
truth, I'm not real sure just what to do now, damn him! If we
take off in the woods in the middle of the night we'll probably
break our fool necks, and if we go in towards the city we'll be
pretty easy to track—and he'll have horses and lots of practice
trackin', I bet. If we go out there we'll be in that creepy mist
for miles and then wind up God knows where."

"You think those vampires he talked about are real?"

Sam shrugged. "Maybe not where he said, but all you got to
do is look at Ladai to know they're probably around someplace, and maybe worse. One thing's sure—we go out there
without somebody who knows what he's doin' and we ain't got
much chance."

"Yeah, but if we stick with him he'll stab us in the back first
chance he gets. You said it yourself. The only reason we're not
already dead or worse is 'cause he's gotta make it look like it's
an accident to keep Boolean from turning him into live sausage
or something. I tell you, I don't see why he just don't hypnotize
us with that jewel of his like he did last night and command us
to betray ourselves. He flashes that thing and commands us to

parade naked down the main street of that city saying 'Here we are—the ones the Horned One wants. *Please* take us to him!' And we'd hav'ta *do* it!''

"I dunno. He acts like he's scared of that thing himself. But if we got centaurs and magic jewels and storms that can change a boy into a monster then the jewel ain't the only possible thing he can use. There's all sorts of drugs—would *we* know a bad drug from one of Ladai's sweetrolls here?—and once he's in the city he'll have magic types he can probably pay off cheap. I figure he don't want to do it here 'cause there's just us and the two of them. Pretty easy to get a full treatment from Boolean, huh? Lots more chances to make a play in the big city, maybe even hope we get nailed by accident and he don't hav'ta lift a finger.''

"The only thing we can do is figure our odds, then," Charley said thoughtfully. "If we run, there's no chance now and he's off the hook. If we stick with him, maybe we got a chance to at least duck. I mean, this country's this Akhbreed, right?"

"Yeah? So?"

"So they talk Akhbreed. Once we're off, no Ladai, there's only humans like us, right? He'll have to do all the talkin' for us to them in their language—and he still don't know *you* know it. At least we'll know what he's planning before he does it, right? That's a chance."

Sam nodded. "I never thought of that. Yeah, sure. Okay. So I guess we figure we're safe for now, huh? Might as well get some sleep. We got to be damned sharp tomorrow."

"Yeah. Sam—one other thing. You're gonna hav'ta clue me in on what's goin' on without him catching on that you know yourself. I wish you knew Spanish—he sure don't—but I been tryin' to think of some edge someplace that'll keep our talk as crazy to him as theirs is to me. It's pretty far out, but I don't think he learned English any more than you learned that other stuff. He thinks in this Akhbreed—that's why he spoke it when he got upset. I think he sorta *wills* it to be translated both ways, to and from Akhbreed.''

"Yeah, so?"

"Well, I been thinking about how you said, like, it wasn't like any language you ever heard of. If that's what his brain's actually hearing, and not English, then there's no way in *hell* he'll ever handle pig latin.''

Sam thought it over and gave a wry smile. "You know, it ightmay ustjay orkway," she muttered aloud.

The "wagon" was sure different. It resembled a Roman chariot, with two big side wheels and an oval-shaped center, but it had a third, smaller wheel in front of the carriage giving it some stability. Inside, the driver had to stand, although there was a kind of bar that allowed him to relax against it, then a bench seat more reminiscent of a rowboat, and some cargo area in back. It wasn't fancy or ornate; it was old, hadn't been painted in years, and had both dirt and splinters. But it held the two trunks and a sack resembling a duffel which was Zenchur's traveling things, and they climbed in and held on for dear life as the navigator climbed in, lowered and latched the wooden safety bar on the side, leaned against the back rest bar, and jerked the reins forward. Two horses, side by side, seemed to have little trouble in pulling it and them, but *man* was that ride *rough* on those wooden wheels! After a while both Charley and Sam's bottoms hurt so bad that they actually envied Zenchur's standing position.

The horses looked pretty much like horses. They seemed a little large, more like the kind of horses that pulled the beer wagon in all those ads, and they looked a lot hairier than the horses they were used to—you could have styled the hair between their ears, in fact—but they were still basically the same sort of animal.

The same went for the countryside. The trees were tall but basically trees, although some had odd colors to their bark, and the grass seemed more blue than green, and every once in a while they'd pass a patch of strange flowers like the bunch of pink ones that looked like roses but grew on separate stalks maybe six feet high and thicker than most people's legs with flowers the size of Zenchur's head, but it was no Alice in Wonderful world—just exotic, sort of like being in another country like Brazil or one of the African ones.

There were birds, many quite colorful, and one fairly large one that might have been some kind of falcon but who seemed to change color and become almost invisible in the trees until spooked by the passing of the wagons. Then you suddenly had what looked like giant leaves taking flight and eventually becoming nearly invisible again as they changed to the gray of clouds or the blue of open sky.

It was good to see the sun again, first in breaks in the clouds and then as time went on more regularly, although the sky was never completely clear. Still, it was damned hot and getting hotter the more sun they got. This was a climate for loin cloths or bikinis, not full dress. The Arabs got away with theirs because their land was so dry their clothes kept in the moisture and that made sense. It was far too humid for that here. The Akhbreed were not only arrogant, they were hung-up assholes, Charley decided.

The road Zenchur had told them about was there, wide and well maintained, but it didn't really help the comfort much. Packed dirt roads only added to the sensation of being on a rolling ship at sea and made the bumps ever harder. Still, the horses needed to rest once in a while and they had to eat and drink, and about a three hours' ride in from the cave they came to a small village that looked with its red slate roofs and white stucco and brick façade like it had been plucked out of some European movie. The thing seemed to be built around a broad, central square with a marketplace all around it. It was not crowded, however; clearly this was a sleepy weekday afternoon and not a main market day.

Zenchur made some preliminary warnings to them. "Remember—say as little as possible, only to each other, and whisper. I doubt if there would be anyone here who would even know about you but be on your guard anyway."

It looked different than the one in Sam's vision, but not any more different than she would have expected going between, say, France and maybe Germany. While there weren't many people about, those they could see seemed to mostly be women, all wearing long, loose, baggy dresses tied off at the waist, the dresses going down to their ankles and looking to be made of cotton or some similar material. All had matching scarves on their heads. The colors were mainly muted reds, browns, or blues, but here and there a woman wore white. What set the white-clad ones apart was that they alone wore not the scarves but rather light white headpieces which covered their entire head and formed almost a hood, and they looked for all the world to be wearing white masks over their faces with only the eyes cut out. They also did not use a tie at the waist, making the dresses so shapeless and sack-like it was impossible to tell anything about them.

"The ones in white are unmarried—virgins of age, or in

some cases past it," Zenchur told them. "They are forbidden to show any more of themselves in public or to anyone outside their immediate household than you see after they undergo a rite of passage on their tenth birthday. They are also forbidden to speak to or even show they hear the speech of any man save their father and brothers. They live like that until they are married and then, as you see, things loosen up a lot."

"I can't see how any of 'em would ever *get* married, considerin' them rules," Sam responded.

Zenchur laughed. "All marriages are arranged—by the mothers, by the way, talking to the groom's father or, if orphaned, the male guardian. Oh, there are stories of romantic trysts and separated lovers, of course, but almost nobody does it. Actually, the girl has some power the man does not, since she can see *him* without his ever really knowing it's her and can make a real case for certain boys and against others with her mother. All the boy gets is a sketch by an artisan known as a Wedding Broker, although in villages such as these he can usually get some information from relatives and friends of relatives."

"The same old story. Women as cattle again, though," Charley noted sourly.

"No, no! The women have rights here. They are given what education they need or can handle, although separately from the boys of course, and they can inherit and have definite rights in courts of law. It is not as bad as it sounds. Most of these shops are run by women and some are even owned by women. This is because, in these conservative societies, the man is the boss but inheritance is through the female line, not the male. I am not saying it is perfect, only that it is not as bad as it looks."

"Still, neither one knows what they're gettin' until they're stuck with it," Sam noted.

"And is it any worse than other ways? Marrying for lust of the moment and then one day you discover you have nothing else in common, or marrying one for supposed wealth or position? I am not defending this system, I am only saying that I have not found the number of successful and happy marriages here any different than other societies' ways."

"Still, with the slim pickings in a village like this and kept apart, I can see why some of 'em would run for the city and sell their bodies rather than take it, particularly if the guy's awful and she can't talk her mom out of it," Charley commented.

Sam looked around. "Somehow, with all them worlds to steal from, I kinda thought this'd be a little more modern than the Dark Ages."

There was a service which unhitched and cared for the horses while you were in town, and they were more than grateful to be out of that box and on their feet again, although both were so sore they had some initial trouble walking. Sam was together enough in a minute or two, though, to note the various signs around the square that all seemed to be filled with little squares and circles and squiggles and realize that her knowledge of the language did not extend to literacy. The letters or symbols or whatever they were seemed to not even have a lot of organizational sense; they were scattered all over and didn't look very consistent at all in their shapes and forms. It reminded her of something that might come out of a kindergarten art class back home.

The one they went into turned out to be a tavern, and a somewhat peculiar one at that. It had the look on the inside you expected going in—round wooden tables, rough, well-worn wooden chairs, sawdust over the wooden, creaky floor, and a long bar with a big polished mirror behind it that just about reflected the whole place. But there were anachronisms as well, things that just didn't make sense.

For example, there were the three Casablanca-style ceiling fans turning slowly above them, keeping the hot air circulating. And the lights, both behind the bar and, subdued, along the side walls, looked, well—not at all primitive. The bottles behind the bar seemed to be of clear glass with fancy labels on them, not the crude stuff of the cave, and when someone yelled to the barman he nodded and drew a tankard of what might have been beer or ale from a *tap* and brought it over. The customers—the only ones other than themselves—were also obviously from somewhere else. One fellow had a loud and ugly voice and a face and body that looked more like a Neanderthal than a modern human, accentuated by the fact that he was wearing a worn fur breech clout and a somewhat matching fur vest over his incredibly hairy chest. His companion was dressed in a fancy bloused top and tights, with fancy pointed boots, and had features far different from those seen in the village—lighter, sharper, with long hair, a black goatee, and a moustache that must have been half wax.

"Don't look now," Charley whispered to Sam, "but I'd swear Conan the Barbarian over there is wearing a wristwatch."

"I noticed," Sam whispered back. "And I think that fugitive from a playing card is smoking a filter-tipped cigarette. This is nuts."

Zenchur gave them a sour look and they shut up. Sam was curious to know what the strange pair was discussing, but the cave man had such lousy command of the language it was hard to make him out most of the time. In a language where a shift of a mere quarter tone could make "I am going to kill you" sound like "I want to make love to a fig tree" she was definitely at a disadvantage only slightly less than Charley's.

"But, my friend, I need five," said the fop, clearly but in a very strange accent. You knew what he was saying but only barely and with some concentration. The people in the changewind vision had also seemed to have odd accents to her, but not this extreme.

"You ask my ass be cake-baked," the Neanderthal seemed to reply. The conversation, thanks to his horrible lack of subtleties, seemed almost comic to Sam, although Moustache seemed to make the right sense out of it.

"But, be reasonable, my friend. Fewer will simply not work."

"I want to lick my pig-sucker," replied the barbarian.

"But there's the watch, the grappler, the—"

"Our names be pudding Daisy loops!"

Sam had to stop listening. The thing made no sense, but if she kept on with it then Zenchur would surely know that she could understand—more or less—if only because she would no longer be able to keep from cracking up.

The barman came over to them. "Yes, sir. How may we serve you?"

"You have food, I take it? You did the last times I was through."

"We do, sir, but there is no kitchen between lunch and dinner and this is off-hours. I could bring a bread, meat, and cheese tray and some fruits or vegetables, though."

"That will do fine. Make it large enough for my companions and bring three cold drafts."

"At once, sir." The barman turned and went back to the bar, drew three very large beers, and brought them over, then went back through a doorway to the right of the bar to get the food. Charley noted that both Zenchur and Sam had the beer set in front of them while the third was simply placed to one side, as if a refill rather than for her.

"Oh, all the respectable types of both sexes will absolutely ignore your existence," he whispered to her. "To them you are to be treated as if you do not exist. But, do not worry—if that old man wanted a fling he'd pull me aside discretely and try and make a deal for an assignation." He paused a moment. "But—please, no more talk for now. I do not like the look of those two."

Charley had never heard of an assignation, but she got the meaning. The usual high moral hypocrites. She did have to wonder what kind of dictionary they'd used to teach him English, though.

The platter that the barman brought out looked like it'd been arranged by a caterer; it had mounds of sliced meats, as well as what appeared to be lettuce, tomatoes, cucumbers—you name it—along with a *very* long loaf of French-type bread and a bread knife. Small canisters with spreaders contained something that looked a lot like mayonnaise, a type of mustard, soft white butter, and two others, one of which seemed a lot like very thin peanut butter. Cutting off a piece of the bread and slicing it, then filling it, was no trouble at all; watching Zenchur eat what looked for all the world like a peanut butter, radish, and roast beef sandwich was harder to take.

Again, as with the plants and birds, the tastes and textures of the sandwich material were slightly off what they would have suspected—the tomatoes, for example, tasted very tomatoey but also had a kick like mild peppers—but nothing was all that exotic and it was pretty good.

Zenchur was a pretty big drinker; he finished off two large steins and was working on his third before he completed his first sandwich. Sam, too, had a big thirst although she was unused to beer or other alcoholic beverages and Charley worried about that. Charley also worried about her own reactions; alcohol always brought out the worst in her, and she just sipped it and tried to eat what she could of her own sandwich concoction. She found to her surprise that her eyes were far bigger than her stomach; what she would have normally packed away with no trouble back home was far too much for her now and she felt stuffed.

Sam had no such limits. Clearly in spite of Boolean's look-alike magic, they were very different beyond outward appearances, something that made Charley actually feel a bit better. Still, it was amazing to see Sam pack away almost as much as the big, muscular Zenchur.

"You are beans! I *will* seduce the governor!" proclaimed the barbarian at the far table in a loud voice, pounding his fist on the table. They all looked at him, a man clearly with too much to drink in the middle of the afternoon, and the fancy dressed man looked nervous.

"This is not the place for more talk," he said. "You are drunk. Can you ride some more?"

"I can sail a fish to the moon!" responded the barbarian confidently. Sam dearly would have liked to have seen *that*, but she was relieved that the pair got up, threw some coins on the table, and made their way out of the tavern. She was having great problems stifling the giggles and stuffed some more sandwich in her mouth to cover it.

"How far are we from this city?" Charley asked Zenchur.

"Not far," the navigator responded. "A few hours. We should be in by nightfall."

Charley groaned. "More hours on that hard seat! Well," she sighed, "I don't think my rear end can get any more bruises. It's tough sitting here now on this chair."

"I think I want a bathroom," Sam said. "They got one or is it out the back?"

"Oh, there's one off the kitchen. Through there. Come—I should go, too."

Charley didn't really have to go but she had this sudden fear of sitting there alone while her two links to this world were both out of sight. "If they have separate rooms I guess I should, too."

"They do. Even in the home there are two bathrooms."

The men's room was surprisingly clean, with two bowl-shaped toilets in two door-less stalls. They looked a lot like pinched oval toilets without seats, and on either wall of the stall were grip handles. Apparently you didn't sit down—you just squatted and held on to the handles. Zenchur was appalled by the idea of a toilet seat. "It would be so—unclean," he said, shaking his head.

Still, he didn't have the problem. He just stood there and pissed into it, while she had to take down her pants, remove the codpiece, and hold on for dear life. You sure as hell wouldn't spend any time reading in *these* johns. She envied him the convenience but couldn't help but stare a bit. My god, it was so—*large!* How did they *walk* with those things between their legs?

Zenchur would have been far more startled had he known that this was the first time Sam had ever seen a male organ except in a picture.

If Sam was having trouble, Charley had to practically undress to be able to go. The toilet was the same sort of hold-on affair but shaped very differently. Still, this was gonna take some getting used to.

Even so, here was another thing that seemed oddly different. Flush toilets—inside plumbing. A small, basic sink with running cold water. And while the toilet paper looked more like Kleenex and came out that way, and was *rough*, it was none the less a manufactured product. Clearly, for all its looks, this was not any Dark Ages civilization.

There was a full-length mirror that was a big aid in rewrapping the dress, but which also gave her a real look at herself. She looked *thin*, thinner than Sam ever looked, and the skin was really smooth. It was a hell of a body, better than she remembered Sam's as being. Even the boyish face looked not at all boyish now but, well, *sexy*. It was more than just the look, though; it was the way you moved and carried yourself and even the way you used your face. She would have preferred a better face than Sam's, but it was, overall, the kind of body she would have *killed* for.

Maybe it was the beer again, but, God! Was she *horny!*

She got ready, then left the bathroom and rejoined the pair already back at the table. She was relieved to see them both; she had this paranoid fear that they would somehow disappear and leave her alone in this world.

As they made their way back to the stable she saw two of the white-robed girls walking hand in hand across the street, their white masks impassive, their features—frankly, even their sex or humanity—impossible to tell. She didn't think she ever could've stood that, although you never know what you'll accept if you grow up thinking that's normal. The sad thing was that little girls probably dreamed of the time when they'd wear the white robes and masks. It was being grown up.

Still, she had to wonder how easy to get those outfits were. They all looked manufactured, that was for sure, but fitted, probably. They'd make one hell of a disguise in a pinch, though—and in this kind of society who would dare pull off the mask and hood and risk being wrong? She bet that such an act would be tantamount to rape for these people.

Before leaving they went into an odd little store and Zenchur purchased a small device that looked something like a spout from the top of a gas can with a long, narrow and bendable base. It wasn't until they were back on the road, however, that he explained it.

"Learn how to use it," he told Sam. "If you learn the proper positioning and get it just right you will not have to sit to pee. It is very handy out in the wilderness where there are few or no bathrooms."

"Yeah—what about those bathrooms?" Sam asked. "Modern plumbing, and I swear those lights and fans were electric!"

"They were. The town is rather modern, as are most. There is a small generating plant at a waterfall not far from here."

"But there were no wires anyplace!"

"So? Your world is so primitive it runs its wires openly? And do your plumbing pipes run atop your streets? How ugly that would be!"

It was time to change the subject. "Those two men back there—who were they? They sure didn't look like nobody 'round *that* town," Sam pointed out.

"I do not know who they were but, you are correct, they are not from anywhere around here. The big hairy one might barely be considered Akhbreed at all, I think. Certainly from some primitive wedge far away from here to the north. The other—I am not sure. He was wealthy but no noble and his speech marked him as coming from elsewhere. Such men hire men like the barbarian to do dirty work they do not wish done themselves. Such men are the sort who usually hire me, in fact."

The countryside grew less wild; the farms seemed smaller and more specialized, the towns a bit larger although still in that European provincial style, and traffic built up, not just on foot or horseback but wagons and carriages of every shape and kind. They made good time, reaching the city before sundown, and it *was* a city—one hell of a city. Sam had expected something on the order of the primitive farming village and castle she'd seen in her vision, but this was something else.

Densely populated and stretching out along the shores of a lake or sea, its central core rose up in great buildings like shining cathedral spires, and out from it spread the rest of the city, smaller buildings to be sure, certainly much lower, but it was sure a big city all the same.

"Tubikosa contains about a half a million people, all Akhbreed," Zenchur told them. "It is one of the largest cities on the planet, and one of the grandest, although it is also one of the most dangerous. If a changewind ever got this far in, there would be no place to really run and hide from it."

Charley frowned. "What's the chances of something like that happening?"

The navigator shrugged. "Who knows? Perhaps tonight, perhaps in a week, perhaps in a hundred years. There has been none through here in more than a century and a half, that is known, and the people are complacent. They choose to ignore the risk, perhaps even the inevitable, just to live and work here."

Charley couldn't get a handle on all this. A civilization great enough to build maybe forty-story buildings, crazy as they looked, with electricity, indoor plumbing, and all the comforts of home, yet one that still used the horse and wagon as a primary means of getting around, with no buses, cars, trains, or anything else, and maybe no TV or even radio, and where swords, spears, and armor were still the rule, and who had a city of half a million people with mostly dirt streets where the women dressed in robes and saris and scarves on their heads and the men dressed like Shakespeare or Robin Hood. It didn't make much sense at all.

It *did* have mass transportation, though, of an old-fashioned sort. Horses pulled big double-decker stagecoaches that looked like buses and acted like them, too, and all over the place fancy-looking three-wheeled enclosed black carriages went about, picking up people and letting them off, and were clearly cabs.

Zenchur took them eventually to an area just off the waterfront and well away from those gleaming spires. It was clearly a low district, with narrow streets and grimy buildings. As darkness overtook the city the lights came on, including many for signs that looked just like home even if you couldn't read them, and the main streets were lit not by lamp posts but by long strips of indirect lighting running along the top of the first floor of buildings on both sides. The secondary streets and back alleys weren't lit at all and looked for that all the more menacing. They went through a district whose nature seemed no different than any back on their own Earth and very easy to spot. In the midst of joints and painted pictures of semi-naked women and muscle men were basically store fronts, lit from within, most having several young and heavily made up women in them, lounging and looking back out at the street, and here and there one with some well-built and well-oiled muscle men wearing only tights doing much the same thing. No white robes and masks around *here*.

Just off this district, Zenchur pulled up to a creaky old place of brick and stone that might have been whitewashed regularly once upon a time, and stopped. It was five stories high and looked and smelled older inside than outside. The reception area was quite small, hardly a lobby and more just a registration desk behind which was a tough-looking middle-aged woman wearing a colorful if threadbare green flower print sack dress and scarf.

"Hello, handsome," she said upon seeing Zenchur. "Been a while since you was through here."

"I just need a room on the street for maybe two nights," the navigator responded. "One that sleeps three. And we have some baggage that's heavy."

She nodded. "Fourth floor, second on the left. Here's the key." She looked at Charley and smiled sweetly. "You know the house gets ten percent if you run anything for profit in the room."

"Nothing like that. Long story not worth the telling, but if you must know she ran away from one of the wedge villages far to the northwest and quickly regretted it, her young and impulsive brother went to find her—and did—and now I am helping them work things out if I can."

"Old story," the woman commented. "She's got all the nice moves and looks like a real nice body. The boy got much potential for anything useful?"

"He's bright but unskilled and neither of them knows the language."

"Well, if you want a quick turnover, you take 'em over to

Boday. A little of Boday's universal love potion and some lessons and she'll be broke in perfect. The boy—without the language best he can do is get much the same treatment. There's a small bunch that likes 'em real young."

"I'm not quite sure what I'm going to do yet with them," Zenchur told her, possibly truthfully. "At any rate I'm going to need to find a good Pilot heading southwest." He took out two large, golden square coins and passed them to her. "This should cover it."

She nodded, picked up, then bit the coins, then stuck them in a slot in the desk, then turned to the back where there was a curtained-off doorway. "Zum!" she shouted. "Haul ass!"

The curtains parted and a huge man entered. He was close to seven feet and had to stoop to get through the doorway, but he was also enormously broad, the kind of man whose muscles had muscles. He was getting on, though; his hair was gray, his face was lined and wrinkled, the skin on his hands was tight, but most unsettling was the expression in his eyes and on his face, that of a rather childlike confusion.

The woman said something to him in an unintelligible tongue, and he grunted and gave an equally unintelligible reply and went immediately past them and out the doors.

Zenchur looked at Sam and Charley and cocked his finger, and after a moment they followed. He led them down a hall, then up four flights of creaky, narrow stairway. The key was one of those massive types, and he fitted it in a lock and opened the door to the room.

It was not exactly the Regency Plaza. A bare, round bulb burned when a button was pressed on an old wall plate illuminating a smelly room with two large windows covered by tattered drapes. There was a sink with a single long, curved pipe for a faucet, a worn bowl, and two porcelain cups both of which were chipped. There were also two beds the size of double beds, more or less, next to each other opposite the sink. Both had twin sets of small, round pillows, a bedspread that looked clean, and, under it, some dark sheets. Charley hoped that they hadn't been dyed to match the stains.

"The toilets are down the hall," Zenchur told them, "and I do mean just that. If you want a bath it's at a commercial bath house down here, and it's public, so I think Sam will have to wait and I wouldn't like to send Charley in alone. Don't worry—as you probably already know, bathing is not something done often here, even by the nobility.''

Charley sat on the bed. It sank down unevenly, was lumpy, and creaked something awful. It definitely was both too old and not built like beds back home. She wasn't sure she wanted to find out how it was, or was not, put together, though.

There was a knock, and Zenchur opened it and found the huge man there carrying one of the heavy trunks in each hand and the duffel on his back. The navigator pointed and the man put them down, then took each one in one at a time and set them near the windows. Zenchur nodded, the man looked pleased, and left.

"*What* is *that?*" Charley had to ask.

"Oh, that is Zum. At least he answers to that name. He has been here longer than anyone now at this hotel. He's from some Outland wedge, and he never was very bright and knows none of the language. You might have noticed that the woman downstairs used a different tongue for him if you have a good enough ear. Because of the language problems with such as him there is a straight and simple language—short, no nonsense, perhaps a few hundred real words—that is used by folks to communicate with such as him. He was probably taken here or wound up here as a boy, fell into selling his body—you saw the men in the windows—and then grew too old or perhaps impotent or both. Now he serves out his days doing the basics for this old hotel, just like the woman downstairs, Argua, who was once young and beautiful and had a thousand lovers before she grew old and fat. Zum will see to the horses and wagon, too.''

"Speaking of fat, when do we eat? Or do we?" Sam asked.

"Yes, we do, and we might as well. As you might guess the service here is not that great, but there is a not very fancy tavern a few minutes' walk from here that serves some decent food and asks no questions. Come, if you are not too tired—but remain mute, particularly around here, when out of this room. No slips. Here the word will be getting around about you.''

Sam glanced at Charley, knowing that her friend must be as dead as she was, but Charley said, "We'll go. I don't think I want to be alone in this place.''

"Oh—you may change if you wish now, Charley," Zenchur told her. "In this neighborhood at this time of day a slit skirt, top, and scarf are appropriate, and it might make you more comfortable. Here—I will show you in the trunk."

Charley was of two minds about this. She didn't like the idea of his suggesting such a radical change—they would still be completely at his mercy and who knew what he might do with her?—but the outfit she'd been wearing was now so tight and uncomfortable she was dying to get out of it. She finally accepted his suggestion, choosing a long pattern skirt slit right up to the thigh and a pullover that matched, sort of, but was so clingy it left nothing to the imagination. Still, she had a freedom of movement in her legs that was more than welcome, and the stuff was dry and clean even if she was not.

"One more thing," Zenchur said warningly to Charley. "For your own safety, be solicitous of us. Open the doors ahead of us, pull our chairs out at the tavern before sitting, and when food and drink comes it will be on a serving tray and you will be expected to serve, always with a smile and no comments."

"Huh?"

"It isn't just sex people want down here. It would be best if it appeared that we were your clients and not merely your companions. That way it seems as if you are already working for someone and, therefore, no one else will make any moves on you. Understand?"

"Yeah," she sighed and looked at Sam. "You got all the luck."

· 6 ·

Backup System

"WAIT HERE JUST a couple of minutes. I will be right back," said Zenchur.

Sam's eyebrows rose. "Where you goin'?" she asked suspiciously.

"It has been a long day. Do you need such constant protection that I cannot go to the toilet?"

Sam shrugged, and Zenchur left.

"Think he's pulling anything?" Charley whispered.

"Maybe. He put us in this sleaze bucket in the worst part of town. I heard that woman down there suggest that he send you over to some bastard called Boday to get "broken in.' They give ya some kind'a potion and you just sort'a love everybody and then they teach you all the right moves and that's it, sounds like."

Charley didn't like that. "Potions are just strong drugs in liquid form. He could slip either or both of us one any time and we wouldn't know. I don't like this, Sam. The way he was talkin' I really don't think he's made up his mind yet, but he's gettin' ideas. What a place! All them respectable folks wearin' fancy clothes and the women all wearin' them robes and virgins them white bags and masks and here we got a district where *anything* goes and no cops show. It's like they took everything bad in them and put it all in these few blocks and said, 'Okay, here's the place of sin. Stay here and we don't bother you.'"

"We got to figure something before he does," Sam said firmly, "and soon, 'cause it's pretty damned clear he's thinkin' real good. Damn it, I don't care *what* his reputation is, he's a

118

flake and a whacko. I can't say I think too much of these wizards if they trust people like him."

She paused a moment and continued, "I dunno. It's kind'a funny, really. I think he was all set to do it, no real problems, and then, well, somethin' happened. He suddenly figured out what all this was about even though he wasn't supposed to. Figured it and changed. I wish we could get him to tell us what is was."

Charley frowned. "You know, he's taking an awful long time in the john, for a man. Damn! I don't like this! We *got* to eat and I got no place to run around here, but it's like in a slasher movie where you're huddled in the closet hoping against hope the slasher won't find you while all the time knowing he will. I wish we could grab that hypnotic jewel he's got. Then *he'd* dance *our* tune! Or at least something we could use as a weapon—just in case."

"I know what you mean. But I don't think he's gonna pull nothin' tonight. He's thinkin', and he's got a problem with us, too, remember. He wants to force *us* into a goof so he won't get the blame."

"You know, I kind of wonder why he just doesn't use that jewel of his on us," Charley mused. "I mean, we'd go out obediently stark naked in these streets and scream, 'Here we are! We're the ones the horned guy's looking for!' until somebody nabbed us. Or just keep mumbling the bad guy's name over and over until he came for us. I wonder why he hasn't? Or has he and we just don't remember or notice. Now *there's* a mean thought."

"I don't think he did. He might if he has to, but for some reason he doesn't want to use that thing on us. Huh! Maybe it's from Boolean! Yeah, that'd explain it. Maybe he's scared that Boolean would know if he used it against us or something. It's a thought."

"Yeah, well I—oops! Here he comes—I hope."

It *was* Zenchur. "Sorry to have taken so long," he told them, "but it was occupied and I had a fair wait. Now, Charley—you remember. Open the doors for us, serve us, speak only when spoken to. Best docile behavior. You might get some propositions, but nobody will think beyond that."

"Seems to me I'm being told to be a sweet little old slave and I don't like it."

"Consider—what you do is not important. But if you do *not*

do it, then many will wonder why and start to ask questions. They will start to compare your features to those out on the wanted contract, and they all know that I have done work for the Akhbreed sorcerers before. They may not be positive, but if the reward is large enough then they will ask questions later."

It was a good point. She opened the door for them and they walked out, her following. She definitely didn't like this stinking world, though, not one bit.

The big city was a bit eerie at night. Oh, the "adult entertainment district" was just what you'd expect, all lit up and very active, but beyond, only a few lights in some of the taller buildings gave a hint that any big city was even there. The contrast was odd but also somehow reassuring; the mere existence of a thriving "adult" district indicated that this place was not as lockjaw fundamentalist conservative as it had seemed to be.

The customers on this three-block walk were equally interesting. The men, mostly dressed in those fancy Robin Hood outfits, you expected, but in just the couple of blocks they saw at least two of the three-wheeled, horse-drawn cabs pull up and, inside, heavily robed women waited alone until the cabbie went to the door, knocked, and someone came out to open the cab door for the woman and usher her inside. Clearly for all the outward appearances to the contrary, women had a fair amount of freedom here and, in a society of anonymous, arranged marriages they took advantages of the services of some of those muscular and well-endowed males to get what their own husbands weren't giving them. Charley found the sight oddly satisfying. The men had been doing it for years; it was about time the women could, too, without falling into disastrous affairs with the postman or some neighbor.

This district, then, was the safety valve for a society that was simply too closed in and structured every place else. In this small area the rules were off; in this small area sin and pleasure were the norm, and frustrations and social claustrophobia could be relieved as needed. It wasn't a nice place; it was merely necessary.

Somehow it seemed to make the role she was told to play less degrading; just another service industry, like butlers, maids, housekeepers, and gardeners. It was a new way to look at this sort of thing, but it was clearly flawed. If such "services" were voluntary, it was one thing—an essential job, perhaps. But one only had to look at the dazed faces in the windows and the eyes of the street procurers to know that many of those who performed the services did so because they were trapped or drugged beyond caring. The trouble with a sin district was that it was inevitably run by people who considered sin simply a commodity and the people just objects, like hammers and nails were to a carpenter. Disposable, replaceable, and they had to be cost effective.

Charley opened the door to the tavern and let the other two enter, then followed. It was fairly late and apparently midweek and so not all that crowded; they found a table with little trouble, and Charley acted like a waitress, pulling the chairs out and getting everything just so before taking her own seat.

The place reeked of food, mostly steaks of some kind on a specially designed long charcoal-style grill in the back. The few waiters and the cooks and barkeeper in the back were all men, but there were a few women in the place, all with groups of men, all acting pretty much like Charley was acting—although these women had a different look to them. For one thing, they had oddly painted faces and bodies, with remarkable designs in bright colors on them. One had eye makeup that surrounded the eye with a design that made great orange cat-like shapes, almost a mask, and most wore very skimpy clothing that revealed intricate body designs as well. Sam, too, could hardly fail to notice them as they jumped up to light cigarettes or cigars or get something for their clientele, always with a smile, always their minds totally on anticipating needs.

Sam leaned over to Zenchur and whispered, "What are they?"

"The top of the class," he responded in a very low tone. "They are neither common whores nor servants but experts. Only the smartest and the prettiest get that position. For a very high fee, for an evening, they will try and fulfill any reasonable wish. *Shhhh! Waiter!*"

A man wearing an apron that was probably white when he'd started work came over. "What do you wish?" he asked in Akhbreed.

"Full steak for the two of us, medium, and give the lady the lady's plate and house wine. We'll take drafts."

The waiter nodded and went back to the cooking area, told the order to the man there, then brought a tray with a huge pitcher of thick, dark beer, two stoneware mugs that must have held a quart each, and a carafe and tall-stemmed glass. He placed it on the table but did not serve it, instead going back to the counter.

Charley had been watching the other women. She got up, poured the beer into the two mugs with some expertise, showing that she'd poured beer somewhere before. The pitcher was well balanced, which was a good thing because it was close to being too heavy for her. She served each from the left, then went back, poured some of the dark red wine into the glass, took it, and resumed her seat, smiling with some satisfaction as Zenchur approved with a nod. Charley thought it was kind of fun; play-acting a fantasy, more or less, while knowing it wasn't real. Besides, those other women were so damned *glamorous* and perfect she instantly felt a sense of competition.

She was a bit nervous about the wine on a mostly empty stomach, but she sipped it and found it surprisingly sweet and very good. In the time it took for the food to come she had mostly finished it and was feeling a rosy glow that made it easy to just put everything out of her mind and pretend she was one of those sexy ladies over there.

The steaks came sizzling on the platter, which the waiter put in front of the other two so Charley didn't have to do much there, and he even put a plate in front of her—on oval-shaped dish which was mostly filled with fruits and salad combined with small cubes of cold meat and cheese. It was, in fact, just what she might have ordered rather than the heavy and greasy steaks, and she was both pleased and amazed at it.

Not that there weren't some mysteries there. What were the blue leaves, for example? She tried one and it didn't taste all that bad. Some of the fruit had odd colors and unfamiliar textures as well—light brown, for example, and almost snow white with little red grains—but nothing looked threatening or repulsive and she tried it, keeping an eye on the other two. You apparently ate it with a little spoon and with your hands. Twice she stopped and refilled their mugs, as well as her own glass, but the more she drank of the sweet wine the easier it was to be this courtesan, the more able she was to tune out all the fears and anxieties and the noise and smells of the surroundings and just *become* this character. She even started trying to imitate the sexy moves of the painted women at the other tables.

Sam was starving and ate heavily, once she'd picked up the system from Zenchur. It had been a little unsettling to discover that the silverware consisted of a very sharp pointed knife, a thin, serrated blade second knife, and a very small spoon, like a demitasse spoon, and nothing else. Clearly nobody had invented forks around here, and you cut the meat by holding it with the sharp knife, cutting with the serrated one, then spearing it with either. The little spoon was used for not just the drippings but also to scoop out the potato—it sort of looked and tasted like a potato although it was kind of purplish inside. Some slicked stalked vegetables were in a small container and proved raw, but tasted all right and gave it whatever balance it might have. Once she'd filled the emptiness inside, though, she also began to observe and to think.

Charley was doing a hell of a job, but she was nothing compared to those others. She wasn't dressed or made up like they were—that eye and body stuff was particularly erotic—and was clearly not in their class. She was good, but she wouldn't fool anybody that she was one of *them*. Then why go through this charade? Was Zenchur just playing games, or what? It seemed to her that Charley would've been less conspicuous wearing the sari and being a new girl in town.

Not that Charley, usually the more suspicious and the brains of the outfit, seemed to mind or question it. She was really getting into, and off on, this stuff.

A man who'd been sitting alone in a corner booth now got up and came over as they finished their meals. "Zenchur! How have you been? Long time," said the newcomer in Akhbreed.

"Well, Kligos. You received my message, then?"

Sam froze. Because Zenchur didn't know she knew the language he was speaking freely. When did the son of a bitch have a chance to send a message? So the toilet was occupied and a long wait, huh?"

"I need Pilots. One for the seven o'clock sector and one again for the five o'clock in the next cluster."

"Malabar, eh? Rough that way, you know. Changewind came through just yesterday and screwed up the hub and a few sectors something fierce. It'll be several more days before we have any accurate information on just what the damage is."

"It did not touch this cluster. I could be halfway there in several more days and closer to the source of the information. By the time I crossed clusters to Malabar the Pilots should have it well in hand. I need ones that keep their mouths shut and know the back ways."

"Woof! You're talking money for security there, my friend. At least a thousand just for services."

Zenchur nodded. "I know. I have full credit in Malabar and I have word that the Palace survived, so that won't be a real problem once I get there. I'm under budget for Tubikosa, though—my employer gave me an extra burden I hadn't counted on, and I had to make it over here fast and on short notice."

"I see. You want to relieve your unexpected burden and enrich your coffers more than enough to make it. Well, you contacted the right organization, old friend. I have been watching and I am impressed. I'll go your five hundred right here and now."

Zenchur chuckled. "I was thinking more about fifteen hundred. You and I know the profit potential from a rare good one. I would be guilty of allowing theft even at that price."

"You take advantage of an old friendship. Seven fifty tops. There is overhead, must preparation and break-in, and I still take a risk. It might not work out and then what do I have?"

"You know what you have, you old thief. This is difficult and risky for me as it is. A sorcerer is involved. Twelve fifty."

"Who you want to work for is your affair and your funeral. We all have our problems. I'm short-handed now because half the low-life in the kingdom is out looking for two Outplane girls dropped by storm here. You want money, go find them. The word on the street says fifty thousand, but only for both. Seems only one is wanted but they don't know which one. For that kind of money I am almost tempted to go look under every scarf myself—except that I know the odds of their showing up here are less than winning the royal lottery. Knowing you, though, if it wasn't for this bit of business I'd be very suspicious of you, too. All right—final offer. A thousand, flat, cash. Take it or leave it."

"Done." They clasped hands, apparently the local form of handshake. "You are aware of the subtleties of the problem?"

"I don't need diagrams. You just go along. Well—good seeing you and a pleasure doing business with you." The man waved, then walked out the door and away from the tavern.

"Who's that?" Sam whispered, not liking this a bit.

"An old friend, but one you cannot turn your back on. He

was friendly enough but I do not like the way he was looking at you two. He brought up the price on your heads and it was enormous. Let us pay the bill and get back to the hotel before he starts looking a bit too closely at you and starts figuring out what sort of girl you might make with longer hair and fewer clothes, if you know what I mean."

Sam nodded, suspicious but still not quite sure what the hell was going on. Zenchur wasn't playing it straight—they had made a deal, and for good money if you could hire somebody skilled and closed-mouthed for five hundred. He hadn't mentioned either the bargaining or the deal, yet he'd pegged the fellow as a bad one and accurately reported the search and reward information and suggested just what Sam was feeling. She wished she knew more about this place.

Zenchur called over the waiter and paid the bill from the coin purse, and Charley then led them out, properly opening the doors and the rest, all with a big smile. She was certainly drunk but it was hard to tell more than that. They began walking back up the street to the hotel, and for a block or so Sam was keyed up. The next block was the darkest, without real street lighting, and she hadn't liked it much on the way down. She just had an uneasy feeling about all this, and with Charley high as a kite she felt very much alone and on her own.

At the end of the second block, three large men turned the corner together and started walking toward them. They were *huge,* but they were no male whores. These guys were dressed in the dark tunics and leggings of Tubikosa but they looked like they'd come straight from Al Capone.

Sam suddenly had an impulse to look over her shoulder and saw three more like these only a few steps in back of them. Where had they come from? One thing was for sure—Sam was scared to death. Zenchur stopped the two girls and grew tense. "Watch it. I don't like this."

"You're the damned protector. *Do* something," Sam said in a low, tense voice.

"With three on either side and two across the street? What do you want me to do—die gloriously? All I can do is try and talk our way through."

They had all stopped now, and the men seemed to be waiting for Zenchur to say something, so he did.

"Hello, my friends. Nice night. Do you wish us to let you pass?"

"Can the crap," said the middle one in front of them. "Just give us the girl and we're gone."

"*Arleychay . . . Aythey antway ouyay,*" Sam said out of the corner of her mouth. *Etgay eadyray ootay unray ikelay ellhay. . . .*"

Charley was already aware that this was no chance encounter and the color started draining from her cheeks. She was sobering up real fast.

"When I move, you run," Zenchur told them in English while keeping a smiling face at the trio. "Meet back at the hotel when you can. . . . *Now!*"

With that the navigator lowered his head and rushed straight at the three men. Sam grabbed Charley's arm and almost pulled her at a dead run diagonally across the street. The pair Zenchur had seen but she hadn't moved equally fast, and the trio in back were right behind them. It was no contest; strong arms, impossible to get out of, grabbed Sam and lifted her right up, one arm pinning her own arms while the other covered her mouth. A second man got to Charley and picked her up like she weighed nothing at all. She yelled and beat at him, struggling to break free, but the man holding her seemed more amused than troubled by it.

Sam managed to get her mouth open and chomped down hard on the hand holding her head. It sunk deep and the man yelled, "Ow! You little brat!" He dropped her, and she started to turn but something hit her head that felt like a ton of cement; there was a roaring in her ears and then blackness.

Sam came to slowly and with great agony. Her head was splitting and she felt dizzy and sick, but she remembered immediately what had happened and opened her eyes. She was back in the hotel room, on the bed, and she could see Zenchur at the sink, washing off what might have been some blood from his mouth.

She moaned. "Charley! Where's Charley?"

Zenchur turned and looked at her. "So you survived that blow. You are tougher than I thought. Your hard head may come in handy many more times before this is over."

"Where's Charley?"

"They got her. I took a couple of good punches but then the three of them pinned me against a wall. I could do nothing. I saw them hit you with the truncheon, but did not know if you were dead or alive. When they took her away, the three gave me a farewell set of punches and then fled themselves. When I could, I got to you and saw that you were still breathing. I thought it best to bring you here as quickly as possible. I hoped you were not seriously hurt. If I had called the medical alchemist it would have been impossible to hide the fact that you were female, and then a lot of people would get ideas about two similar girls, you see."

She managed to get to her feet and felt her head. There was a lump there. With Zenchur's aid she made it to the sink and looked at herself in the mirror. There was a large knot on her head near the back, and some dried blood. She had to admit she looked like she felt, but she couldn't afford to feel sorry for herself now. She dashed some water on her face, then took one of the towels, wet it, and carefully applied it to the lump. It hurt, but it also helped. She turned back to him, leaning against the sink. "Who were they? Why'd they take Charley?"

"Common thugs. I recognized two of them—the ones across the street trying to keep out of my sight. They work for Kligos, the man I spoke to at the tavern. The others I hadn't seen before, but the odds are very good they are Kligos muscle, too. He never travels far without bodyguards. I should have known it—him in the tavern alone. Kligos does not travel, he embarks with full entourage."

"But why Charley?"

"He—he is the largest supplier of full courtesans in the district. Those in the tavern tonight were all his, I think. They are not like common prostitutes, as I said. They require beauty and intelligence and are a special breed. The only thing I can guess is that Kligos decided Charley was one of the rare ones, and he knew his muscle men were outside, and he did not figure he had to pay me to take her. I once did him a disservice in the employ of one of his competitors, although he has also hired me. I guess he was getting even for that other time."

"Yeah, that's all well and good, but how do we get her back?" They really had punched Zenchur out—that was clear—and she wasn't yet ready to give in to her suspicions. Not just yet.

"We do not get her back. She is gone, Sam. Vanished into Kligos's territory in the district."

"But—we *got* to get her back!"

"It would cost much, and we would probably still die. Do

you think it would be that easy to go into his territory and just snatch her back? It might take days just to locate her, never mind actually rescuing her, and by that time she will not be worth rescuing."

Sam froze. "What do you mean by that?"

"You saw the others. First they will drug her and send her to an alchemist to be made to look that good. Then they will give her a potion that will drain her personality, so that she would no longer remember who or what she was and where she came from. Others would then make her mind malleable to remolding as she was trained to be the perfect courtesan. You see? Hopeless."

Sam was appalled. "We have to *do* something! I don't care about the risks—we can't let that happen to *Charley!*"

"Perhaps you cannot. I can."

"But you need both of us for Boolean! He won't be pleased at this!"

"He won't care, really. There was not supposed to be anyone but you. It is *you* they are all interested in, not Charley. She just came along for the ride. Even the two trunks—they were both for you, so we could disguise you as male or female, any way we saw fit or useful. She means nothing to me except someone else to worry about, someone else to drain our finances, which were, by the way, doled out on the basis of my having to protect you alone."

It was all too clear now, and the realization only added to his cold and callous manner. "She was just an extra burden to you, wasn't she? You could find her. You could use that hypnotic jewel of yours and get right to her—but you won't. You won't because *you sold Charley to those men, you son of a bitch!*"

His eyebrows rose and he looked somewhat offended. "You were there. This cut, these bruises. Does it look like a cold business transaction? There were gentler ways."

"I wanted to believe that. That's why I kept hoping. . . . But let's skip *all* the pretendin', you bastard." She switched suddenly to Akhbreed. "I heard and understood your whole conversation, you horse fucker!"

That got him. His mouth dropped and for a second he really didn't seem to know what to do.

"Yeah," she pressed. "I speak and understand it completely. What was to be next for me? A horse that bolts and kills me, or runs away, or something like that? Maybe something Ladai is arrangin' that you don't even know nothin' about so when you go in front of Boolean you can honestly say you tried, right? Well it won't work now."

He sighed and put down his towel. "You are quite right. This does change everything." He stood a few feet directly in front of her, and his hand went to his belt pouch. "I had hoped to avoid using this because it came from Boolean, but now it is the only logical approach. First you, then a good cover story, then I will use it on Ladai and myself so that even we will believe it. In a moment you will feel *very* girlish yourself, you will go over and put on the sexiest outfit in the female trunk, go down, and introduce yourself to someone who will be very lucky getting that reward from Klittichorn."

She hadn't known what was coming the first time he'd pulled out the Jewel of Omak, and so she hadn't paid much attention. Now, though, she saw that it did not shine its nasty light right off, but that the surface, a swirl of white and tan and black like polished onyx, slowly opened, like a camera lens. She weighed rushing him but knew that would be futile; the only hope she had was the oldest, stupidest trick in the book.

At the instant the full glory of the jewel's interior shone forth, she dropped to the floor. The beam struck the bottom part of the mirror behind her and reflected back, striking Zenchur, because of the angle, in the neck. It was unexpected and apparently painful. He cried out, dropped the jewel on the floor, and his hand went to his neck while his face contorted in pain.

Sam's head still hurt like hell but somehow it didn't matter anymore. She lunged for the jewel that was only a few feet from her now on the floor, came up with it, and rolled over with the gem in her hand as Zenchur recovered and whirled to come at her. She held it up in front of her without bothering to get up, and the beam shone and struck his face.

Zenchur froze, the expression of mixed anger and pain also frozen on his face. She whistled some relief. *Just like the freeze-frame on the VCR,* she thought, amazed. She didn't dare move, though. Not yet.

"Okay, lover boy," she said in English. "You will relax, go over and sit on the bed, and you will obey me and answer all my questions. Understand?"

His facial expression softened. "Yes," he mumbled tonelessly, then loosed up, went over, and sat obediently on the side of the bed as told.

Now she could get up. "How long do the effects of this jewel last?" she asked him.

"Six to eight hours," he responded dully.

"All right—you sold Charley to that man, didn't you? The whole kidnapping was a put-up job, wasn't it?"

"Yes."

"You had her actually *auditioning* in there for the courtesan role, and then you sold her for a thousand."

"What you told me about what they'd do to her—was that true?"

"Yes."

That was bad. "How long have I got before they give her the potions that make her forget everything?"

"They do the physical first and that takes a full day and night. They save the rest for after because the potions to do that are far rarer and more expensive than the physical ones. After a full day she would invite Kligos over to give her a love potion. Then she would do anything Kligos said. It makes the rest go very easily."

"All right—so who would they take her to? If you *had* to find her in secret, where would you look?"

"First I would look at Boday's studio," he responded, still in that dull monotone. "The two women in the tavern tonight were Boday's work and Kligos would want the best."

That name again. "Who is this Boday and where would I find him?"

"Boday is a woman. She lives and works out of a studio loft in the warehouse district. She is an expert in artistic alchemy."

Sam frowned. "What the hell is artistic alchemy?"

"She feels she is an artist. She used to be a sculptor but when she came down here she changed. The courtesans are her creations. She thinks of each as a unique work of art."

Well, that explained all the body painting. Kind of sick, though, not just that somebody would think of poor, helpless girls as nothing more than raw material like clay or paint. Even worse that it was a woman. She had—how long?

"How long has it been since I was knocked out?"

"About three hours," Zenchur replied.

Okay, that was something. "So they can't mess with her mind until after dark tomorrow, right?"

"That is the usual way. With Boday it often takes longer. She considers herself an artist and will not be rushed."

"Where is this Boday's place? Exactly—from the hotel?"

Zenchur told her. It wasn't all that complicated, since the warehouse was on the lake, but she made very sure she got it right. Twenty, maybe twenty-four hours. Oops! There was a thought.

"How many hours are in a day, Zenchur?"

"Twenty-four," he responded.

Okay, at least some things were still the same. "This place of Boday's—have you ever been there?"

"Not inside. I have been past it many times."

"Is it guarded?"

"The warehouse is owned by Attum Merchandising. It has many guards there at all hours. Since the only stairs up to Boday's loft are well inside, it is all the protection she needs."

"Uh-huh. And if you wanted to get inside Boday's place without those guards knowing, what would you do? Use the jewel?"

"No. It might not get all the guards and might activate some protective spells. I would hire a thief, small and strong, and get up the outside of the building under cover of darkness, then secure a rope for me. There are large windows like skylights up there, most open to the breezes."

"Huh. It's a wonder thieves don't get up there all the time, then. Or is there something else?"

"Not that I know of, but I have never been inside. Boday would be well protected in any case from such things. She does work for Kligos and for a dozen others, including some procurers for the royal family, yet she has no taste for money or jewelry or anything of major value. Anyone breaking into Boday's would have the instant and total wrath of both the lords of this district and the nobility on their heads, yet probably such a crime would net little. It would not be worth it."

Now *that* made a lot of sense. And most, if not all, of Boday's human raw material would be from the elements where nobody would be looking for them, anyway. It sounded easy—if you had a professional thief.

She clenched the Jewel of Omak tightly in her hand. "I wish I knew how to do it myself," she said aloud.

Immediately, clearly, in her mind, an eerie and inhuman voice responded silently, *Awaiting input/action command.*

She jumped and almost dropped the jewel. "Who said that?"

The hypnotized Zenchur took that as a question directed at him. "You said the last thing."

"No, no! There was a voice—sort of. Like inside my head. Or is this bump doing it?"

"I do not understand."

"Neither do I. I . . ." She looked suddenly down at the jewel in her hand. Was it possible. "Was that you, Jewel of Omak?"

Yes. You stated the activating command. Awaiting input/ action.

"Holy shit. Zenchur—did this jewel ever talk to you?"

"Talk? No."

Well it was sure as hell talking now. And in English, too! She had stated the activating command, it said. What had she said? Just "I wish I knew how to do it myself." Hey! Maybe that was it. This was a land of magic. Maybe you had to wish.

"Jewel—is that it? Do you do something except hypnotize people?"

Yes.

"I wish I knew how to use you properly," she said, hoping it could take a hint.

Operation. Standard feature. Direct mental manipulation of remote subjects by carrier beam centered on forehead. Undocumented features. Manipulation of mind and body of operator as willed subject to energy limits. Access to data information files per specific request. Various protective measures available to bearer. Language used must be English as protective feature. Command must be phrased as wish. End operation guide.

God. Sounded like a computer. "So how come you never talked to Zenchur?"

Zenchur used only standard feature. Never used English until you appeared in speech or thought. Zenchur does not think in English, cannot therefore command access this mode.

"You're from—Boolean?"

Yes. I am backup system in case Zenchur failed. Any attempt by Zenchur to use jewel against Boolean's predetermined interests would have resulted in his destruction.

She grinned and looked at Zenchur. "You don't know it, but I just saved your miserable life." She thought a moment. "I guess the wishes aren't like magic lamps, huh? I can't just wish Charley here and lots of money and all that?"

Impossible. Wishes limited to mind manipulation of others and mind and body manipulation of bearer.

She knew it wasn't gonna be *that* easy. "Zenchur said the effect lasts six to eight hours. Any way to make it longer? Like forever?"

Yes. Aim beam at forehead, express input/action command as wish.

She could command Zenchur to help her, but Zenchur said the only way he could manage it was to hire a thief and she'd had enough of others in this for now.

She stood back, held up the jewel, and put the spot on the navigator's forehead. He stiffened.

"I wish Zenchur would never recognize Charley or me again. Even if we went up to him stark naked and told him he would never recognize us or believe us."

Done.

"I wish that Zenchur would never see me as other than a man, even if he saw me naked or in a slinky dress and everybody else knew what I was. I also wish he would forget he ever knew English, or even what English was, and be unable to ever learn a word of it again."

Done.

She was on a roll now. Power corrupted, particularly when it was on the other side.

"I wish Zenchur would forget about the Jewel of Omak, or that there ever *was* such a thing, and that he could never touch it again, even by accident. And I wish that he would forget Boolean and everything he ever did for Boolean. I wish he would forget everything for the past five days forever."

Done.

"Zenchur—stand up."

The navigator obeyed.

"First, get and give me all your money, anything of value that could be spent in this crazy world."

Zenchur gave her the change purse, which was fairly heavy, then went over to the trunk with the female dress inside and pulled out a small secret compartment. He removed a second bag and brought it to her. It seemed a lot heavier than the change purse. She managed to cram it all into the small leather change purse that was part of her own outfit, although empty.

"So you were gonna have me put on a bikini and go down and wander around offering myself until somebody took me up on it, huh? You bastard. I ought'a just order you to go down and become one of those storefront muscle men, but I won't. Uh-uh. Too easy. But for what you did to Charley, what I might not be able to undo, you deserve something real mean." She aimed the jewel.

"I wish that you only loved men," she said to him, her voice firm. "I also wish that you loved to wear women's clothing and jewelry and cosmetics all the time if you can, and that you had the manner and tongue of one of these courtesans—very swishy and real feminine. And I wish you were scared, terrified, of a lot of things. Scared of all women, for example, Akhbreed or not, and the dark, and lonely streets. I wish you felt completely powerless most of the time, and scared. And I wish female centaurs were the scariest thing to you of all."

Done, said the jewel.

"Okay, get over there and go to sleep, you bastard," she ordered. "Dream nightmares, and when you wake up you'll be a new man."

It felt good, really satisfying, to do in somebody like that. It wasn't until she had done it, though, that she realized she had blown it. He'd already forgotten her and Charley and everything. He could no longer answer the one big question: why she was wanted by so many people.

"Shit," she muttered, dismissing it as a lost opportunity. The real problem was what to do next.

"Boy, I wish I could wish that *everybody* see me as a hundred percent man," she muttered. "That would protect me around here."

Done, said the jewel.

She was startled. "You mean I can really do that?"

You are the bearer. Nothing has changed, but optically and aurally they will see someone male and different. I said I was a protector. Limitations: I can do only physical self; not clothing or inanimate objects. Illusion will also be transparent to higher classes of sorcerers, some non-Akhbreed races.

"Huh. So I can't slip into something of Charley's without lookin' like a man in a dress. Still, it's good enough. It means I won't hav'ta worry 'bout this as much. I'm still real amazed that *anybody* bought it. When that guy looked at Charley and me in the tavern and said that 'bout the two girls I figured I was nailed." She sighed again. "Okay, jewel. I talk to you in English but the one I zap don't hav'ta know it?"

Correct. I will provide the interfaces needed.

"But it'll work on the others, too. Not Akhbreed. Like Ladai."

Yes, but not all. I may also be unable to affect halflings, the accursed, and others of that ilk. Also certain races with intrinsic powers or whose memory and emotive patterns are too different from your own.

She thought a minute. "You can make most folks see a man when they see me. What else can you do to me?"

Question oddly phrased. I can maximize use of anything that is actually a part of the animate bearer. I can give pleasure, dampen fear, speed some types of damage repair, direct energy where it will do the most good, and provide some needed survival reactions and data within the limits of the information available to me. Warning: use me sparingly. I must recharge my energy or my abilities diminish.

She nodded absently. "Yeah, but what I need now is to save Charley and I don't know how. I wish I had the strength, stamina, ability and sheer guts to go after her myself, but . . ."

Done, said the jewel. *Warning: your body will pay a physical price for this later.*

Suddenly there simply was no question in her mind as to what she had to do. Her head stopped its aching, her mind became remarkably clear, although the knot was still there and it was still ugly. She felt strong, confident, wide awake, and cautious, not afraid. She searched Zenchur's bag and the trunks for anything else of use. Not much, and she had no patience to search for secret compartments, not now. Still, in his bag was something solid wrapped in soft crimson cloth, and she took it out and unwrapped it.

It was a knife—no, bigger than a knife. The handle looked more like a sword handle, but the blade was maybe a foot long, perfectly proportioned. She picked it up, felt it, made a few slash and jab moves. It was as if she'd always had the thing and practiced every day.

She took the time to change. There was a soft pullover top of near jet black in there, a pair of black male tights, and a loose but sturdy black leather belt. She tried on the outfit and it fit pretty well, although the top was lifted up a little by her breasts. The body was all girl, though; she searched and found a loose leather jerkin that went over it and concealed a bit. She knew she didn't really need it with the power of the jewel working for her, but you never knew if you were coming back. Her soft leather boots would continue to be fine. The short sword's scabbard fit on the belt, so that was added. She was reasonably satisfied—it was men's clothing, although she didn't look very mannish in it. That jewel's spell had better work. She kind of liked the look, though.

She was almost ready to go when she realized she'd almost forgotten the money purse. That, too, went on the belt, and she hoped it wouldn't jingle much.

Next was finding a way out. She considered risking the stairs, but the less seen the better. She went to the window, stood on the trunk, and with a real effort got it open and looked out. It was four stories down to the street below, but there were ledges and cornices all the way. The fact that she had always been scared of heights and never even climbed trees well as a kid was forgotten; her mind plotted the whole thing carefully, then she let herself out of the window and lowered herself down onto the four-inch ledge. She worked her way along it, carefully but confidently, until she reached the corner of the building, then eased herself down and let her body flow over the side until only her hands were on or held the ledge. The cornices and brickwork at points gave her only an inch to work with, but, very carefully and in fair darkness, she made her way down the side of the building without aids.

The darkness which had been a fearsome enemy was now a friend to her, and she stepped into it and drew the short sword, then allowed her eyes to grow accustomed to the murkiness and made her way along the back streets. She had made Zenchur be very precise; within ten minutes and with no real incidents except a few rats or rat-like creatures, which she ignored contemptuously, she made it to the waterfront itself and looked back on a row of warehouses, one of which in particular interested her.

She made her way completely around it, unobserved in the darkness, studying it with a professional's eye. It was bound on all sides by streets, the smallest of which was maybe fifteen feet. So much for roof to roof; without equipment it was just physically out of reach. That left the warehouse itself. It was about the same distance to the roof as it had been down from the hotel room window, but this was stone and cement block. The only possibility was the rain channels and gutter pipe, which was more of a rounded pipe than the aluminum rectangles back home. The lowest channels that were useful were a good ten or twelve feet from the street level, more than twice her height, and it wasn't clear just how they were set in. She was five-two, a hundred five—okay, a hundred and twenty. Why quibble? The gutters and mounts back home wouldn't take either weight. If these didn't, then she was screwed and there'd be a lot of banging. If these did—then what?

To hell with it, she told herself. *Charley's in there and I don't see another way.*

She removed her boots in an alley that separated two warehouses in back of her target, then used the sword to cut away the bottoms of the tights up to the ankles. She knew she'd be better off if she left the sword and maybe the money as well—even though the money bag also had the Jewel of Omak—but she wasn't about to leave her only weapon behind and certainly not the money or the jewel.

She sized it up from every angle, calculated the timing, speed, and place, then, without considering things further, she took off, hit her mark, and leaped, arms outstretched.

Both hands grabbed the gutter pipe, but then the rest of her body slammed into the stone wall. It hurt and she almost lost her grip, but she held on. Damn! Wasn't she gonna be a sight if she lived through this?

The pipe was solid and held, and seemed to be mounted on thick steel rods embedded in the concrete of the building itself. With supreme effort and contorting more than she ever thought possible she got a leg up, then rolled into the building letting the two inches of clearance between the rods and the side of the building hold her. It took her some more time and much care and breath control as well as strength, but she managed to get up so she was standing on the two inch pipe. She worked her way down to where the vertical pipe from the roof met and merged with the horizontal one and studied it. It went all the way, right up the corner, but there wasn't much to hold on to except pipe and support pins.

Taking a deep breath and willing away the pain, she used the same arms that could not have possibly lifted one of the trunks, let alone Charley, and pulled herself up the side of the building. The roof was a sloping affair of dirty green copper.

Cautiously she moved along it, until she reached the corner and a scary turn to cling to the side facing the water. She hoped Zenchur knew what he was talking about. It would be unendurable to find at this point that this was the wrong warehouse—or that Charley wasn't inside.

There *were* windows, at least—a long string of very large ones, only on this side. Some had been propped open several inches to catch the breeze, which was definitely there, although mostly blowing from the land to the water. She made her way to the nearest window and looked in, praying she was not going to find herself looking down into the warehouse.

She wasn't. It was a room—a big room, with a polished wood floor and tons of stuff all over the place. If definitely looked like an artist's studio—there were even sculptures around on stools and stuff like that. It was definitely what was advertised. Now the only question remaining was whether or not Charley was inside. Zenchur had said that Boday wasn't the only one doing this filthy business, only the biggest name.

Further on down and out of her direct line of sight some lights were certainly on. She had come this far; she had to find out one way or the other. At least, damn it, she made the effort.

It wasn't easy. opening the window more than the pins allowed without them falling back, but she managed it, wondering how the hell Boday opened them in the first place. She managed to get under, just barely squeezing through, until she was hanging, suspended inside, but still a good six or eight feet from the floor.

There was no way around it. She would have to drop and roll, and hope that the sound wouldn't be heard or would be dismissed by any who did.

She let go, falling immediately to all fours and then freezing as the short sword went *thunk* against the wood. Holding it up, she crawled into a dark corner and waited to see if anyone would come to investigate.

Someone did. The figure silhouetted in the far doorway was imposing, but, backlit, it was impossible to tell much more than that she was *very* tall and *very* thin and she wore very high heels.

"Hello! Anybody there, darlings?" she called out in a voice that was deep and rich and very female. The Akhbreed dialect was also heavily accented. She walked into the darkened studio without showing any real fear, and in the darkness various forms and colors seemed to glow, although she was barely visible. It didn't take much imagination to see that the glowing parts were shapes and highlights of her body that made the whole show obscene. In a few steps, she stopped again and was slightly illuminated by a shaft of reflected light from the lakefront outside.

The most obvious thing about her was that she was wearing tall, high-heeled leather boots and matching panties or bikini or whatever. What was anything but apparent for quite a moment was that she wasn't wearing anything else, although that realization restored Sam's confidence in fashion design. The fully lit version of the woman did not have the very obscene shapes, but it was a whole new category of obscenity.

From the top of her small, firm breasts to the top of her boots, the woman was a walking art show. It was like she was tattooed all over, yet it wasn't like that—these were no skin-dulled designs, but bright, flashy colors, and lots of them. Dozens, maybe more, all in loops, swirls, waves, and every sort of shape possible. She looked like a walking modern art sculpture. Even her face had some starburst design exploding from her eyes. Only her arms and hands and shoulders seemed free of paint.

After pausing a moment more, she walked out of the slim light and again there were those glowing patterns, although now Sam realized that it was part of the designs on her body. Like day-glo or something, they glowed softly in the dark. Jeez! Those spirals around the breast and nipples moved when she did and could almost hypnotize you! And the hair. It was long, but she'd never seen spikes that thick or that perfect, going out in all directions maybe a foot from her head—and each a different color, too.

Even without the boots she'd be a tall woman, though. Sam guessed her at well over six feet. Neither she nor Charley would come up much higher than Boday's breasts.

She went to the far part of the studio, unlatched a lock, and opened the door. "Amswaq! Are you there, darling?" she called down into the warehouse.

"Yeah, Boday," came a man's voice from far off. "Problems?"

"Boday thought she heard someone knock. Did anyone come in?"

"No, nobody and I been sitting here all night. Not since

them big bruisers hours ago. You want I should come up and check the place out?"

"No, it's all right, darling! Boday must have simply put something where it was sure to fall over later. She will find it in the light of day. Good night."

"G'night, Boday," the man responded, and the woman closed and relocked the door, then turned and walked briskly back to the lighted doorway and through.

What kind of whacko paints herself like that and then talks about herself like she's somebody else? Sam wondered. *I guess the kind that would think of people as things.* Everybody in this damned world seemed to think about people that way. Weren't there any *good* people in this world?

After waiting to make sure Boday wasn't setting a trap, Sam crept out, keeping low and in the shadows, until, silently, she made it to the doorway. She could hear Boday's voice in there, clearly talking to somebody, although if she had somebody in there why hadn't they come with her to investigate the noise?

The next room was still a large one, although nothing like the studio, but it was a mess. Walls were covered with shelves containing old and musty-looking books, some intermixed with jars and other containers, and one whole wall had only the small jars on it. There was also an old, beat-up looking marble-topped counter in front of the wall full of jars, on which were the odd-looking, Akahlarian equivalents to bunsen burners, holders and stands, and even several mortars and pestles. The whole counter was covered in multi-colored crud. There was also trash and even some ancient garbage on the floor and counters and shelves. Boday was something of a pig.

Boday was clearly working on something—or someone. With a little maneuvering, Sam could see that it was a girl with very long hair standing there, still as a statue, stark naked, on a pedestal. It *could* be Charley, but the hair was colored wrong, and there were designs or markings on the girl's rear end. Boday circled around her, stopping to study or think now and then, a palette balanced professionally on one shoulder and arm, a long, brush instrument in the other. Boday was talking, now and again, to the girl, who gave no reply, no reaction at all.

"Ah, darling, Boday is tempted to create from you a whole pattern of color and design, but that would not be artistically true. No, understated is best with you, my little butterfly.

Boday knows best, including when to fight her impulses and excesses. Oh, those potions have done their work *perfectly!* You are simply *gorgeous*. Boday shall hate to give you away, but that would be selfish, cheating the world of Boday's genius. You must be displayed to be appreciated. How Boday wishes you could speak to her and sing her praises. Ah, but not to worry. Boday could have created this in plaster or clay. Tomorrow comes the true art. Living art." She turned, put down the palette and brush or whatever it was, and looked on the counter, then picked up a black bottle.

"Here, precious one, is Boday's special essence of love which will bind you to your master so you will be protected as Boday's works should be and not get in any trouble." She picked up a green bottle. "But first this, which will sponge away all those memories, all that guilt, all those things you wcrc bcfore Boday remade you. Then you will be a blank slate on which Boday will create the rest of you. The simple tongue—only a few hundred words but all you will ever need. A wonderful creation of times past in which you will only be able to *think* as my creation. You will want for nothing, think of nothing, live for nothing save the *tableau* Boday's living art will teach you, and you will be eager to learn and know nothing else so none will ever spoil the creation. Now—some proper adornments to insure the perfect symmetry, then Boday can rest and you, my sweet, can rest as well and let the potions complete their work."

Sam thought quickly. What the hell could she *do?* Getting here was tough enough, but if that was Charley—should she take on Boday or wait? The multi-colored woman was a big woman, thin or not, and in her own element. She had done a lot already considering it'd been maybe six hours—dawn was breaking fast through the studio windows—and the jewelry and stuff Boday was putting on her was finished off with little dabs of something that caused tiny puffs of smoke and hurt to watch. Still, Zenchur had been right. No love potions or amnesia juices yet. If Boday couldn't give them until all the other stuff had set and taken, then there was no reason to jump the gun and take a big risk. If Charley was "setting" then Boday had to sleep *sometime*.

It was tempting to use the Jewel of Omak and be done, but that might come later. It suddenly occurred to Sam that she had no idea what the range of the thing was—and no way right now to ask the question.

The sun was shining brilliantly by the time Boday finished with her "proper adornments" and seemed willing to let things go. It had been at least two, maybe three more hours; the sounds of the warehouse starting up work for the day came muffled through the floor while other voices and noises came in from the windows as the studio, in particular, heated up.

Finally Boday put out her hands and took the girl's and brought her gently forward off the pedestal, then led her around and out of Sam's sight. But before she did, Sam got a look at the face and felt a thrill. It was Charley, all right! But, boy! If she snapped out of this okay, she was sure gonna be in for a shock when she looked in the mirror.

It would be best, Sam decided, to wait a couple of hours more before going any further. She wanted Boday very solidly asleep and the full din of business outside and below to cover her. She was feeling damned tired, that was for sure. All the aches and pains of the previous night were catching up with her, including a new and growing sensation that every inch of skin was bruised and every bone in her body was broken. She barely made it into a corner where she'd be well hidden behind some boxes. She was just in time, too; Boday came suddenly out of the door, went somewhere in the studio, messed about with something for a little while, then turned and walked back in the other room and perhaps beyond.

God, I'm so damned dizzy and sore I can't move! Sam thought miserably. She was incredulous at what she'd done, but it was wearing off quite rapidly now. The jewel had warned that she would pay a price. She didn't want to rest long, though, certainly not sleep. It would be horrible if she fell asleep and let the worst happen when she'd come this far. It was a plaintive thought, and she wasn't aware of sinking into slumber.

But when she next jerked her head up to stay awake, the studio was no longer lit by sun and the shadows were long and darkening. She was suddenly wide awake, although still feeling some pain.

She was awake—but was Boday? And, if so, had the crazy artist gone too far?

· 7 ·

Personality Changes

SAM REMOVED THE Jewel of Omak and gripped it tightly. "What is your range for hypnotism?" she whispered. "Tell me."

Normal power three meters, the gem responded in her brain. *I am now under severe power down, however. Perhaps one meter. I believe I can maintain your protective disguise for up to two more days without time to recharge, but no other functions fully operative. Last night was a heavy drain. You were warned.*

A meter! That was like three feet! She'd almost have to be kissing Boday to get it to work. "How long will it take you to recharge?" she barely breathed.

If I am not used at all, thirty-six hours should be sufficient.

She put it away. Thirty-six hours! Christ—Charley would be dead meat by then. Not to mention the fact that she herself was feeling pretty drained and achy as hell—and there was no way she was getting down the same way she got up. She was also hungry and thirsty as hell and she was going to burst if she didn't piss pretty soon. This was *great*. Just *great*.

Boday was up and about in there, too. She could hear the artist now moving around, humming an inane tune, and smell some pretty wild smells, a few of which were helpful in making Sam forget how hungry she was.

Sam sat there trying to figure out what to do. Damn it, if she didn't do anything at all Charley was gonna be history, but what could she do? The jewel was no good, and Boday was bigger and from the looks of those arms a lot stronger than she was. Sam went to the short sword which the previous night had

143

felt so light and easy to use and found it so heavy she could hardly manage it. This wasn't *fair,* damn it! It just wasn't *fair!*

But what she had done last night, as incredible, as unbelievable, as it now seemed, was only partly magic. The gem had given her nothing but confidence and some background knowledge skills; she had done nothing she was not capable of doing, only things she would not have dreamed possible for her to do. It was getting dark and she was about to piss on the floor. The hell with it. Without Charley she just didn't want to see what this armpit world looked like, and to hell with Boolean.

Grasping the short sword for all it was worth, she crept around the corner, through the doorway, and into the laboratory, keeping behind a mound of piled up stuff on a table. She could see Charley lying kind of diagonal on a bed with an X-type adjustable frame. Boday was over at the lab counter checking on something. The two little bottles were still on the counter, too, but it was hard to say whether or not they'd been used. Sam had to believe they had not; it was just dark, and it was still not quite twenty-four hours.

Boday was in her usual state of colorful undress, although she was wearing a pair of sparkling pink panties and open-toed sandals now, and she had a bib around her to shield her in case something bubbling on her countertop might splash.

The artistic alchemist had her back to Sam, but she still looked *huge.* Sam felt like David and Goliath—only David had God and a slingshot. Both would be very useful right now.

Boday suddenly dropped something on the floor. "Moonstones and little fishes," she cursed a bit colorfully. She got up slightly from her work stool and leaned down to pick up whatever it was. Sam decided it was now or never.

She summoned every bit of strength she had, leaped suddenly out with sword drawn and rushed the big woman, saying "Yaaaa!"

Boday was so completely surprised she jerked up just in time to see what was coming but not to do anything about it. Sam hit her full force with her body, and Boday, bent over and just in the process of straightening up, went back sharply when hit and her head struck against the marble side of the lab table. Her eyes opened wide, her eyeballs went up toward her eyebrows, and she sank down onto the floor in a heap.

Sam rolled off and managed to pull herself up. It was so

quick and impulsive she hadn't even thought beyond the rush, but now she suddenly was aware that the big woman was lying there in a heap, like some discarded giant colorful rag doll. She stared incredulously at the sight, then thought, *Oh, my God, I've killed her!*

But then Boday moved and Sam realized she had only a minute, perhaps seconds, before things got different. She grabbed one of the bottles off the counter—the black one—and kneeled down beside the artist, who was just returning to consciousness, if not sense. "Here—drink this. It'll make you feel better," Sam said, sounding concerned, and put the bottle to Boday's lips.

The big woman tasted it, coughed a bit, then almost greedily drank the rest of it down. Her big eyes opened hazily and she looked at Sam, then saw the bottle, and the eyes grew suddenly wide.

"Apple cider," she mumbled. "Boday always wondered what it tasted like. How about that . . . !" She sighed, gave a sweet smile, then passed out again on the floor.

Sam had deliberately grabbed one of the potions, of course; it was the only sure way to make sure the big woman didn't come to and turn the tables fast. Now she looked at the bottle and tried to remember what it might have been.

Well, whatever it was, it had knocked the artist out again and that was plenty of breathing space. She wanted to rush to Charley, but first she spied a door at one end of the lab and a somewhat familiar object and headed to it. The piss was almost as sweet as the victory.

That done, she was able to see to Charley, and what she saw amazed her. Boday had been *very* busy with Charley, and if they could do this sort of thing with potions, who knew what magic might accomplish?

Charley had had Sam's old very long straight black hair, but Boday had changed that to strawberry blond with streaks of black and brown, and somehow managed to really fluff it up and thicken it, at least so it appeared. There were differences in the face, too. The lashes seemed extraordinarily long, like the most extreme false ones, and the pronounced overbite was gone, the lips a little turned out more, fuller and thicker like an almost permanent pucker, and colored a deep, rich, solid red. But most noticeable was the face painting around the eyes themselves, each a separate, delicate drawing and a mirror image of the other although they did not connect across the bridge. They were delicate, pale blue butterfly wings, one per side, coming out from the eye and curving gracefully away, yet in the solid color were small, fine lines of white and black that gave it a fascinating look, and from the tops of the "wings" came fine black lines that curved as well and ended in small black dots.

Boday went in for eye painting. She had it on herself and the pair in the tavern had it, too. But it was so intricate, so nicely balanced, that Sam had to admit that the tall woman might be a lot of nasty things, but she was a hell of an artist.

Setting it off were large pierced earrings that would hang down to the jaw line were she standing; thick, more brass than gold but impressive all the same, they were in fact stylized butterflies flying toward the front of Charley's face.

The motif continued on the body painting, although it was, as Boday had said, "understated." The butterfly, mostly in outline but subtly shaded so that it still gave the effect of a solid drawing with gossamer thin wings, used the breasts as the upper wing foundation, blue lines coming off from the wing tips and onto the breasts, circling the nipples and making them appear perfectly round. The wings, outlined in the blue of the eyes, curved down to the navel in which was mounted a matching blue gem, then back out along the hips and back in. The "head" was the pubic hair, dyed to match the new hair color. While it seemed almost an outline, the faint solidity of the wings actually contained hints of many colors, perhaps a very complex pattern depending on how the light caught it or the angle from which it was viewed. The complexion of all the skin, even that untouched by the design, seemed almost wet, glisteny and soft and perfectly smooth. The breasts were the same C cup size, but they seemed rock hard, incredibly firm, and far more prominent. Sam's sagged and drooped, which helped with the boy disguise. There was no way to disguise these, though. They were as firm as a—statue's.

There wasn't a sign of body hair anywhere except pubic hair and even that seemed manicured, and even the duplicate of Sam's old appendix scar was gone. There wasn't a blemish on this body. Not any of Sam's freckles, not a mole or anything.

The fingernails were so smooth and long and perfect they had to be artificial; they had been painted to match the blue of the eyes and the butterfly and had to be an inch or more long.

The toenails were also smooth and painted to match, although trimmed.

More jewelry had been added, to match the earrings. Bracelets and anklets of a twisted braid design, loose but firmly on, and with no sign of any seam showing, and a matching, loose-fitting collar.

Sam knew from seeing her back earlier in the morning that there was another butterfly, same color but different style, cape-like on her back, perfectly following the natural curves and folds of the body as did the one on the front. The colors were bright, vibrant, not at all like tattoos, but Sam had to wonder if this stuff came off.

One thing was for sure. Sam had always had a kind of androgynous look to her, very male in the face and female in the body. Charley had not one trace, one hint, of anything masculine remaining in her looks.

Charley was gonna shit bricks when she saw herself.

"Charley," she called, gently shaking her friend. "Charley—wake up! It's me—Sam."

Charley smiled sweetly and moved a little but did not wake up. It had to be some kind of drug. They'd passed some drugs in the wine last night—that was for sure. Probably more here to make her cooperative and not prone to waking up inconveniently and maybe trying to run away.

Sam heard a sigh behind her and whirled. Boday was stirring again, pulling her legs up and rubbing her temples with her long fingers. She stopped suddenly, looked up across the room, and saw Sam.

Instantly a look spread over her face that could only be described as ecstasy. It was the kind of look one might give when seeing God face to face. "Boday loves you," she whispered in a soft, throaty, sexy voice. "Boday worships you. She grovels at your feet. Whip her, chain her, beat her, but she will always worship you."

Well, that settled that. The black bottle was the love potion.

"Command her! Take her! You are her world, her life. Nothing matters but you! The world revolves about you!" Boday continued in that tone. She got on her hands and knees and crossed to where Sam stood, not knowing quite what to do next, and, without any warning, the artistic alchemist started kissing Sam's feet.

Sam felt embarrassed and pushed her away. "Stop that!"

"Yes, yes, Master. Command me! I instantly obey!" The alchemist scurried back and seemed to be almost whimpering with delight.

Holy shit! That was some potion! was all Sam could think of right off, but then she suddenly began to understand the possibilities.

"What about my friend? What have you done to her?" Sam asked.

"Made her beautiful. That is what Boday does. Creates beauty. She was easier than most. I can see why one of Master's greatness would seek her."

"The way you made her look—that is permanent?"

"Oh, yes, Master, kind Master whom Boday loves. She is beautiful, exotic. One gets so few with fair skin in this region. Do you approve?"

The way the alchemist was speaking and acting Sam thought she was going to have an orgasm all by herself.

"What about—the inside? Have you given any potions to change her brain?"

"No. Well, a few little things to make sure it all remains true to the artistic vision, but not thought, not memory, not personality. The art must be fixed first. See." She rolled and pointed to a small line of bottles. "These change the body chemistry so the body renews itself in my design. Only then, after twelve hours with nothing else ingested, are the potions for love, obedience, and the rest given. Boday was preparing to do it when you came into her life. The girl is still a work in progress."

Well, *that* was a relief. Charley might not like the work of art Boday made from her—but maybe she would—but at least nothing important had been screwed up. She'd been in time! Just barely—from the looks of that potion's effect on Boday.

"Do you remember why you feel the way you do towards me? Do you remember?"

"Oh, yes, Master. Boday drank her wonderful potion—as *you* commanded."

"It don't make no difference that it was that?"

"Oh, *no*, lover, God in the flesh. It can never matter how."

"And it's permanent?"

For the first time she showed a bit of her old pride. "Of *course*, my sweets. When Boday creates, it is *forever!* Isn't it *wonderful?*"

Sam gestured toward Charley. "Can you wake her up—now?" She desperately needed Charley right now to help figure out what to do next.

Boday was on her feet, cat-like, engulfing Sam and kissing her, then over to the workbench. "I obey, Master. Boday lives only for you. Whip her, beat her, she will worship you all the more." She picked up a small jar and uncorked it, then held it under Charley's nose. The unconscious girl made a face, tried to turn away, then suddenly came awake, looking terrified and a little in shock. She stifled a scream.

"Charley! It's me—Sam! It's okay! It's over!"

Charley frowned for a moment, then stared at Sam. "Sam? My God, Sam!" And then she was off the table and hugging and kissing her rescuer like she couldn't believe it and crying all the time. "They were gonna—turn me—into one of *them*," she sobbed, and Charley let it all come out. Suddenly Charley seemed to see Boday and froze. "*Her!*"

"It's all right, Charley." Quickly Sam told her all that had happened up to that point, with one exception. "Uh—I think you better look at yourself in the mirror, Charley, if you're up to it, before we go any further."

Charley froze, then with Sam's help managed to get up and go cautiously over to the three-way mirror as if afraid to look in. The hair tumbled down as she got up and showed not only was it full and colored but it was somehow *longer*, going down to below her ass. Sam couldn't help but think that this was the first hairdresser she'd ever seen who could truly work miracles.

When she did, what she saw took her breath away. "Oh, *man!*" she breathed. "*She* did this?" She wet a finger and rubbed at the thin but colorful design. "It doesn't come off!"

"No. She thinks she's an artist. She says her creations last a lifetime." Sam paused for a moment. "For what it's worth, you are the prettiest, sexiest damned girl I ever saw. It's not really bad at all."

Charley whirled. "That's easy for *you* to say! You don't have a damned butterfly on your body!" She frowned, then approached Sam. "They did something to you, too. Your voice, your manner, even your hair . . . Sam—you're a *guy!*"

"Huh? What the hell do you mean?" She pulled up the shirt revealing her breasts which were still there and, although a bit misshapen and flabbier, every bit the size of Charley's. "Does this look like a guy?"

But Charley wasn't buying. "Your breasts—they're gone! And there's even a little hair on your chest!"

"Such a magnificent chest, my love. So clean and manly," said Boday in Akhbreed.

Sam was so confused she looked down and saw the same old things she'd always seen. "What the hell . . . ?" She pulled the shirt back down and reached into her pouch and pulled out the Jewel of Omak. Sure! The disguise! It worked! Curious, she put down the jewel on the floor and stepped away.

Charley frowned again. "Huh? What the hell . . . ? You're back to normal!"

Sam nodded, reached down, picked up the jewel, and stuck it back in her pouch. "At least I know I'm not the one who's nuts. Man again, right?"

"Uh—yeah. That's like *weird*."

"It's an illusion, a fake. The jewel is causing it. Charley—I figured I been real lucky up to now and this is part of it. At least I think it was luck. Nobody could be *that* smart. Zenchur did a job for Boolean and got this thing in payment. For hypnotizing folks for getaways and stuff like that. But he *really* hired Zenchur for that first one just to give him *this*. It's a lot more than Zenchur thought it was. It's kind'a like, well, like a computer for magic. So long as I have this thing I look like a guy—to everybody, even you. It has lots of other tricks, too; ones that Zenchur never knew. It hypnotized me into thinkin' I was the world's greatest thief and I did things I never would'a dreamed and got here. I just *knew* everything—includin' how to use it. It—*talks* to me, sort of. In my mind."

"Boolean," Charley said flatly. "That's why he didn't answer us. He already had a backup system in place—for you, anyways. And it was in something so handy, so valuable to Zenchur that he'd never let it out of his sight, never sell it, trade it, or get rid of it in any way. Maybe these sorcerers *are* what they're cracked up to be after all."

Charley looked at Boday, who was just sitting there giving Sam the kind of look Sam had only seen girls give to hunks and rock stars. "What about Boday?" she asked. "Is she kidding? Is that love potion really permanent?"

"I think so, considerin' what it was invented for." She looked ruefully at the admiring Boday, who couldn't understand a word of the English conversation, of course. "I just don't know how I'm gonna handle this."

Charley sniffed. "You got a nutty lover, but I get to go through life looking like a member of a fucking freak rock band!" She turned and looked at herself again in the mirror. "Actually, it's not that bad—except I can't take it off!"

"Yeah, well, you got my body by magic 'cause Boolean thought it'd be useful. He was improvisin'. What he can do he can undo, I bet. You got to figure that magic is stronger than chemicals and potions, right? Me—damn it, can't I ever be *normal?*"

Charley lost a little of her self-pity. "Maybe not, Sam. I dunno. What did you do with Zenchur?"

"I used the jewel to turn him into the fairy queen," Sam said, chuckling, "with a fear of women in general and a real terror of female centaurs. After what he tried to pull, he deserved it."

"Yeah, maybe he did, but you blew it. You should have ordered him to go back and kill Ladai and then forget everything."

"Charley! I couldn't do that!"

"Well, maybe it's about time we started getting a little ruthless here. Don't you see, Sam? It's them or us. Period. Sure, you took Zenchur out of it, but you also took away her husband, lover, and only friend. She was outcast from her own people, too. You also took away her access to the ruling class, and, really, her only livelihood. You took away every reason she had for living. Now, put yourself in her place. What would *you* do?"

Sam hadn't considered that angle, but she still wasn't convinced that ordering a killing was the way. "Everybody's tryin' to do us in anyways. Why should we be like them?"

"Because now she's the only one who knows us and can finger us. She'll get in touch with the horned guy—bet on it. She'll tell him we came down near here, that we went into the city with Zenchur. She'll tell what we look like, and that you're disguised as a boy. The heat is gonna be on something fierce around here, and she won't rest until she finds us."

"Um, yeah. But—damn it, I just can't be that cold-blooded. And neither could you."

"Well, I changed a lot more than a nicer bod and butterfly eyes in the past day and a half. You don't know what those bastards are like. Pawing at me, making faces, feeling me up while I was strung up stark naked. They was setting me up for an eight-way gang bang. Only that boss of theirs showing up and ordering them to bring me here immediately, I guess, stopped it—but you don't know how close it was. They all had their goddamned pants down! You better believe if I had *them* and that sword I'd have your nutty friend here bronze eight sets of balls. I have had it with this shit. I may be stuck, but I am sick and tired of being a victim."

Sam sighed and couldn't think of anything else to say. Her eyes went around the room and focused on the now empty bottle of love potion and something else clicked. "Kligos! Holy shit, we forgot about him!"

"Huh?"

"The boss. He was supposed to come tonight so you could take that love juice and fall in love with *him* so he could own you. 'Scuse me.'' She turned to Boday and switched to Akhbreed.

"Boday—Kligos is coming tonight, right?"

Boday frowned, then nodded. "Yes. That's right. It had slipped Boday's mind. It is no longer of importance to her."

"Well, I don't want him to have this girl. I went to a lot of trouble to rescue her. He's a very powerful man, I know, but we have to stall him, or get him no longer interested in Charley. Is there any way to do that convincingly?"

The alchemist thought for a moment. "Well, we could always use a placebo, but that would buy only a few days. Let Boday think. She is a genius. She can solve any disputes.'' She paced for a minute, then snapped her fingers. "Yes! Of course! Royal prerogative!"

"I beg your pardon?"

"Never beg Boday's pardon, my love. You can do no wrong. Royal prerogative. It has happened before. Boday does work for the royal family at times in matters like these. A noble drops by, sees a work in progress, and takes a fancy to it. Even Kligos will not interfere in such a matter. They could shut him down here in hours and fillet him alive on a number of charges if they chose. Boday will simply tell him that the girl was so perfect—and she *is*—that the royal prerogative was invoked. Bad luck. Kligos will be pissed but he will not question it. After all, what does he lose? He just cancels the payment to the procurer, that's all."

"That's great! But won't the warehouse guards be able to tell him that no such royal visitor showed up?"

"No problem, darling! They are three shifts. He will believe. Why should he *not?*"

"Well, do it, then. But that doesn't solve any problems now." She told the alchemical artist about the problem of Ladai. "You see—if Ladai's tale gets back to here, then Kligos is gonna remember the boy and the girl with Zenchur and put two and two together and he'll be back here fast figuring you're just stiffing him for the fifty thousand." She did a quick translation for Charley's benefit.

Charley was also thinking. "I wonder if we're ever gonna get out of the frying pan or the fire? Well, you're right. We can't stay here, but we can't go, either. Once that story gets out they'll be looking for us. They'll have the city and this little country bottled up, maybe for weeks. You're not so bad off, so long as you got that jewel and you aren't around me. Kligos saw you close up but without the magic. That—spell—or whatever it is takes you and cancels out everything, and I mean everything, feminine, and it tightens you up a lot and makes you seem taller. Not real tall, but taller'n me, anyway. I think you can get away with walkin' right past this Kligos, so long as that spell holds, and if not you can zap him with the jewel. Now, he also saw me, and he knows what Boday does, so I think he'd still make me, though. And where can I go in this straight society, like *this*, and without the language?"

Sam explained the problem to Boday, who thought for a moment.

"First, then, my love, you must get your little bauble attached, so to speak. That way the spell holds. Once Boday's genius solves your problem we can think about your friend's, yes?"

She went over to the lab counter, reached down, pulled open a big drawer, and started rummaging through the largest collection of baubles, bangles, and beads Sam had ever seen. She would stop every once in a while, pulling out a wound roll of thin gold chain at one point, then a starburst backing. She reached for a bubbling chemical beaker, then said, "Remove all from the waist up. Let Boday see what she can do."

First a length of thin gold chain was measured so it would fit comfortably around Sam's neck but not with enough play that it could be taken off over the face. "Now your pretty bauble," said the alchemist.

Sam was reluctant to hand it over, even to Boday. "But I will change back into a girl," she noted. "Will you still love me anyway?"

"Not to worry, darling! Boday always has played both sides of the street. She saw you briefly when you proved yourself to your friend. Nice body. Much like hers, I think. Boday could do *wonders* with you."

Sam had forgotten that lapse. So it didn't matter. Whatever bond that potion created was more than just appearance. Or, perhaps, because Boday saw the change there was now no difference in her altered mind between the illusory male vision and Sam's real self.

Expertly, and in very short order, the Jewel of Omak was mounted on a strong backing and held there with folds in the setting and some kind of alchemical bonding. Sam hoped she didn't have it on backward. Then the gem and setting, on a slightly longer chain, was bonded to the neck chain. Again, the fusion appeared seamless, but that thing was *on*. It might be cut off, but never would it fall off.

But the other problems would be tougher to solve. It seemed like every fix they'd gotten into had been resolved more by dumb luck than brains, and there was a limit to how much you could count on that, but that wasn't the real depressing thought. It was that every time a super grade problem had been solved it had created new ones that looked just as or even more formidable.

"Ask her if she's got something to eat," Charley said to Sam. "I'm *starved*."

Suddenly Sam's own hunger and thirst came back full force. "You have anything we can eat? It's been a long time."

Boday brightened. "Anything and everything for you, my darling! Wait, and Boday shall create a *masterpiece!*"

They settled initially, though, for some wine, fresh bread, and cheese, which helped the two of them from getting more nauseous. Boday, however, was in her kitchen making a great racket, but soon the smells coming into the lab were pleasant, overwhelming the chemicals still on the boil.

"It's too bad we can't just stay here," Charlie sighed. "This is the first time I've felt reasonably comfortable in a long time.

It would be nice if it'd last, but I keep sitting here expecting eight big bruisers to crash through the door any minute."

"I know. I been tryin' to figure something but nothing's coming. We just don't know this *town*, let alone this world, well enough, and I keep remembering that sight from the cliffs—the green hills changing like that into tall mountains. Even if we could get out of this place we'd be screwed without somebody to take us. Navigators and Pilots, they call 'em. Like ships. And Kligos told Zenchur that just to get a Pilot who don't talk or ask questions would be five hundred or whatever they call their money here. If we also needed a navigator, it might cost a *fortune,* and we don't even know how far it is we're supposed to go."

To Boday the entire world existed for most people to go about drab, colorless, irrelevant lives while she existed to put artistry there. It extended to her cooking, too, even when doing something essentially quick and dirty in the kitchen. Admittedly some of the colors of some of the items looked more than a bit artificial and odd, but the arrangement, the preparation and look of each item, and, frankly, the smells and taste were really good. They already knew that the food in this part of this world was either basic meat and potatoes or very spicy, even hot, but they had never had things that tasted this uniformly different and good. Neither Sam nor Charley, however, had the guts to ask what any of it was.

Kligos's arrival a bit later, however, forced some improvising. Charley was kept out of sight, but Sam decided it was time to test just what good this magic spell might be before an expert in phoneyness. She had gotten this far on guts and she was beginning to learn confidence in a big way. She was prepared, though, to use the jewel at close range if she had to.

"Oh, darling! Boday has the most wonderful news and the most terrible news!" Boday gushed to the tough but slick-looking gangster. "The wonderful first. She is in *love!* This is Sandwir! Isn't he *cute?*"

"Adorable," the big man grumbled, nodding to but barely giving a second glance otherwise to Sam. Test passed. "He looks like he might take awhile for you to wear out. What's the terrible news?"

"Ah! Boday is crestfallen! She is desolate! Pamquis—he's the ratty little fellow from the Chancellor's Office—came by today to see about something for the regency celebration and he saw your little darling!''

Kligos's face froze into a hard and mean look. "I don't want to hear what I think you're gonna tell me, do I?''

Boday threw an arm up to her forehead in mock despair. "Darling! What can Boday say but what happened? Those two terrible words—'royal prerogative.' He asked who had brought her and I told him, of course, and all he did was grin evilly and—oh, it is confiscation! What must Boday do to atone, but what could she do in the face of those words?''

"Sons of bitches," Kligos grumbled. "She was a lot of trouble to get, too. I wish I'd let my men have at her. *Then* there wouldn't be no 'royal prerogative' with my property! Well, at least no money's been paid yet. Damn! She was worth a hundred a night minimum!''

"Boday *knows*, darling! And she, too, is out much invest-ment. She is as blackmailed as any. What can she say? He insisted on the potion right then and there as usual. Apparently they hold a grudge for that switch we pulled last year. Can you ever forgive this?''

Kligos sighed. "Forgive, yeah. Forget, no. Those highborn royal bastards. It's not enough that we got to pay 'em a percentage just to operate in this town. No, they steal, too, and smile about it. All right, couldn't be helped. But cut rate on the next one, you hear?''

"Boday will create a *masterpiece* for you! She promises!''

The gangster had a look of total disgust, but he turned around and left, slamming the door behind him. He looked in a foul enough mood to go out and torture a few women and children just to get it out of his system.

"*That* is a dangerous man," Sam noted worriedly. "Right now, he's our biggest worry, too. At least he didn't recognize me, I'm sure of that. But he's dangerous and smart or he wouldn't be where he is.''

Boday shrugged. Such things were beneath her notice. "Still, we have a few days. He does not connect you and her, my sweet. Come. Let us go back and you can tell your worries to Boday and she will try and solve them.''

"It's simple. There's an Akhbreed sorcerer trying to kill me by any means he can, and there's another who wants me alive and in his company, maybe just because he hates the other sorcerer so bad he wants something to hold over him. I don't know the reason. *Our* sorcerer can't come to us because he's real powerful, but maybe not powerful enough to match this guy on his home turf. Maybe he's got friends here that can outnumber our man, so our man can't come to us. If we can sneak in and get to him, though, then we're under his power and protection and he can help us. Zenchur was supposed to get us someplace where we could be taught the ropes in this world, then to the sorcerer, but that's out now. I don't even know where this guy is in relation to where we are. I wish I did."

Boolean is chief sorcerer of Masalur, said a familiar voice in her head. *Masalur is two hubs northwest and two hubs due west of that. Add in the seven sectors, or wedges, required for traversal and the nulls as well as the hub traversals and the distance would be approximately four thousand five hundred and six kilometers.*

She had forgotten that the jewel was now against her chest and that a wish was a wish.

"Darling! Lover! What is the matter? Do you feel ill?"

"Yeah, maybe," Sam responded. "I just got the answers to my questions from my magic jewel and now I'm like Kligos. I didn't really want to know. Four hubs, seven sectors—it says the distance is . . ." Suddenly in her mind some measures appeared but they were meaningless. "How big's a leeg?"

"Oh, how can it be put? From here near the water to the tall buildings in the center of town is a bit less than two leegs, my love."

From her rooftop vantage point she'd seen some lights in the spires of those buildings and she now guessed them to be about a mile in. A leeg, then, was about half a mile, and a kilometer wasn't much more than that.

"Would you believe about five thousand leegs, maybe a little less?" *Well over two thousand miles and eleven countries with God knew what!*

"Boday believes all that you tell her, love. That sounds about right. Sectors average about six hundred leegs, give or take, and hubs about four hundred across. This one is four hundred fifteen across."

Then they weren't that standard. Still, it was pretty depressing, and Charley wasn't exactly cheered when clued in, either.

"We can't do that distance on our own," Sam told Boday. The artist nodded. "No one could, not even Boday. You would need a navigator just to start with. Such a one could arrange for the proper Pilots as well as plot the routes and outfit the trip, but this is not cheap. A navigator for such a distance would easily cost two thousand sarkis. Particularly one who would be basically loyal and might defend his client against attack. Say twenty-five hundred just to be sure. Pilots who will just do their jobs and not ask questions are easily five hundred each, and you need—what?—seven of them. No pilots necessary for the hubs. They're all *our* kind, darling, and they stay the same most of the time. Now we are at six thousand. Then there are supplies. One would not wish to walk if it can be avoided, yes? Two thousand more. And then there will be expenses on the trails, and in both sectors and hubs. The more money the merrier but two thousand minimum. Let's see—that is ten thousand sarkis. I think I know where Zenchur was supposed to take you. It is where Boday was perfected! But it is southwest—add six more, you see. Another three or four thousand and another three thousand or more leegs.''

"Yeah? What's so special about that place, anyway?"

"It is—university. You go there, whatever you need to learn, they teach you.''

"Not whatever you want, whatever you need," Sam noted. "And who decides what you need?"

"Oh, *they* do, darling! And they *know*. Those who decide are all Akhbreed sorcerers. Those without positions, those studying further, those who have retired or do not wish positions. They know, lover. They know. Boday was an artist. A good artist. They did not teach her design. No, they teach her alchemy. The secrets of arts and potions. It is where sorcerers learn to be sorcerers, and heroes and heroines learn how to be heroes and heroines, or navigators, or Pilots, or any other great skills.''

"Yeah, and what does it cost to go there?"

"Cost? Precious, it does not *cost!* Only a graduate or a fully ranked sorcerer can send you. Then you must do him service if and when he or she needs it.''

"She? There are female sorcerers?"

"Oh, of *course,* darling! Not many in the hubs thanks to this foul male-dominated system, but many indeed. But why talk about it? It would take probably five thousand to get there at all. How much money do you have now?''

Sam removed the change purse and handed it to Boday, then

gave a running translation of what was going on. "So how much we got?" Charley asked.

"That's what I'm finding out."

"Find out how much *she's* worth, too."

"You have four hundred and twelve sarkis, two illum and seven pillux. A nice sum but it would not even get a Pilot. All that is Boday's is yours, dear one, but money has never been something she has been terribly good at keeping. The filthy pigs of art critics have always insulted her sculptures. The ones here are priceless, of course, but they would bring little money so long as Boday lives. When she dies they will discover her, though, and then they will be priceless treasures. This place is leased, paid up in advance for a year, but no refunds, and subletting a place like this would be very difficult. I have, perhaps, two thousand cash, and another thousand in jewelry and chemicals, but those would bring little if sold in haste or desperation, perhaps a quarter of their worth."

"So we're only halfway if we went to this university or whatever it is," Charley noted after hearing the translation. "And it's south and Boolean's north. So whatever they teach us, if it isn't how to fly we'll wind up dead broke with most of the distance yet to go."

"So you think we shouldn't head there? I mean, that's where Boolean wanted us but it's also not only out of the way but where Ladai might be watchin' and waitin'."

Charley sighed. "We probably *should* go. Somehow I feel it's bound up in all this. And he said we'd be safe there from all enemies, which would be real neat. But we don't dare go broke. Without that extra thousand then when they kick us outta there we're like up shit's creek."

Sam nodded and turned back to Boday. "Stuck again. Not enough money to go most anywhere, it seems. Five thousand for this university, ten thousand to get to Boolean, and fifteen thousand for both. It's a *huge* amount of money, I know. We can't go, and we can't stay here."

Boday looked at Charley. "Boday gets perhaps two, three commissions a month. Kligos is not likely to use us again for a while, so there would be at most two. Even if she is frugal, that is at best a thousand a month less two hundred or so for expenses." She sighed and looked at Charley. "It is a pity that Boday cannot complete her creation on this one. Kligos was right—a hundred a night easily, perhaps more. Satisfied customers have been known to double or triple the payment, and clients of Boday creations are *always* satisfied."

Charley looked at Sam. "What did she say? Come on—I want it all. I saw her looking at me."

"She said at the rate she's doing her girls it'd be one to two years before we'd have enough. She said—well, she said it's too bad you can't be put to work, you might say. Kligos said you was worth a hundred a night minimum, and Boday says, well, there's tips."

Charley looked amazed. "A hundred a *night? Me?*"

"I guess it's true. I mean, Kligos was willin' to shell out a thousand to Zenchur for you and another five hundred or so to Boday. He don't do that 'less he figures you'll make back lots more."

Charley was incredulous. "A thousand to Zenchur and five hundred to Boday? You mean I'd be worth fifteen hundred of these *sarkis* just on my *potential* as a whore? That's ten percent of all the money we'd need?"

"Damn it all, you're lookin' *pleased!* We're talking men paying money and you sellin' your damn *body!*"

"Yeah," she responded, still sounding more amazed than shocked. She realized how terrible she sounded, but she had never been considered pretty or glamorous before, and she had always thought of herself as something of the Ugly Duckling that grew up and turned into the Ugly Duck. The last time she'd gone to bed with a guy she'd gotten a Big Mac, fries, Coke, and mountains of fear and guilt the guy didn't have to deal with at all. The idea that men would pay her, and big, was too ego-boosting for her to dismiss even though she knew it was wrong. Jeez! Kligos shells out fifteen hundred and makes it back in—what?—fifteen days? Impossible. Then he has her for, like, *years*.

Boday couldn't help but interpret Charley's reactions, and smiled. "She is impressed, yes?"

"Yeah," Sam growled, feeling *very* uncomfortable. Damn it, she thought she *knew* Charley, and first this thing about killing and now she's actually impressed by her price. "But to just sell your body . . ."

"Oh, it's not merely *that*. Sex is cheap!" Boday noted. "Boday's creations are no common *tramps*. Not *her* creations! It is an *evening*, with men, perhaps one, perhaps several. Impressing and entertaining business clients, you see. You receive them, prepare and serve a meal that they pay for additionally, then you might entertain—sing, dance, whatever. Make them feel good, feel important. Your client might wish to be bathed, or massaged. Whatever. If he wants sex, you give it to him, whichever way he wants it. He might not even want it. He might just want a sympathetic ear to tell his problems to who'll treat him with sympathy and respect. In the end, he pays you the hundred, maybe more—sometimes much more— if you gave him just what he wanted. It is never quite the same."

"Sounds like Japanese geisha girls," Sam noted. "Still, it's a form of slavery, damn it. Selling your *body* and mind and soul, doing whatever they ask. . . . It's *degrading*. It's bad enough with all them damned potions but at least they don't know what they're doing. Charley would."

But when she translated it all for Charley, the girl with the butterfly eyes nodded, lips pulled in, thinking. "Two hundred days," she said, more to herself than to Sam. "Eight months, tops, and we'd have more than enough without starving—if this guy Boolean's in no hurry."

"*Charley!* Stop thinkin' like that, damn it! You gone completely nuts? Did she give you some of that brain potion anyway?"

Charley stared at Sam. "So what do we do? Hide out in some miserable safe place for two years waiting for your girlfriend there to turn enough new innocent young girls into love slaves so we can go on their blood money?"

"Yeah, if we have to. I mean, they're lost balls anyway."

It was Charley's turn to be appalled. "Listen to you! And *you* called *me* hard!" She took a breath and calmed down. "Look, I'm not sure deep down that I like the idea, either, but you got a better one? If it could be done without this Kligos getting involved . . ."

"Charley! Do you know what you're *saying?* You, the big feminist? Do you know what it'd *mean?* Are you really thinking about that? You're talkin' 'bout servin' and scrapin' and bowin' and maybe *fucking* up to sixty different guys! Maybe gettin' gang banged or worse!"

"Yeah, I know. But it's no feminist thing. I mean, it's a service industry and the money I earned would be for me—for us, not for some corporate pimp. And it's not like getting raped or anything. I mean, it's *my choice*. Maybe I'll hate it. Maybe

I'll regret it to the end of my days. Maybe I'll come back and beg for the drug that makes you forget you're even human. But you got a better solution?"

"It's out of the question! It's—*indecent!*"

"Hah! Look who's talking! You just figured on letting *her* turn like a couple dozen girls into this against their will and for life! Sam—she's nuts but she'll do anything you say. You can save lives with a word, but if you do—then what?"

That stopped Sam for a moment. Finally she said, "But you don't know how. Or have a place, or a wardrobe, or whatever."

"I have a feeling Boday could mix up potions to do temporarily what the others do permanently, and she can teach me. If it came down to it, you could use that thing to hypnotize me, so I'd be just right, and it'd be willing so there'd be no problems with my head gettin' permanently screwed up. And if ten thousand will buy all that, I bet your two or three hundred would buy all the wardrobe I needed."

"I think your brain's pretty screwed up now. Damn it, do you realize what you're almost *begging* me to let you do?"

"Yeah," she sighed. "I do. And I can't believe I'm actually arguing it this way. But—what other way is there? You gonna rob a bank with your magic jewel? I bet they have spells you wouldn't believe on those banks, and it's sure a neat way not to draw attention to yourself. What kind of job you gonna get honest? You may look like a real strong boy but you ain't. I know what you can do. Look at me. *Look at me!* What the hell else can I do in this crazy place? I can't ever play 'respectable' in this burg. Even if one of them robes or dresses or saris covers my body my butterfly eyes and permanent jewelry mark me. I saw the way they looked at me and treated me just in that small town we stopped at. And even if I could somehow mask it, I don't speak the language! I don't speak any language around here. I'm like stuck in ancient times, and the only way I can be a plus and not a minus is like those early ancient women did in the mighty hunter, male-dominated societies. Charge 'em for the only thing I got that has any value."

"I—I can get some kind of job. Anything's better'n that."

"Yeah? What kind of job? We already agree you can't do heavy work, and while you can speak the language you can't read or write it. This may look like a cross between Shakespeare and Robin Hood but it ain't, pal. It's as modern in many ways as where we came from. You don't read or write or have a skill you're up the creek. What's the next idea? Have Boday make up some real strong drugs you can sell to kids?"

"Charley, I—"

"You can go anyplace in this big city. I'm 'beauteous property' wherever I go, and just one look says it. Face it, Sam! We ain't going nowhere without the money and I'm the only one in this group who can get it without exploiting innocent people or stealing it. Maybe I'll be disgusted. Maybe I won't be able to go through with it. I don't know. But right now it's the only thing we got."

Sam, appalled and confused, appealed to Boday for help and alternatives, but she wasn't much good.

"Face it, lover. Why fight it? If she wants to pull in the money then there is more time for *us*. Boday can manage it. It would be nice to see the complete work, too. But if you say no, then it's no."

Sam didn't know what to do but she was still looking for excuses. "She couldn't work out of *here*, or even this district! Kligos would be bound to find out!"

"Oh, piss on Kligos. Boday has many friends and art lovers among the merchant and even noble classes. Many of them would *love* this sort of thing but don't want to be seen down here or are just too scared to come. So we set her up in a nice apartment in a good neighborhood. Boday will decorate it just so. She has often been pressed by people who know her who are upset at enriching the likes of Kligos and his ilk to do something like this but up until now she was not interested in money or business, only art. I will teach her the Short Speech which anyone can learn. It is all they expect a courtesan to know—in speech. Kligos will probably never know, but even if he finds out he will think it is someone at the Palace's doing. And you will stay here with me and we will check on her."

Sam, grudgingly, told all this to Charley, adding, "But you'd be a prisoner in this place. You'd be there, night and day, for months, and I don't think they invented TV here even if you could understand it. And we can check on you and keep you supplied but for safety's sake we'd have to be here, not there. You'd be alone and not even able to call me for help."

"I'll survive," Charley responded. "It's better if we separate. No ideas putting us together. And the time we need should work out, too. Nobody keeps a roadblock and teams of searchers on for months. They'll figure we got out by them somehow and the search will be elsewhere. It's the only way, Sam, considering the circumstances.''

Sam sighed. ''All right, but I got a bad feeling about all this. Damn it, it's *me* they want. I feel like it should be *me* doin' this if anybody does. Go back to bein' a woman and let Boday do her thing on me.''

Charley smiled. ''You're just jealous. No, Sam, it's because they want you that it's gotta be me. And if I'm ever gonna get home again, or even back to me again, then I got to get to that sorcerer, too. This isn't just for you, Sam. It's my only way out.''

The next few days seemed more unreal than real to Sam, although she spent much of it sleeping and regaining strength. The knot on the head went down, until there was only a slight scar from the sapping on the street, and the Jewel of Omak reported that its power was back up to strength, which gave her a real sense of security. Just where it was getting its power from she never thought to ask.

Boday continually attempted to seduce her as well, and she was a pretty easy mark for it considering how she felt. The mad alchemical artist was in fact an artist in all things, including that, although some of the things Boday came up with were more bizarre than anything Sam had imagined. She simply gave up and gave in, partly out of guilt over Charley and partly because she just needed *somebody*. She was getting to be fairly experienced in sex, though, and she still had never had a man and had no idea what it was like. She wondered if she might be gay, but she reserved judgment until the opportunity arose, if ever, to find out if she was or not. She certainly hadn't met very many sexy or attractive men so far.

Watching Boday work was also fascinating. The range of miracles that she could either lay her hands on or concoct in her lab seemed beyond belief, but it wasn't hard after a while to understand how she could make hair grow and change color and even self-streak in a matter of hours, or create an environment where the very bone structure could be expertly manipulated and altered—such as she'd done in altering Charley's overbite to make it sexy rather than intrusive.

Sam had instructed Boday specifically to do nothing more to Charley that was irreversible. That is, that couldn't be undone and Charley brought back to her normal old self. Boday noted that all of the commercially available formulas had absolute antidotes; it was only her special blends that conferred permanency by altering the standard formulas. Thus Sam watched, fascinated, as Boday did to Charley exactly what Sam had gone to so much trouble to prevent, only this time with antidotes available. The result was the same, of course; failing those antidotes, Charley would remain Boday's remade creation.

First was the potion that wiped out all memory, anxiety, inhibition, and fear. She became a wide-eyed, staring, baby-like blank, but she was eager to learn and all that she was taught she grasped quickly. Boday began by teaching her the Short Speech, which was actually a soft and very primitive subset of Akhbreed with certain clever alterations and a lack of any tonalities or subtleties. More interesting, it had only the present tense and mostly second person at that, so that one who thought only in it would have an ego that was always the reflection of another. Charley learned what she was taught while under the potion's influence, but exhibited no curiosity to learn any more than she was given. Without a conscious, repetitive effort to teach, she simply did not learn at all no matter how obvious something was.

By the end of three long days it seemed impossible to Sam that Charley would ever become more than a wooden, childlike puppet. Sam couldn't stand it much anymore, and, following Boday's leads and contacts and with Boday's money, she spent some time exploring the city and ultimately finding an apartment in one of the tall downtown towers with a fine view of the palace, Government House, Royal Gardens, and the rest. As a male, she had considerable freedom to roam and see what the place really looked like, and it was impressive.

There were shops, large stores, bazaars, you name it, there, including many specializing in things from the sectors, the "nonhuman" regions of Akahlar. Many were practical items, some were particular kinds of clothing and materials, perfumes, luxury items of all kinds. The shopping district was divided into single product neighborhoods where everyone sold much the same thing in hot competition. Sam bought a great deal of material at Boday's request to form Charley's outfits, and also discovered that there was a whole industry devoted to very sexy and risque woman's fashions—"for home and husband," of course. There was even a small street selling

magical things—amulets, charms, potions, you name it. Some
magicians advertised that they could weave practical spells
"for business and industry alike," or so the pitchmen proclaimed.

Remembering the jewel's caution about the illusion and
magical powers, she had shopped for and bought several
comfortable but concealing male outfits before venturing onto
that street.

By now she was known to the watchmen as "Boday's new
sex interest" and had no problems going in or out, even with
bundles, although she discovered that men do not help other
men who are overburdened with packages like they help
women. Men, in fact, treated each other far differently than
they had treated her even back home, and she also found by
discussions with the guards that men's talk covered a very
different range than the sort when women got together, most of
it very boring and of no interest to the listener.

Charley had still been mostly a dull-eyed automaton by the
end of the third day, so it was a shock to see her near dark at the
end of the fourth day. She stood there in the studio, a vision of
ethereal beauty, dressed in a flowing blue dress of wispy
material that showed her entire perfect body through the gauze.
She seemed alive—full of life, and almost supernaturally
gorgeous, the eyes lively and attentive, all of the moves so
damned sexy it was turning Sam on just to watch her.

Charley gave Sam a sexy smile and bowed slightly, hands in
the prayer position. "We greet you, our lord," she said in a
soft, seductive whisper. "How may Shari serve?"

Sam dropped the whole bundle of stuff and then heard
Boday's joyous cackle. "Darling!" she cried and ran to Sam,
hugging and kissing her and picking her up almost off the floor.
"Isn't she *wonderful?* Isn't she just simply *marvelous?* Boday
knew she would be good but even she had no idea how simply
stunning it would turn out! Tomorrow she will learn the
technical fine points and then she will be ready! Boday took the
liberty of giving a decorator her sketches, so the day after
tomorrow we can be in *business!*"

Sam just stared at Charley, all sorts of thoughts and emotions
jumbled up together inside her, many in conflict with each
other. One, however, was very personal and more than a little
jealous. *That's my body she did that with! I could look like that!*

Still, another part, from the guilt corner, snuck in and

snapped her back a bit. She was both fascinated and awed by the process, but there was still a strong part of her deep down that made her feel like a common pimp and degrader of women.

"You're gonna keep her like that? So she don't even remember she's Charley?"

"Oh, darling, but of course! Any other way would be a *crime*, not only because it would of necessity spoil the creation but also because it would not be a mercy to *her*. Right now, she will do what she must do willingly, with no guilt, no regrets, no afterthoughts, no reservations. All of her day will be spent preparing for her evenings, and she will get better as she goes along. The more clients, the more perfect she will become, and single-mindedly, to the exclusion of everything else. Look at her now—she barely exists. She exists only through interacting with another. She exists to give pleasure, whatever is required. We will move her in and complete the training there—a few days at best. Then we will look for art lovers."

Sam was feeling pretty queasy about all this, even though Charley had asked for it and she'd argued against it. "You're sure it can be reversed? That we can bring her mind back?"

"But, of course! Do not worry, Boday's sweet flower! Did you not command it? Did we not discuss it with her? It is arranged. In a month it wears off and she will remember everything. Then she decides. To take the potion some more or to come running back here. Every month after she will decide again. It is a pity if she ruins it, though. She is so *perfect*. Well, no matter what, Boday owes you even more for kicking her into this. Never before has she also designed the *setting* as well as the jewel. It is a new challenge!"

Sam just stared at Charley and licked her lips. *And will you be sickened when it wears off?* she wondered. *And will you hate me and yourself for it?*

With the year-long apartment lease, the decorating, the clothes for Charley and for Sam, and the supplies, they'd blown all of Boday's two thousand, and most of the change purse as well. If this unpleasant idea did not make money, they were in a hell of a fix. Charley, damn it all, had to start earning their keep.

· 8 ·

Of Decadence, Demons, and Brassieres

THE PROBLEM WITH decadence is that it is based on decay.

The last of the money went to set up a payment mechanism that would distance both Sam and Boday from Charley just in case anybody in the district thought to check on the new competition, and to arrange for various supplies and services—Charley might well be expected to cook for clients (Boday had taught her three meals which she did exceptionally well), which meant food and beverage had to be provided, and there would be the laundry and cleaning bill. The services were easy to arrange but they could only scrape up enough to prepay ten days' worth. If more money wasn't coming in by then, it would be all for nothing.

Boday did manage to use her contacts to start the ball rolling, but there were only three customers the first week, then five the second. As word of mouth spread, though, and Charley gained practice, things picked up. Still, most of the income was plowed back into the services, leaving little for Sam and Boday. Neither of them had any real business sense, and they had underestimated the start-up costs of even this sort of business and with all the intermediaries doing the work it left them broke and with nothing at all to do for a solid month. Not that they starved, but they wound up buying food that was cheap and easily spiced to disguise its cheapness and they ate a lot of fat and starch.

Sam literally had nothing to do and no place to go. The city offered plenty of diversions but almost none of it was free and Boday was rather limited in the circles she could travel in. With no TV, no radio, no money to go out, no reading material she could read, Sam found herself basically trapped in the loft with Boday who similarly had nothing to do, since Sam, honoring Charley's wishes, had forbade the artist to take any more live commissions and Boday wasn't much interested in the old forms which she dismissed as "dull" and "passe." Not that Boday minded; anything she did was fine so long as it was near Sam. That potion was potent.

By the end of a week Sam was willing to do most anything for a diversion, if only to keep from thinking of Charley over there in that apartment, and Boday had an almost infinite mind for diversions. Sam resisted, though, figuring that if Charley could make this kind of sacrifice she owed it to tough it out for a month after which she was convinced that Charley would be coming back. That left baking and eating the sweet breads and confections that were the easiest to make from their limited grocery budget, and, eventually, letting Boday play out her perversities, which seemed infinite. Boday, after all, was a master teacher of courtesans—and consorts, too—and she knew *everything*. At first Sam was nervous, then repelled, but eventually she found herself drawn to it by sheer boredom and Boday's persistence.

And, after a while, Sam just didn't have reservations anymore.

It was Boday who'd taken the love potion, but that did nothing to dim her dominant personality or to change any of her ways. In the hands of a love object who was equally strong she could have been curbed, restrained, even radically changed, but in this case her love object was a confused, lost, lonely, bored seventeen-year-old girl with little experience and waning self-confidence while the potion-obsessed lover was strong, domineering, experienced in many ways, including the manipulation of others. It wasn't like the fairy tales where the taker of the potion became the submissive love-slave of another; in this case, the tables were turned as the single-minded lover more and more dominated the object of that artificial love.

It wasn't quick; it was a slow, bit by bit breakdown of Sam's old morality, her self-image, her attitudes and behavior. Charley could have stopped it, but when the month passed and the runner informed them that the little vial had been accepted and later picked up empty and that Charley was still there and still the same, it all crumbled. Sam had hoped at least that

Charley would have sent word before taking the potion again, that they could have seen each other, talked. When that didn't happen, and she faced months of unremitting boredom in the loft with Boday, all resistance crumbled. She even gave in to Boday's pleas and allowed the artistic alchemist to begin doing commissions again, even eventually helping out.

But now the money rolled in. Boday was delighted to get an accounting, and drew some of it for fine food and new fashions and a bit of celebration. Their standard of living improved and they even went out a bit, although Boday was clever enough to understand that Sam was best kept on a tight leash, with bright little magical toys a nice reward and diversion, and new clothes for both in the loft and outside for Sam, who no longer even cared what she looked like or how much she ate. At the start she'd tried some diversions like asking Boday to teach her to read the Akhbreed language, but after only a couple of weeks she'd given up. It was like ancient Chinese—almost a character for every word in the rich and colorful language— and she'd never been much good at memorizing anything. She tried art and sculpture but she was awful and she knew it and again quickly lost heart, and any attempt to figure out more than the bottom line basics of alchemy just made her dizzy. She finally simply gave up, and it was the last crushing blow to her ego.

With one day looking much like another and one week looking much like another, Sam lost track of time completely. There was supposed to be an end to it, but the end never seemed to come, one day looking exactly like the next. Boday, quite satisfied, was arranging things, and Sam, so that such an ending might never come and this could go on indefinitely.

Only the nightmares and visions remained uncontrolled. They were infrequent and came at odd times, but they were particularly virulent during times of storms on the waterfront. Twice more she saw the horror of the changewind in remote places far different from Tubikosa, and many more times she was back with the Horned One again, this time watching dark armies grow secretly composed of hordes of mostly nonhuman creatures, some of which were horrible indeed just to look upon. They were secretive, training in small groups all over Akahlar, but for what she did not know.

But every time she had such dreams Boday would be there,

soothing, calming, often with a dream of elixir that induced sweet dreams without thought.

It was late one night when Sam awoke and struggled sleepily into the bathroom. She was having a very bad period, with the worst cramps and heaviest flow she could remember, in spite of Boday's potions that were supposed to keep it from noticeably happening. She made her way to the sink and turned on the small light, then looked at herself in the mirror as something twinkling caught her eye.

It was the Jewel of Omak, and it was shining. It was such a startling, unexpected thing that she frowned and stared at its reflection—and was caught by its beam. Suddenly she was immobile, unable to move or react, and the magic jewel spoke to her mind.

You are now pursuing a course contrary to the interests of Boolean as well as yourself, the jewel told her. *As per my instructions in this eventuality, I must take independent rectification actions. Henceforth you will see yourself clearly as you have made yourself. Henceforth, the drug action will be negated. I will take the appropriate biochemical measures to insure that this brings clear thinking and not suicidal depression but you will not like yourself. What you do for your own appearance and self is not my concern, but I will now intervene. You now have the means. You have had the means for some time. You will proceed to carry out Boolean's wishes. The trip to the university is optional, but you will no longer be permitted to act in a manner not calculated to bring you eventually to Boolean's presence. If you do not do this then I will take command. Boolean requires only your body, not your soul. Protection of the body and its delivery to Boolean alive is the only directive. Demonstration.*

She suddenly felt as if she were falling down a deep well, swirling around in the water, falling, falling. . . .

And then she saw again, but not as she had ever seen before. The image was low, somehow, and it was two-dimensional, slightly distorted, with the middle of things seeming close up and then everything else going away in the distance on both sides. It was a washed-out, strange-looking, ugly vision of herself in the mirror, but she could still see her face, distorted by the contorted lens, if she looked up. It was all she could do. She felt disembodied, a mind without a body, only a single, imperfect eye. There was no pain, no pleasure, no sensation at all.

"Now you see," said a strange, horrible, lifeless voice from her own lips. "My energy comes from the soul and the spirit of the bearer. I do not take much; you never miss it, but it bonds us together. The jewel and the bearer are one."

There was a dizzying sensation as her body turned and the single image whirled for a moment before stabilizing, although it was a bit shaky an image. Now they were in the apartment, now the lab. She turned and walked up to the three-way mirror and her entire body was reflected back to her.

Seeing herself clearly and objectively for the first time in a long while was a shock. Not that she didn't know; until now, it somehow hadn't been something she cared about. Her hair had grown back in well; it was still short but it was now substantial and more or less at an asexual length for this culture. Still, it seemed a lot longer than it should have considering how long it took hair to grow out.

But, lord! Was she *fat!* She hadn't really looked in this mirror in a very long time. Mostly, she hadn't wanted to. Her grossly fat-swollen breasts hung down over a massive beer belly; her arms and legs were very thick, and she had an ass the size of Chicago. Her face, too, showed the weight, and she didn't have to look down much to show a double chin. And this had started with the same body that had created Charley.

It was as if everything within her that was pretty and gentle and nice had gone with Charley, leaving her with the grotesque remains.

"See what you have made of yourself," her body said in that same inhuman whisper. "The same body that your friend has kept beauteous beyond compare. The same body that made three-meter jumps to sneak in here that night and was agile and strong enough to climb drains and move silently across a sloped roof. You are the same one hundred and fifty-seven centimeters, but you weigh one hundred and eleven kilograms. This body grows weary climbing the stairs."

The figures were a shock. *One hundred and eleven kilograms—let's see, each was two point two pounds. . . . My God! I weigh over two hundred and forty pounds and I'm just five-two!*

"No, I weigh that. You weigh under four hundred grams," said her body.

I—I'm in the Jewel of Omak! she suddenly realized. *I'm in the jewel, and whatever thing that dwelled here is now in my body!*

"Yes, quite correct," responded the image. "You thought of me as a computer, which was all right, so long as everything went well. I influenced you and your friends as needed to accomplish the primary mission. I am no computer, Samantha Buell. That is of your world, not of mine or my master's. I am what you would call a demon."

Oh, God! A demon! Visions of Hell and creatures with horns appeared in her mind from her old upbringing. *What have I done? Have I lost my soul?* Suddenly she felt anger. *You! You convinced Charley to do what she did—because it was the only way to get the money!*

"She might have done it anyway. She was inclined that way. I think you know your friend less well than you think. I merely made it easier for her to decide. Just as I used what little strength I had for your charge at Boday, so it would strike perfectly to knock her down. Just as I put the idea in your head for the love potion, since we needed an ally. Just as I put how to do it in Boday's mind. I did not mind your lapse into decadence so long as there was nothing else to do, so long as resources were building up. I fear we demons have rather a taste for decadence. But I am bound to enforce my master's will. That is why I am in the jewel and he is sitting comfortably in Masalur. I do not even particularly like him, but greater power always commands lesser power in all things. I am a lesser power to him and so must obey. You are a lesser power to me. Just as I find being in a human body but with such restrictions repugnant—but if I must possess you, then I must. But I would rather we had an understanding."

You—you have been controlling all of this?

"Naturally, up to a point. Did you think under the circumstances that you could have even survived unaided here for long? I made certain that, when he discussed betraying you, Zenchur spoke Akhbreed, to warn you. When you proved too immature and nervous to act or even plan a course of action, I waited. Do you really believe that one of Zenchur's experience would use the jewel while facing a mirror unless he somehow was prevented from considering that possibility? Do you think you would have had the presence of mind to duck?"

But you let him betray Charley and kidnap her! You could have stopped it!

"Yes, but I have no interest or instructions on Charley. She was not anticipated. Zenchur was a sincere hope, and so long as he did not betray *you* there was no reason to act. When he did, I intervened. Now I must intervene again. Do you like your body now?"

You know I don't! I'm huge! Ugly!

"The outside merely manifests the inside. You have let Boday take over and dominate your mind. You have become complacent with perversity, you have lost your sense of self and purpose. You have betrayed your friend who sacrificed for you. You did not lose your soul. You gave it away."

It was Boday!

"Boday can do nothing that you do not allow her to do. This time could have been put to productive use. You started to do so, but you did not really want to, and at the first sign that learning was work or the first mistake in learning you seized as an excuse to give it up. It was incomprehensible to me that one who would risk everything and sacrifice all to save a friend would have so little sense of self-worth. Your friend was willing to voluntarily lie and be servile to a hundred men or more because she understood that it was the only way to her own goal, to reach Boolean, to get out. To attain something worth attaining, one must sacrifice, do whatever is necessary. She understands that. But you! You never had any goals. You never really succeeded in anything. Charley was the only backbone you ever had, and you used her and wound up dragging her here. Without her, you switched to Boday. Only one thing keeps me from taking complete command, imprisoning you in that bauble and remaining here, possessing your body. Just once, in your whole life, did you have a real goal that did not concern yourself. Just once, you put aside all thoughts of self and risked everything for someone else. I provided the physical stamina and the knowledge and skills needed, but it was your will that used it. I did not send you to save Charley from Boday. That is not my affair. I provided the resources, but you provided the will."

Sam felt very ashamed of herself right then and there. She wanted to cry, but jewels don't cry, or feel any sensations at all. *What would you have me do?* she asked the demon.

"The object was to gain the financial resources to undertake the journey and perhaps acquire some of the skills needed. You have it. In spite of Boday's lavish attempts at spending it down. How long do you think it has been since you abandoned your friend?"

Total confusion. *I—I don't know. Four or five months, I guess. I suppose the way you talk it's a year.*

"It *has* been a year. *Exactly a year today.* Boday in fact is in the process of renewing the lease and taking more rooms for more girls. *You* may not be able to read those papers, but I can read Boday. She has plans to make this permanent. She is the one whose elixirs kept you pleasant but which also induce a massive appetite for sweets. At this weight you will take no other lovers, nor have much energy for ambition. You sleep half the time and the rest you lie around eating and doing whatever she desires. You do not vegetate, you have become a vegetable. You have not left this loft in five weeks, partly because, deep down, you do not want others to see you this way. Boday prepares now for her final coup. She is signing the final papers and leasing a grandiose suite near the Palace into which she will move Charley and the last two girls she did here, which were procured for her use, not as commissions. She is confident now. Then your friend's position will be made—permanent. *She* will teach the others and all the ones who come after her. Soon there will be so much money and power she will be able to eliminate Kligos and the rest."

No! She can't! I wouldn't permit it! I told her about Charley!

"Indeed, you have been very naive. What do you think a love potion does? It directs all of the emotional needs, primitive lusts, whatever, toward a single individual. You fall madly in love with that person—but nothing else changes unless that person changes *her*. You, instead, have given her a free hand. She is protecting you, even from yourself. Do not lovers lie to one another? Do not lovers do something against the other's wishes for what they really believe is the good of the other? That is why I must step in. She must not be allowed to do this thing. This must end now. Either you must end it, or I will. The enemy gathers strength. It builds in secret now, so as not to frighten and unite the Kings of Akahlar, but it builds. When it is strong enough it will move, and millions will suffer, and the fate of all worlds will be decided. You are a player in this matter no matter if you wish to be or not. Many of the soldiers and victims in wars are unwilling and even uncomprehending or uncaring, but they still fight and suffer and die. You are a chess piece in this game. Whether pawn or queen I do not know, but you are none the less important, for even a pawn may capture a king."

I will handle it! I will stop it! I swear to you! I'll kill that bitch!

"No. If you handle it, if you stop it and redirect it, it must be with thought, not emotion. How will you bring Charley back without Boday? How will you access the funds and find the personnel needed and chart the course? She is corrupt. Use her, and prevent her from using you." The demon sighed. "I sense you need some incentives of your own to match your friend's. If you do not act now, your friend is lost. That is the first incentive. Once you recover her you must not be turned again from the objective." Her own brown eyes surveyed her body in the mirror.

"It is fitting, even useful," the demon said, mostly to itself. "The male illusion was for the purposes of disguise but it would not have held up on the trail in any event. It has taken some of my intervention to hold *this* long. But no one, absolutely no one, would recognize you now. I give you back your body, until such time as you give me cause to seize it again. But I also give you my curse. I cannot in any way alter your true body and part of my charge is to prevent that from happening, but *this is* your body, and so it will stay, regardless of spell or potion or three weeks in the wastes without food. If need be the fat will be useful in an emergency to convert to muscle, say, but it will return when not needed. This is the way you will see Akahlar, and this is the way Akahlar will see you. A perfect disguise without illusion. Oh, I will give you strength when needed and undo some of the effects on your mind that keep it dull and sleepy, but this is the way you will look—until you stand face to face with Boolean. And you can look at Charley and think of what might yet be, but only if that meeting comes."

No! she cried from her prison. "Wait!" she finished aloud, in the body. She was back, staring at her reflection in full command of it all, her mind clear. She hated that reflection. She felt the weight, the pressure on her back and ankles. Those huge, sagging, floppy breasts hanging down to a stomach that looked nine months pregnant and wasn't, and a lower body that seemed all rear end. My God, she looked old, too. A lot older.

Still, her mind was clear and the body obeyed. She wasn't gonna be running any races but she felt new strength inside her.

Still, she looked—*gross*. In more ways than one. It would *take* a love potion for anybody to love *this* body. But the demon was correct—she hardly recognized herself. And yet, the demon had been absolutely right. She *deserved* this. Without that damned demon it would have all gone on as scheduled, irreversibly. She was ungainly, obese, ugly—she would have to earn redemption.

She walked to the door of the studio and looked out. Dawn looked to be just breaking. There wasn't a lot of time, and whatever was to be done had to be done quickly. First Boday had to be stopped and brought to heel. Charley had to be sprung, everything then redirected to the journey. This was no time for a test of wills with Boday, although that would surely come.

She fingered the jewel. "All right, demon," she said, "let's put your powers to emergency use." She walked into the bedroom where Boday was sleeping, stood beside the bed, and took the jewel in one hand, aiming its growing light at Boday's head. It struck, and there was that sudden slight stiffening, but Boday was still asleep.

"Boday, can you hear me?"

"Yes, darling! Boday hears," came the sleepy reply.

"Is it true? Were you going to give the permanent potion to Charley and set up your own business? Answer me!"

"Yes, darling."

"Why?"

"Because Boday lives only for you and fears only that you will desert her. This way you will never leave Boday. This way Boday can have you to herself forever."

"No, Boday. If you did that I would never forgive you. I would leave. I would kill myself rather than live with that. I wish you would believe that."

Done.

Boday's eyes opened. "But she has already *done* it!" she exclaimed, sounding horrified. "Boday sent the potion over today so that she would be ready for the move."

"What! Oh, my God! Demon, your clock's off, damn it all! Boday—get up! Put on some clothes that will get you to Charley's place and then wait for me." She turned on the lights and searched through the drawers. Damn! Would *nothing* fit any more? She found some stretch tights that threatened to strangle her lower half or fall down but they had to do. The top was a joke, barely reaching her navel, but the hell with it. Boday had several wrap-around capes that might help. Fitted properly they barely covered her back and went down to the floor, but turned sideways and pinned a black cape made a sort of poncho. It would do. With some difficulty she managed to pull on a pair of the short, soft leather boots, but they pinched like hell. The hell with it!

Boday pulled on a robe with hood and her long leather high-heeled boots. She put up the hood, which covered her head as per regulations and also shaded her face.

"Get some money!" Sam snapped at her. "Then get me to Charley as fast as possible at this time of the morning!"

Dawn was just breaking, but there was always some business in the District. Boday spotted and hailed down one of the horse-drawn three-wheeled cabs and they got in. "Sikobo Royal Tower," Boday ordered, "and quickly!"

The driver was used to picking up strange-looking people here and taking them at top speed back to higher neighborhoods. They also usually tipped real well. He made damned good time, but Sam used it for questions she didn't like the answers to.

"When did you send it over?"

"In the morning. When Boday went to the market."

"Then she's had it most of a day. Did she have any clients today?"

"No. There are never clients on potion day, and none tomorrow, either."

"Then we might be in time. She might not have decided to take it yet."

"No, darling," Boday sighed. "We are too late. In the past she has always had a day to think it over, but the potion she had last time is not due to wear off until next week. She was still Shari, and the bottle had Boday's seal on it and the messenger was told to tell her in Short Speech that her mistress wanted her to take it. Boday did not want her to choose this time. The new set-up would already be in place and she might balk. She took it. There is only 'now' to such as her. She would obey immediately."

"Damn it! *Nothing* is a hundred percent permanent except

death. You made the stuff. Somehow you can make a way to undo it!''

"Darling, there is not. The brain is like Boday's file cabinet. The top drawer is Charley. The next drawer is Shari. The soul is the person going to the cabinet. With no potion she can go to either one with ease. With the regular potion she is able only to open the Shari drawer, but the other drawer is still there. With *this* potion all of the files in the Charley drawer are taken out and burned. Erased. They are no longer there. Only Shari remains. She will remember every bit of being Shari from waking up blank, so to speak, in the studio, but nothing else, not even the in-betweens.''

"If that's true I'll kill you.''

"Boday will willingly die for you at your command.''

And that was the trouble, damn it! There was no satisfaction in this. No satisfaction at all. There was absolutely no way Boday could be punished, not really.

There was a doorman at the Towers, but Boday knew the password. He looked at Sam with gruff disapproval but he let them in. There were two elevators of sorts, but they were of a very odd type, with no doors. They ran all the time, very slowly, and you just waited, stepped on when a floor presented itself, and rode it up until you stepped out fairly quickly onto your floor of choice.

Boday jumped off and Sam followed, falling slightly and hearing a nasty tearing sound. The tights collapsed around her thighs, but she didn't care any more. It was the second door on the right. No key would be needed—the door was always open for the service people.

"How long does it take to work completely?" Sam asked Boday.

"You slip into a beautiful, dreamy sleep for twelve hours, darling. Then the new you wakes up.''

It *was* a gorgeous apartment and quite luxurious. Each room was different but all was styled to match Charley's own features and design. They passed through the living room, dining room. Sam stopped at the entrance to the small kitchen, reached in, and picked up a bottle next to the sink. A little gold bottle with Boday's seal—and it was opened and empty! She threw it against the wall and rushed back to the bedroom, which was dominated by an overlarge heart-shaped bed.

Charley lay asleep on the silk sheets, naked, and Sam was

struck once again by how absolutely beautiful she was. Even
her sleeping position, and the expression on her sleeping face,
was sensual and erotic.

"Charley! Wake up!" Sam shouted. The sleeper shifted
slightly but did not respond. Sam turned to Boday. "Wake her
up!"

Boday threw back her hood and knelt before the sleeping
figure. "Shari. Shari, love. Awake. Thy mistress commands."

Charley frowned, moaned a bit, then opened those big eyes
and saw Boday. She smiled. "Shari greets thee, Mistress," she
said sweetly if a bit sleepily, and sat up on the bed.

"Oh, my God! We're too late!" Sam cried and started
sobbing uncontrollably. Charley looked at this stranger and her
eyes widened a bit at the sight, but she remained passive and
blank. "Mistress want Shari give comfort?" she asked inno-
cently.

But Boday was still hypnotized by the jewel and couldn't
respond to anyone but Sam. "Oh, God! I'm sorry, Charley!"
Sam sobbed in English. "Everything I do turns out wrong! All
I do is hurt people! I'm not fit to live!"

Charley looked at the stranger and frowned. "Jesus Christ,
Sam! Is that *you?*" she exclaimed in perfectly understandable
English.

"Yeah, it's me," Sam sobbed. "Big and fat and—*what did
you just say?*"

"It *is* you! Jeez! I didn't recognize you! How the hell did
you get to look like *that?*"

Sam was in shock. "But—but—you're talkin' normal plain
English! You sound like yourself! The potion—it was there! It
was empty! I—"

Charley yawned. "Sam, if I'd known it was you I wouldn't
have put on Shari. What's the big deal about the potion?"

Still shaking and sobbing, Sam managed to tell her the story.

"Shit! Good thing things turned out the way they did, then."
She looked at Boday. "She's hypnotized, huh? Well, leave her.
Come on up on the bed and get hold of yourself. Jeez! I been
wondering if you'd *ever* show up!"

It took some time for Sam to get a grip on herself, and when
she did it was true confession time. She told Charley
everything—all of it, right down to the demon and the curse.
Charley just nodded and shook her head. *God! She was
beautiful!*

"Sam, you can't completely blame yourself. You can't. Damn it, you just weren't prepared to grow up so quick." She sighed. "I guess I was."

"But the potion—how did you . . . ?"

"Sam, I didn't trust her from the start, but I knew it had to be done. I figured she was too loopy yet to pull anything, so I went along with all that back in the loft. But when it wore off, I sat there and I thought about it. I thought real hard about the life I lived for those first weeks. Then this nice girl, maybe all of fourteen, dressed all in white, you know, with the mask and all, came by and delivered the little jar of potion. I looked at it and then I came back here and I lay down right here and I went over every single day of 'Shari's' life and every one of the clients. It was easy to do—there isn't a whole lot there, you know, in memories, but there's more otherwise than you think. A lot more. My first impulse was to send the bottle back when the cleaning people showed up, which would be the signal to come pick me up, but I couldn't bring myself to do that. Then I opened it and looked at it and knew I couldn't bring myself to take it, either. I left it there in front of me and thought some more."

"Why didn't you just get out of here?"

She sighed. "Sam—that was the thing. I didn't *want* to go back there. I—this may be hard to understand—didn't want to give this life up. I'm sure it wasn't any of Boday's tricks. I *liked* being Shari. I used to lie in bed some nights and fantasize about this. Being beautiful, glamorous, sexy. So beautiful that men would pay a fortune for just my company. It was more of an Arabian Nights meet Las Vegas kind of fantasy, but this was *it*."

"But all those *men* . . ."

She smiled: "Yeah. I always figured if I ever did wind up like this I'd get the bottom of the barrel types—ugly, middle-aged, stinking breath and drooling, the whips and chains types. But they weren't like that. It was more like my fantasy. Some were middle-aged, sure, and some were younger, but they were mostly nice-looking men with good jobs from their looks and manner. Successful types with something missing in their lives. All of 'em probably had those forced blind marriages. Hell, some of 'em were so inept in bed you kind'a wonder if they had *any* sex life before. Some wanted a few things—oral stuff, mostly—I guess they just couldn't get. A couple of the young ones, I think, wanted some experience before they got married so they wouldn't seem fools. More than one just wanted to be babied, or hold someone. It didn't go all the way every night. One guy just clung to me on the sofa out there and talked and talked and finally cried his eyes out. That's all he wanted. Didn't make no difference I couldn't understand but three words he said."

"Jeez! That's *weird!*"

"No, just a little sad. They had no place else to go, nobody to unload on, to get the tensions out. Oh, I'm not saying there weren't a couple with odd wants in sex, but I kind'a liked that, too. I sat here and I realized that I really liked the sex. But the main thing was I was doing something these guys needed and they were willing to pay top money for me. *Me!* I knew I should feel real guilty about it all, but I just didn't. I still don't. So, finally, I poured the potion down the sink and washed it away and decided I'd try it cold. I just wanted to see if I was really nuts."

"Yeah?"

"It was better. With a little practice I discovered I could shift to Shari, actually thinking in that language, and just tune out and go along for the ride. But it was easier with the whole me there. I could figure out the clients better, give them more of what they wanted and maybe some new things, too. In a way, I turned the tables just like Boday did with you. I was in control. I could handle the bad ones cleverly without pissing them off and I could give the good ones extra. And when I got off, I *really* got off! Weeks went by and I still wasn't tired of it. I'm still not. But it was kind'a dull on the off days and in the days. I wanted a way to get out, to be *completely* in control of my destiny, and I figured it out. It wasn't that hard. They paid the money to the account, right? I never saw that. But they also left tips—bigger tips after I stopped the damned potion, if you want to know. Every day the White Virgin would show to collect, but I knew she wasn't no unmarried virgin. In fact, I ain't even a hundred percent sure 'she' was a 'she,' and that gave me an idea. So I started holding out on the tips. Didn't take long to build up a nice little nest egg. I knew the golden ones were the sarkis and I could count."

She got up and walked to a closet, opened it, then went in. Sam followed, not quite over the shock yet and not knowing what to say.

In the closet, a walk-in type, were lots of sexy outfits all designed for Shari, but well in the back and hidden was another, which she revealed and brought out. It was a white robe, white hood, and face mask.

"I knew that my collector couldn't be real. No self-respecting girl of that status would be seen *near* the docks or the District. I didn't know much of the language, but it wasn't hard to get the message across with gestures. If she or he or whatever would get me an outfit like that and not tell Boday or anybody, I'd give her a small fortune. She didn't even wait til the next day. She had the outfit back that afternoon. The first day off I had I put it on and walked out and went down and walked around the block. It was a *wonderful* sense of freedom and total anonymity. I was a little worried at first that the bracelets on my arms would give me away or that somebody would notice the earrings under the hood but nobody ever said a thing. The hair was a bigger problem. I had to let it go down under the hood and then down so it was completely out of sight, but then I had troubles sitting down. You learn."

Sam listened, feeling more ashamed than ever that she'd allowed herself to, well, vegetate was the right term, while Charley was figuring.

"After maybe three months," Charley continued, "I had lots of money, freedom of movement, and with a lot of concentration I picked up enough of the language to make my wants known. I don't speak it, really, but I can understand a lot of what's said if I really concentrate. I always was good at languages and I didn't have much else to do. Reading's different—they have like *thousands* of characters—but I know the most common ones, like which is the ladies' room and 'store,' 'restaurant,' and stuff like that. I bought different foods to try, got a bunch of nice other things, and after I spotted a couple of the goons who'd mugged us staking out this building I bought a knife and a blow gun. The blow gun's neat. But they never came in. I figured, though, that was why you never looked in. I didn't *dream* you were having such a bad time. When the time passed and there was a tenth little bottle—I kept careful count—I figured the heat was still on or maybe expenses were high. I really didn't care. This was the best time I had since getting sucked into this place." She paused, and added, in a slightly more distant tone, "It's the best time overall I ever had in my life."

She looked at Sam and then kissed her gently on the cheek. "Poor Sam! Well, your demon's right. I kind'a think that neither one of us come close to the descriptions. You know, I wonder what Boday could do with you as you are?"

"Huh? Charley—look at me!"

"I know, I know. I don't mean body painting, and I don't mean me, but maybe she can make the best of a bad situation. We have a ways to go."

Sam stared at her. "Charlie—you just finished soundin' to me like you don't wanna go, don't wanna give this up."

"I don't," she admitted, "but you need me. You don't *know* what this has done for me, Sam. But, anyway, a girl can't operate independently in this society, and you need Boday. Don't hate her too much for this, Sam. She did it for you, but she also was kind'a being a secret revolutionary. Women would control all the vice in this town, top to bottom. That's power, Sam. And influence, if you know the names of the ones who use it most. Come on—get out of that ridiculous set of tatters and tell Boday to go to sleep in the corner, then get some rest yourself. Order her to wake us up if she wakes up first. Once we're rested we can find out how much we're worth and go from there."

Sam stripped, which wasn't hard and gave great relief, but she didn't just sit Boday in a corner. She used the jewel.

"Boday—I wish that you would be totally obedient to my needs and wishes," she said. "I also wish that from this point on you will be incapable of lying to me or to Charley, of doing anything concerning me or Charley without telling me first, and that you will obey any order that either of us gives to you. I wish that from now on your sole interest in me will be satisfying my desires, not anticipating them."

Done! said the demon, and there was a bit of satisfaction in its usual cold tone.

Boday was not exactly a changed woman when they awoke, and had no regrets, but now she wanted only to be cooperative and promised that she would never *think* of doing something like that again.

She had a perfect eye for figures, even bad ones, so they sent her out that afternoon to find out just how much money they had, to cancel her deals, and to buy some appropriate clothing for Sam while Charley cooked breakfast. Sam did more than clean her plate. In fact, she ate most everything that was left in the kitchen.

Charley watched, fascinated in spite of herself. "How much *do* you weigh, anyway?"

"The demon says about two forty-five. Don't say it. I'm a walking bowling ball with two huge fingers and I know it. I'm gonna eat compulsively and I got to live with it. At least I don't hav'ta worry 'bout my figure."

Charley smiled, but she knew it was killing Sam. It was the perfect demonic punishment. Sam would get to Boolean or die now. Her friend just hoped that the near perfection that would accompany that journey would inspire rather than breed envy and resentment.

Charley had a couple of saris she'd bought in case she had to make a run for it. They were kind of pretty but her eyes and jewelry would mark her, of course, as one of *those* kind of women. She didn't care anymore. Boday returned with a cotton robe with hood that fit loosely and a pair of sandals and a lot of material. "Darling—much more in your size Boday will have to make," she said apologetically. Shari's costumes and few personal belongings were packed in two black bags. The bags were there anyway; Shari, after all, had been set to move. Where they moved was back to Boday's loft.

The account information was not bad, less than great. Between fees and tips Charley had earned in the year more than thirty thousand sarkis, and Boday, with her "art" for others, had brought in another ten thousand and still had two of her creations. Charley didn't like it, but it was too late to do much for them. They would bring perhaps two thousand five hundred more. That was forty-two hundred, and Charley had held out about a thousand, of which she had something like five hundred now. Forty-two five in sounded good. But almost six thousand had gone for Charley's support services, and their initial money had covered only the first and last month on Charley's apartment, and there went another six thousand. The loft had been renewed for another two thousand. Another eight had gone for Sam and Boday's food, clothing, living expenses, Boday's materials, and close to five for a deposit and decorating on the new place. The cash on hand actually amounted to a bit under fourteen thousand two hundred sarkis.

"I can't believe it!" Sam exclaimed. "One whole fucking year and we're still *short?* Not just short—*way* short! Can't we at least get the deposit back on the new place? That'd add another two thousand.''

Boday shook her head. "Sorry, darling. Once the decoration and furnishings were done there was no way out.''

"I could always take the two girls in there and run them with me in the new place for a little while," Charley suggested. "If we ran seven days and all got booked we'd have it in another month. After a year, what's another month?''

Sam sighed. "Yeah, and so we take in eight grand and we spend three on expenses. That makes it two months. But in two months we owe two more grand in rent. Three months. My demon will have shit fits by then, and so will I.''

More delay is unacceptable, the demon agreed. *Money or not, you have enough to start. I will give you thirty days to do so. Every day you are in Tubikosa beyond that you will gain another kilogram. With your height, weight, and frame, another thirty kilograms and you will be unable to walk or get up on your own.*

She was close to tears. "But, damn it, we don't have enough! Besides, it's counterproductive. What does it gain *you* if Boday has to pull me in a rickshaw or whatever—if she could? Besides, I bet I eat fifty sarkis a day worth. That adds to the cost.''

You eat whatever would otherwise be spoilage, but your weight will be maintained if you eat relatively normally. I will suppress hunger until necessary. You are giving up again. Giving up before you even try.

Sam tried to repeat the conversation but gave up and just broke down and sobbed. "I'm so *miserable!*" she cried. "I'd kill myself if they'd let me!''

Charley sat back and thought. Finally she said, "Look, we can probably scrounge up enough stuff by liquidating the new place's furnishings and what has value here. And we can't afford to be fussy about this navigator and these Pilots. We take what we can get for the money, that's all. Calm down and ask Boday what ways we can do this on the cheap.''

The artist thought it over. "The old price was for our own navigator and secure Pilots. If we just sign on with someone else's trip and take it as far as it is going, then found another and so on, and were not fussy about the company or the accommodations, it would be much cheaper.''

"I understood her," Charley said, quieting Sam's translation. "I'm getting pretty good at it. Can't speak it worth a damn, though, except some single words and the Short Speech. I just play mute and communicate real fine. Okay, that's a lot, and we got your demon jewel to help out, too. If it's the one in the all-fired hurry, it should be ready and willing to help pull the weight. So will we, wherever we can. And if we get stuck and broke real close to the goal line, then we can find some kind of work or other. Hell, Boday's an alchemist and you could stomp grapes if you had to, and as for me, I kind'a think that if we're in human territory my special skills are universal. Maybe old Boolean will get antsy and break his tails and come get us or send help if he really wants you, particularly if we get close and no cigar. Cheer up. We may still be on the wanted list but ain't nobody gonna finger us as the ones, and after this long they probably wrote us off."

Sam stared at her. "You make it sound so *easy.*"

"No. It's gonna be hard and nasty and probably real unpleasant, but if it wasn't possible Boolean wouldn't'a stuck you with that demon. Too bad we can't afford to go to that university, though. I bet they could figure out a thing or two and tell us what all this is about, too. I figure I just been to graduate school. I think maybe I want to see a little bit of this world and what's out there."

Sam sighed. "You're not only beautiful, you got the guts I wish I had and the brains to use 'em. God, I feel miserable."

"Hey! I'm scared shitless by this. That apartment—that was *safe* after one hell of a series of scares nobody should have to go through. But I grew up a whole lot this past year and I know you can't keep hiding and feeling miserable for yourself all the time and do anything worthwhile." She looked at both of them. "Three women against a whole world. One fat broad, one lovesick painted loony, and one high-class call girl. It's the stuff of which legends are born. But, first things first. I looked at the material and at Boday's sewing stuff and I got an idea that'll help you a whole lot. I think it's about time somebody in this shitty burg invented the bra."

Boday was actually thunderstruck by the design and the concept. She was built so she'd never need one, and Charley had been designed never to need one, but it wasn't just Sam who did. Charley managed the basic sketch and, with gestures, pretty much described the thing and how it worked. It took some help from Sam, but once Boday got the idea her designer's mind was off in a tear. The first few tries didn't really work—not stiff enough, not enough support stitching— but after a while she got it. It wasn't Playtex or Maidenform, but it worked, relieving a lot of back stress and balance difficulties and revealing inevitable irritating chafing under Sam's pair.

Boday worked like she, too, had a demon pushing her, and after she explained they didn't stop her.

"But, darlings, don't you see? This is *revolutionary!* Think of the market for this in large women in Tubikosa alone! Tomorrow Sam and Boday go back into the shopping district again. She needs more stuff anyway. Only she wears *this* and we take these design sketches and patterns. We show these to the wear-at-home bosses and bluff that we have applied for a Royal Patent. If we can find one run by a big-breasted woman we are home free. Even if it is a man, he will buy it—if only to make certain his competitors do not. Strictly cash."

Sam was open-mouthed at that. Finally she asked, "What could we get for it, do you think? Five hundred?"

Boday laughed. "Boday intends to ask for ten thousand and perhaps get argued down to five or six."

"But—these courtesans are only going for a thousand! You mean the idea for a *bra* is worth more than *human beings?*"

Boday smiled. "Girls are cheap and in good supply. Original ideas that fit a need are very rare. They will be robbing us blind at the price!"

"Wow!" said Charley. "I wonder what they'd pay for tampons?"

· 9 ·

The Long Road to Boolean

IDEAS TURNED OUT to be worth a fair amount at that. Because they insisted on cash or convertibles, they had to take a beating, but they still got more than five thousand sarkis for the bra idea even though it was hard bargaining and Sam for one didn't think anybody was really interested. They got a fair amount of material thrown in, including some nice, stiff, reinforced stuff and heavy-duty threads, and with that Boday, using her strange kind of manual sewing machine and with Charley's help, was able to come up with several pairs that would help Sam.

Sam had never paid a lot of attention to her clothes, even back home, but Charley, it appeared, was something of a would-be designer, although she had to defer in the end to Boday both to make proper patterns and to put them together correctly. The fact was, those super-long glamor nails made much that required manual dexterity not all that practical. That was okay, but it was hard to convince the artist to leave out her own outrageous embellishments.

What they came up with, over a period of a couple of weeks, was an ensemble of clothing not just for Sam but for them as well, since much of what could be gotten off the rack in Tubikosa was pretty dull stuff. The buyer of the bra idea even offered to loan them a couple of seamstresses at low cost and gave them some access to the small sewing sweatshop, an offer they accepted in spite of the fact that they knew the real motive of the generosity was probably to steal designs and ideas for nothing. That was all right with Charley; she thought this place could use a little flair.

They concentrated most on stretch fabrics that would protect but would breathe. The lack of the invention of the zipper hampered them somewhat, but since neither Sam nor Charley, when they thought about it, understood just how a zipper worked well enough to show how to make it, they forgot about it and concentrated on more solid fasteners. With this they were able to make Sam a series of fitted outfits that gave when she did but didn't pinch. Boday's talents were prodigious when doing a fitting; they had the look of one-piece outfits that exactly clung to the contours of the body. That was of little comfort to Sam, whose body definitely didn't need the clingy approach, but it was comfortable, it worked, and, somehow, dressed all in a black or brown outfit, it looked at least reasonable. Charley wasn't satisfied, though, and came up with the idea of a Mexican *serape*—basically a cape-like garment with a hole in the center through which you poked your head. The effect was about as good as you could do with Sam's figure.

Charley was delighted to find that there was an equivalent of jeans here, but, of course, it was men only. It was asking too much even for the seamstresses to come up with custom jeans, but she found some boys' pairs that she was able to have shaped and modified. Those, some tops made out of the same sort of clingy material they'd used for Sam only in brighter colors, and a couple of body suits of the same material for her and she felt she was ready for the trip, too. Nothing she made for herself left much to the imagination of an onlooker, though.

Boday went with her custom leather outfits and long capes. With those on her long, lanky, six-foot-two-inch frame and in the high-topped leather boots with the thick high heels she looked, well, imposing. Charley learned not to be too flip around her, though. When she remarked that all Boday needed was a leather whip, Boday produced one.

The busy whirl of getting ready to go helped Sam somewhat, but not completely. She was still depressed, particularly about herself, and she had such ambivalent feelings around Charley she felt pulled this way and that. On the one hand, she needed Charley badly to see her through all this. Her old friend's take-charge attitude and confident, sympathetic ways were essential. But Charley had changed. She was no longer the schoolgirl chum; she was suddenly wise, mature, very adult, very strong. Sam still felt very much a kid. Charley was beautiful and sexy without even having to work at it much. Sam felt ugly, clumsy, and she had to work at it constantly just to keep doing things. The fact that her looks and weight were not the result of any magic spells or evil potions but were largely self-inflicted didn't help matters a bit.

To top it all off, Charley was a whole lot smarter than she was. It hadn't been obvious when they were just pals together, but Sam had been working at high capacity and Charley had her brains in coast. Now she had learned a language, pretty much on her own, that even Zenchur had said you almost had to be born with to speak. That might have been true to speak it, but Charley rarely needed help in translations to understand what was being said now. The plain fact was she was *smart,* and no magic spell made her that way. Back in junior high, when Sam was trying to get into a special course she really wanted, one of the guidance counselors had looked at her record with her mom there and all and said, "I'm afraid that course load just might be too much for her. I know she reads all right and her grades are good, but she's at her maximum capacity now and it wouldn't be good to frustrate her when she's doing so well. Her IQ is a hundred and she's doing exceptional for all that where she is. Don't be upset—it's average, just not exceptional." And she'd looked it up and discovered that "average" was a hundred to a hundred and ten, so she was just *barely* average. And she'd just sorta quit after that, because what was the use of knocking yourself out when you were damned stupid? And what the hell did straight *B*s mean if it was in a class of stupid kids?

She didn't *feel* stupid, but maybe stupid people didn't feel stupid. So what was the use of trying? Mom was a lawyer and Dad was a contractor, but maybe she just didn't get the brain part. Charley had seemed a kindred spirit at a time when her folks had split and she'd moved. Hell, they'd liked the same things and really hit it off. But now she realized she never really knew Charley. Maybe Charley hadn't really known Charley, but she sure as hell wasn't "barely average."

She loved and needed Charley, but it was impossible not to hate somebody like that, too.

And she'd been afraid *Charley* would hate *her!*

At first, Sam was pretty self-conscious when going out. She wondered what the warehouse people would think when they saw a girl instead of the guy but nobody seemed to bat an eyelash. Sex changes weren't exactly the rule in Tubikosa, but these guys had been around the place so long they just weren't surprised by anything that came out of Boday's place.

On the street, even dressed in the conventional, "respect-able" ways, she felt everybody would be staring at her, that they'd be thinking "Look at the tub of lard," but the fact was nobody gave her much notice and people she had to deal with treated her as a normal person. After a while the worries simply faded. It was true that no guys were whistling her way or putting the make on her but they never had before, either. Her self-consciousness vanished quickly and she felt much better. In fact, with that out of the way, it was a relief. No more play-acting; just be what you were and the hell with it. Somehow, some of the tension she'd lived under since running away to the mall seemed to vanish with that acceptance.

Arranging for transport was done through halls of the Royal Guilds, no matter what your class or status. Instead of trying to hire a navigator for a special trip, though, they looked over the list of trips to see who was going where. Even though Sam couldn't read the lists, she knew each squiggle beside a number squiggle was a trip and there were *hundreds*. Boday *could* read them but they didn't help much. Nobody was going all the way through to Masalur and most of the destinations meant little. Boday was a native of Tubikosa; her odd accent was mostly put on while she studied at the university and just stuck, and that trip had been her only one outside her homeland. Maps appeared useless on Akahlar; they had to see a Guild dispatcher.

It was decided that they wouldn't ask for a direct trip to Masalur; the odds were if Boolean were really dangerous to this enemy, whoever and whatever it was, they'd be specially interested in *anybody* out of the ordinary who booked to there. It made more sense to book to Covanti, the halfway point more or less, and then take stock from there. The university was out of the question; they were now reasonably flush but not that flush, and they had wasted too much time. The demon was uncharacteristically neutral on that, but Sam wanted this *over* with and the distance was still huge.

Although class and social rules meant nothing to navigators, who'd seen and done it all and disdained most local customs, Sam found it fascinating that even the dispatcher basically addressed *her* as the leader or spokeswoman. Perhaps it was because she was wearing one of those stock sack dresses and a scarf and had on no makeup or jewelry and thus she had to be the leader because she was "normal." If only they knew!

"I can't get you to Covanti directly for another six weeks," the dispatcher told her. "Tubikosa only does some seasonal business with them, and a minor flurry of changewinds have made the direct route too risky anyway." He showed them a map that showed the hemisphere with Tubikosa in the middle, but showed only the hubs in detail. The rest were blank, the hubs looking like the center of flowers surrounded by petals.

"Now, then," he went on, "the only reasonable route is southwest to Mashtopol, even though it's a little out of your way, then northwest to Quodac, then up to Covanti. I can get you to Quodac with no troubles, and I'm sure you can get something from the Guildhall there to get up to Covanti. That by-passes the unstable regions. You say it's three women traveling in a group?"

Sam nodded. "Just the three of us. But I don't like it. We're adding a lot of distance and extra expense that way."

"Well, I can get you a break on the Tubikosa to Quodac leg since it's related to poor conditions, but your supply budget and time will be greater. If you wanted to change navigators at Mashtopol and were willing to have as much as a week's layover there, we have something going tomorrow. If you want it through to Quodac it'll be leaving sixteen days from today. Your share of the navigator's fees plus the Pilot's charges would be—thirty-five hundred sarkis for all three, plus supplies. That's to Quodac. You are advised that this paticular route may be hazardous."

Buddy, you don't know what hazardous is, Sam thought sourly. "How long is it to Quodac?" she asked. "As opposed to direct to Covanti?"

"It varies," the dispatcher told her honestly. "but the average straight through, before the troubles, was fifty days direct, give or take a few and depending on local conditions. Now it's about sixty. Quodac should be about the same—closer to fifty than sixty, I'd say. Another thirty or so to Covanti depending on how long you would have to wait in Quodac for a trip. It's not great, but it *is* a safer route these days anyway. You get stuck in a sudden changewind and you wouldn't ever be able to come back to a hub."

It was a good enough argument. "All right, then. The one sixteen days from now is best, I guess. How do we work it?"

"You fill this out. If you cannot read I'll fill it out for you and take your mark. Then you pay me fifteen hundred cash now, with the balance due to the navigator directly when you start your trip. I'll give you a list of basic supplies you'll need to buy and your routing when you pay me."

She nodded. "This woman will pay you and fill out the form," she said, nodding to Boday, who took the paper and an inkwell-style pen and started in on it. Another of Sam's discoveries made her feel less inadequate about this. The damned writing language was so complicated that very few people could read any old book, including Boday. You learned what you needed for your profession and for functional literacy. That was Charley's discovery as well. The practical vocabulary of most people in day to day life was at best a few thousand words; the rest were used only for more specialized things. There were lots of people who never could manage much reading even in Akhbreed society, and deliberately so. Outside of royalty, the better you read and the more you could read the higher you could rise. That meant that even the lowest might rise close to the top if they were smart enough. That was one reason women, even low in status, ran a lot of the stores.

Boday read the form to them. "Names, ages, sex—Boday always wants to write 'yes' in there—spouse, clan, and occupation. Nosy, aren't they? Well—Boday is easy enough. She is thirty-one, female, artist-alchemist, she has renounced her clan before they could renounce her—*peasants!*—and what is your real name, my love?"

"Samantha Rose Buell, but do we hav'ta put that? It's kind'a a giveaway of me bein' from someplace not usual."

Boday thought a moment. "Then why not Susama? An odd name but not a bad one. Boday has met someone of that name before and it will let you keep using 'Sam.' We will make you of the clan Pua'hoca. It's a big sector clan, so big the name is used if one does not wish to give a real one."

"Like Smith or Brown back home," Sam understood, nodding. "I once knew a guy really named John Smith and nobody ever believed it." Good. That gave her some legitimacy—if she could remember the damned name.

Charley looked over their shoulders. "Uh—I can't read this

stuff, but the mark under 'spouse' is different for the two of you. What did you put?''

"Why, darling, Boday puts Susama as her spouse and Boday as Susama's. Her legal name would then be Boday Susama, and Sam would be Susama Boday.''

"Hmmm . . . Won't that cause some problems or raise some eyebrows?''

"Not at all. Is the law of Akhbreed. If you cohabit in all ways with one partner only for a year and a day you are legally married under the law. In fact, we should register it.''

Sam didn't like that. "What are you trying to pull now, Boday?''

"Boday is serious. You are a woman. Your age is eighteen. You do not wear the white nor live with family and you are listed as apprentice to Boday but you have no husband and there is no records on you except cohabiting with Boday. Marriage to a citizen is the only way to get travel documents unless you are *sent* someplace by authority as Boday was sent to university. You are obviously no courtesan. It is the easiest way out without getting into a lot of very fictional stories that might betray you.''

"Yeah, but—in this straight a society, what will they say if you registered two women?''

"The law was designed for foreigners, but with an address in the District it will not be disallowed. And once we are on the trail it will not be questioned. Things are different out there. Trust me, darling! This happens more than they want to admit, particularly with men.''

Sam looked at Charley, who shrugged. "I don't know. I keep feeling she's pulling something again, but she's also right. If they allow it, then you're suddenly a somebody instead of a nobody and that'll keep things even less suspicious.''

This time Sam decided to take no chances. She turned away from the busy hall and pressed the jewel against her. "Demon, is what she says correct?''

She cannot lie to you. Yes. It is legal and the easiest way to get total legitimacy as if you were a native. It completes the disguise.

"I'm not gonna be stuck limited to just her by this, am I?''

Question interpreted and understood. If married people could not and did not cheat here there would be no District and no business for those like Charley.

It was a good enough point that she decided to do it. The hell with it. After the last year it was nothing more than the truth, and, considering her looks, it was Boday or nothing anyway.

For Charley they put down "Shari, 18, female, no clan, Beauteous Property under contract to Susama and Boday." There wasn't, after all, much way to hide what she was.

They paid the money and got the supply list. Boday read it over as they walked from the Guildhall to the Royal Ministry of Records. They got a lot of stares from the city crowd, with Charley getting the most from both sexes, but aside from treating them like they had leprosy the others gave them no problems. Sam was glad they were blowing this kind of place.

"Boday thinks we should get a wagon rather than horses and pack animals," the artist said. "You are not much good riding horses, you say, and this will be just as good. Besides, a decent one will provide some cover in bad weather. No sleeping out under the stars, either. The basic foods list is manageable and we can take more than that if we pay a bit for preservative spells. It is worth it—you never know what you might have to eat out there. Clothing—jackets. We will have to pick up some jackets. And perhaps hats and gloves. Tubikosa is always very warm but there are cold places out there. And Boday will take an alchemical kit. Not bad. Ah—here we are. Here we will register and then use the certificate to get the documents. 'Shari' is already registered, of course."

The marriage registrar looked more bored than shocked, although perhaps it was because of the looks of the women in there. "You swear that you have cohabited for a year and a day or more and that you have during that period been intimate with each other and with nobody else?"

"Yes," they both answered. Sam felt uncomfortable with this but she could see the practical reasons if they allowed it. This sure as hell wouldn't be allowed back home, but here it was actually a law!

"Dip all five fingers in this solution and then place them where I point on the document," the registrar instructed. The stuff tingled, and when Sam pressed her fingers on the paper there was a hot sensation. It made a nice embossed set of prints, though.

"You understand that this pairing is unorthodox and by registering it the Kingdom does not imply that it condones or approves such unions but that it allows this only to ratify an existing fact so that legal ejudication of disputes, property, powers of attorney, and so forth can be maintained in an orderly manner," said the registrar in a tone so routine and bored it sounded even more soul-less than the demon.

"Yes," they both answered.

"Dip both palms completely in the solution and then place palm against the palm of the other," the registrar instructed. "If you have sworn falsely to this you will feel a painful shock at the end of this."

Some kind of truth stuff, Sam thought. They really wanted to make sure of this. Of course, it protected the pair, since if they'd cheated it would tell, but it also forced a somewhat embarrassing admission in public and on the record that indeed you had sex with another woman. She and Boday pressed palms.

"Say aloud your given name and then the given name of the other," the registrar said. "Be exact, for from that point on that will be your only legal and true name."

"Susama Boday," she said, and Boday said, "Boday Susama." There was a sudden but not unpleasant shock and their palms were stuck together for a period. Sam felt a little dizzy and seemed to black out for a moment, then it was gone except for a slight headache. They let go, and the registrar stamped the document and then gave them a certified true copy.

They left and went out into the main hall. Sam was mad and Charley saw it. "Got you *again?*"

"I don't know. Damn it all. Oh, I don't *feel* much different, even about her, but—it's hard to explain. I'm *really* married to her. It's a spell or something. I can't shut her out, I can't really act without considering her. It's not sex. Nothing like that, although I can't deny her her rights in that. But, somehow, a tiny part of her is inside me and I guess the other way around. I could fool around all I wanted to but I couldn't be not married to her as long as she lives. I can't dump her, run away from her, or shut her out. And I'm Susama Boday. Everything inside me says that that's me. Damn it, demon! You said she wasn't pullin' nothin'!"

She wasn't. As I said, it was the easiest and best way. You need her to survive, to read, to protect. From my point of view it completes the disguise in an almost iron-clad manner so long as no one runs a skin or hair sample or something like that—and why would they? Even under truth potions and spells you will say that you are Susama Boday, legal consort of Boday Susama, and she the same. You cannot slip anymore. All you need is to take care to use English sparingly and you are beyond suspicion. She now has a tiny bit of your soul and you have a tiny bit of hers. Since it is your body, not your mind or soul that is required, this was a permissible deviation. You will never miss it, but it is vital. Even some magics will be fooled. Do not worry. I assured you that you could cheat, didn't I? And thanks to the potion, she won't.

She growled but said nothing. This damned demon was her master, and that was the most galling part of all.

The marriage document smoothed the way for her to get whatever legal documents she needed, though, just as promised. Boday showed her how her name was written in Akhbreed script and it wasn't all that complicated, but it saved a lot of time. The full documents would have to be picked up in ten day's time, the usual bureaucratic thing, but they issued her a citizenship and identity card. For the first time she could open or close an account, sign or make contracts, and have all the legal rights of a citizen. Socially and religiously, of course, she was an outcast, but legally she was a real person in this world. The most unsettling thing of all was the near reversal when clerks and others dealt with them. *She* became "Madame Boday" and Boday became "Madame Susama." Sam was still Sam, of course, but the trouble was she had no problems knowing which one they were speaking to, and it was aggravated by Boday's new use of "Madame Susama" to refer to herself—still in the third person, of course. That got to her and she blew her stack.

"Boday! You're still Boday and I'm still Sam, okay? Now cut out the Madame crap!"

And to her surprise Boday responded meekly, "Yes, Sam."

Sam thought long and hard about herself over the next few weeks, and about the other two as well. After all her fantasies and play-acting at being a man, here she had a chance to be legitimately butch and she found she didn't want it anymore. It hadn't been the fun of her fantasies at all. Maybe it was the spark of Boday inside her that got all the right things in balance, but she wanted to be all woman now. She shaved her arms and legs, took some time styling her hair, and applied a little perfume and makeup.

The link with Boday also gave her an odd sense of security and identity that somehow hadn't been there before. She no longer cared what other people thought; the vision in the mirror no longer repulsed her, it just *was* her. The reflection became her identity. She had no illusions that the shape with the monster tits and ass and the two spare tires was gonna knock 'em dead and drive men wild, but she didn't dwell on it anymore, either. It was sure as hell a body that *two* men wanted on this world, two big and powerful ones. And even some of her resentment of Charley faded as she stumbled into facts she simply hadn't considered. It had come out of a very simple situation.

"Hey—the bags and trunks for the trip are in," Sam said to Charley. Boday was off pricing other stuff and shutting down her interests, such as they were, and without her Sam was stuck with a splitting headache and no alchemical remedies. "I just can't make it now."

"You kidding?" Charley replied. "Sam, I can't go out alone. Not unless I pull my virgin trick and around here that's a sure way to get yourself snatched or arrested."

"Huh? Why not?"

Charley sighed. "Sam, *think*. Both you and Boday are full citizens of the master race here. You have rights and separate identities and can come and go as you please. Sam, I'm *property*. Legally I belong to you and Boday. Oh, they go through this contract business because they don't allow slavery, but that's just a sham. Legally and officially I have no rights at all. In fact, under this law I'm treated as if I were a baby, mentally incompetent to make any decisions for myself. It's illegal for me to own anything—even the dresses and stuff. It's illegal for me to have money, let alone spend it. It's even illegal to give me anything, or even to talk to me or me talk to them, without your permission. In fact, it's illegal for me to be out of my quarters unaccompanied by a responsible citizen who's either you, Boday, or somebody delegated by either of you. It's even illegal for me to use anything but the Short Speech, although in your company and outside the earshot of strangers they can't do much. My prints and documents are on file this way and have to go with me. Didn't you *know* that?"

"Uh—no, I didn't. Jeez, Charley—that's the pits. No *wonder* you didn't want to stay here."

"Well, it would just have been a matter of transferring my

contract to somebody else, but I couldn't be on my own. In fact, if I fail to act within the law, even to the slightest degree, then the punishment must be a public whipping by my—contractors. You or Boday. A real one, too."

"Come on! I could never allow that!"

"Then if you couldn't you forfeit your contract and I'm either sold to the highest bidder around who has to do it or I must be put to death. I like being taken around to all these places but I got to be on my best Shari behavior. Didn't you even notice how I opened the doors and stuff like that?"

The truth was, Sam hadn't. "Charlie—the only way anybody'd know is if somebody told them, right? I mean, Boday has the eye makeup and more body painting than ten of you."

"And she has to show her citizen's card a lot, too, and she doesn't even look the part of a courtesan. I do. Boday also reads, writes, and speaks the language and I think she's a known character in this town. I'm not supposed to—and I don't. Oh, maybe I could get away with it once, but if I got caught the penalty is too much for the risk. I kind'a hope that once we blow this country the laws won't be all that strict but, face it. Those other places aren't our kind of people, and the Akhbreed system, I think, is pretty consistent in its basics. Oh, I understand there are some places where the girls are loose and high fashion and maybe even some where they run the place, but there are men of my status, too, remember. I think there's a certain—standardization—in the basic system no matter how different they are. I'm resigned to it. I envy you your freedom here but we have to take what we're dealt and make the best of it."

Sam looked at the stunningly beautiful woman who none the less was an alternate version of herself and couldn't believe it. "*You* envy *me?*"

It was inconceivable, yet, the more she thought about it, the more obvious what her friend said was true. Charley liked being a courtesan, it was true, but if Sam was as smart and pretty as Charley and had the kind of adventurous spirit Charley had and found that the price of being a courtesan was irretrievable slavery . . . Well, maybe. Damn, this was a lot more complicated than it looked.

All of the documents came through, and they went shopping for things on the list to take with them—other than food, of course. That would come last, as it must. Somehow neither

Sam nor Charley had envisioned this trip as Wagon Train, but that's pretty much the way it looked. Oh, the wagon was oddly styled and had fancy suspension and a comfortable driver's seat, but it was still a covered wagon. It was not pulled by horses, either, but by odd-looking animals called *nargas*, which looked like a cross between a big mule and a humpless camel but tan and white striped like a zebra. They were strong if not swift, could survive on almost any known grasses alone, and if need be could go without water for up to ten days. They were tough, muscular bastards not native to any of the hubs but an import from one of the sectors, but they were highly recommended for wagon travel. They had long, skinny, snake-like tails with big tufts of tan hair at the ends that they carried looped up on top of their bodies most of the time—but you found that those tails were *very* prehensile and that a favorite narga sport was to swat you hard in the behind if you had your back turned to them. Apparently they thought it was funny.

The wagon was cleverly designed. You carried most of your stuff in compartments underneath, putting only what you needed every day inside. The area behind the seat was lined with a soft, thick material like a mattress, and another compartment came off the back end when stopped and turned into a kitchen-like area, although, of course, you had to build your fire on the ground away from the wagon. It had compartments for carrying water and two more for wine, and it also had a small box with a cut-out that was sort of a toilet, although it appeared that whatever you did in it just dropped down onto the road.

"More like an early American Winnebago," Charley commented.

They also bought a sleeping bag—it was as roomy as it could be but kind of cramped sleeping for three, although in really bad conditions it would do in a pinch—and some cold and foul-weather clothing, giving in to Charley's pleas in her case to buy her a fur jacket. It looked like mink and was pretty well styled, but if it was, then mink were cheap and common around here. Sam finally found a sheepskin coat, man's type, that fit even if it did come down to her knees, and Boday, of course, stuck with leather.

Charley was pretty good at helping them hitch up the team and showing them how to drive the thing. She'd driven buckboards and hay wagons when still a kid at her relatives' ranch where she often spent the summers, and she knew most of the tricks that also proved true for nargas. "By rights and status I should be the driver," she told them, "but I don't dare. It's not possible for beauteous property to get or wear glasses and they never invented contacts here. Neither Boolean nor Boday was able to change my nearsightedness. It's not awful— I can see to the lead narga, but beyond it's just a blur."

Sam hadn't considered how little change had really been necessary in Charley to make her look a twin. "I'm still farsighted," she told Charley. "I guess I figured you were, too. Since I can't read this stuff I haven't really thought about it much. I know Boday's got decent vision so I guess you teach us to drive this thing. At least you know how to hitch 'em up and unhitch 'em, and the care and feedin' and all. They seem to like you, too."

"Yeah, we got things in common. We both got the same owner, we're kind'a pretty, we go where we're told and we don't own nothin'."

Buying the food was the last thing, and it was a real expedition, although there were a couple of companies specializing in this sort of outfitting who even had magicians in their employ giving preservative spells, then packing it all nice and neat and stowing it in the wagon. Counting what they would have to give the navigator the next day, their fortune was already down almost seven thousand. They did a final check to make sure the expedition was really kicking off the next day— delays were the rule—and found it on schedule. The navigator had been vacationing here and so was starting fresh.

All three of them were excited by the idea, if a little apprehensive. They were setting off in near total ignorance of their destinations on a trip few generally took who were not in trade, finance, politics, or the military and diplomatic corps, and they hadn't the slightest idea why or what might await them at their destination.

The square in front of the Guildhall looked like a scene from an old western movie in spite of the alienness of the buildings and setting. People scurried here and there, there were a number of wagons laden with who knew what, and men on horseback looking like they were out of an old cowboy movie, hats and all. Somehow, both Sam and Charley had thought of the navigator as a single individual, a guide or something like that, but clearly this was part of a company. The actual navigator was a middle-aged man with thick, long gray hair and a white, neatly trimmed beard dressed in buckskins with fringes and, of all things, a buckskin tan top hat! He gathered all of the people around who would be making the trip other than his "crew"—all apprentices only a few of whom would ever make navigator.

He went around to each in turn, introduced himself as Gallo Jahoort, although his crew and most others addressed him as "Master Jahoort" in respect for his position, checking travel documents, and collecting and counting the money. He didn't blink an eye at Sam and Boday, although he certainly spared one for Charley. She gave him the shy, sweet smile and he almost forgot his count. Charley, for her part, appreciated the reaction. She had learned that power came in a lot of unexpected forms and it was nice to see she had it.

That finished, Jahoort gathered everyone around. "All right—first things first," he bellowed in a loud, booming baritone that could probably be heard through a thunderstorm. "How many folks we got here who never been in the bush before?"

Several, other than just Sam and Boday, raised their hands. Charley, who wasn't supposed to understand this, just kept smiling sweetly.

"All right. Today we're gonna start gettin' some practice and see where the weak links lie," the navigator went on. "It's a hundred ninety-two leegs to our jumping off point but it'll still be country riding for the most part. We want to average sixty leegs a day minimum, but we should do much better while still in Tubikosa. In three days we'll be at the border, and the next mornin' we're gonna cross into buffer null and make the first sector. I'll tell you more about that when we get there. For now, we have three days for breakdowns, for findin' out you got clipped, your horses or nargas are all geriatric cases or psychopaths, your food's spoiled, you don't know how to build a campfire, and you forgot to buy toilet paper. Once we cross, it's too late to learn that. Me and my crew will be checking on everything, seeing that it's all in shape for the trip, teaching you what you don't know, and all that. But once we start this mornin' we ain't gonna stop. If we can't fix it and you can't get it on the way, we're gonna just give you a refund and leave you here."

He paused to let that sink in. Charley found she couldn't

follow much of what the man was saying, so she surveyed the others who would be coming along. They were mostly men but there were a few women, too, none it appeared unaccompanied by men. She made it as four wagons and six on horses with pack nargas. The half dozen or so tarp-covered flat wagons were obviously some kind of trade goods going from here to somewhere else on consignment. This was after all a shipping company. There were even a couple of kids in one of the wagons. The boy looked to be thirteen or fourteen, the girl maybe nine or ten—getting close to the time when she'd be putting on white and being segregated. Tubikosans had a certain look about them and most of these people and most of the crew didn't have it. There were almond-eyed Oriental-looking men, although a lot bigger than she thought of Orientals as being, some with brown skin, some with olive skin, all sorts of hair, and lots of different features. Clearly the Akhbreed encompassed a lot more than one race as she understood race.

The crew of about a dozen men looked rather young and even dressed in their cowboy outfits they almost seemed to be boys playing at cowboys rather than the genuine article. Some smoked and a few had beards but that didn't change the impression. Apparently the buckskins were the uniform of navigators; only Jahoort wore them, as Zenchur had.

One fellow who was making the trip on horseback with pack narga looked familiar. For a while she wondered if he hadn't at one time been one of her clients, but it didn't seem like it. She would have remembered that outrageous moustache.

And then she had it. It was a long time ago and almost a lifetime away, or so it seemed. In the tavern in that little town they'd stopped at with Zenchur. He hadn't been wearing a black trail outfit then; he'd been dressed like some kind of rich Shakespearean character, and he'd been talking to Conan the Barbarian with the wristwatch. It had been a short period of time and long ago, but she was dead certain it was the same guy. Both Sam and Zenchur had thought he was making some kind of shady deal with the big Neanderthal in skins. She wondered what he was doing here—and if it was a coincidence. The odds of them ever meeting again, let alone under these circumstances, were pretty damned slim. Of course, if it *was* him it just *had* to be coincidence, no matter how remote. They looked nothing like they did then and if he knew or even suspected that they were the two girls old Horned Head was looking for and knew it well enough to make this wagon train, then he would have known where they were all along and turned them in long before.

Still, he would bear watching.

The train was organized by the crew, and they moved out slowly and carefully, taking the lake front route right past Boday's old loft warehouse and continuing on even as they began to leave the city. Sam looked at the warehouse a bit wistfully and saw that Boday had a slight tear, the first she'd ever shown. "Regrets?" Boday asked, looking at Sam. "Boday can still cut that damned thing off your neck and we can go back, you know."

Sam shook her head. "No. I already had that once. All I got was boredom and two and a half times my weight. Any future I have is straight ahead."

She knew that what she said was true, but there still wasn't much enthusiasm in her for this. After all, Charley really just wanted to stay here and keep at her—trade. She had done it initially because, as the demon had said, it was the only way possible to get home, but now Sam wasn't all that sure Charley wanted to get home. As for her—what was so big about getting to this sorcerer, anyway? Seeing how this world worked, it was just as likely he wanted to use her body in some kind of human sacrifice or something as anything else. She sure wasn't vital enough for him to take no risks. All the risks had been theirs. Back there she had rights now and a name and place, somebody who loved and watched over her while making few demands, and, now, a friend to talk to when need be. The only thing was, she didn't love Boday, although she'd gotten to know the crazy artist so well that she had a lot of affection for her in spite of her treachery and her numerous faults. All she really needed was to take some of Boday's love potion herself and they'd live blissfully ever after.

And she'd been tempted, too, particularly during those terrible months of sloth and drifting. She wondered why Boday hadn't figured that one and slipped her some potion during that time. The demon, probably. Protecting her by putting the thought out of Boday's mind every time it surfaced.

The pace was slow, stately, but deliberate, and men rode up and down keeping everyone and everything at the proper distance and pace. There were a few problems, mostly with the wagons or with improperly tightened cinches or unbalanced loads, but these were quickly and professionally solved.

That night they camped in a farmer's field by prior arrangement. Charley built the campfire expertly and did the cooking and serving and it was probably the best in the train by far. Charley, as was custom, ate apart from them and by herself.

While camped the crew dug a pit toilet that had little modesty but some remoteness. The hole-in-the-wagon approach just wasn't that practical while standing still. It was while Boday was over waiting her turn after dinner that one of the crew came by. He was a good-looking guy, at most in his early twenties, with a full but short-cropped brown beard, long, trimmed curly hair, and built a bit burly but not at all bad. Charley, watching from the other side of the fire, thought he had a cute ass.

"Hello—Madame Boday, isn't it? I'm Crindil. I wanted to check and see if there were any problems today we missed." His voice was a pleasant middle tenor, and his accent was sort of folksy, although not so much as Jahoort's.

Sam smiled at him. "*Sam,* please. It's so much better than Susama or Madame Boday. No, no real problems that I know of, but it's early yet and I'm always the one for problems. Will you have some of this? Shari is a superb cook and if somebody doesn't eat it I will and the last thing I need is more food."

He looked at the dish and smelled it. "Oh, I don't know. I always liked women with some extra paddin'. There's more to look at and like." But he took the rest and started in on it.

Sam knew a line when she heard it but it didn't make it any less effective being exactly what she wanted to be told. She knew he was probably angling for a crack at Charley but she found herself instantly attracted to the man anyway. "You're kind to say it, anyway."

"No, I mean it," he responded between bites. "Uh! That girl of yours is one fine cook and a pretty good rigger, too. That was the best-rigged team we had today and it was taken down just as good. But, gettin' back to the subject. I never met a lady with weight who didn't think she was ugly, and I never met a woman without a weight problem who didn't think she had one. But, uh—you really married to the tall woman? I mean, *married?*"

"Yes," she admitted. "But it's not quite how it looks. I was lost, penniless, stuck, in the city through circumstances I'd rather not describe, and I wasn't exactly built for *her* line of work." She gestured to Charley. "Anyway, there was a kind'a freak happening—Boday's both an artist and an alchemist—and Boday accidentally swallowed some love potion she was making for a client. I was the only one around when she came to, and you can guess the rest. I had no place else to go and no other alternatives."

Crindil looked at her with an amused expression on his face. "Well that's the damnedest story I ever heard. Love potion, huh? So you sorta got trapped into it. And you married her to get a new citizenship, a new start. I can see that." He put down the now empty dish and got up and sighed. "Well, that's real interesting. I'd like to talk more but I got more rounds to make and duties to perform. Maybe we'll have a chance to talk again on this trip. How far you goin'?"

"Well, we're supposed to be going to Covanti. Your guild recommended this route as safer, if longer."

"Yeah, well, it's sure longer. Then you'll be with us all the way to Quodac. Well, we'll have plenty of time then. Nice talking to you, and my regards to your—wife? Maybe I'll talk to her, too. We often got use for an alchemist out there. And don't you listen to nobody else on your looks. For the record you're kind'a cute."

She smiled and got up and was startled when he took her hand and kissed it. She felt almost an electric shock at the gesture, and her eyes followed him off to the next campfire. God! He was charming! Ten minutes and he'd bummed a good meal and had her swooning over him like she never did with a man before.

Charley came over to collect the dirty plates. "Real Romeo," she whispered to Sam as she cleaned up. "Three women alone and he's drawn like bees to honey the first night. You watch out for his type or you'll wind up givin' him the money and me in the bargain."

"You're just jealous 'cause he came on to me and not you." She paused a moment. "I never had a guy come on to me before."

"Oh, he was lookin' at me. He'll seduce you to get to me, if you let him, though."

Sam felt a flush of anger. "Just do the dishes and shut up!"

"Yes, Mistress. Y'm," Charley said mockingly, but she didn't press it.

Boday returned and sat down. "Sorry to be so long, darling, but while waiting over there at least three men came to Boday wanting to know if they could have a bit of Charley. Peasants, mostly. They offered little. The first one, the big fellow with the beard, Boday deferred to you."

Sam suddenly felt angry and betrayed. Deep down she'd known all along that Charley was right but she didn't really want to have it proved to her. She got up and walked to the side of the wagon, out of view of the other two, and felt the Jewel of Omak against her breast, and she thought of its power so seldom used by her. The demon *owed* her for what it had done to her. She had the power to have any man she wanted no matter how she looked or sounded. Up to now all her sexual experiences had been with women. Maybe she *was* one of "them," and if so, that was okay—she certainly enjoyed it. But there would certainly be differences with a man. Big ones. Hell, Charley had done it with her in the shack and Charley was a real man-lover. Charley's power was beauty, but she had power, too. She was through being a patsy. It was time for Sam to take a little.

From Zenchur's cave to the city had been only forty miles or so; the trip to the border where the train would leave Tubikosa was maybe a hundred in the other direction, counting having to go around part of the big lake. The trip was already just starting to settle into a big and potentially boring routine when they reached that border.

Tubikosa ended in a flat plain here, but it still gently sloped down into that glowing mist. It had been so long since they had seen it that it was almost like seeing it for the first time. Tubikosa was a mixture of the primitive and the modern but it was still a large, cosmopolitan city. It was easy to forget that it was such a small part of a new and very alien world rather than just a remote part of their home.

Across the mists another land could be seen, one not very appetizing to look at. A mass of tall, green trees that seemed to cover virtually everything in sight. From their distance it looked just plain green, but with the aid of strong binoculars borrowed from one of the crew it looked like a pretty creepy and dark jungle.

There was a large staging area at the border and a large building for officials, sort of like a customs and immigration station, although it was pretty large and included barracks in back and seemed to be run by the black-clad professional army troops. Sam didn't remember any such things where they'd come in and suspected that, like most borders, you could get in and out of this one secretly if you knew the territory and if you really had to.

There wasn't much incoming traffic, but waiting at the border post was another wagon, this one guarded by four heavily armed men wearing uniforms of a different sort. Private security. Mercenaries. Sam was startled by the sight of both the private and national troops; it was the first time she had seen guns here. They were sleek and oddly curved and shaped yet, oddly, they appeared to be single-shot short rifles, and even the pistols had no barrels—you put in one bullet and that was it. Charley, from the conservative southwest and no stranger to firearms, figured they had to be pretty good shots, since you might not have the time to reload.

"I sure hope so," Sam responded worriedly. That jungle looked pretty mean, and on top of that it looked like it was raining buckets over there. The weather here was cloudy, with the clouds in rapid motion in that somewhat circular pattern, but it wasn't really bad.

That night they had a campfire meeting with Jahoort, this time around the new and still guarded wagon.

"All right, we shook you down and we didn't lose nobody," the navigator commented. "That's pretty good. Now the easy part's out of the way. Tomorrow it gets tough, and we'll have to go through that ground fog you see. Now, we'll all be sittin' high enough up that we'll be able to see each other, but fix cold sandwiches for tomorrow 'cause we won't be stoppin' in it unless we have to. The area extends about forty leegs"—that was a little under twenty miles, Sam knew—"and then we're out of the hub completely. The weather will likely take some real turns for the worse, too. Lots of overcast at least in the region closest to the hub and probably some nasty weather. Be prepared for it but don't let it get you down. It don't last a long ways in and then the weather gets more like normal—which means unpredictable. Normal weather we can handle, I think. Your first mud bath will try your strength and your patience but you'll soon take it in stride. The only kind of storm you really

have to worry about you probably won't meet—and pray you
don't. But you better know what to do just in case you meet
one.''

He got up, walked over to the wagon, and pulled back the
tarp, then pulled out what looked like a large blanket or rug
made of woven wool the color of dull gold.

"This is Mandan gold, and it's fairly heavy although not as
heavy as regular gold. Some of you may have seen it before
and know all this but listen anyway. Self-confidence gets more
folks killed or worse than any other cause. Each of you is
gonna get one of these blankets about this size and we'll stow it
for you. You don't own it—Mandan's worth more than all of us
put together, particularly in this form—and we'll take it back
when you leave us, but for the duration it's yours. If we get
much changewind warning, we will stop, the crew will handle
your things, and we'll all pitch in and dig a series of bunkers—
holes in the ground, really—and get in, lying as flat as
possible, with these blankets covering the entire hole. Don't
worry—you won't suffocate, you'll just feel like you will. Air
passes through the blanket, but Mandan is the only known
substance that insulates against the effects of a changewind.
You stay down and under it no matter how long it takes until I,
personally, or one of my crew comes and tells you it's all clear.
Understand. No peeking out, no feeling to see if it's still going,
nothing like that. Any exposed area of your body will be
permanently affected by the changewind.''

Sam shivered at the vision, remembering her own changewind nightmare. So *that* was why all the villagers crowded into
the underground bunker! And why that castle and even the big
door looked golden. It was Mandan coated, inside and out.
Inside, they were protected. All but that poor boy. . . .

"Now, changewinds could blow any time—even here,"
Jahoort warned. "At least two hubs have been hit in the last
five years. Both had a great deal of warning, although ones like
Tubikosa with large cities simply like to play with the fates.
But the odds of a changewind hitting here, or hitting us, are
slim—but not as slim as they used to be. There's been a
dramatic upsurge in the number of them, mostly very small and
localized, in the past year and a half. The unique conditions of
a hub prevent many of these small local ones from happening
here, but they are not that uncommon in the sectors and can
come without much real warning at all.

"If you hear this," he continued, blowing a sharp, shrill, unpleasant air-powered horn that startled them and the animals alike, "then don't even *think*. Grab the Mandan blankets, get on the ground, and under them. If you're caught in the open and can't get to the blankets quickly enough, take cover in any enclosed or depressed area you could, particularly one that's sheltered from the wind. It might not save you, but it's the only chance you got. Now, we'll practice and drill and drill and practice as we go along. Don't grumble at the drills. It might save more than your life."

Charley stared at the big, heavy golden mats and shivered a bit. She had trouble following Jahoort's rapid-fire and dialect-tinted speech, but she understood the basics: the mat was the only protection against the changewind. She had never seen a changewind and knew of them only from Sam's terrified account of her vision, but she wondered very much if she had the strength to lift or carry one of those things.

"Now we'll distribute these tonight, before you go to sleep," Jahoort went on. "Hopefully we won't need them. I've plotted a course that should take us away from where any changewind activity has been seen for a fair amount of time. Be ready for a changewind, but don't worry about them. We have far more probable things goin' wrong than that. Our route is gonna take us first through a land called Bi'ihqua, which has some dangerous terrain we'll try and steer clear of but is peaceful, friendly, and pretty rich in agriculture. Just stick to the trail and the train and don't sight-see and you'll be fine. The trouble will come when we leave this cluster and cross into the Kudaan Wastes. Right at the start is a sort of no man's land, a refuge for bandits, escaped prisoners, changelings, and the accursed. That will be the dangerous time, but we have to go there. I have cargo to be picked up at the mining stations. If we pass the close end of the Wastes we'll be fine. If all goes well, we'll have you safe and snug in Mashtopol in twenty-two days. That's all for now. Wakeup is zero five-thirty, push off is at six-thirty sharp. Be ready."

They walked off a ways back toward the wagon. "Boday does not like this Wastes with bandits," the artist commented. "Still, it might give inspiration. Perhaps she will paint a bit on this trip, make a record of it."

"Not a bad idea," Sam replied. "But I think I'm scarder of the changewind."

"Do not fear, my little flower! Boday tells you that lightning and meteors falling on your head are as common as change-winds. She has lived here her whole life and traveled as far as this leg and never seen one. The journey will be dangerous enough without worrying about something that is strictly fate. Did you think about tonight?"

Boday and Sam had both been approached by a fair number of the crew about spending an evening with Charley. Boday thought that a few careful favors might pay off on the trail in extra protection and service. Sam knew it probably would, but she felt uneasy about it. "Charley? What do you think?"

"Hell, Sam, I been horny as hell around all these nice-looking guys who are seducing me with their eyes and I haven't been able to do a thing about it. I'd love to do it."

She sighed. "All right, then, but I can't stomach it. Boday, you set it up. I have some other worries about it, though. Can you make up some potion to make her just Shari just for the night?"

"Not with the kit we brought, no. Why do you wish this?"

"Just in case somebody notices that Charley's a little brighter and more talkative than the usual girl of her kind. I don't want any slips right away. Of course, I could always use the Jewel. I'm sure His Demonic Highness wouldn't have any objections to that. Charley?"

"Just so long as you bring me back and I remember it all. No problems. It can work both ways, you know. I can overhear things they don't think I can understand."

It was getting quite dark now, but they walked right past Crindil, who gave them a smile and a nod. He'd continued to be friendly but he'd been a bit busy for much conversation. Sam thought it over. Charley was gonna be away and Crindil was now winding up his duties, looked like. Tomorrow onward they'd be in alien lands and under who knew what pressure? Tonight was the best night.

She reached under her tunic, brought the locket out, and aimed it at Charley. The "eye" opened and the usual stiffening occurred. "Jewel, I wish that when I say 'Charley be gone' that only Shari will be in that body, and that she will continue to be Shari until I say 'Charley return.' Then Charley will be back in charge but will remember all that happened as Shari."

Done. I will make it a standing command so you may do this whenever you like.

She hadn't even considered that, but the power of it gave her a slight thrill. She judged distance, then made a sudden move and shined the light on to Boday's head. "Jewel, I wish that when I snap my fingers Boday will be back to normal, such as that is, but that she will still be under my power and not know it. She will make the arrangements for Charley, then return here and go to sleep in the sleeping bag out here and not be awakened until I wake her up."

Done.

"You know what I mean to do?"

Yes.

"And you have no objections?"

No. I never object to such things so long as they do not interfere with my charge. I am a demon, after all. Like you, I am trapped. I may only find freedom by fulfilling my commission.

Oh, wow! She hadn't ever considered that. She snapped her fingers and Boday was as if she'd just finished with Charley. "Boday, go set it up."

"At once, darling." The tall artist left, leaving Sam with Charley who was still in a sort of trance and would be until one of the commands was given. "Charley, be gone," she said, and her friend was once again animated, but not like usual. The brightness, the spark, was gone from her eyes, and there was little thought behind them.

"Wait here for Mistress Boday," she ordered, and Shari nodded. "Yes, Mistress."

Sam then left to find Crindil, who was checking on the riders' horses before the start tomorrow and was pretty well by himself. He turned, smiled, and nodded to her and she returned it. "Hello, there! Any problems?" he asked nicely.

"You all finished for the night?"

"Just about. I should get some sleep, though. Long day tomorrow."

"I just wanted to show you this," Sam said, pulling out the jewel. He frowned, stared down at it, and it caught him.

"I wish," Sam said, "that when I say, 'Crindil love,' you will find yourself suddenly very horny and attracted to me, to the point of lust. You will want to have sex with me. From that point on you will treat me as the most beautiful, desirable, sexy woman you have ever made love to and you will make mad, passionate love to me until I tell you to stop. Then, when you leave my presence, you will forget it ever happened and go to bed."

Done, said the demon.

"Now show me what normal is, Crindil love," she said softly, feeling the power.

·10·

Power and Privilege in Akahlar

SAM HAD ALL sorts of things to do fast when the navigator's blast woke her up at five-thirty. For one thing, she needed several more hours of sleep; for another, she was alone in the wagon. Well, not quite—Charley was curled up asleep on the seat and now stirred and looked up sleepy and confused. Sam spotted her and yelled, "Charley! Get up and get going! I got a lot to tell you later on!"

But Charley just stared blankly and said, in Short Speech, "Pardon, Mistress. Shari not understand."

"Oh, shit," Sam growled. "Charley—come back!" And Charley was back—quickly, but no less sleepy. She shook her head as if to clear it, then looked in. "Jeez, Sam! Where's Boday?"

"Nuts," Sam growled, and jumped out of the back of the wagon. Everybody was stirring and running around and there was Boday in the sleeping bag dead to everything. "Boday! Wake up! Time to get up and go!"

Boday stirred, opened her eyes, then frowned and looked around. "What in—how did Boday come to sleep here?"

"Nevermind! Just get out of there now and let's get packed up! You sleep okay?"

Boday slithered out of the bag, still fully dressed from the previous night. "Yes. The best sleep Boday has had in weeks. Odd. Perhaps she should consider this more often."

"Good. Then you're gonna drive 'cause I feel like I got no sleep at all."

Charley came around with a tray with a steaming pot and two mugs. The Akhbreed had excellent if very strong coffee

215

and in the year with Boday Sam had gotten hooked on it, with a
fair amount of sugar. Boday drank it black and only in the
mornings. A huge amount, almost a cauldron, was always on
when the train camped for the night and all were welcome to it.
Charley couldn't stand the stuff—never could—and somewhere in the process of her becoming what she was she'd lost
her taste for almost all stimulants, as well as her taste for meat,
although she prepared it well. She did like wine and fruit
juices, though, and although there weren't any juices along and
the concept of sipping wine in the morning to wake up was
incredible to both Sam and Boday, that's what she had. She
went back and brought the last of the sweet breads, noting that
somebody was going to have to bake in primitive style or they
would be eating dried preserved hard biscuits.

"The woman with the kids seems to be doin' pretty good,"
Sam noted. "I'll have to ask her just how to do it and when I
learn I can teach you. I know we got the equipment, anyway."

Boday and Sam went into the wagon and closed the flaps and
used some of the water to sponge each other off before they
changed. It was going to be a long trip. By the time they'd
finished, Charley had found the narga team and was in the
process of rigging it. Even so, almost nobody seemed quite
ready an hour later to get going except the crew.

They lined up in formation, a rider checking each horse,
pack horse, and wagon to see that all was there and secure, and
then they waited for Master Jahoort. Across and beyond the
customs station was the mist in the first light of dawn, and
beyond . . . Well, it was hard to tell without binoculars but it
sure as hell looked like a pretty bleak sandy desert, and a dry
one at that. It sure wasn't any green jungle.

Jahoort came by them on his huge tan horse—Charley
suspected he'd bought it because it matched his outfit—as he
circled the train. And then—they waited. Now each and every
rider in the group was checked by the black-clad soldiers, and
identity papers were inspected.

Charley, knowing that Boday could understand no English,
took advantage of the delay, coming up in back of Sam. "You
did it last night, didn't you? That's why all the rush and Boday
out in the sleeping bag."

Sam nodded but didn't look back at her. "Yeah, I did. I used
the jewel. He don't remember nothin'. I figured, hell, we don't
know what's out there but why should you have all the fun?"

"And? And?" Charley prompted.

"It was—interesting. Not bad. Not what I thought it would be, either. So much of it was the same, 'though I liked that beard. That was neat. He was rougher, though. Not gentle where he should be. I'm sore in places. Messier, too, but it felt good goin' in. That was something new. And it was quicker. A lot quicker. I wanted more than he had. I just don't know. I'm glad I did it, glad I've done it, but it's an itch that got scratched. I know this much: women's bodies are a whole hell of a lot prettier to look at than men's. I dunno. I wouldn't *not* do it again, but only if it's for real. I won't force it ever again. You?"

"Well, maybe all that with Boday just jaded you. I know she knows things that have *never* been in books. Maybe he wasn't much good. A lot of men aren't, you know. Sometimes I wonder how people have kids. I had—fun. It was kind of a group thing, which was neat, and it was on the grass, which was fun. I sure as hell wouldn't mind doing it regular on this trip. Anybody except Mister Moustache, that is. There's just something about him that just gives me the creeps."

"Yeah, well, it was so long ago. Your memory's better than mine. All I remember is that big guy in skins with the speech impediment. I had my back to 'em, anyway."

Boday asked about the conversation, and Sam told her about the fellow with the fancy waxed moustache and Charley's suspicions.

She frowned. "Boday, too, has seen him somewhere. She had been trying for three days." She snapped her fingers. "Now, suddenly, it comes to her! She has seen him several times with Kligos!"

"Kligos! Then he *is* a scoundrel! He works for Kligos?"

"No, no. It was as if they were friends. Equals. Boday does not know more, but perhaps our little Butterfly is correct. We should keep an eye on him, particularly if he continues on with us. Ah! Here come the inspectors."

Boday handed them the passport, which covered both her and Sam, and which contained the clearance stamps, as well as the small document that certified that one Shari was contracted to them for life as beauteous property. They looked at them, gave a few looks like "We're glad to get rid of the likes of you," then went on. Charley pointed to the little fold-over card that was her only ID. "Don't lose that," she cautioned. "That is the only identity I have here. Lose that and I'm fair game."

It took a few more minutes for them to clear everybody, and Sam stared out ahead at the mist beyond. She was nervous and confused and didn't know quite what to think about herself. Instead, everything came around in circles to Charley's comment on her little card. This wagon was *her* card. Not just all she had, but everybody who loved her and cared about her. Both of them. Charley was her true friend and confidante, her trusted companion who was both big and little sister. That had never changed. But Boday—it was crazy, but she was fond of the tall woman's outrageousness and often awed by the talent there. Boday's devotion, whether chemically induced or not, was real down to the core of her heart and soul, even if it was kind'a like making a deal with the devil sometimes. You had to be real careful around Boday or she could smother you. That had finally been worked out now. She suddenly looked at the slim body, long fingers, strong but attractive face, and saw Boday in a new way. Okay, so it wasn't "normal," wasn't accepted, but it was real. More real than what Charley had—or maybe needed—and more real than what Crindil had, too. Maybe more than most people.

She'd been around men, lived for a time with men and kept company with them as one of them, and now she'd had one, and, on the whole, she liked the company of women better. So be it. The hell with fantasies. Like Charley said, you take what you got and you make the most of it.

The border soldiers rode back past and Master Jahoort gave a cry of "*Hooooo!*" and they started to move.

"Oh boy," Charley muttered nervously to herself, "here we go."

By the time they passed the border station and descended into the mist Jahoort was already well ahead. They were the first of the high, covered wagons but were in about the middle of the train. The desert landscape still held, and all looked normal as the sun rose, although behind them the clouds were gathering and it looked like a possible storm at the exit point.

They were above the mist, but it came up to about the center of the wagon wheels and up to about the middle of the nargas, making a pretty weird sight. Jahoort, leading the way on his big horse and unmistakable with his top hat and buckskins, seemed to know just exactly where he was going, and the crew, those not driving the cargo wagons but on horseback, moved up and back along the train, keeping it tight but not congested. All Sam could think of was the old song *Ghost Riders in the Sky*. That's sure what it looked and felt like as they went back and forth, their animals' legs lost in cloud.

It took a couple of hours to cross the region, and then the riders began to direct traffic much like mounted traffic police, putting many of the wagons side by side and stopping them, with all the passengers on horseback with pack animals behind. They were now no more than a hundred yards from that fearsome-looking desert, and they could even feel some of the dry heat.

Jahoort rode out so that he was about in the middle of the parked train, and just ten feet or so in front of them, and he just sat there, looking like some Old West painting, staring at the desert for enough time for Boday to sketch him. She was really good, too.

And then, in front of them, the desertscape started to change, and not subtly like the visions Sam and Charley had seen while "falling" down that storm-created tunnel to Akahlar. No, it was more like slides, like one slide fading out as another faded in, only in full three-dimensions and brilliant, life-like color. Slowly, at first, then faster, until they were going by at a good clip and it was hard to categorize them as more than types before they were gone. Several different colored deserts with wildly different landforms, certainly; a number of jungles, one of which had purple and pink trees and no green in sight; rolling hills manicured like a golf course that looked complete with water hazards and sand traps—everything but a hole, flag, and putting green; a shore looking out on a vast ocean-like body of blue-green water; tall mountains, short mountains, green mountains, white mountains. . . . It just went on and on.

Still, while there were infinite variations in color and placement and in some of the vegetation, the fact was that there were only a few basic landscapes. There were mountains, valleys, hills, deserts, plains, jungles, and seashores both sandy and rocky. The variety of them, however, startled and impressed even Boday, who'd seen it before. In most, it was overcast; in some, it was raining—or even snowing, although they knew this was the equatorial region of the planet.

"Are *we* moving or is *that?*" Sam asked.

"Neither, darling," Boday responded. "All of it is in the same place at the same time."

"Well—which one's Akahlar?"

"Darling—they are *all* Akahlar!"

"She's right about one thing," Charley said, coming back forward. "I just got dizzy looking at that and checked out the back. It still looks just the same."

Sam translated and Boday nodded. "Of *course,* because it *is* the same. All sectors intersect with the hub, but none with each other. That is why they can all be there but all are Akahlar. What you are seeing, though, is something that only a master navigator like Jahoort can do. He is flipping through all of the wedges intersecting this point for the one he wants. This Bi'ihqua, which is not an Akhbreed name. You can expect to see a native race, my darlings. It will be the first time, yes?"

"Second," Sam responded. "We met one before that we sure as hell don't want to meet again."

"Yeah," Charley agreed. "Tell her if we're ever near Ba'ahdon to give it a wide miss."

The end came very suddenly, when a view simply locked in before them. It was a very pretty view, but not one of the most friendly looking.

A valley and well-traveled dirt road opened before them, but on all sides were high mountains dotted maybe two-thirds of the way with lush greenery but with barren peaks, some with large patches of snow showing just how high they were. Thick gray clouds were overhead, cutting off the tops of some of the mountains from view, but it wasn't the mountains that was most impressive. Even on their greenest sides, there were dark, black, ugly scars, some quite wide and imposing, a few coming down into the valley and looking like blobs of oozing black rock suddenly frozen in mid-ooze. At various points around the valley and even near the trail the ground seemed to be on fire. At least, there was constant smoke and steam rising there.

"Looks like a cross between Yellowstone and Hawaii. I hope those bubbling places smell better here than there."

Now Jahoort motioned with his hand and gave his cry, and the mounted crew reformed the train and had it start to move out after Master Jahoort. There was no question as to where to aim for; there was only that road.

As they got to the edge of the land and came up out of the mist they discovered that Charley's wish did not come true. While the air was mostly decent and humid, now and again they would get a whiff of sulphur and even the telltale rotten egg smell of hydrogen sulfide. Even the nargas snorted their disgust.

They pulled onto the road that seemed to come right out of the mist, and Charley looked back. The mist was there, and she could see around the next wagon and beyond, but there was a darkness of sorts at the other end of the mist. All view of the hub seemed to have gone. In a few minutes all sight of the mist was gone, and they were in the volcanic landscape.

The temperature was down but it still wasn't all that chilly; Sam guessed it was maybe high sixties or low seventies, but after just leaving ten or more degrees warmer you really knew it.

Charley was trying to figure out how the hell the world was put together. "Like a crazy kind of flower, maybe," she suggested. "You know—the hub is the middle of the flower, and then there are the petals all around, like on the maps. Only the maps just show a view from the top, seeing the top petal. Suppose there were a hundred or a thousand petals all stuck to the middle of the flower at one point—that mist—but leaning away from each other, drooping down and giving a little space between? And each petal was one of those places. I dunno how the hell that's possible, but it's gotta be something like that."

Sam suggested the analogy to Boday, who liked it. "Yes, Boday has heard that before. It is very much like that, in fact. Is it not wonderful to have such variety? And there are forty-eight flowers, each with twelve series of petals. Darlings, only in Akahlar can every place and everything be possible!"

Conversation stopped as they heard what sounded like a very large group of barbershop quartet singers sounding off one note at a time at random—and very loudly.

They were passing a pretty but ugly-smelling area very near the road that seemed to be boiling colored mud. Sam looked at it, fascinated, but she wasn't sure what variety she wanted. The singing notes were coming from it; as each bubble burst, it gave off a noxious-smelling gas and a note that sounded just like a tenor or a baritone in one of those groups singing "ah Ah AH AHH!" only not in any ascending or descending order. It was kind of funny and a little neat, but she preferred her mud unboiled and she wasn't too keen on the ground singing to her.

She also wondered if there were any alto and contralto and soprano mud boils about. As it turned out, there were, and it sounded just awful as the sounds of one blended in with the sounds of others.

Charley just couldn't resist, even though she realized how precarious her position was. "The hills are alive with the sound of music," she said, giggling.

Sam turned and gave her a look and for a moment was tempted to turn her into just Shari.

They stopped just a half mile or so into the valley, but were not given much of a break or told to form a camp. Instead, Jahoort seemed to be waiting for somebody, and that somebody showed up fairly promptly. He was a rather dashing figure dressed all in khaki, with a small, upturned matching hat with brin, atop a chestnut brown horse. He had a large and comfortable-looking saddle and two large saddlebags mounted just in back of it, as well as what might have been a bedroll rolled up between the two bags. It was hard to tell detail at this distance, but he appeared to be ruddy brown from the sun and younger than Jahoort, although perhaps as experienced. It wasn't just the newcomer that caused attention, however, but his two companions.

"My God! What are *those?*" Sam asked.

Boday frowned. "Most likely the man is the Pilot," she answered. "The other two are probably natives of some sort. Odd little ones, are they not?"

Odd was not the word. The pair on either side of the Pilot were hardly half his height and seemed little more than brown humanoid blobs, but they were riding in tiny saddles atop what looked like the largest mice in all creation, and mice that not only had saddles on their backs but stood on their hind legs and hopped like kangaroos.

The Pilot shook hands with Jahoort, then looked back at the train, nodded, then turned to look ahead. He barked some orders to the little creatures, and they whirled their strange mounts and went forward, hopping rapidly, until they were perhaps a hundred feet ahead of the lead. Then Jahoort gave the cry, and they started forward once again.

The valley twisted and turned before it opened up into an enormous expanse flanked by high volcanic peaks. The valley had several large rivers and streams running through it, and seemed about as lush and green as it was possible to imagine. It seemed to go off in the distance forever.

The road dipped down into it and then followed a broad and fairly straight river. At the road's junction with the water there was a—well, a village. There seemed to be hundreds of conical grass huts of varying shapes and sizes, all built atop stilts at least ten feet in the air and some far higher. There were no ladders, no stairs, but there were small porches in front of the oval-shaped door openings, and there were people on some of them, as well as below on the ground.

Well, not people, exactly.

They were small, all between three and four feet high, and they all seemed to have broad, muscular brown bodies that seemed hard and tough as leather or maybe rock, with small, thick legs and short, stubby arms and heads that were very round and hairless, with enormous bulging brown eyes, thick, flat noses that ran half the distance of their face, and mouths that ran the entire distance. They were ugly as sin and they all looked kind of alike, although you could tell the males from the females. The females had small, round, hard breasts and were also, it seemed, a few inches taller on the average than the males. Most wore brightly colored loincloths and nothing else; the younger ones wore nothing at all.

They ran by the dozens out to greet the train as it passed, all yelling and gibbering in some odd-sounding language that was high-pitched and totally unintelligible. Others popped out of the stilt huts to join them, simply jumping out off the little porches and sliding down the not very smooth-looking stilts like firemen answering an alarm. When they got real close to the slow-moving wagon and seemed to be shouting up at her and grinning with those incredibly wide mouths, Sam felt repulsed and tried to shrink away lest they jump up or try and touch her. Charley, looking out from behind the seat, was finally able to see them as well. They *were* ugly, even repulsive in a way, but she felt no particular fear of them. This was, after all, probably *their* land.

Their fellow Bi'ihquans who were working with the Pilot whirled on their mounts and hopped back, coming down either side of the train and shouting at the natives and pushing them away with whip-like tools that looked like giant wicker dusters. They weren't hurting anybody, but the crowd moved back.

Giant brown and gray tailless mice were the best description for those mounts, too, although the creatures were clearly bipedal, with very large and powerful rear legs oriented that way and very small forelegs mounted on thin, short arms. Charley was less tolerant of their sight when she could finally see them; she had never been very fond of mice.

"Boy, I'd hate to be a cat in this place," she remarked, still being flip, but not really feeling funny right now.

Those creatures could *hop*, though. There wasn't a horse that could move that fast or turn that much on a dime. For the little people who could ride them, they were an amazingly versatile form of transportation.

They were past the village in no time, but others could now be seen popping up in the distance. In fact, they seemed to be scattered, yet pretty numerous; in between were lush fields that were obviously carefully cultivated. In one they could see lots of the little people walking down neat rows of plants taller than they were, carrying baskets and picking something or other. From the plants nearest the road Sam guessed it was the local Tubikosan style of banana. It tasted like one, but it was green on the outside all the time *and* green on the inside as well.

There were still occasional thermal areas but they weren't as pervasive as at the entrance to the land. Some steaming blue pools here and there, and off in the distance there could be seen an occasional geyser spouting off, sending its plume high into the air.

The banana seemed to be the main crop of the land, but every once in a while they would see a large amount of acreage planted with other fruit trees, or bushes bearing large, almond-colored nuts, and here and there what might have been a purplish relative of sugar cane. Mostly the small villages dominated, but here and there in the distance they saw some very large if conventional-looking houses with massive barns and other outbuildings that looked entirely out of place here, and areas that were cleared of all but thick grass and which had horses and monstrous-sized longhorn cows grazing.

About four hours in they pulled off the trail and toward one of those large houses, stopping just short of it in a large grassy field. Charley looked at the house—it was almost a mansion—

and then around at the fields. "Kind'a looks like *Gone With the Wind*," she noted. "Sure looks more like plantations than farms or ranches."

They set up in the field, allowing the horses and nargas to get water and do a little grazing, and allowing themselves to stretch and fix something to eat. The crew warned them that this would be just a ninety-minute stop, so they ate as fast and light as possible in order to have some time to look around.

Master Jahoort and the Pilot had gone into the big house and emerged only about forty minutes later, along with a young-looking couple and their four children, all Akhbreed. The woman and two of her daughters wore the long saris of the Tubikosans, and scarves, but clearly the business of young unmarried girls going in white and masked was out the window here. This was less formal.

Work was going on around the place; dozens of the little people were scurrying this way and that, carrying large things on their heads with balanced ease and hauling and repairing and cutting and sawing and all the rest. Two females attended the Akhbreed family.

Sam had Boday point out a couple of the train crew who had been part of the company Charley kept the previous night and walked over to them. She was curious. One of them, called Hude, a tall, lanky guy who always had a cigarette in the corner of his mouth but never seemed to light or smoke it, felt talkative.

"Yeah, most of these are big places," he told her. "It's the usual thing. Most of the produce here will be shipped by a train goin' where we just come from back to Tubikosa's markets. Them, they're the relatives of rich or powerful folks back in Tubikosa but they got the life out here. Hell, I bet they live as good as some kings and queens, only they don't got all the politics and shit you do if you're royalty."

Sam nodded. "But it's the land of these little people, right? I mean, they look so poor and primitive."

"Yeah, but they're ugly little brutes. All this volcanic stuff makes some of the richest farmland anywhere. Just drop anything at random here and it grows. They never did nothin' with it, though. Just squatted in their little huts and went out and picked wild fruit to eat back in ancient times. The Akhbreed come in, they made it a science. Growin' ten times as much, gave the little buggers medicine and sanitation and stuff like that. Taught 'em the work ethic. They never had it so good."

"Yeah, maybe," Sam responded, but she wondered if Charley's first impression of the old slave-owning South might not be a better example, or maybe some of the colonies in the old days when the English and French and others went all over the place "civilizing" the world. These little people didn't seem much better off than Hude said they were before the Akhbreed "made it a science." It was real clear to see who was bringing the tea to who, and who was dressing good and living in mansions and who was living in primitive huts, carrying water back to their places on their heads, and begging wagon trains.

Charley though so, too, but she wasn't all that surprised. "It's like we were told at the start, remember? The Akhbreed run all this. 'Sectors!!' 'Wedges!' They should call 'em what they really are—colonies!"

The Pilot and the navigator, along with the plantation owner, walked toward the rest, still talking, and their conversation now could be overheard.

". . . Much real trouble?" Jahoort was asking.

"Only out near the nulls," the Pilot, who kind of looked to Sam and Charley like a shaved Mark Twain in a bush outfit, responded. "We're getting some cross banditry whenever the synchronicity is right. We've asked for more troops but it's the usual story, you know. Things are pretty good here, you should see what some of the others are facing, we're spread thin, that sort of crap."

Jahoort shrugged. "Yeah, well, I've been talking to some of the other navigators at the Hall and they say there's been scattered outbreaks of outright resistance in some of the wedges, particularly in the more permissive kingdoms. Would you believe it? *Resistance! Natives* killing Akhbreed! And it's spreading. Mark my words, we're going to have a nasty mess on our hands if we don't stop it now, but the damned monarchs and their asshole advisors can't even agree on when to go to the bathroom, let alone unite."

"Laxity, that's the root of it," said the young plantation owner. "We've gotten too gentle and too permissive as a race over the years. Keep a tight rein and a whip and treat them fair and you'll have no trouble, I say. You don't see any of that rot seeping in *here!* Fairness and toughness, that's the answer. You talk as if it was some sort of worldwide conspiracy afoot."

As he said that Charley noticed a little native behind them pick up a melon and make as if to throw it at the owner. He didn't, but the thought was there. Charley smiled at him and he grinned. If they were bold enough to even show off like that, she thought, this idiot was in for a lot of trouble and couldn't see it if it was right in front of him. This place was grand, but it was dependent on native labor and the next Akhbreed plantation was a good ways from here. They were very vulnerable; only the threat of reprisal kept them alive and in this arrogant and ignorant state of wealth.

"Some think it *is* a conspiracy," the Pilot remarked. "I take trains through from all over. There's lots of talk about whole villages of natives disappearing in some sectors, and there's been more changewinds reported in the past year than in any one year in my entire memory. None here, yet, thank the gods, but you never know."

"You really think there's some dark conspiracy that might overthrow the Akhbreed?" the plantation owner asked in a very skeptical tone.

"I can't see how they could actually overthrow us," the Pilot admitted, "but if somebody was mean and powerful enough they could cost massive loss of lives and property and break the system. The hubs have gotten too damned soft and dependent. Jahoort can tell you. You stop the imports from the sectors and you'll have starvation, unemployment, maybe revolution."

The plantation owner chuckled. "Oh, come on! I can't take you two seriously! Revolution indeed. So one king and clan is traded for another. The army and the sorcerers still suppress things and that's that. Besides, it would be an inconvenience, nothing more. Why, it would take the revolt by a majority of sectors to more than irritate the hub. Besides, nobody in their right mind would foment such a disastrous and doomed uprising. There would be no gain in the end, only losses all around. Even the unhappiest of natives wouldn't follow such a course when it meant defeat and possible genocide for their people. I can see some power mad madmen dreaming of it— there are always psychotics—but actually getting a following? Come on, gentlemen! When the gods gave the Akhbreed the power, this system was *ordained*. One can scratch it, but hardly alter it."

It was an interesting debate, and one neither Sam nor Charley wanted any part of. In the end, the owner was right. The Akhbreed were in power because they *had* the power. Their sorcerers were demi-gods, the navigators alone could go where they like and bring troops to bear on any problem area while any revolt would have to trust to luck for help from anywhere else. But you had to wonder . . .

Boolean had said that whatever it was about Sam involved the fate of everybody, and not just Akahlar, either. Suppose somebody like the horned wizard *had* figured out a way to solve the problems? Suppose his biggest problem was convincing enough sectors to support and go along with him? It'd take lots of time, but these sorcerers had that time and the natives of all these worlds would be offered hope for the first time.

Suppose, just suppose, you could lock up the Akhbreed in their hubs so only the ones out here were around. If the sorcerers and the troops couldn't get out for some reason, then these Akhbreed would be outnumbered by a whole lot. And all sectors led to the hub. . . . What if most of the natives from most of the sectors all decided to attack the hubs at the same time?

"Impossible, darlings," Boday assured them. "Such a thing could not be. Only Akhbreed has sorcerers of such general and unlimited magic. No other race could do it but we against ourselves and that was settled in wars long ago. It is like everything, darlings. We have the power. There is no way to take that power away and we alone have it. You worry about everything, I think."

Sam remembered her strange visions and the horned sorcerer. "Yeah, but suppose some of the sorcerers went real bad? A lot of 'em?"

Boday laughed. "They are all insane, my love. Such power does that to the best of them. And some do go rogue, as it is called, and can be very, very dangerous. But to get two rogues with all that power to agree to do *anything* together—that is against nature."

But both Sam and Charley wondered about such confidence. Neither of them understood enough of this world to either accept or contradict the prevailing view, and neither had enough experience or education to compare it to their own world—if it could be compared—but it smelled. Something sure smelled.

When they were back on the trail, though, they couldn't stop discussing it. "Suppose Horny *did* figure a way," Charley theorized. "And suppose Boolean caught on? Remember— even Zenchur kind'a said that was up."

"Yeah, and the demon said the armies were gathering and the enemy gainin' strength," Sam responded. "I wish it would say more but it can't or won't about that. I don't think it really cares 'cept it wants to deliver me before all hell breaks loose. It's just trapped and wants out."

Charley nodded. "So in the tunnel this horned guy is blocked for the first time by somebody. Boolean had to come out of hiding to save us from him. Remember how surprised the Horned One was? So now Boolean's an enemy to the horned guy, right? He's too strong to take on, but I bet you Boolean's run into the same kind'a guff that plantation guy and Boday are giving. It ain't possible. It don't make no sense. Go away and stop with your conspiracies. Only Boolean's got something up to either prove it or give Horny fits. You. Only Horny knows it and he wants you out of the way. He now knows Boolean's his enemy so he has him covered. If Boolean reveals where you are, Horny pulls out all the stops. Maybe he can't zap Boolean, but he sure as hell could zap you. So *you* got to sneak in to *him*. It all makes sense. Zenchur's supposed to be the old dependable native to get us through with me as decoy, but Zenchur catches on and plays us dirty 'cause he hates his own kind. So the backup, the demon, comes in. It ain't human and it don't really give a damn about us, so it gives you Boday as a Zenchur replacement and makes you too fat to be recognized. Yeah, it really hangs together, except . . . ."

"Yeah, 'cept why the hell would a girl from another world who don't know much 'bout nothin' and sure as hell don't know sorcery or Akahlar or nothin' be the key to stoppin' all this? Why *me?* What in hell could I do against a sorcerer like *that?*" she sighed. "And the worst part is, from what I seen so far, I ain't even sure I like the game. It's the same feelin' I had when Zenchur first explained it all. I kept thinkin' that I went along more with the guy who was tryin' to kill me than the one tryin' to save me."

"I noticed you didn't get real fond around these natives," Charley noted.

"Well, yeah, but this is *their* place. I don't think I could ever kiss one of 'em but that don't mean they aren't *people*. I saw that bit with the melon, too. I don't like it, Charley. I don't like it at all. It seems like if we make it, somehow, and I do whatever it is Boolean wants, I'll keep thousands, maybe millions of people enslaved forever even if I get a gold star and fame and beauty and money and whatever. It'd be blood money. But it seems that if I don't, I *die,* and I don't wanna die right now. I ain't the hero type but I'm not smart enough to figure out a way out of this."

"I don't know who is," Charley sighed. "We don't know enough. Like, why do these sorcerers speak English with American accents yet? Your demon, too."

"Actually the demon sounds kind'a English. I don't know. But I sure don't like bein' pushed and that's all I've been since I got here. So pushed around that I almost gave up everything. It's nuts. I'm goin' where I don't wanna go—to do, if I get there, something that'll keep all these people from freein' themselves from their masters and lock in the Akhbreed for another ten thousand years or whatever, which I hate. That or die."

Charley sighed. "Well, we just play it by ear and try and figure it out. It's a long trip yet. Maybe we'll learn enough to figure it all out before we hav'ta make a decision. Or maybe we'll find some people who are smart enough to figure it out." She shook her head. "I dunno. Maybe we should spring for that university place. They *got* to know, and somebody there has got to be smart enough to figure it all out."

"Well, I can't do nothin' but play it by ear," Sam noted sourly. "But I don't think that university would help us figure out a way to beat the system. I mean, it's Akhbreed run, right? They *invented* the system. They might know what it's all about, but they sure wouldn't be no help to me."

Boday's sketches were getting very good and very elaborate as they went along, although she was running out of paper fast. She hoped that Jahoort would have some, or that there would be some available at one of the stops.

The days and nights went by with little change in the routine and little worry. The scenery changed a bit, but only occasionally, and they would pass from one valley up and through a pass and into another that might be growing some different things but was still pretty much the same plantation system. At least they could get fresh fruit and fresh fruit juices as they went along.

There were surprisingly few Akhbreed, all in plantations, and no non-native towns in evidence. The plantations were supplied by and supported by the trains that came through and dependent upon them not only to get the luxury goods and materials in, even importing skilled workmen when needed, but also to get their products out. Special trains just for this were employed using junior navigators; the long-haul trains generally dealt only with inter-kingdom commerce.

Sam eventually broke down and bargained for a pair of binoculars just for them, since most of what was worth seeing was well away from the roads and the "host" plantations were all ready for them.

One thing was obvious, particularly through the binoculars. The farther away they got from the hub, the looser the Akhbreed living in Bi'ihqua were as well. On their farms and generally secure, there was little sign of robes or saris on the plantation women around the places they were not set to stop at. Practical work clothes, even pants, were the rule and not the exception, and Boday once caught an excited look at a couple of women reclining by a pool about a half mile back who seemed to be wearing nothing at all, and twice Sam thought she saw a couple of women wearing work pants but topless. The men, too, seemed more casual but they had less distance to go to be that way.

The natives began to fascinate them as well. It was the first time either Charley or Sam had ever seen or heard of a race more advanced than spiders where the women were bigger and stronger than the men, on the whole—and clearly the bosses in their society. Both decided that they liked the idea. Boday couldn't care less. At six two and with her personality the concept was irrelevant.

The seventh day was notable because it rained torrentially and was one of the most miserable experiences any of them could remember. The wagon was in fact waterproof, but when you had to sit in the seat and drive it wasn't much help, and with poor visibility and several wagons getting stuck and having to be pushed out, including theirs, it was a really rotten time. It was not, however, a thunderstorm, and for that much

Sam was thankful. The last thing she needed that day was more visions and nightmares.

Still, it took Boday to put it into perspective. "Look at it this way, darlings. Suppose you were one of those on horseback?"

On the eighth day in, they saw a strange and scary sight that brought the reason for the repeated changewind drills home to them no matter how they griped about them. They sat atop another mountain pass looking down on yet another valley, but it was not the same as before. Well, it *was* for part of the way, but right through the middle, visible from the heights, was a vast and strange scar that seemed several miles long and a mile wide. It was gray and yellow and when they reached it there were in it the remains of what had once apparently been a dense forest. The change was so sudden and dramatic and the result so creepy they had to ask about it. Charley thought it was volcanoes; her folks had taken her to Volcanoes National Park in Hawaii when she was thirteen and she'd never forgotten the sight.

"Volcanoes, yeah," they were told, "but not directly. Oh, them things do pop their corks now and again and it can look real ugly for a while and cover the place in ash a krill deep"—a *krill* was roughly five or six feet—"but that's just how the land stays so rich. Nothin's growin' again here 'cause the soil's all wrong. Poison for these plants. This was a changewind come in maybe twenty years ago. You can see where there were eruptions around that time and it's already grown back. Not here. The land's wrong. It was some kind of nasty forest that didn't belong here, but the effect also opened up a hot crack and set the whole thing on fire. Nothin's grown here since or will, and the tree remains just stay there, mostly petrified."

The Pilot, who was old enough to remember, agreed. "Used to be a native village over there," he told them. "Just like all the rest. Only when the wind was done they was stone huts and the natives were foul-lookin' red buggers with lots of teeth and tails like reptiles who just started off tryin' to eat anything and anybody they could. Took months to root 'em all out and kill the last of them. They was just startin' to breed." He shuddered.

At that Sam's mind went back to that horrible vision of the boy turned monstrous by the changewind. He'd looked horrible, but he'd been the same scared little boy inside. That was why it was so awful, them killing him. But turning these pleasant little natives into demonic killers—maybe there was a reason why they killed them. Maybe it could change you inside sometimes, too. Or maybe the natives just found themselves about to be hunted anyway but now with a form able to do some damage, so they did. Hard to tell.

Still and all, the Akhbreed killed all changewind victims they could catch as policy because they no longer fit. Everything and everybody had its place here, and those changewind victims had the least power of all.

They all felt better when they were through the desolation.

Late on the afternoon of the ninth day in Bi'ihqua, they met the soldiers. They were a tough-looking bunch of men who'd obviously been out in the field a long time. They weren't all sharp and spiffy and totally clean-shaven like the ones back in Tubikosa, but they looked like the kind of men you'd want on your side in a fight. It was only a patrol, a dozen or so men under a junior officer and an old sergeant, but they were doing their business and it was something everybody learned soon enough.

"There's been some banditry off and on for months along the border," the officer told them. "They're a special kind of bandit and we've been hunting them for half a year to no avail, although we don't know how they could hide in this land for that long. They're ruthless when they have to be but they're only after one thing, or so it seems. They take the Mandan gold and leave most of the rest. Oh, they'll take something if it strikes their fancy, but that's their target. Been a rash of these things at or near the borders. We're escorting all trains through to the Null from here, though."

"Hard to believe that few enough bandits to be able to hide in this country could take a train," Jahoort noted. "Ain't like the old days, I'll tell you."

"Yeah, we've had the natives out looking into every nook and cranny and we can't come up with 'em. Can't figure out why they're so hot just for the Mandan, too. It's valuable enough, sure, and rare enough, but it's not characteristic of bandits."

". . . *We've had the natives out looking* . . ." Sam couldn't help but wonder if maybe the natives were deliberately not looking in the right places. These people were so used to running the show and also so used to thinking of the natives as primitive children it just might not ever occur to them that the natives could be in cahoots with the robbers. They'd dismiss it. What's the motive? The natives would be wiped out if it were discovered, but couldn't profit without being obvious, right? Maybe it was just the satisfaction of doing something, however small, against their arrogant bastard masters.

"Where'd they come from?" Jahoort asked.

"Probably when the Kudaan Wastes synchronized with here. The timing's about right. But we figure it wasn't any impulse thing. They had their hiding places prepared in advance for sure. They don't hit every train, just a few, but it's best not to take chances. Could be they got a deal in collusion with some of *our* bad ones. Might be partly an inside job. There'd be big money in exporting Mandan."

The Pilot sighed. "Yeah, some people will do anything for a sarkis. Glad to have you, officer. I was arguing for this policy for months."

Charley frowned. She'd gotten the gist of it and whispered to Sam, "Aren't we going to this Kudaan Wastes? Jeez! We're goin' where they *came* from!"

"Kudaan Wastes," Boday repeated. "It is not even a pleasant name. You wanted something real to worry about, darlings. Boday thinks this is it."

As if in confirmation, Jahoort said, "Well, I'm goin' right into the Wastes. I'm supposed to have a patrol from the Mashtopol Forces meet me at the border there. Until I talked to Ganny, here, I hadn't expected much trouble til I got there. I'll order all my men armed from this point anyway."

The officer spat. "The Mashtopol Forces. That motley lot might be more dangerous to you than the bandits." When they left Bi'ihqua they would also leave the Kingdom of Tubikosa and enter the Kingdom of Mashtopol; it would be another country's jurisdiction.

"I can't say I ain't worried," Jahoort responded rather casually, "but I been through the Wastes many times and I got a few surprises if anybody makes a try on me there. You just get me to the border and we'll be fine."

Although it had seemed a long trip already, and they had far to go, in many ways Sam and her companions were sorry to reach the end of this place, with its spectacular geysers, singing mud pots, colorful mountains and rich land. It had been an education in how things worked on Akahlar, but it had not been unpleasant until the patrol showed up. After then, every time they reached a point where the road went through thick growth or sloped down, presenting rocky outcrops on either side, their eyes combed for any signs of movement and the friendly land seemed filled with potential menace.

Charley was positive that Mister Moustache was the inside man and that he would somehow signal and bring down a horde of fierce bandits on them at any moment, but while the odd little man kept to himself pretty much he did nothing of a really suspicious nature. Perhaps he just decided that this one wasn't worth it; there'd be easier pickings on later trains.

Along the way, too, Sam had gotten to know a number of the people, both travelers and crew, including Madame Serkosh, the married woman traveling with husband and kids. Rini, as she insisted she be called, had the art of trail cooking and packing down pat. "You have to, with five along," she said practically. Her husband seemed somewhat withdrawn and aloof, but she and the kids were outgoing types, delighted to show a newcomer the art of baking on the trail and lots of other practical things, and seemingly not at all put off by the unusual nature of the female trio Sam represented. They were headed home after showing off the kids to her brother-in-law, who managed a luxury hotel in Tubikosa. They lived in a Mashtopol sector off the southwest of that hub, and would change there for the final few days home.

"You'll like Mashtopol after Tubikosa," she told Sam. "Things are a lot more fun and a lot less strict there. The capital's not very big compared to Tubikosa, but it's a nice little city that minds its own business and lets you mind yours. I wish it had the markets and bazaars of Tubikosa, though. Seeing the variety there compared to what we're used to was just amazing."

Their own sector, which was called Shadimoc, apparently was involved in some kind of manufacturing, although just what it produced—and what sort of inhabitants really produced it—wasn't all that clear. Sam didn't press it; with all the possibilities of this world it didn't seem worth it, and besides she was still getting used to the little Bi'ihquans.

Neither of Rini's boys—Tan, eleven, and Jom, seven— would have much to do with Sam; she suspected their father feared those weird women would infect them with some kind of debauched ideas. Apparently he didn't care about his daughters getting corrupted, though, or thought they were too smart to be corrupted, since he seemed to have no objection to their talking not only with Sam but even with Boday, who showed an unexpected soft side for kids. Charley, at first, had felt stuck, since she really wanted some company, but felt she had to play Shari at all times around them so they wouldn't be going back to their parents with news that the pretty girl was smart and clever. After a couple of days, though, it was clear that while Charley could fool adults, she had little chance of fooling kids. The language barrier, at least, kept things at what seemed to be a safe level. Both dressed in long pullovers and pants, apparently the standard garb for Akhbreed colonials where they came from. It wasn't all that fashionable, but it was practical; they had all clearly left the strict codes of Tubikosa, or at least had exchanged them for looser ones.

Rani was thirteen and already pubescent, only just so, and still trying to deal a bit with what that all meant and what her body was doing to her. She was thin, with her parents' dark olive complexion and her father's rather prominent nose, with thick black curly hair and eyes that seemed just as dark, and she was already about five feet tall, almost to Sam and Charley's height. She looked like somebody from the Middle East, as did her parents. She wasn't all that pretty, with a mouth too large and a nose too prominent, but she wasn't ugly, either, but to Sam, at least, the girl seemed both ordinary and exotic. She was a rather quiet child, but she warmed Boday's heart by looking at the eccentric artist's sketches with awe and wonder. Boday instantly decided that this was the most tasteful and intuitively brilliant child she'd ever met.

Sheka was nine, and had that same mouth, but her nose was a bit better proportioned, her eyes large, and her hair straight, and she was chubby—not fat like Sam, but chubby. She was also more outgoing and inquisitive, and seemed fascinated by Charley. She was also capable of asking embarrassing questions in total innocence like why Charley waited on them like a *serk*—apparently the name of the natives of Shamidoc—and if the butterfly eyes came off and how much of Boday's body was covered with designs and pictures—and why. With the aid of Rani, who seemed constantly embarrassed by her sister's questions, they managed to deflect the hardest to answer.

Both were allowed to come over now and then, usually together, when they stopped for the evenings, and even though their stays were brief they were welcome ones.

The last day's journey was through rough, less developed country and rugged, volcanic terrain, and it was easy to see why this place would be ideal for bandits, but when they reached the end of the road nothing had happened. It seemed almost anticlimactic, but neither Sam nor Charley nor Boday could say they felt disappointed. So far so good. Over four hundred miles and the worst that had happened overall was a good drenching.

The end of Bi'ihqua was not like the beginning. The road did not just end; only the land changed just beyond the border posts. The change was dramatic, but there was nothing to suggest anything odd or magical here. The road did not end; it continued on past a border control post and fort, and a few hundred yards beyond, the volcanic terrain simply ceased and was replaced by a thick, northern-style forest. The road changed at that point, too, from the rich black hard-packed earth of Bi'ihqua to a hard, unrutted red clay. The road seemed better maintained on the other side for all the soldier's remarks about Mashtopol, even to having drainage cuts on either side. There was a small border post there, too, with far fewer soldiers wearing blue, not black, uniforms and colored epaulets on their shoulders.

They disembarked and set up for the night on the Tubikosan side, just outside the border fort. Sam couldn't help noticing that while the Tubikosa border was heavily double-fenced as far as you could see in both directions, the Mastopol one was not. After getting set up, she wandered over to the Serkosh family wagon and found Rini. "*That* is the Kudaan Wastes?" she asked them. "It looks pretty nice to me!"

Rini laughed. "Oh, no! That's Kwei, I think. It's hard to keep track but I thought I heard the Pilot say so. I wish we *were* going that way, but few trains do. Kwei wood goes almost entirely to the rest of Mashtopol; little is exported. Unfortunately, the international trains coming back almost always go through the worst and ugliest sectors. That's because it's cheaper to get *them* to pick up the dangerous or heavy cargo and bring it in for free in lieu of transit fees. If we'd known someplace like Kwei would be up when we got here we would have arranged a special transfer through to it, but there's no way of knowing what you'll get when you come here and it's too late now.'' She sighed. ''Too bad, too. I'd much rather pick up some nice wood furnishings cheap than go through a damned desert.''

Sam felt disappointed. The land in front of her looked so *pleasant*. ''Then that's why they call it the Wastes? Because it's a desert?''

Rini nodded. ''They'll take on a water wagon here, I bet, and maybe more. I've heard the Wastes are pretty, though. It's just that down this end they're pretty dangerous. The land is so rugged it's a perfect hideout for anyone who, well, needs to hide out and can somehow get there. Ten armies wouldn't blast you out of there if you didn't want to be blasted out, so they don't try. There's a *wonderful* lot of books written set in the Kudaan Wastes. It's very romantic. They just quarantine the area and have a military escort the first hundred and fifty leegs. Nobody usually bothers the inbound trains anyway, though; not much to steal. So they only pick up the ores inbound. See? Oh, it'll be exotic but I don't think we'll be molested. If we thought there was a real danger we'd never go through there with the kids. There's a number of spots like Kudaan, and most of these navigators have deals, anyway. We might even see some of the accursed or changelings.''

Sam wasn't sure she was too excited about seeing anybody called accursed or a changeling but she let that pass. Charley seemed genuinely excited by the description; it sounded much like her own native desert southwest. Boday seemed interested only in the artistic possibilities, but she did explain two terms.

''Changelings are those poor unfortunates caught in a changewind who manage to make it to such places,'' she told them. ''They are often horrible or grotesque, and not all were Akhbreed to begin with. Some are partly changed—only a part of them received exposure and the result was able to live—and they are the halflings. The accursed—they may look similar or look ordinary, but their troubles are due to more deliberate magic. The changewinds are random; the accursed are truly that. Often they change in the dark or under special conditions from normal to quite mad, or from man or woman to beast. The others—criminals, malcontents, political refugees, zealots. Boday thinks most will keep well out of sight, particularly if we have troops with us. Most are there because they do not *wish* to be seen."

The next morning dawned bleak and dreary. Kwei was gone; in its place was a slimy, creepy-looking swamp that was being wet down by a light, misty rain. The road still continued on; this one, however, was not in nearly as good shape as the one into Kwei; it was hard-packed and looked paved and slightly elevated and it had potholes in it that looked mean enough to bounce a wagon to the moon. There was a tiny border post there but it appeared unmanned. Boday read the sign on it that said, "Mashtopol Entry Point. All entrants should report to Customs Office in the Village of Muur, one hundred and six leegs."

"They're real worried about their border, aren't they?" Charley noted sarcastically.

"About as much as they are about road maintenance," Sam responded, eyeing those potholes. "This is one I'm glad we *don't* have to go through."

Jahoort got them all assembled as if it were just another day's journey, but this was different. For one thing, all of the crew, including Jahoort, were now packing weapons. Sam saw pistols, rifles, shotguns, even fancy crossbows. They looked loaded for bear, that was for sure. Some of the people traveling with them also now were armed, a few with swords, fewer with guns which were generally prohibited to the public in Tubikosa.

The navigator stood a moment with the Pilot who'd brought them through with no trouble. "I'll be picking up an inbound sometime tomorrow if he's on schedule," the Pilot was saying. He offered his hand. "Well, good luck. It's been a pleasure, as usual. Take care through that armpit you're going into and shoot anything that don't shoot you first."

Jahoort took the Pilot's hand. "Well, can't say I'm fond of taking paying passengers this route, but in a choice between saving money and risking lives the Company always chooses the money. I been that way dozens of times, though. It's not as bad as it's cracked up to be." He pointed to the swamp across the way. "Now, *that* just shouldn't be allowed. I'd rather go through Kudaan than risk horses, nargas, and wagons on that kind of road."

With that, he stepped out, mounted his horse, then rode right up to the gate at the border, and stared out at the swamp.

Again the scenes changed, first slowly, then more rapidly. Again infinite variations flashed before them, and again it suddenly stopped and there before them now the road led into the Kudaan Wastes.

"Bleak," said Sam.

"Beautiful," said Boday.

"Oh, wow!" exclaimed Charley.

·11·

When the Desert Storms

THE MISTY RAIN and the humid feel suddenly vanished and they were hit by a sudden blast of incredibly dry, superheated air.

Charley had not been far off in her guess. The Kudaan Wastes resembled the Four Corners area of New Mexico, Arizona, Colorado, and Utah; the land where most western movies had been made, the land so pretty but so bleak nobody had even *wanted* to take it away from the Indians.

It was a broad, flat plain punctuated with tall mesas and buttes of multicolored rock, twisted spires and places where the land ended in great gashes revealing more rock layers as you looked down into canyons. The colors were red, purple, black, white, tan, orange, even blue, in all sorts of shades and hues. The road was little more than a worn dirt track on the parched and cracked desert floor and it seemed to go off into the distance forever.

Jahoort didn't immediately signal a forward advance and it was fairly clear why. He had said that troops were to meet them here and escort them beyond the no man's land before them, but there was not a living thing in sight and sight extended a fair ways. No military also meant no Pilot, and that meant they were on their own with no warnings of what was ahead. He gave a hand signal and all members of the crew went forward to meet with him, the ones driving the wagons jumping down and walking over there or doubling up with the horsemen and riggers.

"Gentlemen, the safety of this train is our responsibility," Jahoort told his men, "and particularly mine. As you can see, no troops, no nothing, and I cannot maintain this synchronicity for very long, certainly no more than an hour. Any thoughts?"

Donnah, one of the older hands and the cargomaster, spat, then said, "Hell, boss, if we could drop the passengers I'd say go for it, but I wouldn't go in *there* with paying customers for nothin' if I could avoid it. 'Course, I'll do what you order."

"You know better, Donnah. We drop the passengers and make it, we're goona have to refund their whole damned passage and send a safe special back for 'em. Might be penalties, too. I ain't old enough to retire yet, let alone get kicked out on that account. Either we all stay or we all go. How say you?"

It was Crindil who spoke for most of them. "You know we're game for it, boss. Been kind'a dull lately. I haven't been through here in six, seven months, but I didn't have much trouble with Sanglar and I don't expect none with you. Seems to me we go and we got a real club to hold to Mashtopol's head. Still, there's too many women and children this trip for me to just bravo it. I say we ask them."

Everybody else gave their advice as well, but much of it was conflicting and contradictory. Still, the consensus was to go.

Jahoort was asking for advice, though, not a vote. He was an absolute monarch in the end and the final choice was his. "No," he said. "I'll not have the blood of a child on my hands because her father was a damn fool." He took out a pocket watch and looked at it. "Forty-nine minutes. If them troopers get here within that time we'll move in. If not, we'll try again tomorrow and the day after that until we get sick and tired of it and go someplace civilized."

He would have liked the option of simply defaulting to a better sector, but he really didn't have it. Those border posts that were staffed would not let them through if their papers said otherwise, and those that were not staffed were as bad as this one.

They held in position, as instructed by the outriders, waiting for Jahoort to signal go ahead or abort. Sam waited impatiently, the reins in her hands, and scanned the terrain with her binoculars. Nothing much to see. Time dragged, and even the nargas grew bored and restless.

Jahoort, too, sat atop his horse scanning the road, as immobile as a statue, except that every once in a while he'd take out his watch again and look at it. He was just about to give up and tell everybody to return to camp formation when he gave one last look down the road. There, in the distance, he could see riders coming toward them, kicking up a bit of dust, definitely in formation. They had four minutes really to cross, and he had a split second to decide. He turned and made the call of "Ahead at full speed," and they began very suddenly and quickly to move, the outriders screaming at them to hurry up and cross and never mind the formation or the road. They'd fix it later.

They were through the border before anyone even had time to wonder what would happen if they didn't make it—or, worse, made it halfway. Later they were reassured to learn that that simply did not happen, although the shift could occur the instant you were across.

Jahoort wasted no time in reforming the train, and everyone was so busy that they could pay attention only to themselves. It was Charley, looking out of the back of the wagon, who wondered idly where some of the riders had gone and worried for a moment that some of the crew might have missed the crossing, but she dismissed the thought. She could not, after all, see everything, and nobody else seemed concerned. As soon as everyone was formed up and ready to go another reality hit them that began to occupy their attention.

It was hotter than hell here, and so dry that perspiration seemed to evaporate as it formed on the skin. It bothered them all almost immediately, but it didn't seem to concern Jahoort, who had to be broiling in those buckskins. His attention was entirely on the oncoming riders.

In back of them, the landscape was now tall, seemingly impenetrable mountains rising up through clouds. It was as barren a landscape as this one, but it looked a lot cooler. Wherever Bi'ihqua now was, it wasn't connected to them anymore.

Jahoort waited for the riders, letting them come to him. There were ten men, in the blue uniforms of the Mashtopol Forces, but wearing white headdresses that sheltered their faces and left their dark, brown features to peer from folds of cooling white. Considering the dark blue uniforms had to soak up the sun, nobody could figure out how the hell they stood it.

The man leading the ten-man patrol approached Jahoort and saluted. "Pilot Captain Yonan, sir. Sorry we were delayed. I hope we didn't inconvenience you."

"Quite all right, Captain," Jahoort responded, looking over the men. They were a motley lot, and a couple looked like they had beards beneath those burnooses. "I'm most anxious to clear the Furnace Region by nightfall. If you like, I can have the water wagon release some into the portable trough so your horses can replenish. Then we'd best be off."

The officer thought a moment. "Kind of you, sir. I believe we will."

The navigator gave one of his signals and the water wagon driver lowered the trough and then turned a valve releasing water into it to a depth of perhaps six inches. Enough for all of them, three or four at a time.

"That's the filthiest, motleyest crew of soldiers Boday has ever seen," the artist commented as they went past. "Look at that. Dirt all over, and even rips in their uniforms."

Charley scurried back to get a good look, then went over and opened one of the trunks. "Sam—warn Boday. Here's that short sword of yours. Be ready for it. I'm getting my knife and blow gun."

"Wha—what's the matter."

"Sam, those aren't tears in some of those coats, and they're dirty for a reason. Hides the blood stains, but not completely. I guess the lead ones had the most intact uniforms." She saw that Sam still didn't get it. "Sam—they're not soldiers, and in that condition they can't play-act being soldiers real long."

"Jesus!" Sam turned to Boday. "Charley says they're not soldiers. They're a gang in soldier's uniforms."

Boday did not have an emotional reaction, but simply responded, "Good."

"*Good?*"

"Yes. Boday would hate to think any so mangy could be real soldiers. Tell Charley to hand her the whip."

Jahoort maneuvered around on his horse just to one side of the gang as they went for the precious water, then drew his two pistols. "Pilot Captain!" he yelled. "You should tell your men to shave. And uniform means uniform—including bullet holes!"

They turned and drew their own weapons, but as they did the navigator fired and the top of the water wagon suddenly swung out on hinges and four rifles fired simultaneously. The maneuver was obviously carefully planned and perhaps a standard for the crew; as five raiders fell without firing an accurate shot, one jumped to the water wagon and the other four turned to run before there was a reload. They didn't make it; the three remaining mounted riders of the crew opened up, cutting two down, then took off after the other two.

The one who'd jumped on the water wagon, however, struggled with the driver and then managed to sock him hard on the chin and push him over. The raider then grabbed the reins and started off, yelling at the narga team to make speed.

Boday stood on the running board of her wagon and waited. When the water wagon came close to pass, her whip snaked out and actually caught the driver, who was not hurt but was so startled he dropped the reins. The nargas weren't all that fast, but they were fast enough and now had no control. The top-heavy wagon overturned, breaking the hitch and crashing to the hard ground, while the team continued on. The huge, keg-like wagon cracked a bit, and water began spilling out of one of its seams even as the men in the compartment up top struggled to get out.

Jahoort made for the water wagon and got there just as the raider was picking himself off the ground. He stared into a reloaded pistol and raised his hands, palms out.

The three outriders were even then returning—empty-handed. "Two got away, boss," Hude told Jahoort. "They made it into the rocks over there and it could be all day catchin' 'em. We figured it was better to get back here."

"Help the men out of there and tend to any injuries," the navigator ordered. "This scumbag is going to talk if I have to get that alchemist woman to make him fall in love with a narga."

The wagon drivers checked on the rest of the fallen band of pseudo-soldiers. A couple were still alive, but they were badly wounded and needed attention they did not get.

Jahoort and Crindil stripped the one surviving raider stark naked and staked him down face up on the desert floor. He looked better with the uniform on, Sam decided. He was an ugly, hairy brute whose body seemed full of scars. He looked mean as hell, though.

The navigator took a sword from its saddle scabbard and then stood over the man. As he did there was a series of yells from the area of the overturned water wagon, and everyone looked to see what was happening there. The water had almost completely seeped out, wetting down the immediate area heavily enough that it should have been soaked through, yet it was drying even as they watched. Then, suddenly, they saw what the yelling was all about.

From everywhere under and around the overturned water wagon thick, green shoots like tentacles shot up—hundreds of them, growing, or oozing from the hard rock, whichever— with lightning speed and in a matter of a minute completely engulfed the wagon. One of the crew from the top, injured, had been pulled away just in time before the long green fingers came up right where he'd laid.

Boday turned to Sam. "Get Boday her kit. Some of those men might need help!"

Sam idly turned and picked up the small alchemical kit and handed it to Boday, at no time taking her eyes off the wagon which was now engulfed in the long, waving tendrils. Boday jumped off and went to see to the injured crew.

"My God, Sam! They're *alive!*" Charley breathed, watching the spectacle. "They're *moving!* Crushing the wagon!"

And that was exactly what they were doing to the entire wagon. Enfolding it, grasping it, then crushing it, tearing it slowly and methodically to shreds.

Sam frowned. "Are they plants—or what?"

Charley shook her head. "I think they are. I guess out here everything's below the ground and when water activates them or wakes them up they do all their living in a few moments. They're tearing that thing to pieces looking for the smallest extra drop of water still left, Sam!" She looked nervously down at the ground on which their wagon sat. "Do me a favor, Sam—don't spill anything. *Please* don't spill anything!"

On the other side of the still immobile wagons, Jahoort was fairly free with his sword over the captive.

"I'd like to pour some water slowly over you, but I can't spare none," the navigator said matter-of-factly. " 'Course, if I was to prick an artery along here and let the blood flow down it'd come to the same thing, wouldn't it? Only a lot slower." He kicked the man in the side. "What do you say, friend? Or do I maybe cut your balls off and let the blood make the *sippiqua* rise? That'd be a pretty neat entry into the body, wouldn't it, friend? They'd slowly drink you dry from the inside."

The man glared at him, but looking in Jahoort's eyes he saw

immediately a reflection that scared the hell out of him. He saw himself.

"What do you want to know, you old fart?"

Jahoort smiled sweetly. "What happened to the troops? What's this raid all about, anyway? We don't have nothin' worth this kind'a risk."

"All I know is this changeling's got hold of some kind of repeater gun. Mowed all ten of them Whiteheads down in nothin' flat. Never saw nothin' like it. Neither did they. We was picked up, recruited for odd jobs. Good money. They told us to pretend to be the soldiers and make sure we met you soon enough for you to see us and too late to backtrack. Whatever we found was ours. Only thing *they* want's the Mandan cloaks. If you was too tough, we was to blow the water and scram. I'd'a got away, too, if that bitch hadn't got me with that fucking whip! All your horsemen were off chasin' the others."

"Mandan gold again! *Why?* Folks out here don't need no Mandan gold cloaks. They already been touched by the changewind. They can smell 'em so far away they can warn all Creation to keep out of its way."

"I dunno."

The sword moved; sharp as a razor at its tip, it traced a thin, bloody line on his thigh.

"I don't know, I tell you!" the man screamed. "I swear it! You don't ask no questions in this business, Cap. You just do it and take your reward or your lumps!"

The answer seemed to satisfy the navigator. "This changeling—what's it like? He or she? How's its shape and form? How would we know it?"

"All I can tell you is that it's a woman," the raider replied. "Wore a dark purple cloak that covered her up good. Sharp, nasty voice. Sounded like my ex-wife. Caught a glimpse of the face—not a bad looker, but you see them arms and the shape of that cloak and you know. Black, nasty arms. Devil hands with claws. I can't tell you no more. I swear it!"

"Oh, I believe that, son," said Master Jahoort, and slit the man's throat with the sword. He turned and walked away as the man still struggled, strangling on his own blood, which was seeping into the ground. . . . "Shoot any survivors in the head!" Jahoort ordered his crew who were looking over the wounded raiders. "I know everything I need to know and I don't like it! Circle for camp! Crew conference in twenty minutes!''

Three shots rang out. Eight of the ten raiders were dead, but they weren't very competent or clever enemies. They had merely been sent by competent and clever enemies. It had been an easy victory overall, and that bothered Jahoort as much as a tough fight.

Of the four men in the ambush compartment atop the water wagon, two had mainly bruises and a few cuts, one had a broken arm and rib, and the other was in worse shape. Boday was doing what she could, but without her full lab she could only set and treat and ease the pain; she couldn't do much in the way of repairs.

''All right, boys, they cut us down to size on this one,'' the navigator told his men. ''I got suckered even though I'm an old pro at this. Somebody banked on even the most experienced pro's weakness for the schedule. They cut us down to size, that's for sure. I got to hand it to that crazy alchemist, though. Without her that bastard would'a disengaged the wagon and crashed it and got away with four good nargas. We couldn't chase him and save the boys up top and he knew it. Smart one. He should'a been leadin'. 'Course, if he had we'd be taken now and all of us'd be dead. Crin, how's the remaining water?''

''Not too bad,'' Crindil responded. ''Everybody filled up like they were told to at the fort. I'd like more but I don't think anybody's gonna die of thirst.''

Jahoort nodded. ''All right. Whoever sent those ten men with the collective IQ of a narga probably didn't figure they'd take us. They probably just wanted to slow us down. Men like that are cheap, and, who knows, they might'a got lucky. But now we know. We got a changeling with some kind of repeater gun up ahead and I don't figure she's even trusting to that. I'll bet you a thousand sarkis that band that was raidin' in Bi'ihqua was just sittin' there well away from the fort waiting for either Kudaan to come up or somebody like me to bring it up.'' He looked in back in both directions, ignoring the majestic mountains of the other sector that also blocked any retreat for a short time.

''I figure they'd cross south, maybe thirty, forty leegs or more just to be on the safe side,'' Jahoort continued. ''Cut that fence and come on through. It's fairly flat down there, an easy cross with no surprises but far enough down we couldn't see 'em. We go forward, we got the changeling with the repeater in front and them in back of us. They know we can't stay here 'cause the risk is almost certain somebody's gonna spill things and then the sippiqua'll cause us more problems than they could. From the looks of them mountains somebody involved has got navigator skill and I bet there won't be nothin' useful come up to retreat to before they close on us. I could go in a test of wills but that might take hours and I still might not win. You never know with these changeling types. If they didn't think they could at least hold me they wouldn't have tried this. And without a Pilot we're up shit's creek if we go off this road."

"I don't see where we got a choice," Hude commented. "I been through here myself once before. You go much this way or that without a guide and you'll be in a canyon or chasm or worse. Let's just get on that road and depend on some decent scouting ahead. I'd rather risk that repeater, now that we know it's there, than who knows how many pushin' us in back? Ain't but so many places you can put and hide a repeater, and we know they can't be more than maybe two hours ahead allowing for horse speed rather than wagon speed. Keep on both sides, never bunch, and if anything opens up go like hell!"

It wasn't a very satisfactory plan, but considering the alternatives it was the best available. At least they knew now what they were dealing with, if not the location and exact numbers. The train was formed up yet again, the people were briefed and, if they could handle them, given arms. Then they pulled out.

A little over an hour later they all saw where the ambush had to be. The open desert area was growing wilder and nastier as they went, and in a few miles more the road would descend from the cracked desert with the tendril-like lurking plants and into a canyon formed by a now dry riverbed that, either in the past or on rare occasions now, had lots of rushing water in it. The canyon narrowed around the road in at least two places, either one of which had perches that seemed impossible to reach but, if they could be reached, would be ideal spots for ambushers. For now, though, they were still on the sippiqua flats, a fact that made everyone a bit nervous.

Jahoort stopped the train with the intention of sending men forward on either side with binoculars and rifles, with the hope of spotting the ambush and, if not taking them out, at least making it very hot for whoever sat there. If there was enough of a crossfire from enough rifles and pistols, one bullet at a time or not, then the wagons might be able to haul ass through the narrows before they could be cut down. The road was also very well defined through the area; Jahoort, if he knew the location of the gun, might risk running the thing at night.

From the rear of the train came the sudden shout of "Dust behind!" which put an end to such thoughts. The raiders from Bi'ihqua, as the navigator had figured, had closed on the train and were now riding full in to force them forward into the slaughter.

Jahoort quickly rode back to the rear of the train. "How many you make it, Dal?"

"Shit! Must be a dozen at least. Maybe more. Remember, they been hittin' *trains* in Bi'ihqua and gettin' away with it!"

Sam and Boday had jumped down to see what was going on, just like some of the others. The dust cloud approaching told the story, and they knew as well as the crew what had to be ahead.

Boday let loose her whip. "Well, little flower, we die together!" she sighed. "They shall never take you unless it is over the body of Boday! Do not be downcast! It was meant to be! And the heroic death of Boday will awaken the critics who will proclaim her a legend and the greatest artist who ever lived!"

Even Charley was pretty glum right now. "All this for nothin'. Damn! Wish I had a couple of guns right now!"

Sam had just stared at the cloud, not believing that it could really be happening. Not now. Not to her, and Charley, and Boday. Not to those nice kids. . . . She clutched the Jewel of Omak. "Demon, get us the hell *out* of this!"

You expect miracles or something? asked the demon. *I'll save you if I can but you know my limitations.*

"Damn it! You forced me into this!" she screamed, suddenly terrified.

Charley sighed behind her. "I sure wish we had one of your damned thunderstorms *now*," she sighed.

"What?" Sam was hardly even sane anymore as she continued to stare.

"One of your damned thunderstorms. Can't you see what would happen if it rained on them? Especially *here*?"

My God! Why not? Sam thought crazily. *They came every time before!*

Distances were deceiving on the flats; the crew was circling and setting up the train for defense methodically, with no sense of hurry.

Sam looked up at the sky. A few wispy, white clouds in a pale blue field, nothing more. Just like back at the cabin long ago. . . .

"Okay!" she screamed up to the heavens, loud and forcefully. "You blood-sucking nightmare storms! You been huntin' me and huntin' me! Well *here I am!* Come and get me!"

The wispy clouds started to move. The fact that they actually did both awed and startled her, and at first she didn't believe it, but *they were actually moving!* Thickening. Drawing moisture from behind them—from whatever sector of Tubikosa was now along the border maybe ten miles back!

Now there was a near solid wall of clouds in the distance, going from horizon to horizon, a weather front so straight you could have drawn it with a ruler. On their side it was sunny and blue, sucked of any clouds, but at that line it was dark and rumbling. . . .

"Holy shit! You *did* it!" Charley exclaimed, a little awed herself.

No, not *quite* ruler straight. Centered perhaps right over the road there was a prominence coming out from the front, forming . . .

A head. A clearly defined picture of a face in the clouds sharp as a cheap photograph and just as solid. A face and a neck going down to the shoulders, with arms out, infinite arms, that were the front itself. . . .

A face she knew.

Charley might have been awed but she was more scared than that and she had a sudden horrible thought. "Sam! Boday! *Get in the wagon! Get us the hell off this mesa or we're gonna be sucked up, too!*"

Sam just continued to stare and Boday did not understand, so Charley went up and actually shook Sam and repeated her panicked warning.

"Charley—the clouds! There's a face in the clouds!"

"I don't give a fuck if there's God Himself in the clouds! We gotta move and you got to warn the rest!" Charley was nearsighted. She could see the storm as an approaching line of darkness but could not make out even so huge a detail.

Jahoort and the others weren't so oblivious, either. They yelled and screamed and told people to forget anything and just do a firm hitch and get into the canyon and stop. They had to beat that rain.

That Boday heard and understood as well, and she practically yanked Sam away and back into the wagon, which they'd never even gotten into defensive position. Charley needed no persuading—she was back inside quicker than they could get on the seat and jiggle the reins.

Nargas weren't very fast animals even when pushed, and the dip down into the canyon was narrow, really no wider than two wagons' worth if that, and a bit more than a mile away at the start. It was going to be a very near thing for most of them as the front with the strange head came ever on.

Sam peered back nervously. "But it's gonna catch me this time!"

"One damned problem at a time!" Charley yelled, wondering if they *would* make it? Some of the professional and veteran drivers, sure, and maybe all the ones on horseback, but she was dependent on two citified novices doing all the driving.

But Sam suddenly snapped out of it and took the reins like a pro, getting the nargas into a rhythm and making the best possible time without becoming unbalanced. The demon of the jewel couldn't handle ambushes and small armies, but it sure as hell knew how to drive a wagon.

They drew abreast of a cargo wagon going at top speed and the nargas, seeing the competition, matched pace, but they were mere inches apart. A mistake on the part of either driver or the nargas themselves would bring the two into a side collision at speed.

Then they *did* bump—once, twice! It was all Sam could do to control the nargas and keep them straight but she managed. Charley was holding on for dear life and looking back out the back flap. She couldn't see any horses or wagons and figured they had to be last, but she sure as hell could see that dark approaching mass. "It's gonna *catch* us!" she muttered, teeth tightly clenched.

The edge of the rain shield raced after them, darkening the

parched desert and causing in its wake a veritable jungle of thin, waving tentacles to rise all across the plain, turning it from a sun-baked nightmare into an instant sea of living, active plants.

And then they were down, down into the canyon, the walls rising up, as rain suddenly overtook and then enveloped them. Sam started to pull up but Charley yelled, "No! Keep going if you can see!"

"But the ambusher!"

"The hell with the bushwacker! If he can see to shoot anything in this shit he *deserves* to get us!"

This thought had not occurred to everybody, and there was almost a traffic jam at the bottom for a moment. Jahoort and his crew, though, were there, drenched by the rain, screaming at people to keep going. They no longer cared about the bushwacker; this much rain would cause a flash flood of this dry riverbed very quickly, and that narrow ambush spot would be like target zero when the dam burst in a very short time.

Sam needed no urging. Demon-driven, she made her way expertly around those too scared or dense to move and made it full speed for the opening ahead. Already the dry riverbed was starting to fill, and there was almost a waterfall behind them.

Something went *smash! ping!* inside the wagon but she didn't stop and was soon on the other side and pulling to the side, off the road, where it was higher ground. Still she didn't want to stop, though; others would come through and would need room as well.

The highest point available wasn't very high, particularly with the crush and in the near-blinding rain, so she picked the best spot she could and stopped, then turned around. "Charley? You okay?"

"Yeah. I *think* so," her friend muttered. "Jesus, Sam! There's a line of fucking *bullet holes* through the wagon and half our stuff! That's no repeater—that's a damned *machine gun!*"

"Take the reins, Boday," Sam said, handing it off to the artist, and went back where at least it was nominally dry. There were holes in the canvas top, though, through which rain was coming, and wood was splintered in a neat diagonal line. Charley had taken a small knife and was busily trying to pry one of the spent bullets out. After a while she exposed part of it, enough to see what it was.

"Thirty caliber, copper jacket," she said, shaking her head. "That gun's regular Army issue. With guns and ammo like that it's no *wonder* those soldiers got mowed down. Without that rain there was no way to keep that sucker from taking out the whole train easy. They got nothing to fight *this* kind'a stuff." She stopped a moment, thinking. "You know, with enough of these just a few could really hold off a whole damned Akhbreed army. Son of a bitch! I think maybe they really got a chance to pull their revolution off! Imagine a couple of these in the hands of a couple of little Bi'ihquans instead of melons!"

Sam nodded absently. "Charley—there was a face, a head, in the clouds."

"Yeah? So? What's got you so hung up? Never seen faces in clouds before?"

"Charley—it was *your* face. It was your face in the clouds, bringing on the storm like a cape."

For a moment Charley was taken aback, then she got it. "Uh-uh, Sam. Not *my* face. *Your* face. I'm the gal with the big nose and the chubby cheekbones, remember? This is *your* face, only prettied up a bit and still thin."

Sam shook her head slowly from side to side. "Uh-uh. I always had a boy's face. This face was real feminine-lookin' even though it had short hair. That's how clear it was. And it had somethin' on its head or around it—a headband or crown or tiara or somethin'."

"Sam, there's a lot more that goes into a face than that. It was yours—and, even though I know it sounds crazy, if there *was* a face in there it *should'a* been yours. All this time you been running from those storms and you *call* 'em. You called this one, crazy as it sounds."

"I didn't call those other storms. They were *hunting* for me." But, dimly, she remembered that last one at the mall, the one that had scared her half to death. She had told it to go away—and it had.

"You gotta think magic around this place," her friend reminded her. "If you can call a storm and make it do tricks, then so can other people. So now we know there can be good and bad storms, right? Sam—this is important! Not just now, 'though Lord knows if you hadn't done it the rest wouldn't make no difference, but in general. Sam—*you can do magic.* Not Boday's potions, and maybe stronger than your pet demon's tricks."

The storm was letting up; it had almost passed now, with just some light rain and dreary mist on its back side. Suddenly the wagon started to jerk and lurch, and both women moved forward.

"Darlings! The nargas will not hold still! There is some kind of noise—you hear? The ground seems to be shaking. . . ."

Charley was born and raised in the southwestern desert and it didn't take her long to figure it out. "Cut the team loose!" she said sharply. "Cut 'em loose!" She stood on the seat and looked around. Damn! It was near sheer cliffs around here. There might be a few holds here and there but there wasn't much time.

"What d'ya mean, 'cut 'em loose'?" Sam responded.

"For God's sake cut 'em loose and climb up as high and fast as you can for dear life!" she screamed. "Sam—*it's a flash flood!* Any second now!"

Sam didn't have to hear any more. "Boday—cut loose the team and climb the walls! Flash flood!"

Boday jumped down, knocked loose the pin, then made sure Sam was down and made for the walls. In back of them, they could see remnants of the train scattered all over the canyon floor, some still inside that narrow stretch that would be flushed like a toilet any minute. There was no way to do more than scream warnings as they got up as high as they could. Charley was way ahead of them, her hands holding onto a very narrow rocky outcrop. She intended to pull herself up if she could, but she turned and saw the wall of water coming and could hardly believe her eyes. The surge looked like some dam had busted.

As if in slow motion she watched the narrow end of the canyon as horses reared and started to run while others, just stick figures, turned and watched what was coming in sheer panic.

The water hit her like a brick wall and instantly she, who had gotten the highest up, was none the less in the water and being carried at high speed toward the rock wall of the narrows, back where she'd come from.

She kicked off her boots, took a deep breath, and went under, hoping to ride the center surge.

Charley came to in what seemed to be dense brush. For a moment she didn't know what had happened or where she might be, but after she'd coughed up a little water and taken several deep breaths she suddenly thought, *I'm alive! I made it!*

But—to where? The top of the canyon? Not likely. Somewhere high up in that narrows section where there were lots of ledges. She got up, feeling a bit bruised in the ribs but otherwise surprisingly good. Her long hair was waterlogged and it took a lot of wringing out before it was manageable enough to forget for the time being.

It was only a few yards to the edge and she saw she was just where she thought—on some fairly wide and lengthy ledge about two thirds of the way up the canyon wall. At least the bushes here didn't drink your blood—although it probably wouldn't matter if they did right now. After that drink *they'd* had, there was no way they could take any more for a while.

The water was already receding and, frankly, gave little hint of what it had been not long before. The clouds were breaking and the sun was actually coming out. It seemed good at first, but as soon as the heat and tremendous evaporation hit she began to wonder if clouds weren't better.

She couldn't see well enough at this distance to make out details, but it looked like loads of debris scattered all over the canyon floor, maybe even the bodies of drowned horses and nargas. Maybe the bodies of people, too, she thought suddenly. Sam, Boday, those really nice kids . . .

She had survived, although it looked mostly like luck. Maybe others had as well, although she wasn't at all sure how good a swimmer Sam was. Maybe that demon knew all the swimming tricks, though. It was a hope. The water level had been high enough but not so high as to wash anybody up out of the canyon, that was for sure, except maybe right at the end— and that would have washed them right into those creepy crawlies that lived there. Of course, they were so saturated that somebody might have a chance if they weren't so full of water they couldn't come around in time to get back.

Still, she knew she had to face facts. She could *hope* they survived, hope that *everybody* survived, but from a practical point of view she was alone and it was one hell of a long way down without a rope.

She examined herself. A few scratches, probably from the bushes, and the bruises, nothing more. She was oddly undressed, though. She'd been wearing one of the stretch pullover tops and that had come through fairly well, but when she'd contorted to get the boots off she'd also slipped off the pair of work pants that threatened to drag her down with their extra waterlogged weight. She was naked from the waist down, a rather odd feeling. She slipped off the top and wrung it out as best she could, then went over to lay it out on one of the bushes to dry. Better something than nothing with this sun. She was about to stretch it out when she suddenly saw a hand and gasped. She cleared away as much as she could and found a man there.

He was dead; no question about that. It was Fromick, one of the quieter crew, who had been one of the men who'd set out after the two surviving raiders. His clothes were bloodstained and ripped to shreds—he must have hit the rocks and not much use, but, oddly, his gunbelt was still on and the twin pistols still in their holsters. She didn't like touching dead men, but if she could have made use of the shirt or pants she'd have done so. She undid the belt and managed to get it off him. Most crew kept their personal stuff in the crew wagon, but these belts often had compartments, pouches, whatever, for practical stuff.

It was well worn; a veteran's gunbelt, but it was also very well made. She examined it, felt it—it felt heavy and looked a bit too thick. There were also some pouches which she opened and checked, knowing that they were supposedly waterproof.

Some money—the hell with that. What good would it be here, anyway? A silver-plated cigarette case containing fifteen cigarettes and a small flint activated lighting stick. That might come in handy. The cigarettes were dry; the odds were she could build a fire if she had to. A partly eaten bar of dark chocolate—*that* was a godsend. A tiny, toy-like penknife. And, all along the lining in a clever series of folds, bullets.

She examined the pistols. They were nicely balanced, if a bit strange to look at. No barrel. Somebody could make machine guns with thirty-caliber copper-clad ammunition, but nobody official had more than a single-shot weapon. Weird. Surely these people could figure out the principles involved. It was like there was a law against repeaters or something.

And, of course, she realized that this must be it. It must be, in fact, the explanation for a lot of crazy things like people with flush toilets, electric ranges, and elevators, who *didn't* have

cars or trains or telephones or even telegraphs and whose guns
had single shots so their swords wouldn't be obsolete. It was
like a code. If the Akhbreed controlled everything, they also
controlled what knowledge was permitted to get out and what
could be made in the colonial factories. No repeaters. Not
honorable or something.

But you didn't make fancy machine guns and the kind of
ammunition they used without big factories, machine tools,
standardized parts, lots of supplies. Either some king himself
was with the opposition, which seemed improbable, or else
that gun came from the same kind of place she did—
somewhere else. If people dropped down now and again, then
maybe machine guns did, too. But with bullets? Enough to
make it worth toting around and using? It was still not making
sense.

She ejected the bullet in the chamber, then stuck a dry one in
and snapped it closed. Not bad, she thought. The shells were
man-stoppers, more like forty-fours than police specials, but it
was nicely balanced. She had—let's see—twenty-four bullets
now. When the leather dried out, she had at least a weapon and
one she felt she could shoot. Just like on Cousin Harry's ranch
back home.

That sun was really mean, so she went back a bit until she
had some shade from the canyon wall itself. The evaporation
was so intense she felt like she was trapped in a steamer, but
there was nothing to do except wait it out and try not to cook.
She settled back in the shade, put the pistols beside her, and
worked with the penknife on the gunbelt until she had a little if
not very neat-looking hole where she wanted it. She tried it
with the belt buckle—one of those fancy green stones that
looked like a design cut to oval shape and mounted in a big,
fancy brass setting sort of like the truck drivers wore back
home—and it fit and seemed to hold. She got up and tried it on
and it worked, although, of course, the belt was *way* too long
after the hole and it was still a bit wide, although it hung nicely
at an angle on her hips.

She was suddenly struck by how she must look, stark naked
with a wide gunbelt and holsters with twin pearl-handled
single-hot pistols and nothing else. It seemed at one and the
same time the most erotic and damned stupid silly vision she
could think of. *Watch out, Akahlar!* she thought crazily. *Here*

comes the Butterfly Kid and she's hot to prowl! She needed something silly to think about right now, and she laughed about the vision, then took off the belt, cut some of the extra length off, removed the pistols and kept them with her, then stretched it all out to dry just beyond the shadow where the sun would be right on it. Then she sat against the rock wall and just tried to get some rest and eventually, in spite of herself, she did nod off.

She awoke what had to be hours later because the shadow was now very thin and even her legs were in sunlight; she started, and looked around. There was a strong wind up now, and a dry, hot one. It no longer felt all that humid but it still felt like an oven. She'd simply traded the steamer for the bakery. She was hungry and thirsty but there wasn't much she could do about the thirst right now and she didn't want to eat the chocolate for fear the extra dryness it might bring would drive her mad for a drink.

The gunbelt had flipped over and actually been blown several feet; the wind up here was pretty good as the climate returned to its former state with all deliberate speed. She retrieved the belt and then went over to the swaying bushes to discover that Fromick was getting very gruesome and very smelly and her top had blown away someplace. *Great,* she thought. *My only protection, such as it was, from this damned sun.* She briefly considered undressing Fromick and making what she could from his tattered clothing, but the look and the smell were just too much. She couldn't bear to touch that body, not for anything.

The noise the wind made blowing through the narrows made it next to impossible to hear anything else; no use listening for people or cries or whatever now, and she was too damned nearsighted to tell even if there had been an ice cream wagon in the canyon.

She checked the sun. Might not be long until it was beyond the other wall, and when it was it would get dark real fast around here. If she had any chance of getting off this place without help, now was the time to explore. The Butterfly Kid was on the prowl for sure.

The ledge or whatever it was was larger than she thought, and followed a curve around the rocky wall. Just beyond there was another bushy outcrop and it looked recently occupied.

She drew one of her pistols and walked cautiously to it, then knelt down. Shells. Hundreds of them. And several spent cartridge belts as well. She suddenly tensed. *This was the ambush spot!* But there was no mysterious lady changeling, whatever that was, around now, and no machine gun, either. The fact that the assassin wasn't there was not unusual, since somebody from these parts could be expected to have some abilities to get around here. She got *up* here, after all. But machine guns—this wasn't the Al Capone type, this was the Army type. They were bulky and heavy. If this mystery bushwacker could have levitated a machine gun she wouldn't have needed one. And she and it hadn't washed off—not if the shells were still on the ground. That meant there might be some way off this place!

She followed the rock wall along very closely and it didn't take long to find it. You don't expect to find a wide, flat piece of wood around this area. Two ropes secured it, nicely tied off to make an effective scaffold. *Hot damn!* She didn't even consider that there might be danger at the top; if she didn't get off here it didn't matter, and if they came back later and took this all away she'd be stuck anyway. She holstered the pistols as tight as she could, grabbed on to one of the ropes, and with a lot of effort started up the cliff.

She was amazed when she made it to the top. She never would have believed that her arms had the strength for it, but, then, she had a lot of motivation as well. The arm muscles hurt like hell and she felt exhausted, but she was up and out.

It was a crude wooden winch at the top, anchored by steel pins driven hard into the rock, but it was more than enough to haul up a machine gun, maybe all in one piece, and definitely pull up a person, too. That meant at least one, probably two people up here as well, most likely very big and very strong. Of course, it may have been the pair who escaped come back to rescue their boss, but Charley doubted that the brain behind this would trust to ones like them.

She surveyed the terrain. It was pretty jagged and some of the connections between sheer drops were pretty damned narrow, but she would have no trouble with it—if the light held. At least she had more of it up here, maybe an hour or more additional. It was like following a maze to get all the way to some safety, but aside from being pretty hot on the feet it was also easy. The right route wasn't that hard, either. They apparently hadn't taken or risked horses or other pack animals in here, but tracks of a small, narrow, wheeled cart or something were easy to make out wherever the rain had softened fill or dirt. It wasn't a continuous track, but it wasn't hard to spot, either. Probably the mount for the machine gun. And there *was* a trail of sorts, worn right into the rock. Clearly this was a favorite vantage point to look down on the road and not be seen.

Here and there, too, were hard natural rock depressions in which there was still collected rainwater. The rock was too solid for seepage and the depressions just a bit too deep to be evaporated in one day. She eagerly went to one, then carefully tasted it. It tasted like rocky rainwater, so she drank, and even took some and rubbed it on her body. The wind evaporated it quickly, but it felt good and at least she wasn't gonna die right off of thirst. She celebrated with two bites of the now nearly liquid candy, then reluctantly continued on. Light was failing and you couldn't afford a misstep in *this* country.

It apparently ended in a sheer rock wall, but when you got right to it you could see that the trail veered sharply to the left and continued on up. It was real nasty badlands, all right, but clearly *somebody* lived around here.

The trail reached the top, then followed it for a bit, then continued on part way down the other side. There was no way to get much farther today, and nobody, but nobody, human walked the badlands at night. She found a rock-ringed depression that gave some shelter from the wind and wasn't *too* uncomfortable and settled in. Both pistols were loaded with dry bullets; it was *some* comfort, but not much. Sooner or later she'd have to find somebody or starve or die of thirst or exposure. If that person were Akhbreed she'd be his or her slave instantly under the law—or else. If it was somebody else, it would most likely be somebody allied with the woman with the machine gun and that wasn't too thrilling an idea, either. One day at a time, one problem at a time. At least she was still alive and in one piece.

When it got dark out here, it got *very* dark *very* fast. The wind died down to nothing, though, causing for a while an eerie stillness. She slept for a while, never very long and never very deep, and then she'd wake up for periods, during some of which she would be unable to keep from dwelling on her fears. She'd been brave and tough long enough; she couldn't hold it back anymore, and during more than one waking period she couldn't help crying until she was just more or less cried out.

Then she'd just sit there, trying to see *anything* in the blackness. The stars overhead were pretty thick but blurry, and what moon there'd been went down not long after the sun. So she sat there, staring into the blackness, and after a while she swore she heard voices. Imagination? Wish fulfillment? She strained again to hear. Definitely somebody, maybe a lot of people, and some animals, too. Where? She carefully made her way back onto the trail and tried to look down and around. *There!* A sort of blurry glow like a big campfire or something. She wished she had better vision or glasses, but that was the best she could do. Now the question was, what to do about it?

There was nothing to do but try and make for it. Even if it was the bushwackers, it might be the only chance she had. She'd be going down the trail blind and in the dark, so take it slow and easy girl, but the trail up had always had one side against solid rock. The trick would be figuring the curves. Slow and easy . . .

It took her quite some time, perhaps two hours or more, to get down, but finally she was close enough to really see where she was going. It was a big, mostly level area just off the main trail, set into a huge natural stone arch. There were horses there, and a few small wagons, and some people, too. She needed to get closer. It looked like a couple of guards down there, with rifles, but they weren't looking *her* way. Who could come from *this* direction, after all?

That allowed her to get in very close, close enough to see just what was what in the encampment. What she saw both excited and repulsed her.

There were two men with rifles all right, one at the head of the trail and the other by the fire. The one closest to the fire was wearing a dirty blue uniform; definitely one of the pair that escaped. The other might have been the other one; it was hard to tell for sure. There was also somebody asleep in the arch, maybe two. There were also four horses and a pair of nargas tied up there docilely.

Laid out to her right and the right of the fire was a grisly scene. There were bodies, lots of bodies there, all stripped naked, all terribly mutilated. Maybe five or more. All looked to be men, although it was hard to tell from that distance and in their condition.

To the left and nearest her were more bodies stretched out, but some of these, at least, were definitely alive. They were all lying naked on their backs, spread-eagled, their arms and legs apparently tied down with rock bolts securing heavy rope. All were female, and all appeared to have gags or something stuck in their mouths. She counted four and she knew them all. Boday was easiest to spot—long and looking like an abstract painting. Sam, too, was there, in all her corpulent glory, and the other two . . .

Sweet Jesus! The Serkosh girls! Rani and Sheka! Those *bastards!* It didn't take Sherlock Holmes to figure this out.

After it was safe, these men and their confederates had gone hunting for loot and maybe survivors. They'd found both, from the looks of it. They might even have saved a few lives—but not out of the goodness of their black hearts. The loot was piled up in front of the fire, with the Mandan gold blankets neatly separated off to one side. Sam—it was hard to tell but it didn't look like she had anything around her neck. Ten to one the Jewel of Omak was in that pile as well, the demon helpless with Sam probably unconscious and maybe half-drowned, while they cut the neck chain off her and tossed it in their loot sacks. Helpless now because there was nobody to aim the damned thing.

The male survivors had been brought here and then apparently tortured to death, either for revenge over the morning's work or just for fun. The women had been stretched out and, well, it didn't take much of a leap of imagination to figure out how they'd been used. Sheka—she was only nine years old, her sister just thirteen! *Damn* these monsters!

But what could she do about it? Two guards, and at least two more in the arch, probably with weapons nearby. She spotted the machine gun on its little cart, but it was well on the other side from her and looked packed down, anyway. Useless. She had two single-shot pistols. She had always been a good shot, and even with the distance she thought she could take the far guard, which would alert the one by the fire but wouldn't give him anyplace to hide or a clear target to shoot at. She might take both of them—but then she'd be at the mercy of the ones in the cleft until she reloaded, and that would take precious seconds. During that time those others could take cover—and use the stretched out and helpless women in between as a bargaining chip. Sam had twice come to her rescue. There was no question of not doing something, only what to do without getting her and them killed?

She had maybe an hour til dawn to figure that out.

·12·

A Choice of Evils

IT TOOK CHARLEY several minutes to realize that the guard by the fire was asleep. It figured; he'd had a long day, although not as long as she had. Let *him* survive a raid, a chase, an ambush, and a flash flood and wind up in fairly good shape! Still, she'd experienced nothing like those prisoners there, and nothing like what they might experience if she couldn't figure this one out. She had no demons or magic jewels to help her, no special powers, but she *did* have weapons she knew and superb control of her body and whatever brains she'd been born with. They would have to do.

The real question was the other guard. If he was the other raider and he was asleep as well, then there was a chance. He had a rifle, perhaps other guns, and a very good field of fire for the whole area. If she had *his* position, then she might not be able to rescue the prisoners but she sure as hell would have a point-blank field of fire into the arch. Her long vision was poor enough that she might not be able to hit still forms in there, but she sure as hell could detect and hit moving ones, while she would be in darkness and behind some cover. She also wondered what a few rifle shots rattling around inside that arch might hit.

But first she had to get over there.

The fire was down but it still gave off pretty good illumination; there was maybe a twenty-foot section of trail that was lit, if dimly, by the flickering fire and its reflections against the deep rust red of the rock arch. If the trail guard had either nodded off or was concentrating entirely on the trail in the other direction, and if she was quiet enough, she had a chance. She just hoped there weren't two trail guards there; she would have to shoot the bastard from the start and then try and nail the other one before he reacted to the first shot. If there was somebody else up there or farther down the trail she was dead meat.

She had no reservations about shooting these men, though. In fact, if it hadn't been for her courtesan life where she'd met some pretty decent guys and had seen a slice of normal life, she might have had the impression that, here in Akahlar at least, all the men were vicious, brutish monsters, even the good ones. Even Jahoort and his crew had butchered those wounded raiders without a qualm; the only real deep down difference between them seemed to be that one was official and the other criminal. Just like in the Old West, where the only way most times to tell the difference between the psychopathic killer and the marshal was that the marshal wore a star.

No matter what, though, nobody with any guts at all could have any feeling for these men, not with the grisly sights laid out right here in front of them. The problem was, could she do it alone? Everything she saw told her that all she'd be doing would be adding another victim to these bastards' scalp belt even if she got one or two of them. Still, she would have to try.

She looked at the looming cliff wall that followed the trail opposite the camp; that went up who knew how far into the darkness and she wondered if there was any possibility of another route over to the other side. She backed off and decided to see if there was any way short of a direct walk down the trail where either of the guards might, if he wasn't really asleep, pick her off with ease.

Still, she didn't relish the climb. It might end in a sheer drop for all she knew, and it'd be pretty close to pitch dark up there. If it had been easy or a real threat to them they'd have put a guard up there, too.

That was a nasty thought. Maybe they did. Looking at the potential field of observation and fire such a post would present such a guard, she knew she damned well had to find out.

It wasn't an easy climb, but the rock was mostly layered shale on the far side and there were footholds, if tenuous at times. Still, it was very slowgoing in the darkness; for all she knew a single misstep might send her plunging a mile or two down into some nameless canyon.

After twenty minutes or so it began to level out, but just as she felt she had a real chance she sensed something in the darkness ahead and froze.

"*Shhhh!*" somebody whispered in Akhbreed. Then it added, in the lowest of whispers, "Come ahead, girl. I won't hurt you. I'm from the train as well."

She wasn't sure if it was a trick or not, but considering her position there wasn't much she could do but act as if it was not. She hauled herself up and sat, breathing hard. She could see the figure of a man now propped against a rock outcrop, but it was impossible to tell more about him.

"You are the courtesan," he said softly. "The butterfly girl. I always thought you were a lot smarter than you were supposed to be. Can you understand me?"

She groped for the words and hoped they came out all right. The trouble with the language wasn't learning the words but duplicating the complex intonations. "Saa," she whispered back. "Ducadol, nar prucadol." *Yes. Understand. No speak.*

He gave a low chuckle. "You just told me you want to speak to my ass, not blow it, but I think I get the meaning. I saw you down there with the two pistols trying to work it out. I know how you feel. I was a mess when I crawled out of that damned ravine after hiding from them scavengers, but I made it after 'em. I was already busted up somethin' fierce; this just about's done me in. Kind'a hoped you'd try this route, though. I thought I could get the drop on 'em but wasn't much I could do. Might plug one or two of 'em but the rest would get me or hold them women hostage. They's bloody monsters, they are. Don't worry 'bout them hearin' me. Wind's wrong at this low pitch."

"Who?" Charley managed.

He coughed and seemed to shake a bit but got hold of himself. "Who, you mean? Them two guards is the ones who hit us and got away. There's four more in the cleft. One's Zamofir, the little fellow with the moustache from the train. He's banged up bad and wasn't with them but they knew him and took him in. He's a bad 'un. Two more are big suckers, maybe changelings. Hard to say. Their leader's mighty strange. Changeling sure. Woman in purple cloak and robes, real sharp tongue, but there's a lot more movin' under them robes than should be. She was the gunner—and the leader."

"Who?" Charley repeated, somewhat impatiently. She

didn't like the idea of fighting six of them, not one bit—and if one or more were inhuman . . .

The man seemed to grope for a moment, then understood. "Oh—you mean me. I'm Rawl Serkosh. The two young ones down there are my daughters. It's why I had to follow and why I haven't been able to act." He shook again, this time in rage. "You don't know what it's been like, or how long I been wonderin' if causin' their deaths wouldn't be a mercy." He sighed. "Rini's dead. So's Jom. I don't know about Tan. Right now, though, them girls is all I got left."

She crawled slowly over to him. He had a gun—maybe more than one. One was a rifle, anyway, and maybe there was ammunition. He saw her feel it and sighed. "Yeah. Took it off a dead narga. One of the pack animals. Rifle, couple'a pistols, even a crossbow. What good does it do me? I'm busted up bad inside. Bleedin' inside, too, I think. I ain't goin' nowheres now."

Her mind raced as she thought of how to use this poor man to best advantage. She struggled, then came up with a few words she needed. "Knife?"

"Yeah. Still got mine. Why?"

"Me cut girls loose. You—protect. Up here."

For a moment there was no response, and she was afraid that he was dead, but suddenly he said, "Maybe. If they ain't been drugged or magicked or somethin'." Again a slight cough. "Been thinkin', though, what I could do if I was able to move right. That big repeater of theirs. See them boxes right there? That's the bullets. Somebody stick a fire under that, all hell would break loose. Might blow up, might shoot all over. Yeah, I know, might kill the women, but they're better off dead if they can't be rescued. Go down, toss a fire under that gun wagon, then get back and cut 'em loose—I'll cover. Get 'em to the rocks on this side if they can move, otherwise leave 'em. When it goes, we shoot the guards under the cover of the bangs and booms. The ones in the cleft will stay put til its over, then come rushin' out, not knowin' we're here. By that time we'll have reloads. We have to nail 'em before they know they're bein' nailed." He paused a moment, as if expecting a reply, then sighed when none came.

"Yeah, I know," he sighed. "Odds are they'll spot you first thing. I'm sure both them guards are out cold—the one down by the fire ain't moved in two hours—but who knows how hard they sleep? One little thing goes wrong and it's all over. It was just the best I could do."

"Give crossbow, knife. Load guns." It was the craziest plan she'd ever heard and sure to get her killed or worse, but damn it it was worth a try!

"You know how to use a crossbow?"

"Saa," she responded confidently. She was ready to do this now, before she thought about it too much and realized how insane it was. The truth was, she really *didn't* know the crossbow, but the thing resembled a rifle with a bow and arrow set on top. She figured she could use it at the distances she'd be dealing with—and maybe without waking people up.

"You keep live. Shoot straight," she told him, knowing it sounded all wrong but that he'd get the idea. If nature didn't crush him at the critical moment, in which case she was at least no worse off than before, there was a glimmer of a chance. "That way safe?" she asked him, thinking that this would be better from the go-around position.

"Yeah. *Now* it is. Good luck, little beauty. May the gods bless you with success or death."

She made her way past him and for the first time saw why this was a safe route. There was a body next to Serkosh; a dead, rumpled heap that was all that remained of the guard who'd been posted up here.

"Arrow or knife right in the throat," he told her. "Slow death but they can't yell for nothin'."

Getting down was not all that much easier on the other side than getting up, and now she had extra things to carry. She was nervous that the crossbow might hit against the side of the rock and awaken the guard below, but she was loath to give up any added weapon.

The snores she heard from below gave her the first feeling of optimism she had. If the fellow by the fire was asleep, and this one was as well, then they were a pretty confident, complacent bunch—or stupid. They had, after all, depended on sheer numbers and brute force against the train. Effective, but not exactly subtle plotting.

This one was certainly dead to the world. She managed to get almost all the way down, and not as silently as she would have wished, without his breaking his snoring rhythm. He had a shotgun in his lap and a pistol on his hip, but neither had moved.

She carefully threaded the arrow into the crossbow and pulled it back until it latched, then crept toward the guard. For the first time she wondered if she could really do it. Kill somebody in cold blood, that is, rather than in a fight. She knew she could shoot him if he were awake or even became aware of her, but, like this, she wasn't so damned sure anymore. Easy enough to tell Sam to do it, but this was her and this was now.

She stood up, barely two yards from him, and raised and aimed the crossbow. If it had been loaded right, if she figured it out and it worked, she could hardly miss. She stood there a moment, frozen, all thought really gone, then she pulled the trigger—or tried to. It was jammed, somehow. It wouldn't fire! She realized instantly that there had to be a safety catch, fumbled for it, and found it, sliding it forward. She raised the crossbow again and took aim through its sights when suddenly the man jerked awake and turned and started to stand up!

It was almost as if the world had turned to slow motion, but she adjusted with a proficiency that only danger gave her and pulled the trigger. The arrow went off and went straight into his head, missing the neck and throat. He fell back from its force, then to her horror twitched, then started to pull himself up again! The force of the arrow had split his skull wide open; blood was pouring from his head, yet he still moved! She dropped the crossbow and went instinctively for her pistol, but then the man stood up absolutely straight, froze for a moment, then toppled back down atop his rocky perch.

Shaken, she dropped the crossbow—no more arrows anyway—and approached his body. She reached out and pulled the shotgun, a double-barreled type, from under his body as if he might turn and rise again at any moment. *That* was one tough son of a bitch!

The other one was asleep at the dwindling fire. That fire was beginning to die now from not having been stoked or fueled once again, and it was the only source she had for her own little bonfire. There wasn't any way around it; she'd have to quietly but boldly go right to that fire, get something useful and still burning, and torch the ammunition wagon, then make it all the way back to the captives before it went off. The hell with it; either she had cover or she didn't. She wasn't sure about Serkosh's long-term prospects, but as long as his daughters were down there she felt he'd keep alive on sheer will alone.

She gripped the shotgun, took a deep breath, then walked out into the exposed flat, keeping to the back of the guard at the fire, and alert for any signs of movement from him. Serkosh was certainly right, though; even if she had to blow this guy's head off and wake up the others, the first and only real priority—and hope—was torching that ammo.

A horse snorted and shifted slightly over to one side, and a couple of nargas echoed the sounds, which reverberated eerily in the camp, but the man remained still and there was no sign of real movement from the arch-like cleft. She circled around before going to the fire, so that it was between her and the sleeper, then knelt down. There weren't many trees in these parts; they had been burning the remnants of a wagon, and there were curved wooden pieces of ribbing there. She hauled one up, thankful that she'd been good at pick-up sticks as a kid, and got it free—but it wasn't actually aflame, just glowing red. She gingerly put its glowing tip back in the small remaining flame and caught it again, then slowly withdrew it, all the time looking up at the man on the other side of the fire.

Now it was slow going, guarding that flame, as she went back to the ammunition wagon. She reached it, but just as she did her flame went out again. She put down the shotgun and tried blowing on it, then swinging it in the air to get some oxygen to it. It glowed brightly, but wouldn't keep a flame. The hell with it, she decided, and touched it to a rope, then blew on it with all her lung power until the rope began to char and then smolder and then, with more blowing, she got a flame in the rope. It was tenuous, but it might work. She waited, oblivious to the danger, until it caught fairly well, then finally used it to re-light the stake. She touched off the covering over the ammunition crates and, when she felt she had enough small fires going, she threw the stake on top.

So far so good. She crossed back to the other side as if she owned the place, always with one eye on the sleeping man, and reached the staked out prisoners. She went to Sam, knelt down, and shook her. Sam stirred, then began to say, loudly, without opening her eyes, "No! *No!*" Charley put her hand over Sam's mouth and stifled any further outburst, and Sam seemed to settle back down. Serkosh had been right; they were drugged or something. That complicated things.

Charley took the knife from her gunbelt and sawed away at Sam's ropes. It wasn't easy; the ropes were fairly thick. Finally she got one, then a second, then the feet. By the fourth and final rope she was getting good at it; she knew by now where to cut for maximum speed and efficiency. Sam did not move even when less restrained; Charley hadn't expected her to.

She had freed Boday's arms when she suddenly stopped and froze. There was a sound from the arch, and she retreated back into the shadows and watched, glancing over at the ammunition wagon with the machine gun. It was smoking pretty damned good now but there wasn't any visible open flame.

A man emerged from the arch. He was big and covered with thick black body hair as well as a full beard and very long hair in back, and he was stark naked. The smoke was really pouring from the wagon now; Charley was certain that the man had to see it and got ready, but he went to a break in the rock near where the nargas were tethered and pissed.

When he was done he returned, but he was awake enough now to look at the man by the fire. He stopped, swore, then stalked to the sleeper, reached down, carefully got the guard's rifle, then pointed it at the sleeping man's head. "Sarnoc! Wake up you sleeping son of a bitch!" he snarled, and pushed at the man.

The guard stirred, then reached instinctively for his rifle and found it not in front of him but rather a few inches from his head. He whirled, saw who it was, and seemed to relax a bit. "Don't *do* that to me!" he exclaimed, more in relief than anger.

"I should blow your stupid lazy brains out," the hairy man responded. He looked out at the trail. "By the condition of the fire and the first slight lightening of the horizon I'd say it was only an hour to dawn. Did you ever relieve Potokir?"

The guard frowned. "He—he never come and got me. Never yelled or nothin'. Hell, Halot, he must'a gone fast asleep, too." They both turned in the direction of the guard and then suddenly spotted the near volcanic smoke coming from the vicinity of the machine gun. "*Holy shit! The ammo!* Hey! Everybody! The ammo's on fire!"

There was some stirring in the cleft, and just about that time the nicest little set of flames Charley ever saw popped up right in the center of the covering on the wagon.

"Get some water!" Halot yelled. "We got to get that thing out before it goes!"

Charley wondered if the thing would *ever* "go." It might not

be very worthwhile to wait and find out; if the mere threat of it
could bring out the others, and if Serkosh were still alive and
capable of shooting up there, then between them they might
well be able to take them out. There had been six, Serkosh had
said; now there were five, and if one of them was Moustache
he wasn't in any great shape himself.

Another man came from the cleft; a big, dark, ugly sucker
pulling up a pair of pants. He had a shaved head and looked
more like a professional wrestler than a gangster, but he sure
looked mean. "Where are Potokir and Tatoche?" he thun-
dered. "Halot! Fetch Potokir! I don't like the looks of this!"

That was too much. Praying that she was as good a shot with
these things as she was with her dad's pistols back home and
also praying that Serkosh took the hint, she took steady aim
with the first pistol and fired. Halot cried out and pitched
forward, a small wound in his back. Immediately she saw her
mistake; she should have shot Baldy first, since he was closest
to shelter, then sleepy, and finally Halot. She aimed at the bald
man who was starting to duck down and look around
suspiciously and fired again, but this time she missed as the
man dropped and rolled back toward the arch.

There was a sudden extra sharp report from overhead and to
her right, and the bald man suddenly cried out and fell back.
He wasn't dead, but he was hit pretty bad.

Charley reloaded, leaving any targets of opportunity to the
man above them, and she heard another shot—and then
several. Sleepy seemed to have figured out where the sniper
had to be and gotten his guns; using the nargas for cover, he
was shooting up into the darkness at Serkosh—but he was
shooting blind.

Charley had to wait. The distance was too great for accuracy
with these pistols—hitting a big man walking away was one
thing, but this was an armed man behind cover and wary, and
almost at the limits of her vision's resolution. It was a standoff,
though; neither Sleepy nor Serkosh could move and neither
could hit the other from where they were at. It was a Mexican
standoff, and since those in the camp didn't and couldn't know
just how badly hurt Serkosh was or even who or what he was,
they were very much at a disadvantage. That had to occur to
Sleepy and the pair still in the cleft; they would have to make a
move or stand an indefinite siege, and daylight would give a
potential sniper a clear view of everyone and everything.

Sleepy might have been sloppy and a sound snorer, but he was definitely a survivor in a hard life, once it was him or them. He startled both Serkosh and Charley by suddenly breaking free and into the open, using the shadows of the near dead fire and firing two shots wild up at his unseen assailant to cover his movements. Serkosh fired three times at him and missed, closely, all three times. It wasn't easy when you were dying and you also had to pick up a new gun each time.

Sleepy made it to the darkest shadows near where the captives lay. He took time first to reload his pistol and rifle, then looked around and spotted the cut bonds on Sam and Boday.

"You up there!" he cried out, his voice reverberating around the rock walls. "You throw down your guns and you come down—*now!* I'll count five, then I'm gonna start blowin' some beauties' brains out!"

He paused a moment, then shouted, "One! Two! Three! Four! Fi—"

That was as far as he got. Charley stepped out not ten feet from him and fired both pistols into his hulking black form. He screamed and fell back from the shock of being hit, and both his guns fired harmlessly in the air, the bullets ricocheting dangerously around the almost amphitheater-like camp. The effect gave her an idea and she cursed again her inability to really speak this tongue as she reloaded.

Serkosh, however, had the same idea, but when he spoke he sounded like someone already dead and rotting, a living corpse somehow alive and dangerous. "You in there! Come out with your hands up!" he yelled, his hollow, ghostly voice, amplified by the reverberations, sounding even more ghastly. "I wonder if you thought about how it would be if I pumped bullets into that arch cave of yours? Got lots of bullets. They'll make a nice *ping! ping! ping! ping!* sound, I bet. Might even hit somebody. Let's see."

He fired three shots at two-second intervals, about the best speed he could make with three guns. He was right about the sounds; being in there must be scary as hell. Charley liked that; these people should suffer a bit. She wondered why he should have all the fun. It was still just a dark hole in spite of the rapidly lightening sky, but she only had to fire into that dark hole. Two shots, then a reload even as the bullets continued to *ping* around inside. She was about to do it again when, at last, the ammunition wagon went up.

There was a tremendous explosion and a plume of fire, and then all sorts of small explosions and now the effect was not just on those in the cave, but on Charley and the captives as well. Horses and nargas reared and panicked, trying to pull away from their tethers and in some cases succeeding; in others falling to the sudden hail of random bullets.

Suddenly a tall, looming shape took form out of the sudden illumination of the cave, and the fire and small explosions and everything suddenly seemed to freeze and then be drawn— *sucked* was more appropriate—toward the dark form who seemed to absorb the energy and take on an unnatural blue glow.

A shrouded arm went out and up, and a stream of fire and bullets sped like a solid thing to the top of the cliff overlooking the camp, right at Serkosh, landing there with a flare and the sound of a hundred bullet reports. Charley heard a last, pitiable scream from on high and knew suddenly that she was alone once again.

She was also stunned by the incredible power that action had demonstrated. Damn it, if their boss was some kind of wizard why the hell hadn't she or he or it saved her men? Maybe, just maybe, the creature had only so much magic to use and saved it for self-preservation.

And now it came forward, a female figure in a dark, shimmering blue robe and hood. This, then, was the machine gunner and the mistress of all that had happened. What was it Serkosh had said? There was something odd about her, not quite human, as if she were hiding far more than a female form under that blue wrapping? Charley could see what he meant. The creature was large, menacing, and moved very oddly.

"Well done, well done indeed, my dear," said a sharp, crisp female voice from inside the hood. "You must realize that your bullets have no effect on me, and I know you must be over *there*. That trail is a dead end, as you must know. Come—I will make it easy on you. You saw how much I absorbed from the explosion. There were thousands of rounds in those cases and I used barely half to finish off your friend. Shall I, then, use the rest of them on your friends over there? Shall you watch them be ripped apart, into bloody messes, before I still come for you?"

Charley figured on this, but it didn't make much difference. What would be the fate of Sam and the others if she *did* surrender?

When there was no immediate surrender this also occurred to the blue-robed woman. She thought for a moment, trying to decide whether or not to go through with her threat or not. Charley hoped, even suspected, she would not; if she killed them all there would be nothing left to bargain with, and she couldn't be that selective. Those bullets went in a stream. There were clearly strong limits to this one's magic, but it sure as hell was better than no magic at all.

The blue-robed woman sighed, then reached a hand into a hidden pocket in her robe and pulled out something. "Jewel," she said—in perfect English, although in a *very* English accent, "who is this one I am facing and how do I deal with whoever it may be?"

Charley realized with a start that the villainness had the Jewel of Omak! But what would that damned demon tell her?

The woman in blue laughed. "So!" she said loudly in Akhbreed, "your name is Charley. How quaint. And I need but say a simple phrase in your native English to banish all but the courtesan in you. Did you even know that?" She paused, then said, in English, "Charley be gone!"

It was sudden and absolute. Charley no longer existed in a practical sense; only a very scared and very confused Shari.

"Come here, girl!" the woman in blue ordered, and she obeyed, totally bewildered and terrified. "Ah!" The woman in blue saw her now as she approached and knelt before her. "So! *You* are the one! I saw your face in the clouds you summoned that cleverly dispatched my men—at the cost of dispatching your train. What fun to have you in this state! How . . . *tempting* to keep you that way."

She put out a long, slender finger and pointed at the kneeling courtesan.

"Take off that ridiculous gunbelt with the guns in it and throw it as far away as you can, dear," said the woman in blue. Shari, who hadn't even realized she had such a thing on, immediately obeyed. The throw was pretty far for someone like her.

"This is such *delightful* fun," said the witch, adding, in English, "Charley return!"

Charley immediately came back to consciousness, now well

aware of her complete vulnerability. *Damn* Sam! These little power trips were gonna kill them all!

"Ah, now the return. *Fascinating!* You may speak, my dear. I'm afraid that all of this complicates my plans a great deal, and your unexpected appearance after so long raises possibilities long discarded. I must think of this."

The blue cloak and hood effectively covered the strange witch from any real view, but Charley got a glimpse of a dark, beautiful face inside that cowl, and long, slender fingers with dark, long nails emerged from the sleeves.

"Who are you?" she asked the witch. "How do you know English? And how could you permit—*this?*"

The blue witch laughed. "I am Asterial," she responded, "and I am of no place but this wasted land. Once I was of the Akhbreed, like yourself, and a building sorceress, but then I was kissed by a changewind, forced to flee here, forced to seek my revenge on those who cast me out. Most had given you up for dead, you know, even myself. Only Klittichorn remained convinced that you lived and were not in Boolean's hands or his control. Now you are in mine, although I never expected it. A fascinating new set of possibilities unfolds."

Suddenly Charley realized why she was still alive. Ironically, Boolean's little trick had worked. The woman in blue thought that she, Charley, and not Sam, was the woman the Horned One sought. Not that it was doing much good, considering Sam's state at that moment. The demon inside the jewel apparently had gone along with Asterial so far because it did not threaten Sam, only Charley. The most practical thing probably seemed to the demon to let the witch kill Charley and believe the deed done, then handle Sam's own rescue in a less obvious way. It was an unsettling thought, but whatever worth it had to the demon was now negated. Clearly this powerful and ambitious sorceress was not going to kill her; at least not for some time.

"At least you could tell me what all this is about," Charley prompted, feeling a bit more secure and hoping that conversation would keep those damned words away and keep her mind whole. "I've been snatched from my own world after many attempts to kill me, tracked all over, and I really don't know what this is about."

"Ambition, my dear, and power, as usual," replied Asterial. "A great wizard has turned against his own kind and works to

bring an end to Akhbreed rule. Quite naturally he couches this
in liberation terms, but his true aim is to rule—first here, then
everywhere. We all know it and even his allies suspect it, deep
down, but they go along dealing with the devil in the
knowledge that he is the only hope, perhaps for thousands of
years, to overthrow this wicked system. They join him with
prayers that perhaps they can find some way to stop him as
well. You, my dear, represent a dagger at his throat. You see,
whosoever defeats the Akhbreed will need the changewind as
his weapon. Even Klittichorn cannot control the changewind,
but the Storm Princess can influence, call, direct, nudge *any*
storm.''

"You mean—I'm the Storm Princess?"

Asterial laughed. "Of course not, my dear! How *could* you
be? You are of the Outplane, not a native of Akahlar. No, my
dear, you are her double, her parallel. Genetically identical in
spite of different worlds, different ancestry, everything. The
Outplanes contain all things that might have ever been, and
certainly they include a few parallels of most everyone. But the
forces of Probability have no way of telling one from the other
except location. Here, on Akahlar, you have access to the same
powers as she. You are identical, unless touched by the
changewind or otherwise altered in your basic makeup. Here,
her powers and your powers are indistinguishable. Here, you
may, with the proper training, cancel the other out, and with it
Klittichorn's ambition.''

So that was it! She remembered when they fell through the
great tunnel or whatever it was; the scene of the cabin region
where the deer had changed, bit by bit, into something totally
different. All those worlds. . . . And by sheer probability, on
a few of them would be ones like Sam, perfect doubles, which
an enemy of Klittichorn could turn. One by one the sorcerer
had been seeking them out and killing them off. Sam's girl in
the red car . . . Not Sam, but Sam all the same. Boolean
hadn't been kidding them. Right now, Sam was probably the
most important person on Akahlar.

Charley looked over at the captives, relieved to see no sign
of wounds. They hadn't moved during the whole thing. "What
have you done to them?"

"A bit of a test. I recognized this gem around the fat one's
neck as an amulet of power. I simply put them under with it.
The restraints were earlier, and remained on because I did not

and do not know the limits of this amulet's spell. I am told that the painted one is an alchemist. When we get back to my lair I shall have her create potions that will create the perfect slaves. You have cost me most of my organization; it is therefore fitting that you all should become my obedient slaves and rebuild. But no potions for you, my dear. A few words are all it takes for you to become my willing and obedient slave—with your full self about as insurance against Klittichorn. After he wins it all, you will be there to give *him* a taste of the changewind. With the greater sorcerers gone and you at my side I shall exterminate the Akhbreed and myself rule."

"Good plan," Charley muttered dryly. She now knew the basics of it all and she didn't like the position they were in. It sure was gonna be a hell of a shock to this witch, though, when she trotted out Charley to do old Horny in and discovered she had somebody whose magic powers were less than nothing. Boolean must have much the same plan, but after revealing himself to Klittichorn it was impossible for him to act—if, in fact, he knew just where they were all this time. "And when's this war supposed to break out?"

"Ah! It will be a complex affair. Great armies as well as great magic will be required, and as for the magic it will not get two chances. Klittichorn may be destroyed but not aged, although the withering old fart is bad enough now. He has time to build and train and practice—and teach his little Storm Princess. In the meantime, he pays well for the Mandan gold cloaks we steal from the trains and whose manufacture is limited and very tightly controlled. One cannot use the changewind unless one's army is protected from it. Oh, we shall have a long, long time together before this all comes about, my sweet. Why, it might be many *years* before you are needed."

Charley thought fast. She'd come this far on bluff and bravado and sheer luck; this time it might well run out, but it was worth the chance.

She looked around. "Your gang's pretty well wiped out," she noted, "and the horses and nargas that didn't spook are dead or soon will be. You ain't gonna be able to move this shit, and you don't know who else survived with a gun and is sittin' around someplace waitin' for sitting ducks. Me, I don't wanna be Shari for the next ten years, but I got no axe to grind. I don't like what you and your boys did, but they paid for it. Now I got to think of me. Boolean or you is all the same to me since you got reason to keep me alive and kicking, but I don't owe old Green Robes anything. He sure dumped me in a vat of shit and left me there to sink or swim. I'm stark naked, marked for life, and I got nowhere to go. You, and this place, is as good as any. Seems to me, though, that I'm no match for my twin sister or whatever she is. Sure, I called the storm, and I sent one or two away, but strictly out of emotion or fear. Your horned boy is teachin' her the fine points and he's got years to do it in. You keep me around as some servile little ass-licker and when it comes time for the showdown they're gonna wipe the floor up with me.''

Asterial paused. "Go on. Just what are you proposing?"

"Not exactly what you got in mind. More the same kind of relationship your big boy has with my twin sister. We get a sort of partnership. You teach me the magic and I'll handle the guns and work with you. You got nothin' to lose, after all. Like, all you do is say the words and I'm gone even if I got ten storms comin' in on you and five guns aimed at your head.''

The proposition was really tempting to the sorceress, but she simply could not be sure. "I would *like* to trust you. Anyone who can pull this off is someone quite exceptional. You have done to me what armies could not. But seeing all this, even knowing those words, how could I ever be certain? You have not truly seen me. You are repulsed by what I permitted here tonight, even though it was merely payment to those men who were all I really had left. I believe you are from too moral a background to be trusted.''

"I'll show you how valuable and trusted I can be—and how trusting," Charley responded, feeling her stomach tighten and hoping her nerves didn't show. "Use that jewel and bring one of the captives over here. The fat one—I already cut her bonds so she's the logical choice. I'll show you how to make a devoted, obedient slave without potions or new spells.''

"But I was told she was your friend and companion.''

"She is—but she also stuck that go away and come back on me, and I stuck out my neck once too often. She can still be my friend, she just will also be your slave. That's fair enough.''

Asterial thought a moment, then said, "I will do it." She held up the jewel and let it open and its tiny beam fall on Sam, who stiffened when it hit her forehead. "Arise and walk to me," the sorceress commanded.

Sam got up, with some difficulty, and walked rather wobbly over to them, still in a trance state.

"Now," Charley continued, "you just shine that jewel on her and say, in English, 'I wish that you will forget all about Boolean and will instead become my obedient and abject slave for life beyond the ability of any spell or potion to change.' Don't forget the 'I wish' part and make sure it's in English."

"This grows interesting," the sorceress muttered to herself, too interested in the potential new powers of this thing to think beyond it at the moment. "I wish that you will forget Boolean or even that he exists and will instead become by abject and obedient slave, willingly and joyfully serving me as your only reason for living, and that this will be so permanent that no spell or potion may change it."

Suddenly there was a strange, hollow voice in Asterial's head, one she neither expected nor was able to cope with.

Command inconsistent with prime directive. I am not going to stay forever sealed in this fucking thing until the end of time!

Suddenly the jewel seemed to transform, growing in an instant from a tiny bauble to a huge, amorphous, sinister shape that was dripping both power and evil. It was unlike anything Charley had ever dreamed even in her wildest nightmares and she felt repulsed, unclean; she wanted to turn away, to run, but she could not. She had to watch.

Waves of amber-colored energy both enveloped and outlined the thing, and it reached out with a horrible, monstrous roar and took hold of the blue-clad sorceress, the energy waves growing to envelop her as well.

Asterial screamed and threw off her blue cloak, and Charley's mouth dropped. The sorceress *was* beautiful, but it was the beauty of the new dawn against the millions of tiny scales over her body reflecting every color and hue. The head and upper torso were human, but the rest of the body was like a giant insect, the two human arms the forelegs and the other six thin and spiny, and from her back suddenly emerged great sets of wings which began to unfold and begin a terrible buzzing.

My God! She's a six-foot-tall dragonfly! was all Charley could think.

Both figures rose into the air now, several feet off the ground, and the sounds from the two of them were horrible, the energy flowing through, around, and out from them like some fantastic lightning show.

There was a sudden great roar as Asterial expended the last of her acquired energy and all those bullets into the *thing* that had sprung from nowhere, but to no effect. It simply absorbed them and roared with a horrible ferocity and enclosed the insect woman in an ever-tightening embrace. There was a sudden brilliant, blinding flash, and both figures shimmered a moment and seemed to blend, then they simply faded out.

Quite suddenly there was a dead silence in the amphitheater, and, a moment later, something small dropped from a height and clattered against the rock floor, rolling near Sam's feet. It was the Jewel of Omak.

Sam began to sway a bit, then collapsed on her knees and went down on all fours, shaking her head as if waking up from a deep sleep. The others began to groan and shift, the two girls still bound and Boday's feet still held by the rope and stakes.

Sam looked up, appearing both haunted and confused, and suddenly saw Charley standing there looking at her. "Charley?" she called weakly. "My God! Charley!" And then she suddenly started to cry hysterically.

Charley rushed over to her and just held her and rocked her back and forth for a while. Boday, seeing the scene and having her hands free, managed to undo the knots around her ankles and then retrieve Charley's knife and free the two girls. For a while they were all stunned, all in shock of one kind or another, but suddenly Sheka, the cute nine-year-old, spotted the body of Halot, grabbed the knife where Boday had put it down, rushed over to the body with a cry and started stabbing Halot's still form again and again and again.

Sam got hold of herself, and Charley was able to get free enough to reach down and pick up the Jewel of Omak. "It must'a been tough," she said as calmly and sympathetically as possible. "Maybe you should use this to give her a little bit of peace."

Sam stared at the incessant stab, stab, stab, as the child cried and cried, and she shook her head negatively. "No. One day, yes. She'll need more help than this stupid demon can give anyway. Maybe we all will. But, right now, she should hate. If she hates, she might yet survive."

Charley started to respond, but she couldn't think of anything to say. Finally she managed, "You okay—otherwise?"

"I'll live." Sam was starting to think clearly again for the first time in the whole day of terror. She suddenly looked around at the dead bodies, the jewel back in her hand, the new carnage, and she was acutely aware that only she and the four others seemed to still be alive. "My God, Charley! All this— how'd you do it? Where's your army? And that—thing. That bitch. She was *evil*, Charley. I've seen a lot of bad people, but I never before saw pure evil." She was suddenly awed. "You did all this—yourself?"

"I had a little help. He's dead now. I—" But Charley could say no more. Suddenly she felt land and sky heave and she passed out cold on the rocky floor.

Things were different when Charley came to, not the least difference being she herself. She ached all over and she felt more tired than she ever had in her life. She was also incredibly thirsty, and everything was so damned blurry. She made out a figure sitting nearby and tried to call to her but only a croak came out.

Boday jumped at the sound, then rushed to her with a canteen. "Drink slowly," the alchemist cautioned. "There is plenty of water but too much at once will make you sick."

In fact she had to be forced to stop, then had a fit of coughing and dizziness, but her voice loosened a bit and she felt a slight bit better. "What—what happened?" she managed.

"We have been near dying to ask *you* that question. Even Boday had her doubts, it must be admitted. Captured, a night of horror, then put out by the jewel in the midst of a powerful and evil changeling and her cohorts, and suddenly—they are all dead or gone and here you are. But rest, relax now. Boday will not press you. We have been waiting almost two days for the story; it will wait a bit longer."

Charley felt her mind reel. "*Two days!* You mean I've been out for two days?"

Boday nodded. "You performed miraculously, my beauty, but you were not designed for this. Climbing, hiking, shooting, and who knows what else, with no rest and nothing to eat or drink from the looks of it. Boday wishes she had her kit to give you some help but it is all gone. You will feel this for some time. You pushed yourself well beyond your limits, and we are all blessed that you are not dead because of it."

She *felt* half dead, anyway, and sank back on the cot. How

the hell *had* she done all that? My God, it was like some kind of weird dream. She couldn't believe it herself.

Using the canteen some more she splashed water on her face and rubbed her eyes. God, she needed a bath! A nice, warm, extra-long bath. . . .

By the time she was in reasonable shape to talk and feel some degree of normalcy returning, Sam was there, and they hugged and talked until morning and filled each other in on just what had gone on.

The flash flood had been more devastating, more likely, than Asterial's machine gun might have been to the train. It wasn't like an old-fashioned Earth flood which would have taken far longer to build, but it might well have been typical of what to expect in the Kudaan Wastes. Still, even with little warning, there had been some time to get ready for it and a fair number of survivors managed to swim to dryer high areas. It wasn't until later, when the waters receded, that the gang went into real action.

With Asterial as a spotter from her high perch, the quartet of henchmen was easily able to spot a number of living and dead and they had the expertise and equipment to get to them. The dead were stripped and left to rot; five male survivors in varying degrees of shock and injury were hauled out along with the four of them. Boday had clutched Sam with tremendous force and even the action of the flood hadn't separated them, but by the time they made it to a rocky butte they were all in and simply collapsed until found and taken captive. The other two girls had an even more miraculous escape, being washed straight through the narrows and onto the sides of the bowl-shaped canyon. All the captives had been stripped and tied with their arms behind them linked to a rope collar. If they struggled or failed to keep up, they might well have strangled themselves.

But they had some time to recover because their rescuers, Halot and the one called Tatoche who'd been later killed by Serkosh, had gone scavenging over miles of valley terrain, foraging for everything they could find. Some of the discoveries were astonishing—two wagons intact, although their covers had been torn off, and even some live horses and nargas. They put all the loot they could find in the wagons, then began their march around to the camp at the arch. Waiting there for them were Asterial and the two others who'd helped get her gun and equipment out of the ambush spot. It was unlikely that Asterial needed any help herself; Charley, from what she saw, was convinced that somehow the changeling could fly, at least for short distances.

Then, well after dark, when they had stowed away all they really wanted to keep and broken down and burned the rest, the night of horror had begun. Asterial encouraged it like some demonic queen; she seemed to take a perverse pleasure in torture and mutilation, although she did not participate—she presided.

The men—two paying passengers, three trail crew—were brutally questioned about almost everything they knew, then tortured, mutilated for sheer fun, and eventually killed. One man took a very long time to die. The women expected much the same, but while they were horribly brutalized, tied up, made to do most anything imaginable, and ultimately repeatedly raped, they were by Asterial's expressed command not mutilated or killed. She was a creature of some magic and so felt the magic in the jewel taken from Sam; she had experimented with it and in the process, of course, knocked them all mercifully out cold.

"What about Moustache?" Charley asked. "Zamofir, I think his name is."

"He was here and in pretty good shape," Sam told her. "He seemed to know them and they seemed to know him and he sure wasn't treated bad, but he looked real uncomfortable at their blood orgy and stayed back in the cave. You didn't see him?"

"No, not at all, but Serkosh said he was there and he hadn't seen him leave, either. He didn't even come out when the fire started. He's not there now? You looked?"

"Nowhere. Some signs that he was there but nothin' else. I guess you were right about him, but he didn't seem to have nothin' to do with *this*. I'm pretty sure he had nothin' to do with the trap and didn't even figure on it."

"No difference. He works for the same master as they do. He's just the more genteel, brainy, sly kind of monster. The kind that don't care how many folks get murdered or raped or enslaved or anything like that but who can't stand the sight of it themselves. Instead they pay somebody else and order it done out of their sight and mind. I don't like the fact that he's disappeared so well here, either. He could'a answered a ton of questions for us and given us the lay of the land. More, I sure as hell would like to know *when* he split. He could paint a big target right on my butterfly eyes, you know. And if he knows any English he might know how to turn me off and on at will. Say—will you do me a favor? Use that damned thing and get rid of that? It's like a sword over my head. If Asterial hadn't been so damned arrogant in bringin' me back we'd all be slaves now."

Sam sighed. "I can't. I tried the jewel—it doesn't answer. There's not even any little beam of light. It stays closed and silent, like so much junk jewelry. That—*thing* you saw come out of it—could it have been the demon?"

Charley shuddered. "Could be. I hadn't thought of that. If it is we're well rid of it even if it was powerful and on our side. The damned thing—you said Asterial was pure evil, but she wasn't. She was just an evil creature, like a lot of others we've met this trip. This thing was. Pure, unadulterated, undiluted evil of a form and kind I just can't describe to you. I dunno. Maybe it figured a way to spring itself on its own. Maybe Asterial drew it out. Maybe they're both still alive." That gave her another chill. "If so, my neck's had it. Asterial will spend all eternity hunting me down and she knows just how to nail me, damn it."

Sam sighed. "I'm sorry. It was the demon who suggested it. Did it almost on its own, really, although I went along. All that power . . . You just can't not use it."

Charley sighed. "Well, it's done. At least we showed we're no pushovers. You looked for any more survivors?"

"Yeah. The girls went out. We couldn't stop 'em, so one of us would stay here with you and the other would go with them. Not much left even now down there, but well up the canyon past where we got—and we was the leaders, I thought—I swear there were wagon tracks. And somebody'd dug several graves. It could be that some of the train not only managed to escape Asterial's boys but actually put together enough to push on. Hard to say. They sure as hell pushed on without *us*. Trouble was, they wasn't much useful to us, neither."

"What have you got?"

"Well, we got five horses, if that's anything. I guess it is. All the wagons pretty much burned or blew up. Nothin' that could be done about that. We got lots of guns but only a few boxes of ammo that were in the arch. Plus some assorted knives, swords, spears—that kind of shit. Nothin' much for clothes. A few blankets, maybe, that kind of thing, and a couple of bedrolls. Saddles, too, if we can manage to get 'em on the horses. They're *heavy* sons of bitches. Took all of us to saddle up and go back down there today. The kids ride good, though, and I'll manage. Also six or seven of them Mandan gold blankets. Talk about *heavy*. They looked like dyed wool but they ain't, I'll tell you. Plenty of water here—there's a natural spring back there—and lots of these rock-hard biscuits. Could be worse."

Charley nodded. Daylight had broken by the time they'd finished, and she struggled up and insisted on getting to her feet. She still felt like every bone in her body was broken, but she knew it wasn't. In the end, it would go away, and she'd return to some semblance of normalcy. What worried her most was that the sun was up now and it was quite bright, but everything was still pretty damned blurry to her. Real clarity lasted only inches beyond her outstretched arm; after that the world just dissolved into blurry, indistinct shapes that, after ten or fifteen feet at best, became a nothingness. That one frantic night she'd seen with a clarity she hadn't remembered for years, but this was far worse than her usual nearsightedness now. It could be that her eyes were just like the rest of her— pushed by will beyond their limits, overused, overstrained, and that this would pass. She hoped it was so, but she had to wonder if that supernatural bout she had witnessed on top of it all hadn't given off more damage than it seemed. Right now, from maybe ten or twelve feet, she couldn't tell short, fat Sam from tall, painted Boday. They were just blurry, indistinct shapes.

She decided not to tell them, not just yet, but to wait and hope that vision returned. She could fake it for a while, considering her condition. They all had enough problems without her going blind. The crazy thing was, a good eye doctor and a decent pair of glasses would probably restore her vision to better than theirs, but the only eye doctors were in places where girls like her couldn't wear them, and there seemed a real lack of medical help in the Kudaan Wastes.

Later, when all were awake, they held a council to decide what to do. The kids were a bit withdrawn but not nearly as

much as Charley thought she might have been at their age
going through what they'd gone through. It was also sort of
embarrassing to discover that, to them, she was some sort of
incarnate superwoman. She could easily have had the default
leadership role if only she spoke the language. It fell to Sam to
coordinate, with Charley kibbitzing.

"We should all turn 'round and go back," Boday suggested.
"The loft is still ours."

"Yeah, and Kligos ready to take us all out," Sam noted
sourly.

"Kligos!" The artist spat. "After Asterial, what is such a
pimple to us? Boday is in her element there in any event. We
have papers there. We are recognized, known."

"Yeah, but we'd have to get back through that damned
desert with the creepy crawlies all alone," Sam pointed out,
"and after that we'd have to cross who knows what land to get
back to Tubikosa. No navigator, no Pilot, no choice."

"Oh, we might have to wait a dangerous day," Boday
admitted, "but all we would need is one with a proper border
post. The tickets, the passage, included insurance, darling! We
make contact with a company train and we get a new wagon,
new provisions, all of it. Or a free ride home on the first train
going that way and a settlement."

"Yeah," Sam sighed. "And we're right back where we
started from again. Maybe I don't have no demon pushin' me,
but I didn't get fat and lazy 'cause of no demon. I did it to
myself. This insurance works both ways, don't it? I mean, if
we can make it farther on to some outpost it's one and the
same. Maybe a little wait for the documents to be sent and
catch up but that's all."

"It may be more complicated than that," Boday responded.
"Besides, it would be hundreds of leegs yet to anything
approaching civilization. We are no army and these are
dangerous lands. Many days we would have to go without so
much as clothes to protect us or anyone to guide us or warn us
of the dangers."

"Yeah, there's never a mall around when you really need
one," Charley commented sourly. Sam did not bother to
translate.

"And who knows the level of corruption?" Boday pressed.
"Two women, two children, and a courtesan, naked and

vithout means but with large claims on a powerful company able for those claims. Far cheaper to delay, stall, misdirect 1ose papers, let us rot at some isolated army post. And have ou not forgotten that we were raped by men with near magical apacities? What if one or more of us is with a rapist's child, tuck there in the middle of nowhere without resources snared 1 bureaucrat's tape? We must go back, Sam! It is the only easonable thing to do."

Sam looked at Rani, the oldest girl and one of those who night well have that problem on top of being orphaned and rutalized. "Rani—what do you and your sister want to do ow? What can we possibly do for you?"

"We want to stay with you," the girl responded unhesitatngly. "If we go back, you see, we will be—unclean. Our amilies will disown us. We would have nothing and no one."

Sam was appalled. "But you were attacked and *raped* hrough no fault of your own, damn it! Surely they can't hold hat against you!"

Boday broke in, conscious that while Rani had grown up a great deal in forty-eight hours she still wasn't adult. "They are colonials, but they are all that is left of the colonial branch where they were," she tried to explain. "From what I gather heir parents became colonials because their clan is strictly traditionalist. Their bad fortune would be considered then the wrath or curse of the clan gods. Desecrated as they were, they would be expected to commit ritual suicide so that they could be cleansed and then be reborn pure. Not all clans are that strict but the ones that are have a lot of volunteers to be colonials."

Sam looked at Rani. "That right?"

The girl nodded somberly. "We have no family now, and no clan. If we were to get out of this hellish place we would be forced to sell ourselves or die."

"Die," said little Sheka firmly. "Ain't no *man* ever gonna touch me 'gain. I hate 'em! I hate 'em all!"

Charley stepped in. "Remind her that her father was a man. And one hell of a man, too. He gave more than he imagined he could give for them. Tell her to remember that."

Sam did. It didn't immediately illicit a response, but after a while it was clear that Sheka was softly crying.

Sam sighed. "For what it's worth, you have one, maybe three new mommies as of this moment and I have two daughters."

Rani gave a slight gasp, then got up and practically thre
herself at Sam, hugging her, and Sam returned it. Finally th
new mom asked, "But there's some things you got to know
too. About Boday and me, for instance."

"We know," Rani replied. "Mom—our real mom—sort
told us. It don't matter. You want us and we want and nee
you."

Well, that settled that part of it, and it was up to Sam, wit
some help from Boday, to explain exactly who they were an
what was going on as best they could, at least on the level of
one wizard bringing them here and then losing them, the othe
trying to kill them. She also spared nothing in explaining wha
Boday had done for a living and what sort of underworl
they'd lived in and which Boday was urging a return to.
wasn't clear just how naive they might be, but they seemed t
get the general picture.

"And if we get to this Boolean, what then?" Rani asked her

"I don't know. All I know is that we'd be among rich an
powerful people who have a stake in keeping me alive an
maybe the power to really do it."

"I think I know, Sam," Charley said, forgetting until nov
that she was the only one. "I think he wants to train you. Mak
you a sorceress, a mistress of the storms. This horned guy tha
they all worked for, the same one who tried to get you—he ha
this sorceress he's trained who can do what nobody else can
Control or influence the storms, maybe even the changewinds
He's gonna use her to try and take over, first here, then every
place. Become like a god. The only other one with that kind of
power is you, Sam—but it's raw, untrained. This Boolea
wants to train you like the other guy trained *her*, and when th
war comes set you against her. Asterial told me—when sh
thought I was you."

Sam thought it over. "Well, it's something, anyway. Now
know the power's real and why this all happened. Don't d
much good, though, 'less I can figure what to do about it.
figure we got three options, no more. We can go back—but tha
might make us sittin' ducks if Zamofir's around or Asterial'
still alive and maybe if they're not. It'd also turn these
two kids into the bastard daughters of a pair of dykes. You and
I know how they'd wind up in a culture like that. And I'd wind
up a fat, corrupt, brainless vegetable. And that's if Zamofir and
Kligos and Asterial and all the rest would leave us alone."

"I know," Charley replied, nodding.

"Or we can keep on going to Boolean and probably get the girls and maybe the rest of us killed or worse—now I know there *is* worse. Or we can say the hell with all of 'em and try'n find some quiet place where nobody knows us or cares and where we can live our own lives."

"Until Horny launches his war," Charley pointed out. "And we—all of us—will be targets just because we're Akhbreed. And you'll be sittin' there watching him make himself a god, the kind of guy so evil that things like these guys here and Asterial actually *work* for him, and know maybe, just maybe, you could'a stopped it."

"But this whole fucking system's so *evil* right now," Sam noted. "It's a different kind of evil—nicer, maybe, and quieter, 'cause we're all on the ruling side, but evil just the same. And if I *could* stop this thing, I'd be cementin' this evil in place for many lifetimes. Charley—what do I do? It ain't fair to be offered a choice of evils. You're tellin' me that if we get out of here and if we live through all this and if it all comes out right I get to choose between killin' millions or permanently enslavin' like *billions*. It just ain't fair, Charley."

"I know it isn't, kid, but that's what there is. Five naked broads stuck in the wilderness and we got to decide it for 'em no matter what. Me, I'd just like to find out why all the damned magicians here speak English. Why not French or Chinese or Hindu or something we never heard of? It's been drivin' me nuts. So I guess I got a stake in this; sort of. And there's tons of little worlds out there filled with people and things we never would guess. We've seen so little of this crazy world I think I want to see more before I give up on it. Besides, until you're secure someplace I'll never be. I'm target number one."

Sam gave her an odd half-smile. "We've come such a long way already," she noted.

Charley nodded. "And we got such a long way to go. . . ."

Sam got up and turned and looked out at the trail and the sun-parched but colorful landscape beyond. "Well, everybody, it's time we got going," she said.

"Where?" asked Boday.

Sam pointed. "Out there. Someplace. Until we find a mall, or a good motel, or Boolean. Whichever comes first."

Somewhere, far in the distance, something shimmered and changed, and the changewinds shifted and bounced and flew about in new and unexpected patterns as if a new randomness had been introduced that they were keen to follow.

Far away, in his spacious Palace tower quarters overlooking an exotic and beautiful city, a man wearing a green robe who also had a strange, pea-green monkey-like creature perched on his left shoulder, sensed it, and gave a slight smile.

"Well, Cromil, it might work after all," he said softly to the little creature. "It just might work out in spite of the odds."

"More likely she'll just get her ass blown off or worse," responded the green creature in a shrill, nasal voice. "She'll never make it here and you know it. Look how long it's been already!"

He sighed. "If she cannot make it here then she has no hope against the powers of Klittichorn and no prayer of countering the Storm Princess. We take what we can get and make of it what we must, my friend. When she started she was a frightened, ignorant, vacuous schoolgirl with the active intelligence and self-confidence and ego of a carrot. If she makes it here, then she will already have developed the confidence and skills and toughness required to make her one of the most dangerous survivors on this planet. That is someone I can take and revolutionize the world. If she does not—well, she is not the only one, as you know. Relax, Cromil. We will still all probably lose out and die I know, but, just for now, just this once, let Klittichorn do a little bit of stomach-churning."

And, half a world away, inside a great castle set into and partially cut from a towering purplish snow-capped mountain peak, a tall, gaunt figure in a crimson cloak was walking down a hall when he suddenly felt a sudden and mysterious chill. He stopped, frowned, and tried to figure out what it was, but failed. He didn't like it, though. He didn't like it at all. He continued walking and went into the Council chamber, unable to shake this new and, for now, merely unpleasant chill. "Alert all agents and commands," he ordered crisply. "Something very odd just happened and I don't know what. Until I do and we remedy it, spare no effort in finding and isolating it. And triple the magical guard on Boolean. If he scratches his ass I want to know it."

"At once, sir," responded the Captain General. "Uh—sir? Any idea what we are looking for?"

He shook his head. "A random equation seeking a definite solution. It floats, seeking its own answer. I prefer not to solve it." He went over to a blackboard and picked up a small object. "The easiest path is to erase it. Find it, Captain General. Find it and erase it before we all catch our death of cold."

The *Changewinds* saga continues
with *Riders of the Winds.*

BESTSELLING
Science Fiction
and
Fantasy